T0171669

More Praise for *Bitten*

"Clever, quirky, hip, and funny, skating between genres with style and grace."

—Joanne Harris, author of *Chocolat*

"[Something] for the she-wolf in us all."

—Shannon Olson, author of *Welcome to My Planet*

"Sometimes there's nothing more fun than an excellent debut novel, and Kelley Armstrong's *Bitten* fits the bill. It's a witty, suspenseful, and well-paced tale. [Armstrong] spins an intricate but comprehensible plot around compelling characters. Bring on the sequel, we're ready for more."

—*Houston Chronicle*

Kelley Armstrong lives in rural southwestern Ontario. *Bitten* is her first novel. Her second novel, *Stolen,* Book II of *Women of the Otherworld,* will be published by Viking in the summer of 2003.

Bitten

Women of the Otherworld:
BOOK I

Kelley Armstrong

A PLUME BOOK

PLUME
Published by the Penguin Group
Penguin Putnam Inc., 375 Hudson Street, New York, New York 10014, U.S.A.
Penguin Books Ltd., 80 Strand, London WC2R 0RL, England
Penguin Books Australia Ltd, 250 Camberwell Road, Camberwell, Victoria 3124, Australia
Penguin Books Canada Ltd, 10 Alcorn Avenue, Toronto, Ontario, Canada M4V 3B2
Penguin Books (N.Z.) Ltd, 182–190 Wairau Road, Auckland 10, New Zealand

Penguin Books Ltd, Registered Offices: Harmondsworth, Middlesex, England

Published by Plume, a member of Penguin Putnam Inc. Previously published in a Viking edition.

The Library of Congress has catalogued the Viking edition as follows:
Armstrong, Kelley.
Bitten / Kelley Armstrong
p. cm.
ISBN 0-670-89471-0 (hc.)
ISBN 0-452-28348-5 (pbk.)
1. Werewolves—Fiction. I. Title.
PS3551.R4678 B58 2001
813'.6—dc21 00-068590

PUBLISHER'S NOTE
This is a work of fiction. Names, characters, places, and incidents are either the products of the author's imagination or are used fictitiously, and any resemblance to actual persons, living or dead, business establishments, events, or locales is entirely coincidental.

148055521

To Jeff ❧ *For always believing I could*

Acknowledgments

This being a first novel, I have a lot of acknowledging to do, not just for help with this book, but for help with every short story, poem, and literary rambling that came before it. Thanks to my family, friends, instructors, fellow writers, everyone who ever offered a word of praise or criticism. Special thanks to my old writing group (Anonymous Writers of London). This novel was born at that group and, without their encouragement, it would have died there.

Now, for those who helped this book from concept to publication. To Brian Henry, writing instructor, who saw the promise in the story and recommended it to my amazing agent. To Helen Heller, aforesaid "amazing agent," who worked nothing short of miracles. To Sarah Manges and Carole DeSanti at Viking for their enthusiasm and dead-on editorial suggestions. Finally, to my husband, Jeff, for knowing that a closed study door meant it was his turn to make dinner, and to my daughter Julia, who grew up knowing that a closed study door meant she could help herself to all the snacks she could eat.

Contents

Prologue

I HAVE TO.

I've been fighting it all night. I'm going to lose. My battle is as futile as a woman feeling the first pangs of labor and deciding it's an inconvenient time to give birth. Nature wins out. It always does.

It's nearly two A.M., too late for this foolishness and I need my sleep. Four nights spent cramming to meet a deadline have left me exhausted. It doesn't matter. Patches of skin behind my knees and elbows have been tingling and now begin to burn. My heart beats so fast I have to gulp air. I clench my eyes shut, willing the sensations to stop but they don't.

Philip is sleeping beside me. He's another reason why I shouldn't leave, sneaking out in the middle of the night again and returning with a torrent of lame excuses. He's working late tomorrow. If I can just wait one more day. My temples begin to throb. The burning sensation in my skin spreads down my arms and legs. The rage forms a tight ball in my gut and threatens to explode.

I've got to get out of here—I don't have a lot of time left.

Philip doesn't stir when I slip from the bed. There's a pile of clothing tucked underneath my dresser so I won't risk the squeaks and groans of opening drawers and closets. I pick up my keys, clasping my fist around them so they don't jangle, ease open the door, and creep into the hallway.

Everything's quiet. The lights seem dimmed, as if overpowered by the emptiness. When I push the elevator button, it creaks out a complaint at being disturbed at so ungodly an hour. The first floor and lobby are equally empty. People who can afford the rent this close to downtown Toronto are comfortably asleep by this time.

My legs itch as well as hurt and I curl my toes to see if the itching stops. It doesn't. I look down at the car keys in my hand. It's too late to drive to a safe place—the itching has crystallized into a sharp burn. Keys in my pocket, I stride onto the streets, looking for a quiet place to Change. As I walk, I monitor the sensation in my legs, tracing its passage to my arms and the back of my neck. Soon. Soon. When my scalp starts to tingle, I know I have walked as far as I can so I search for an alley. The first one I find has been claimed by two men squeezed together inside a tattered big-screen TV box. The next alley is empty. I hurry to the end and undress quickly behind a barricade of trash bins, hide the clothes under an old newspaper. Then I start the Change.

My skin stretches. The sensation deepens and I try to block the pain. Pain. What a trivial word—agony is better. One doesn't call the sensation of being flayed alive "painful." I inhale deeply and focus my attention on the Change, dropping to the ground before I'm doubled over and forced down. It's never easy—perhaps I'm still too human. In the struggle to keep my thoughts straight, I try to anticipate each phase and move my body into position—head down, on all fours, arms and legs straight, feet and hands flexed, and back arched. My leg muscles knot and convulse. I gasp and strain to relax. Sweat breaks out, pouring off me in streams, but the muscles finally relent and untwist themselves. Next comes the ten seconds of hell that used to make me swear I'd rather die than endure this again. Then it's over.

Changed.

I stretch and blink. When I look around, the world has mutated to an array of colors unknown to the human eye, blacks and browns and grays with subtle shadings that my brain still converts to blues and greens and reds. I lift my nose and inhale. With the Change, my already keen senses sharpen even more. I pick up scents of fresh asphalt and rotting tomatoes and window-pot mums and day-old sweat and a million other things, mixing together in an odor so overwhelming I cough and shake my head. As I turn, I catch distorted fragments of my reflection in a dented trash can. My eyes stare back at me. I curl my lips back and snarl at myself. White fangs flash in the metal.

I am a wolf, a 130-pound wolf with pale blond fur. The only part of me that remains are my eyes, sparking with a cold intelligence and a simmering ferocity that could never be mistaken for anything but human.

I look around, inhaling the scents of the city again. I'm nervous here. It's too close, too confined; it reeks of human spoor. I must be careful. If I'm seen, I'll be mistaken for a dog, a large mixed breed, perhaps a husky and yellow Labrador mix. But even a dog my size is cause for alarm when it's running loose. I head for the back of the laneway and seek a path through the underbelly of the city.

My brain is dulled, disoriented not by my change of form but by the unnaturalness of my surroundings. I can't get my bearings and the first alley I go down turns out to be the one I'd encountered in human form, the one with the two men in the faded Sony box. One of them is awake now. He's tugging the remnants of a filth-encrusted blanket between his fingers as if he can stretch it large enough to cover himself against the cold October night. He looks up and sees me. His eyes widen. He starts to shrink back, then stops himself. He says something. His voice is crooning, the musical, exaggerated tones people use with infants and animals. If I concentrated, I could make out the words, but there's no point. I know what he's saying, some variation of "nice doggy," repeated over and over in a variety of inflections. His hands are outstretched, palms out to ward me off, the physical language contradicting the vocal. Stay back—nice doggy—stay back. And people wonder why animals don't understand them.

I can smell the neglect and waste rising from his body. It smells like weakness, like an aged deer driven to the fringe of the herd, prime pickings for predators. If I were hungry, he'd smell like dinner. Fortunately, I'm not hungry yet, so I don't have to deal with the temptation, the conflict, the revulsion. I snort, condensation trumpeting from my nostrils, then turn and lope back up the alley.

Ahead is a Vietnamese restaurant. The smell of food is embedded in the very wood frame of the building. On a rear addition, an exhaust fan turns slowly, clicking with each revolution as one blade catches the metal screen casing. Below the fan a window is open. Faded sunflower-print curtains billow out in the night breeze. I can hear people inside, a room full of people, grunting and whistling in sleep. I want to see them. I want to stick my muzzle in the open window and look inside. A werewolf can have a lot of fun with a roomful of unprotected people.

I start to creep forward but a sudden crackle and hiss stops me. The hiss softens, then is drowned out by a man's voice, sharp, his words snapped off like icicles. I turn my head each way, radar searching for the source. He's farther down the street. I abandon the restaurant and go to him. We are curious by nature.

He's standing in a three-car parking lot wedged at the end of a narrow passage between buildings. He holds a walkie-talkie to his ear and leans one elbow against a brick wall, casual but not resting. His shoulders are relaxed. His gaze goes nowhere. He is confident in his place, that he has a right to be here and little to fear from the night. The gun dangling from his belt probably helps. He stops talking, jabs a button, and slams the walkie-talkie into its holster. His eyes scan the parking lot once, taking inventory and seeing nothing requiring his attention. Then he heads deeper into the alley maze. This could be amusing. I follow.

My nails click against the pavement. He doesn't notice. I pick up speed, darting around trash bags and empty boxes. Finally, I'm close enough. He hears the steady clicking behind him and stops. I duck behind a Dumpster, peer around the corner. He turns and squints into the darkness. After a second he starts forward. I let him get a few steps away, then resume the pursuit. This time when he stops, I wait one extra second before diving for cover. He lets out a muffled oath. He's seen something—a flash of motion, a shadow flickering, something. His right hand slips to his gun, caressing the metal, then pulling back, as if the reassurance is enough. He hesitates, then looks up and down the alley, realizing he is alone and uncertain what to do about it. He mutters something, then continues walking, quicker this time.

As he walks, his eyes flick from side to side, wariness treading the border of alarm. I inhale deeply, picking up only wisps of fear, enough to make my heart pound, but not enough to send my brain spinning out of control. He's safe quarry for a stalking game. He won't run. I can suppress most of my instincts. I can stalk him without killing him. I can suffer the first pangs of hunger without killing him. I can watch him pull his gun without killing him. Yet if he runs, I won't be able to stop myself. That's a temptation I can't fight. If he runs, I *will* chase. If I chase, either he'll kill me or I'll kill him.

As he turns the corner down a connecting alley, he relaxes. All has been silent behind him. I creep from my hiding place, shifting my weight to the back of my foot pads to muffle the sound of my nails. Soon I am only a few feet behind him. I can smell his aftershave, almost masking the natural scent of a long day's work. I can see his white socks appearing and disappearing between his shoes and pant legs. I can hear his breathing, the slight elevation in tempo betraying the fact that he's walking faster than usual. I ease forward, coming close enough that I could lunge if I want to and knock him to the ground before he even thought to reach for his gun. His head jerks up. He knows I'm there. He knows *something* is there. I wonder if he will turn. Does he dare to look, to face something he can't see or hear, but can only sense? His hand slides to his gun, but he doesn't turn. He walks faster. Then he swings back to the safety of the street.

I follow him to the end and observe from the darkness. He strides forward, keys in hand, to a parked cruiser, unlocks it, and hops inside. The car roars and squeals from the curb. I watch the receding taillights and sigh. Game over. I won.

That was nice but it wasn't nearly enough to satisfy me. These city backstreets are too confining. My heart is thudding with unspent excitement. My legs are aching with built-up energy. I must *run.*

A wind gusts from the south, bringing the sharp tang of Lake Ontario with it. I think of heading to the beach, imagine running along the stretch of sand, feeling the icy water slapping against my paws, but it's not safe. If I want to run, I must go to the ravine. It's a long way, but I have little choice unless I plan to skulk around human-smelling alleyways for the rest of the night. I swing to the northwest and begin the journey.

Nearly a half hour later, I'm standing at the crest of a hill. My nose twitches, picking up the vestiges of an illegal leaf fire smoldering in a nearby yard. The wind bristles through my fur, chill, nearly cold, invigorating. Above me, traffic thunders across the overpass. Below is sanctuary, a perfect oasis in the middle of the city. I leap forward, throwing myself off. At last I'm running.

My legs pick up the rhythm before I'm halfway down the ravine. I close my eyes for a second and feel the wind slice across my muzzle. As my paws thump against the hard earth, tiny darts of pain shoot up my legs, but they make me feel alive, like jolting awake after an overlong sleep. The muscles contract and extend in perfect harmony. With each stretch comes an ache and a burst of physical joy. My body is thanking me for the exercise, rewarding me with jolts of near-narcotic adrenaline. The more I run, the lighter I feel, the pain falling free as if my paws are no longer striking the ground. Even as I race along the bottom of the ravine, I feel like I'm still running downhill, gaining energy instead of expending it. I want to run until all the tension in my body flies away, leaving nothing but the sensations of the moment. I couldn't stop if I wanted to. And I don't want to.

Dead leaves crackle under my paws. Somewhere in the forest an owl hoots softly. It has finished its hunting and rests contented, not caring who knows it's around. A rabbit bolts out of a thicket and halfway across my path, then realizes its mistake and zooms back into the undergrowth. I keep running. My heart pounds. Against my rising body heat, the air feels ice-cold, stinging as it storms through my nostrils and into my lungs. I inhale, savoring the shock of it hitting my insides. I'm running too fast to smell anything. Bits of scents flutter through my brain in a jumbled montage that smells of freedom. Unable to resist, I finally skid to a halt, throw my head back, and howl. The music pours up from my chest in a tangible evocation of pure joy. It echoes through the ravine and soars to the moonless sky, letting them all know I'm here. I own this place! When I'm done, I drop my head, panting with exertion. I'm standing there, staring down into a scattering of yellow and red maple leaves, when a sound pierces my self-absorption. It's a growl, a soft, menacing growl. There's a pretender to my throne.

I look up to see a brownish yellow dog standing a few meters away. No, not a dog. My brain takes a second, but it finally recognizes the animal. A coyote. The recognition takes a second because it's unexpected. I've heard there are coyotes in the city, but have never encountered one. The coyote is equally confused. Animals don't know what to make of me. They smell human, but see wolf and, just when they decide their nose is tricking them, they look into my eyes and see human. When I encounter dogs, they either attack or turn tail and run. The coyote does neither. It lifts its muzzle and sniffs the air, then bristles and pulls its lips back in a drawn-out growl. It's half my size, scarcely worth my notice. I let it know this with a lazy "get lost" growl and a shake of my head. The coyote doesn't move. I stare at it. The coyote breaks the gazelock first.

I snort, toss my head again, and slowly turn away. I'm halfway turned when a flash of brown fur leaps at my shoulder. Diving to the side, I roll out of the way, then scramble to my feet. The coyote snarls. I give a serious growl, a canine "now you're pissing me off." The coyote stands its ground. It wants a fight. Good.

My fur rises on end, my tail bushing out behind me. I lower my head between my shoulder bones and lay my ears flat. My lips pull back and I feel the snarl tickling up through my throat then reverberating into the night. The coyote doesn't back down. I crouch and I'm about to lunge when something hits me hard in the shoulder, throwing me off balance. I stumble, then twist to face my attacker. A second coyote, gray-brown, hangs from my shoulder, fangs sunk to the bone. With a roar of rage and pain, I buck up and throw my weight to the side.

As the second coyote flies free, the first launches itself at my face. Ducking my head, I catch it in the throat, but my teeth clamp down on fur instead of flesh and it squirms away. It tries to back off for a second lunge, but I leap at it, backing it into a tree. It rears up, trying to get out of my way. I slash for its throat. This time I get my grip. Blood spurts in my mouth, salty and thick. The coyote's mate lands on my back. My legs buckle. Teeth sink into the loose skin beneath my skull. Fresh pain arcs through me. Concentrating hard, I keep my grip on the first coyote's throat. I steady myself, then release it for a split second, just long enough to make the fatal slash and tear. As I pull back, blood sprays into my eyes, blinding me. I swing my head hard, ripping out the coyote's throat. Once I feel it go limp, I toss it aside, then throw myself on the ground and roll over. The coyote on my back yips in surprise and releases its hold. I jump up and turn in the same motion, ready to take this other animal out of the game, but it scrambles up and dives into the brush. With a flash of wire-brush tail, it's gone. I look at the dead coyote. Blood streams from its throat, eagerly lapped up by the dry earth below. A tremor runs through me, like the final shudder of sated lust. I close my eyes and shiver. Not my fault. They attacked me first. The ravine has gone quiet, echoing the calm that floods through me. Not so much as a cricket chirps. The world is dark and silent and sleeping.

I try to examine and clean my wounds, but they are out of reach. I stretch and assess the pain. Two deep cuts, both bleeding only enough to mat my fur. I'll live. I turn and start the trip out of the ravine.

In the alley I Change then yank my clothes on and scurry to the sidewalk like a junkie caught shooting up in the shadows. Frustration fills me. It shouldn't end like this, dirty and furtive, amidst the garbage and filth of the city. It should end in a clearing in the forest, clothes abandoned in some thicket, stretched out naked, feeling the coolness of the earth beneath me and the night breeze tickling my bare skin. I should be falling asleep in the grass, exhausted beyond all thought, with only the miasma of contentedness floating through my mind. And I shouldn't be alone. In my mind, I can see the others, lying around me in the grass. I can hear the familiar snores, the occasional whisper and laugh. I can feel warm skin against mine, a bare foot hooked over my calf, twitching in a dream of running. I can smell them: their sweat, their breath, mingling with the scent of blood, smears from a deer killed in the chase. The image shatters and I am staring into a shop-window, seeing nothing but myself reflected back. My chest tightens in a loneliness so deep and so complete I can't breathe.

I turn quickly and lash out at the nearest object. A streetlamp quavers and rings with the blow. Pain sears down my arm. Welcome to reality—changing in alleyways and creeping back to my apartment. I am cursed to live between worlds. On the one side there is normalcy. On the other, there is a place where I can be what I am with no fear of reprisals, where I can commit murder itself and scarcely raise the eyebrows of those around me, where I am even encouraged to do so to protect the sanctity of that world. But I left and I can't return. I won't return.

As I walk to the apartment, my anger blisters the pavement with every step. A woman curled up under a pile of dirty blankets peers out as I pass and instinctively shrinks back into her nest. As I round the corner, two men step out and size up my prospects as prey. I resist the urge to snarl at them, but just barely. I walk faster and they seem to decide I'm not worth chasing. I shouldn't be here. I should be home in bed, not prowling downtown Toronto at four A.M. A normal woman wouldn't be here. It's yet another reminder that I'm not normal. Not normal. I look down the darkened street and I can read a billet on a telephone post fifty feet off. Not normal. I catch a whiff of fresh bread from a bakery starting production miles away. Not normal. I stop by a storefront, grab a bar over the windows, and flex my biceps. The metal groans in my hand. Not normal. Not normal. I chant the words in my head, flagellating myself with them. The anger only grows.

Outside my apartment door, I stop and inhale deeply. I mustn't wake Philip. And if I do, I mustn't let him see me like this. I don't need a mirror to know what I look like: skin taut, color high, eyes incandescent with the rage that always seems to follow a Change now. Definitely not normal.

When I finally enter the apartment, I hear his measured breathing from the bedroom. Still asleep. I'm nearly to the bathroom when his breathing catches.

"Elena?" His voice is a sleep-stuffed croak.

"Just going to the washroom."

I try to slip past the doorway, but he's sitting up, peering nearsightedly at me. He frowns.

"Fully dressed?" he says.

"I went out."

A moment of silence. He runs a hand through his dark hair and sighs. "It's not safe. Damn it, Elena. We've discussed this. Wake me up and I'll go with you."

"I need to be alone. To think."

"It's not safe."

"I know. I'm sorry."

I creep into the bathroom, spending longer than necessary. I pretend to use the toilet, wash my hands with enough water to fill a Jacuzzi, then find a fingernail that needs elaborate filing attention. When I finally decide Philip has fallen back asleep, I head for the bedroom. The bedside lamp is on. He's propped on his pillow, glasses in place. I hesitate in the doorway. I can't bring myself to cross the threshold, to go and crawl into bed with him. I hate myself for it, but I can't do it. The memory of the night lingers and I feel out of place here.

When I don't move, Philip shifts his legs over the side of the bed and sits up.

"I didn't mean to snap," he says. "I worry. I know you need your freedom and I'm trying—"

He stops and rubs his hand across his mouth. His words slice through me. I know he doesn't mean them as a reprimand, but they are a reminder that I'm screwing this up, that I'm fortunate to have found someone as patient and understanding as Philip, but I'm wearing through that patience at breakneck speed and all I seem capable of doing is standing back and waiting for the final crash.

"I know you need your freedom," he says again. "But there has to be some other way. Maybe you could go out in the morning, early. If you prefer night, we could drive down to the lake. You could walk around. I could sit in the car and keep an eye on you. Maybe I could walk with you. Stay twenty paces behind or something." He manages a wry smile.

"Or maybe not. I'd probably get picked up by the cops, the middle-aged guy stalking the beautiful young blonde."

He pauses, then leans forward. "That's your cue, Elena. You're supposed to remind me that forty-one is far from middle-aged."

"We'll work something out," I say.

We can't, of course. I have to run under the cover of night and I have to do it alone. There is no compromise.

As he sits on the edge of the bed, watching me, I know we're doomed. My only hope is to make this relationship so otherwise perfect that Philip might come to overlook our one insurmountable problem. To do that, my first step should be to go to him, crawl in bed, kiss him and tell him I love him. But I can't. Not tonight. Tonight I'm something else, something he doesn't know and couldn't understand. I don't want to go to him like this.

"I'm not tired," I say. "I might as well stay up. Do you want breakfast?"

He looks at me. Something in his expression falters and I know I've failed—again. But he doesn't say anything. He pulls his smile back in place. "Let's go out. Someplace in this city has to be open this early. We'll drive around until we find it. Drink five cups of coffee and watch the sun come up. Okay?"

I nod, not trusting myself to speak.

"Shower first?" he says. "Or flip for it?"

"You go ahead."

He kisses my cheek as he passes. I wait until I hear the shower running, then head for the kitchen.

Sometimes I get so hungry.

Human

I STOOD AT THE DOOR BEFORE RINGING THE BELL. IT WAS Mother's Day and I was standing at a door holding a present, which would have been quite normal if it was a present for my mother. But my mother was long dead and I didn't keep in touch with any of my foster mothers, let alone bring them gifts. The present was for Philip's mother. Again, this would have been very normal if Philip had been there with me. He wasn't. He'd called from his office an hour ago to say he couldn't get away. Did I want to go alone? Or would I rather wait for him? I'd opted to go and now stood there wondering if that was the right decision. Did a woman visit her boyfriend's mother on Mother's Day without said boyfriend? Maybe I was trying too hard. It wouldn't be the first time.

Human rules confounded me. It wasn't as if I'd been raised in a cave. Before I became a werewolf, I'd already learned the basic mechanics: how to hail a taxi, operate an elevator, apply for a bank account, all the minutiae of human life. The problem came with human interactions. My childhood had been pretty screwed up. Then, when I'd been on the cusp of becoming an adult, I'd been bitten and spent the next nine years of my life with other werewolves. Even during those years, I hadn't been locked away from the human world. I'd gone back to university, traveled with the others, even taken on jobs. But they'd always been there, for support and protection and companionship. I hadn't needed to make it on my own. I hadn't needed to make friends or take lovers or go to lunch with coworkers. So, I hadn't. Last year, when I broke with the others and came back to Toronto alone, I thought fitting in would be the least of my concerns. How tough could it be? I'd just take the basics I'd learned from childhood, mix in the adult conversational skills I'd learned with the others, toss in a dash of caution and voilà, I'd be making friends and chatting up new acquaintances in no time. Hah!

Was it too late to leave? I didn't want to leave. Taking a deep breath, I rang the doorbell. Moments later, a flurry of footsteps erupted inside. Then a round-faced woman with graying brown hair answered.

"Elena!" Diane said, throwing the door open. "Mom, Elena's here. Is Philip parking the car? I can't believe how packed the street is. Everyone out visiting."

"Actually, Philip's not—uh—with me. He had to work, but he'll be along soon."

"Working? On a Sunday? Have a talk with him, girl." Diane braced the door open. "Come in, come in. Everyone's here."

Philip's mother, Anne, appeared from behind his sister. She was tiny, not even reaching my chin, with a sleek iron gray pageboy.

"Still ringing the doorbell, dear?" she said, reaching up to hug me. "Only salesmen ring the bell. Family walks right in."

"Philip will be late," Diane said. "He's working."

Anne made a noise in her throat and ushered me inside. Philip's father, Larry, was in the kitchen pilfering pastries from a tray.

"Those are for dessert, Dad," Anne said, shooing him away.

Larry greeted me with a one-armed hug, the other hand still clutching a brownie. "So where's—"

"Late," Diane said. "Working. Come into the living room, Elena. Mom invited the neighbors, Sally and Juan, for lunch." Her voice lowered to a whisper. "Their kids are all out West." She pushed open the French doors. "Before you got here, Mom was showing them your last few articles in *Focus Toronto.*"

"Uh-oh. Is that good or bad?"

"Don't worry. They're staunch Liberals. They loved your stuff. Oh, here we are. Sally, Juan, this is Elena Michaels, Philip's girlfriend."

———

Philip's girlfriend. That always sounded odd, not because I objected to being called a "girlfriend" instead of "partner" or anything as ridiculously politically correct. It struck me because it'd been years since I'd been anyone's girlfriend. I didn't do relationships. For me, if it lasted the weekend, it was getting too serious. My one and only lengthy relationship had been a disaster. More than a disaster. Catastrophic.

Philip was different.

I'd met Philip a few weeks after I'd moved back to Toronto. He'd been living in an apartment a few blocks away. Since our buildings shared a property manager, tenants in his complex had access to the health club in mine. He'd come to the pool one day after midnight and, finding me alone swimming laps, he'd asked if I minded if he did some, as if I had the right to kick him out. Over the next month, we'd often found ourselves alone in the health club late at night. Each time, he'd checked to make sure I was comfortable being alone there with him. Finally, I'd said that the reason I was working out in the health club was to ensure I didn't need to worry about being attacked by strange men and I'd be defeating the whole purpose if I was nervous about having him there. That had made him laugh and he'd lingered after his workout and bought me a juice from the vending machine. Once the post-workout juice break became a habit, he worked his way up the meal chain with invitations to coffee, then lunch, then dinner. By the time we got around to breakfast, it was nearly six months from the day we'd met in the pool. That might have been part of the reason I let myself fall for him, flattered that anyone would put that amount of time and effort into getting to know me. Philip wooed me with all the patience of someone trying to coax a half-wild animal into the house and, like many a stray, I found myself domesticated before I thought to resist.

All had gone well until he'd suggested we move in together. I should have said no. But I hadn't. Part of me couldn't resist the challenge of seeing whether I could pull it off. Another part of me had been afraid of losing him if I refused. The first month had been a disaster. Then, just when I'd been sure the bubble was ready to burst, the pressure eased. I forced myself to postpone my Changes longer, allowing me to run when Philip was away on overnight business trips or working late.

Of course, I can't take all the credit for saving the relationship. Hell, I'd be pushing it if I took half. Even after we moved in together, Philip was as patient as he'd been when we were dating. When I did something that would raise most human eyebrows, Philip brushed it off with a joke. When I was overwhelmed by the stress of fitting in, he took me to dinner or a show, getting my mind off my problems, letting me know he was there if I wanted to talk, and understanding if I didn't. At first I thought it was too good to be true. Every day I'd come home from work, pause outside the apartment door, and brace myself to open it and find him gone. But he didn't leave. A few weeks ago he'd begun talking about finding us a bigger place when my lease was up, even hinting that a condo might be a wise investment. A condo. Wow. That was almost semi-permanent, wasn't it? A week later and I was still in shock—but it was a good sort of shock.

It was mid-afternoon. The neighbors were gone. Diane's husband, Ken, had left early to take their youngest to work. Philip's other sister, Judith, lived in the U.K. and had to settle for a Mother's Day phone call, phoning after lunch and speaking to everyone, including me. Like all of Philip's family, she treated me as if I were a sister-in-law instead of her brother's girlfriend-of-the-hour. They were all so friendly, so ready to accept me that I had a hard time believing they weren't just being polite. It was possible they really did like me but, having had rotten luck with families, I was reluctant to believe it. I wanted it too much.

As we were washing dishes, the telephone rang. Anne answered it in the living room. A few minutes later, she came and got me. It was Philip.

"I am so sorry, hon," he said when I answered. "Is Mom mad?"

"I don't think so."

"Good. I promised to take her to dinner another time to make up for it."

"So are you coming over?"

He sighed. "I'm not going to make it. Diane'll give you a ride home."

"Oh, that's not necessary. I can take a cab or the—"

"Too late," he said. "I already told Mom to ask Diane. They won't let you out of that house without an escort now." He paused. "I really didn't mean to abandon you. Are you surviving?"

"Very well. Everyone's great, as always."

"Good. I'll be home by seven. Don't make anything. I'll pick up. Caribbean?"

"You hate Caribbean."

"I'm doing penance. See you at seven, then. Love you."

He hung up before I could argue.

"You should have seen the dresses," Diane was saying as she drove to my apartment. "God-awful. Like bags with armholes. Designers must figure by the time women need a mother-of-the-bride dress they don't give a damn what they look like. I found this one gorgeous navy number, probably meant for the father-of-the-bride's new young wife, but the middle was tight. I thought about crash dieting to fit, but I won't do it. It's a matter of principle. I've had three kids, I earned this belly."

"There's got to be better stuff out there," I said. "Have you tried the non-bridal shops?"

"That's my next step. I was actually leading up to asking if you'd come with me. Most of my friends think bags with armholes are great. Middle-age camouflage. Then there's my daughters, who won't look at anything that doesn't show off their belly-rings. Would you mind? I'll throw in a free lunch. A three-martini lunch."

I laughed. "After three martinis, any dress will look good."

Diane grinned. "My plan exactly. Is that a yes?"

"Sure."

"Great. I'll give you a call and we'll set it up."

She drove into the roundabout in front of my apartment. I opened the door, then remembered my manners.

"Would you like to come up for a coffee?"

I was sure she'd offer some polite refusal, but instead she said, "Sure. Another hour of peace before reentering the trenches. Plus a chance to give my little brother proper hell for tossing you to the sharks today."

I laughed and directed her to visitor parking.

Summons

MAYBE I'VE GIVEN THE WRONG IMPRESSION BY MAKING SUCH A big deal out of my quest to live in the human world, as if all werewolves cut themselves off from human life. They don't. By necessity, most werewolves live in the human world. Short of teaming up and creating a commune in New Mexico, they don't have much choice. The human world provides them with food, shelter, sex, and other necessities. Yet, although they may live in that world, they don't consider themselves part of it. They view human interaction as a necessary evil, with attitudes ranging from contempt to barely concealed amusement. They are actors playing a role, sometimes enjoying their turn on the stage, but usually relieved to get off it. I didn't want to be like that. I wanted to live in the human world and, as much as possible, be myself doing it. I didn't choose this life and I damn well wasn't about to give in to it, surrendering every dream of my future, ordinary, mediocre dreams of a home, a family, a career, and above all, stability. None of that was possible living as a werewolf.

I grew up in foster homes. Bad foster homes. Not having had a family as a child, I became determined to create one for myself. Becoming a werewolf pretty much knocked those plans into the dumper. Still, even if a husband and children were out of the question, that didn't mean I couldn't pursue some part of that dream. I was making a career for myself in journalism. I was making a home in Toronto. And I was making a family, albeit not the traditional family, with Philip. We'd been together long enough that I'd begun to believe some stability in my life was possible. I couldn't believe my luck in finding someone as normal and decent as Philip. I knew what I was. I was difficult, temperamental, argumentative, not the sort of woman someone like Philip would fall for. Of course, I wasn't like that around Philip. I kept that part of me—the werewolf part—hidden, hoping I'd eventually slough it off like dead skin. With Philip, I had the chance to reinvent myself, to become the kind of person he thought I was. Which, of course, was exactly the kind of person I wanted to be.

The Pack didn't understand why I chose to live among humans. They couldn't understand because they weren't like me. First, I wasn't born a werewolf. Most werewolves are, or at least they're born carrying the blood in their veins and will experience their first Change when they reach adulthood. The other way to become a werewolf is to be bitten by one. Very few people survive a werewolf's bite. Werewolves are neither stupid nor altruistic. If they bite, they intend to kill. If they bite and fail to kill, they'll stalk their victim and finish the job. It's a simple matter of survival. If you're a werewolf who has comfortably assimilated into a town or city, the last thing you want is some half-crazed new werewolf lurching around your territory, slaughtering people and calling attention to himself. Even if someone is bitten and escapes, the chances of surviving are minimal. The first few Changes are hell, on the body and the sanity. Hereditary werewolves grow up knowing their lot in life and having their fathers to guide them. Bitten werewolves are on their own. If they don't die from the physical stress, the mental stress drives them either to kill themselves or raise a big enough ruckus that another werewolf finds them and ends their suffering before they cause trouble. So there aren't many bitten werewolves running around. At last count, there were approximately thirty-five werewolves in the world. Exactly three were nonhereditary, including me.

Me. The only female werewolf in existence. The werewolf gene is passed only through the male line, father to son, so the only way for a woman to become a werewolf is to be bitten and survive, which, as I've said, is rare. Given the odds, it's not surprising I'm the only female. Bitten on purpose, turned into a werewolf on purpose. Amazing, really, that I survived. After all, when you've got a species with three dozen males and one female, that one female becomes something of a prize. And werewolves do not settle their battles over a nice game of chess. Nor do they have a history of respect for women. Women serve two functions in the werewolf world: sex and dinner, or if they're feeling lazy, sex followed by dinner. Although I doubt any werewolf would dine on me, I'm an irresistible object for satisfying the other primal urge. Left on my own, I wouldn't have survived. Fortunately, I wasn't left on my own. Since I'd been bitten, I'd been under the protection of the Pack. Every society has its ruling class. In the werewolf world, it was the Pack. For reasons that had nothing to do with me and everything to do with the status of the werewolf who'd bitten me, I'd been part of the Pack from the time I was turned. A year ago I'd left. I'd cut myself off and I wasn't going back. Given the choice between human and werewolf, I'd chosen to be human.

Philip had to work late the next day. Tuesday evening, I was waiting for his "I'll be late" phone call when he walked into the apartment carrying dinner.

"Hope you're hungry," he said, swinging a bag of Indian takeout onto the table.

I was, though I'd grabbed two sausages from a vendor on the way home from work. The predinner meal had taken the edge off, so a normal dinner would now suffice. Yet another of the million tricks I'd learned to accommodate to human life.

Philip chatted about work as he took the cartons from the bag and set the table. I graciously shifted my papers to the side to let him lay out my place setting. I can be so helpful sometimes. Even after the food was on my plate, I managed to resist eating while I jotted down the final line of the article I was working on. Then I pushed the pad of paper aside and dug in.

"Mom called me at work," Philip said. "She forgot to ask on Sunday whether you could help her plan Becky's wedding shower."

"Really?"

I heard the delight in my voice and wondered at it. Throwing a shower wasn't exactly cause for high excitement. Still, no one had ever asked me to help at one before. Hell, no one had even invited me to one, excluding Sarah from work, but she'd invited all her coworkers.

Philip smiled. "I take it that's a yes. Good. Mom will be happy. She loves that kind of stuff, all the fussing around and planning."

"I don't have much experience with throwing showers."

"No problem. Becky's bridesmaids are giving her the main shower, so this will just be a little family one. Well, not exactly little. I think Mom plans to invite every relative in Ontario. You'll get to meet the whole bunch. I'm sure Mom's told them all about you. Hope it's not too overwhelming."

"No," I said. "I'll be looking forward to it."

"Sure, you can say that now. You haven't met them."

After dinner, Philip went downstairs to the fitness center for some weight-training. When he worked normal hours, he liked to get his workout in early and get to bed early, wryly admitting that he was getting too old to survive on five hours of sleep per night. For the first month we'd lived together, I'd joined him in his early workouts. It wasn't easy pretending to struggle bench-pressing a hundred pounds when I could do five times that. Then came the day when I was so engrossed in conversation with one of our neighbors that I didn't realize I was doing a sixty-pound lat pulldown one-handed and chatting away as casually as if I were pulling down a window blind. When I noticed the neighbor double-checking my weights, I realized my goof and covered it up with some bullshit about an incorrectly adjusted machine. After that, I restricted my workouts to between midnight and six, when the weight room was empty. I'd told Philip some story about taking advantage of a late-night second wind. He bought that, as he'd readily accepted so many other of my quirks. When he worked late, I went down to the health club afterward with him and did my swimming and running workouts as I'd done when we first met. Otherwise, he went alone.

That evening after Philip left, I switched on the TV. I didn't watch it much, but when I did, I wallowed in the dregs of the broadcasting barrel, flicking past educational shows and high-grade dramas to tabloids and talk shows. Why? Because it reassured me that there were people in the world who were worse off than I was. No matter what went wrong with my day, I could turn on the TV, watch some moron telling his wife and the rest of the world that he's sleeping with her daughter and say to myself Well, at least I'm better than that. Trash television as reaffirmation therapy. You gotta love it.

Today *Inside Scoop* was following up on some psycho who'd escaped from a North Carolina jail several months ago. Pure sensationalism. This guy had broken into the apartment of a total stranger, tied the man up and shot him because he—quote—wanted to know what it felt like. The show's writers had peppered the piece with words like "savage," "wild," and "animalistic." What bullshit. Show me the animal that kills for the thrill of watching something die. Why does the stereotype of the animalistic killer persist? Because humans like it. It neatly explains things for them, moving humans to the top of the evolutionary ladder and putting killers down among mythological man-beast monsters like werewolves.

The truth is, if a werewolf behaved like this psychopath it wouldn't be because he was part animal, but because he was still too human. Only humans kill for sport.

The show was almost over when Philip returned.

"Good workout?" I asked.

"Never good," he said, making a face. "I'm still waiting for the day when they invent a pill to replace exercise. What are you watching?" He leaned over my head. "Any good fights breaking out?"

"That's Jerry Springer. I can't watch Springer. I tried once. Watched for ten minutes, trying to get past the profanity to figure out what they were saying. Finally figured out the profanity was all they were saying—a break between wrestling bouts. The WWF of daytime TV. No, strike that. At least WWF has a story line."

Philip laughed and rumpled my hair. "How about a walk? I'll grab a shower while you finish your show."

"Sounds good."

Philip headed to the bathroom. I sneaked to the fridge and grabbed a hunk of provolone that I'd hidden amongst the vegetables. When the phone rang, I ignored it. Eating was more important, and since Philip already had the water running, he wouldn't hear the ringing, so he wouldn't know I wasn't answering it. Or so I thought. As I heard the water shut off, I shoved the cheese behind the lettuce and jogged for the phone. Philip was the sort who'd answer the phone during dinner rather than subject someone to the answering machine. I tried to live up to his example—at least when he was around. I was halfway across the apartment when the machine clicked on. My recorded voice sang out a nauseatingly cheery greeting and invited the caller to leave a message. This one did.

"Elena? It's Jeremy." I stopped in midstride. "Please call me. It's important."

His voice trailed off. The phone hissed with a sharp intake of breath. I knew he was tempted to say more, to issue a call-me-or-else ultimatum, but he couldn't. We had an agreement. He couldn't come here or send any of the others here. I resisted the urge to stick out my tongue at the answering machine. Nyah-nyah-nyah, you can't get me. Maturity is highly overrated.

"It's urgent, Elena," Jeremy continued. "You know I wouldn't call if it wasn't."

Philip reached for the phone, but Jeremy had already hung up. He lifted the receiver and held it out to me. I averted my gaze and walked to the couch.

"Aren't you going to call back?" he said.

"He didn't leave a number."

"He sounded as if he expected you to have it. Who was it anyway?"

"A—uh—second cousin."

"So my mysterious orphan has family? I'll have to meet this cousin someday."

"You wouldn't want to."

He laughed. "Turnabout's fair play. I inflicted my family on you. Now's your chance for revenge. After Betsy's shower you'll want to sic your worst on me. Dig up the mad cousins who've been locked in attics for years. Though, actually, crazy attic-dwelling cousins would probably be the best kind. Definite dinner party interest. Better than the great-aunts who've told you the same story since childhood and fall asleep over dessert."

I rolled my eyes. "Ready for that walk yet?"

"Let me finish my shower. How about giving 411 a call?"

"And get dinged with a service charge whether they find the number or not?"

"It's less than a buck. We can afford it. Call. If you can't find his number, maybe you can get someone else who can give you his number. There must be more of these cousins, right?"

"You think they have phone service in those attics? They're lucky if they get electric lighting."

"Call, Elena," he said, giving a mock growl as he disappeared into the bathroom.

Once he was out of the room, I stared at the phone. Philip may have joked about it, but I knew he expected me to call Jeremy back. Why wouldn't he? It was what any decent human being would do. Philip had heard the message, heard the urgency in Jeremy's voice. By refusing to return what seemed to be a very important call, I'd appear callous, uncaring. A human would call back. The kind of woman I wanted to be would call back.

I could pretend I'd made the call. It was tempting, but it wouldn't stop Jeremy from phoning again . . . and again . . . and again. This wasn't the first time he'd tried communicating with me in the past few days. Werewolves share some degree of telepathy. Most werewolves ignored it, preferring less mystical ways of communication. Jeremy had refined the ability to an art, mainly because it gave him one more way to get under our skin and harass us until we did his bidding. While he'd been trying to contact me, I'd been blocking him. So he'd resorted to the phone. Not quite as effective as bombarding someone's brain, but after a few days of filled message tapes, I'd cave in, if only to get rid of him.

I stood next to the phone, closed my eyes, and inhaled. I could do this. I could make the call, find out what Jeremy wanted, politely thank him for letting me know, and refuse to do whatever it was he demanded, knowing full well he was going to demand something of me. Even if Jeremy was the Pack Alpha and I'd been conditioned to obey him, I didn't have to do it anymore. I wasn't Pack. He had no control over me.

I lifted the receiver and punched in the numbers from memory. It rang four times, then the machine picked up. A recorded voice started, not Jeremy's deep tones, but a Southern drawl that made me fumble to hang up before I heard the entire message. Sweat broke out along my forehead. The air in the apartment seemed to have shot up ten degrees and lost half its oxygen. I wiped my hands over my face, gave my head a sharp shake and went to find my shoes for my walk with Philip.

Before breakfast the next morning, Philip asked what Jeremy had wanted. I admitted that I hadn't been able to get in touch with him, but promised to keep trying. After we ate, Philip went downstairs to get the newspaper. I called Jeremy and once more got the answering machine.

As much as I hated to admit it, I was starting to worry. It wasn't my fault, really. Being concerned about my former Pack brothers was instinctive, something I couldn't control. Or, at least, that's what I told myself when my heart pounded on the third unanswered call.

Jeremy should have been there. He rarely went far from Stonehaven, preferring to rule from his throne of power and sending his minions to do his dirty work. Okay, that wasn't a fair assessment of Jeremy's leadership style, but I was in no mood to be complimentary. He'd told me to call and, goddamn it, he should have been there when I did.

When Philip came back, I was hovering over the phone, glaring down at it as if I could mentally force Jeremy to pick up.

"Still no answer?" Philip said.

I shook my head. He studied my face more closely than I liked. As I turned away, he crossed the room and put his hand on my shoulder.

"You're worried."

"Not really. I just—"

"It's okay, hon. If it were my family, I'd be worried. Maybe you should go there. See what's wrong. It sounded urgent."

I pulled away. "No, that's ridiculous. I'll keep calling—"

"It's family, hon," he said, as if that answered any argument I could come up with. For him, it did. That was one thing I couldn't argue with. When Philip and I first became serious, the lease on his apartment came up and he'd made it clear he wanted to move in with me, but I'd resisted. Then he'd taken me to his family reunion. I'd met his mother and his father and his sister and seen how he interacted with them, how integral they were to his life. The next day I'd told him not to extend his lease.

Now Philip expected me to go to the aid of someone he thought was my family. If I refused, would he think I wasn't the kind of person he wanted? I wouldn't take that chance. I promised to keep trying. I promised if I didn't get hold of Jeremy by noon, I'd fly to New York State to see what was wrong.

Each time I called over the next few hours, I prayed for an answer. The only reply I got was the click of the answering machine.

Philip drove me to the airport after lunch.

Prodigal

THE PLANE LANDED AT SYRACUSE-HANCOCK AT SEVEN P.M. I TRIED Jeremy's number, but only got the answering machine. Again. By now I was more annoyed than worried. As the distance between us lessened, my memory improved and I remembered what it was like to live at Stonehaven, Jeremy's country estate. In particular, I recalled the resident phone-answering habits, or lack thereof. Two people lived at Stonehaven, Jeremy and his foster-son-turned-bodyguard, Clayton. There were two phones in the five-bedroom house. The one in Clay's room was connected to the answering machine, but the phone itself had lost the ability to ring four years ago, when Clay whipped it across the room after it dared disturb his sleep two nights in a row. There was also a phone in the study, but if Clay needed to use the line for his laptop, he often neglected to plug the phone back in, sometimes for days. Even if, by chance, there was an operating telephone in the house, both men had been known to sit five feet away and not bother picking it up. And Philip thought my phone habits were bad.

The more I thought about it, the more I fumed. The more I fumed, the more determined I was not to leave the airport until someone answered the damned phone. If they summoned me, they should pick me up. At least, this was my excuse. The truth was that I was loath to leave the bustle of the airport. Yes, that sounds crazy. Most people judge the success of a plane flight by how little time they have to spend in the airport. Normally, I would have felt the same way, but as I sat there, taking in the sights and smells of the nearly empty terminal, I reveled in the humanness of it. Here in the airport I was an anonymous face in a sea of equally anonymous faces. There was comfort in that, the feeling of being part of something larger, but not at the center of it. Things would change the minute I walked out of here and into Stonehaven.

Two hours later, I decided I couldn't put it off any longer. I made my last call to Stonehaven and left a message. Two words. "I'm coming." It would do.

Getting to Stonehaven wasn't easy. It was in remote upstate New York, near a small town called Bear Valley. As my cab pulled away from the airport, it was already night. Syracuse glowed somewhere to the south, but the cab turned north once it reached Highway 81. The lights of North Syracuse appeared to my left, faded fast, then vanished into the night. A dozen miles later the driver turned off the highway and the darkness was complete. In the quiet of the country night, I relaxed. Werewolves weren't meant for urban life. There was no place to run, and the sheer crush of people often provided more temptation than anonymity. Sometimes I think I chose to live in downtown Toronto simply because it was against my nature, one more instinct for me to defeat.

As I looked out the window, I ticked off the time with the landmarks. With each passing mark, my stomach danced faster. Trepidation, I told myself. Not anticipation. Even if I'd spent the better part of ten years at Stonehaven, I didn't consider it my home. The concept of home was difficult for me, an ethereal construct emerging from dreams and stories rather than actual experience. Of course, I did have a home once, a good home and a good family, but it didn't last long enough to leave more than the most fleeting impression.

My parents died when I was five. We'd been coming home from the fair, taking a back road because my mother wanted to show me a miniature pony foal she'd seen at a farm along there. I could hear my father laughing, asking my mother how she expected me to see anything in a field at midnight. I remember him turning to look over the seat, grinning at me while he teased my mother beside me. I don't remember what happened next, no squealing tires, no screams, no careering out of control. Just blackness.

I don't know how I got on the side of the road. I'd been seat-belted in, but must have crawled out after the accident. All I remember is sitting in the gravel beside my father's bloodied body, shaking him, talking to him, pleading with him to answer and not understanding why he didn't, knowing only that my father always answered, never ignored me, but all he did now was stare at me, eyes wide and unblinking. I remember hearing myself start to whimper, a five-year-old, crouched by the side of the road, staring into my father's eyes, whimpering because it was so dark and there was no one coming to help, whimpering because my mother was back in the crushed car, not moving, and my father was lying here in the dirt, not answering me, not holding me, not comforting me, not helping my mother get out of the car, and there was blood, so much blood, and broken glass everywhere, and it was so dark and so cold and no one was coming to help.

If I had any extended family, I never heard of them. After my parents died, the only person who tried to claim me was my mother's best friend and she was refused on the grounds that she was unmarried. However, I only spent a couple of weeks in the children's home before I was snatched up by the first couple who saw me. I can still see them, kneeling before me, cooing and ahhhing about what a beautiful child I was. So tiny, so perfect with my white-blond hair and my blue eyes. A porcelain doll, they called me. They took their doll home and started their perfect life. But it didn't work out quite that way. Their precious doll sat in a chair all day and never opened her mouth, then at night—every night—she screamed until dawn. After three weeks they returned me. So I went from one foster family to the next, always taken by the ones utterly charmed by my face and utterly incapable of handling my scarred psyche.

As I grew into adolescence, the couples who picked me from the home changed. It was no longer the wife who chose me but the husband, picking up on my childish beauty and my fear. I became the favored choice of male predators who were looking for a very special kind of child. Ironically, it was through these monsters that I first found my strength. As I grew older, I began to see them for what they were, not all-powerful bogeymen who slipped into my room at night, but weak creatures terrified of rejection and exposure. With that realization, the fear slipped away. They could touch me, but they couldn't touch *me,* not the me who lay beyond my body. As the fear subsided, so did the rage. I despised them and their equally weak, blind wives, but they weren't worthy of my anger. I wouldn't let myself be angry at them, wouldn't let myself waste time and effort better spent elsewhere. If I wanted to escape this life, I had to do it myself. That didn't mean running away. It meant staying and surviving. It meant studying hard and making the honors list even if I rarely went a full year without switching schools. Succeeding at school would mean acceptance into university, which would mean a degree, which would mean a career, which would mean the kind of life my social workers and foster families assumed was beyond me. At the same time, I discovered another source of power—the strength of my own body. I grew tall and rangy. A teacher signed me up for track-and-field, hoping it would help me get close to other children. Instead I learned to run, discovering the absolute bliss, the unparalleled pleasure of the physical, feeling my strength and my speed for the first time. By the time I was midway through high school I was lifting weights and working out daily. My foster father wasn't touching me by then. I wasn't anyone's idea of a victim by then.

"Is this it, miss?" the driver asked.

I hadn't felt the car stop, but when I looked out the window I could see we were at the front gates of Stonehaven. A figure sat on the grass, ankles crossed as he leaned against the stone wall. Clayton.

The driver squinted, trying to make out the house in the dark, as blind to the brass nameplate as to the man waiting by the gate. The moon had gone behind a cloud and the coach lamps at the end of the drive were unlit.

"I'll get out here," I said.

"Uh-uh. No can do, miss. It's not safe. There's something out there."

I thought he was referring to Clay. "Something" was an apt description. I was about to say, unfortunately, that I knew that "something" when the driver continued.

"We've been having ourselves some trouble in these woods, miss. Wild dogs by the looks of it. One of our girls from town was found not too far from here. Butchered by these dogs. Buddy of mind found her and he said—well, it wasn't nice, miss. You just sit back and I'll unlatch that gate and drive you up."

"Wild dogs?" I repeated, certain I'd heard wrong.

"That's right. My buddy found tracks. Huge ones. Some guy from some college said all the tracks came from one animal, but that can't be right. It's gotta be a pack. You don't see—" The driver's eyes went to the side window and he jumped in his seat. "Jesus!"

Clay had left his post at the gate and materialized at my window. He stood there, watching me, a slow grin lighting his eyes. He reached for the door handle. The driver put the car in gear.

"It's okay," I said, with deep regret. "He's with me."

The door opened. Clay ducked his head inside.

"You getting out or just thinking about it?" he asked.

"She's not getting out here," the driver said, twisting back to look over the seat. "If you're fool enough to be wandering around these woods at night, that's your problem, but I'm not letting this young lady walk God-knows-how-far to that house back there. If you want a ride up, unlock the gate for me and get in. Otherwise, close my door."

Clay turned to the driver, as if noticing him for the first time. His lip curled and his mouth opened. Whatever he planned to say, it wasn't going to be nice. Before Clay could cause a scene, I opened the opposite door and slid out. As the cab driver rolled down his window to stop me, I dropped a fifty on his lap and skirted around the back of the cab. Clay slammed the other door and headed for the front walk. The driver hesitated, then sped off, kicking up a hail of gravel as a parting shot of disgust at our youthful foolishness.

As I approached, Clay stepped back to watch me. Despite the cold night air, he wore only faded jeans and a black T-shirt, displaying slim hips, a broad chest, and sculpted biceps. In the decade I'd known him, he hadn't changed. I was always hoping for a difference—a few wrinkles, a scar, anything that would mar his model-perfect looks and bring him down to mortality with the rest of us, but I was always disappointed.

As I walked toward him, he tilted his head, his eyes never leaving mine. White teeth flashed as he grinned.

"Welcome home, darling." His Deep South drawl mangled the endearment into a "*dah*-lin" straight out of a country-and-western song. I hated country music.

"Are you the welcoming committee? Or has Jeremy finally chained you up to the front gate where you belong?"

"I missed you, too."

He reached out for me, but I sidestepped back onto the road, then started down the quarter-mile lane to the house. Clay followed. A breeze of cool, dry night air lifted a tendril of hair from my neck, and with it came a dusting of scents—the sharp tang of cedar, the faint perfume of apple blossoms, and the teasing smell of long-devoured dinner. Each smell loosened my tense muscles. I shook myself, throwing off the feeling and forced myself to keep my eyes on the road, concentrating on doing nothing, not talking to Clay, not smelling anything, not looking left or right. I didn't dare ask Clay what was going on. That would mean engaging him in conversation, which would imply that I wanted to talk to him. With Clay, even the simplest overtures were dangerous. As much as I wanted to know what was happening, I'd have to hear it from Jeremy.

When I reached the house, I paused at the door and looked up. The two-story stone house seemed not to loom over me, but to lean back, expectant. The welcome was there, but muted, waiting for me to make the first move. So very much like its owner. I touched one of the cool stones and felt a rush of memory leap out to greet me. Pulling away, I flung open the door, threw my overnight bag to the floor and headed for the study, expecting to find Jeremy reading by the fireplace. He was always there when I came home, not waiting at the gate like Clay, but waiting nonetheless.

The room was empty. A folded copy of Milan's daily paper *Corriere della Sera* lay beside Jeremy's chair. Stacks of Clay's anthropology magazines and research publications covered the couch and desk. The main phone rested on the desk and appeared to be intact and plugged in.

"I called," I said. "Why wasn't anyone here?"

"We were here," Clay said. "Around, anyway. You should have left a message."

"I did. Two hours ago."

"Well, that explains it. I've been out by the gate all day waiting for you, and you know Jer never checks the machine."

I didn't ask how Clay knew I was coming back today when I hadn't left a message. Nor did I question why he'd spent the entire day sitting at the gate. Clay's behavior couldn't be measured by human standards of normalcy . . . or by any standards of normalcy at all.

"So where is he?" I asked.

"Dunno. I haven't seen him since he brought out my dinner a few hours ago. He must have gone out."

I didn't need to check the garage for Jeremy's car to know Clay didn't mean he'd gone out in the usual sense. Common human phrases took on new meanings at Stonehaven. Going out meant he'd gone for a run—and that didn't mean he'd gone jogging.

Did Jeremy expect me to fly all the way here, then wait on his convenience? Of course he did. Was it punishment for ignoring his summons? Part of me wished I could accuse him of that, but Jeremy was never petty. If he'd planned a run for tonight, he'd have gone, regardless of whether I was coming or not. A sliver of hurt ran through my anger, but I tried to disown it. Did I expect Jeremy to be waiting for me like Clay? Of course not. Didn't expect it and didn't care about it. Really. I was pissed off, nothing more. Two could play this game. Jeremy valued his privacy when he ran. So what was I going to do? Invade that privacy, of course. Jeremy may never be petty, but I sure as hell could be.

"Out?" I said. "Well then, I'll just have to find him."

I swerved to pass Clay, heading for the door. He stepped in front of me.

"He'll be back soon. Sit down and we'll—"

I sidestepped Clay on my way to the rear hall and the half-open back door. Clay followed at my heels, keeping pace a step behind. I walked through the walled garden to the path leading into the forest. The wood-chip path crunched underfoot. From beyond, the night smells began to sift in: burning leaves, distant cattle, wet soil—myriad inviting scents. Somewhere in the distance a mouse shrieked as an owl snatched it from the forest floor.

I kept walking. Within fifty feet the trail dwindled to a thin path of trodden grass, then disappeared into the undergrowth. I paused and sniffed the air. Nothing. No scent, no sound, no sign of Jeremy. At that moment, I realized I heard no sound at all, not even the clomp of Clay's footsteps behind me. I turned and saw only trees.

"Clayton!" I shouted.

A moment later the reply came back in a crashing of distant bushes. He was off to warn Jeremy. I slammed my hand into the nearest tree trunk. Had I really expected Clay to let me intrude on Jeremy's privacy that easily? If so, I'd forgotten a few things in the past year.

I pushed through the trees. Twigs lashed at my face and vines grabbed my feet. I stumbled forward, feeling huge, clumsy, and most unwelcome out here. The path wasn't made for people. I didn't stand a chance of heading off Clay like this, so I found a clearing and prepared for the Change.

My Change was rushed, making it awkward and torturous and afterward I had to rest, panting on the ground. As I got to my feet, I closed my eyes and inhaled the smell of Stonehaven. A shiver of elation started in my paws, raced up my legs, and quivered through my entire body. In its wake, it left an indescribable blend of excitement and calm that made me want to tear through the forest and collapse in blissful peace at the same time. I was home. As a human, I could deny that Stonehaven was my home, that the people here were my Pack, that the woods here were anything more than a patch of someone else's land. But as a wolf in Stonehaven's forest, one chorus trumpeted through my head. This forest was mine. It was Pack territory and therefore it was mine. Mine to run in and hunt in and play in without fear of partying teenagers, overeager hunters, or rabid foxes and raccoons. No discarded sofas to block my path, no rusty cans to slice open my paws, no stinking garbage bags to foul the air I breathed, or dumped chemicals to pollute the water I drank. This wasn't some patch of woods claimed for an hour or two. This was five hundred acres of forest, every acre crisscrossed with familiar paths and stocked with rabbits and deer, a smorgasbord supplied for my pleasure. *My* pleasure. I downed huge gulps of air. Mine. I darted out of the thicket to the well-worn path. Mine. I rubbed against an oak tree, feeling the bark scratch and pull away tickling clumps of dead fur. Mine. The ground shuddered in three low vibrations—a rabbit thumping somewhere to my left. Mine. My legs ached to run, to rediscover the intricate world of my forest. Somewhere deep in my brain, a tiny human voice shouted No, no, no! This isn't yours. You gave it up. You don't want it! I ignored it.

There was only one thing missing, one last thing that differentiated these woods from the lonely ravines of Toronto. Even as I was thinking this, a howl pierced the night; not musical night singing, but the urgent cry of a lone wolf, blood calling to blood. I closed my eyes and felt the sound vibrate through me. Then I threw back my head and responded. The small warning voice stopped yelling invective, anger taken over by something closer to dread. No, it whispered. Not that. Claim the forest. Claim the air and the paths and the trees and the animals. But don't claim that.

The bushes crackled behind me and I whirled around to see Clay in midair. He caught my forequarters and knocked me flying onto my back, then stood over me and nipped at the loose skin around my neck. When I snapped at him, he pulled back. Standing over me, he whined and prodded my neck with his nose, begging me to come play with him, telling me how lonely he'd been. I could feel the resistance somewhere within me, but it was too deeply buried. I grabbed his foreleg between my jaws and yanked him off balance. As he fell, I leapt atop him. We tumbled into the thick undergrowth, nipping and kicking and fighting for the top position. Just as he was about to pin me, I wriggled free and leapt away. We circled each other. Clay's tail lashed against my side, running along it like a caressing hand. He inched closer and rubbed his flank against mine. As we circled the next round, he put a leg in front of mine to stop me and buried his nose against my neck. I could feel his hot breath against my skin as he inhaled my scent. Then he grabbed me by the throat and threw me over backward, giving a yip of triumph as I fell for it—literally. He didn't hold the victory spot for more than a couple of seconds before I dethroned him. We wrestled a while longer, then I leapt free. Clay stepped back and crouched, leaving his hindquarters high. His mouth hung open, tongue out and ears forward. I hunkered down as if preparing to meet his attack. When he pounced, I sprang to the side and started to run.

Clay tore after me. We raced through the forest, crossing acre after acre of ground. Then, just as I was circling back toward the front of the property, a shot exploded the peace of the forest. I skidded to a stop.

A shot? Had I really heard a shot? Of course I'd encountered guns before, guns and hunters were an expected danger when you roamed strange forests. But this was Stonehaven. It was safe.

Another shot rang out. I swiveled my ears. The blasts had come from the north. There were orchards far to the north. Was the farmer using one of those devices that mimicked shotgun blasts to scare off birds? It had to be. Either that or someone was hunting in the neighboring fields. Stonehaven's forests were clearly marked with fences and signs. The locals respected the boundaries. They always had. Jeremy's reputation with the locals was peerless. He may not have been the most sociable landowner, but he was respected.

I headed north to solve the mystery. I'd barely gone three yards when Clay leapt in front of me. He growled. It wasn't a playful growl. I stared at him, wondering if I'd misinterpreted his meaning. He growled again and I was certain. He was warning me off. I put my ears back and snarled. He blocked my path. I narrowed my eyes and glared at him. Obviously I'd been away too long if he thought he could boss me around like he did the others. If he'd forgotten who I was, I'd be willing to give him a refresher lesson. I curled my lips back and growled one last warning. He didn't back down. I threw myself at him. He met me in midleap, knocking the wind from me. When I regained my senses, I was lying on the ground with Clay's teeth locked in the loose skin behind my head. I was out of practice.

Clay growled and gave me a rough shake, as if I were a misbehaving pup. After a few rounds of this, he pulled back and stood up. I got to my feet with as much dignity as I could muster. Before I was even fully standing, Clay butted my backside with his muzzle. I turned to give him an indignant glare. He butted me again, driving me in the opposite direction. I went along with it for nearly a quarter mile, then swerved to the side and tried an end run around him. Seconds after I flew past him, a 200-pound weight dropped on my back and I skidded into the dirt. Clay's teeth sunk into my shoulder, deep enough to draw blood and send a stab of pain and shock through me. This time he didn't even let me get to my feet before he started herding me back to the house, nipping at my back legs if I showed signs of slowing.

Clay drove me to the clearing where I'd Changed and made his own Change on the other side of the thicket. My Change back to human was even more hurried than my Change to a wolf. This time, though, I didn't need to rest afterward. Fury gave me energy. I yanked on my clothes, ripping the sleeve of my shirt. Then I strode out from the clearing. Clay was there, arms crossed, waiting. He was naked, of course, his clothing abandoned in a clearing deeper in the forest. Naked, Clay was even more perfect than when he was dressed, a Greek sculptor's dream come to life. Seeing him, a slow flush of heat ran through me, bringing to mind memories of other runs and their inevitable aftermath. I cursed my body's betrayal and strode toward him.

"What the hell were you doing?" I shouted.

"Me? Me? I wasn't the idiot running toward men with guns. Where the hell was your head at, Elena?"

"Don't give me that crap. I wouldn't leave the property and you know it. I was just curious. I'm back an hour and you're already testing the waters. How far can you push me, how much can you control—"

"Those hunters were on the property, Elena." Clay's voice was low, his eyes locked on to mine.

"Oh, that's a load of—" I stopped and studied his face. "You're serious, aren't you? Hunters? On Jeremy's land? Are you getting soft in your old age?"

The barb struck deeper than I hoped. Clay's mouth tightened. His eyes went hard. Rage simmered there, mere degrees from explosion.

The anger wasn't directed at me, but at those who had dared invade his sanctuary. Every fiber in Clay would rebel at the thought of allowing armed men on the property. Only one thing would keep him from hunting them down—Jeremy. So Jeremy must have forbidden him to take care of these trespassers, forbidden him not only to kill them, but even to use his infamous scare techniques, Clay's usual method of dealing with human trespassers. Two generations of local teenagers in search of party sites had grown up passing along the story that Stonehaven's backwoods were haunted. So long as the tales involved spooks and phantasms, with no mention of werewolves, Jeremy allowed it, even encouraged it. After all, letting Clay scare the locals was safer and far less messy than the alternative. So why wasn't Jeremy letting him do it now? What had changed?

"He should be inside now," Clay said. "Go talk to him."

He turned and headed into the woods to find his clothing.

As I walked to the house, I thought about what the cab driver had said. Wild dogs. There were no wild dogs here. Dogs wouldn't set foot anywhere near werewolf territory. Nor did dogs run around slaughtering healthy young women. Huge canine tracks found around the body could only mean one thing. A werewolf. Yet who would be killing that close to Stonehaven? The question itself was so unfathomable it could have no answer. A non-Pack werewolf would have to be suicidal to cross the New York State border. Clay's methods for dealing with trespassers were so renowned that one hadn't come within a hundred miles of Stonehaven in over twenty years. The story goes that Clay had dismembered the last trespassing werewolf finger by finger, limb by limb, keeping him alive until the last possible moment, when he'd ripped off his head. Clay had been seventeen at the time.

The idea that either Clay or Jeremy could be responsible for the woman's death was equally ludicrous. Jeremy didn't kill. That wasn't to say he couldn't kill or even that he never felt the urge, but simply that he realized his energy was better channeled elsewhere, as an army general must forgo the heat of the battle and devote himself to matters of strategy and leadership. If someone had to be killed, Jeremy ordered it done. Even that was done only in extreme cases and rarely involved humans. No matter what the threat, Jeremy would never order the killing of a human on his own territory. As for Clay, whatever his legion of faults, sport-killing humans wasn't one of them. Killing them would involve touching them, which meant lowering himself to physical contact with them, which he didn't do unless absolutely necessary.

When I reentered the house, it was still silent. I went back to the study, the heart of Stonehaven. Jeremy wasn't there. I decided to wait. If he was in the house, he'd hear me. For once, he could come to me.

Jeremy ruled the Pack with absolute authority. That's the law of wild wolves, though it hadn't always been the law of the Pack. At times, the history of the Pack Alphas made Roman imperial succession look downright civilized. A Pack werewolf would scramble to the top of the heap, hold the Alpha position for a few months, maybe even a few years, then get assassinated or executed by one of his more ambitious Pack brothers, who would then take over until he met his own—almost certainly unnatural—demise. Pack Alpha-hood had nothing to do with leadership and everything to do with power.

By the second half of the twentieth century, the Pack was falling apart. The postindustrial world wasn't kind to werewolves. Urban sprawl swallowed deep forests and wide open spaces. People in modern society were far less likely than those in feudal England to respect the privacy of their wealthy, reclusive neighbors. Radio, television, and newspapers could spread stories of werewolf sightings across the globe within hours. New methods of police work meant a strange canine-like killing in Tallahassee could be swiftly linked to similar ones in Miami and Key West. The world began to close in on the Pack. Instead of banding together, they'd begun fighting one another for every last vestige of security, even going so far as to steal prime territory from their own Pack brothers.

Jeremy changed that.

Although Jeremy could never be considered the best fighter in the Pack, he possessed a strength that was even more important for the survival and success of the modern Pack. Jeremy had absolute self-control.

Being able to master his own instincts and urges meant he could see the problems the Pack was facing and deal with them rationally, making decisions untainted by impulse. As suburbs consumed the land surrounding cities, he moved the Pack farther into the countryside. He taught them how to deal with humans, how to be part of the world and outside of the world at the same time. As stories of werewolves travelled faster and more easily, he exerted his control over not just the Pack, but the non-Pack werewolves. In the past, non-Pack werewolves—known as mutts—were seen as second-class citizens, beneath the notice of the Pack. Under Jeremy's rule, mutts didn't gain any status, but the Pack learned that they couldn't afford to ignore them. If a mutt caused enough trouble in Cairo, it could resonate all the way to New York. The Pack started keeping dossiers on mutts, learning their habits and tracing their movements. When a werewolf caused trouble anywhere in the world, the Pack responded quickly and decisively. The penalty for endangering the security of the Pack ranged anywhere from a rousting to a beating to a swift execution. Under Jeremy's rule, the Pack was stronger and more stable than ever, and no one contested it. They were smart enough to know when they had a good thing.

I shook off my thoughts and walked to the desk, looking at the nest of papers piled there. "Excavation Reveals New Insights on the Chavín Phenomenon" read the title of one article. Peeking out from under it was another about ancient Chavín de Huántar jaguar cults. Fascinating stuff. Yawn. Though it came as a shock to most who met him, Clay had a brain, actually a brilliant brain, one that had earned him a Ph.D. in anthropology. He specialized in anthropomorphic religions. In other words, he studied man-beast symbolism in ancient cultures. His reputation was built on his research, since he didn't like to deal directly with the human world, but when he deemed it necessary to make a foray into the live world of academics he'd take on brief teaching stints. That was how I'd met him.

Again, I shook off my thoughts, harder this time. Turning from the mess of Clay's papers, I sunk onto the couch. As I glanced around, I realized that the room looked exactly as I'd left it fourteen months ago. I pulled up a picture of the study from memory, compared it with what I was seeing and found not a single difference. That couldn't be right. Jeremy redecorated this room—and most of the house—so often it was a running gag that we could blink and see something different. Clay said once that the changes had to do with bad memories, but he wouldn't elaborate. Soon after Clay brought me here, Jeremy had recruited me as his decorating assistant. I could remember entire nights spent poring over catalogues, dragging around furniture, and holding up paint chips. When I looked up at the ceiling by the fireplace, I could see hardened lumps of wallpaper paste, still there from a four A.M. wallpapering spree that had turned the study into a battleground, Jeremy and I too exhausted to do anything more than lob clumps of paste at each other.

I remembered staring at those hardened lumps the last time I'd been in this room. Jeremy had been there, standing before the fireplace, his back to me. As I'd told him what I'd done, I'd ached for him to turn around, to tell me that it wasn't wrong. But I knew it was wrong. So completely wrong. Still, I'd wanted him to say something, anything, to make me feel better. When he hadn't, I'd left, promising myself that I wouldn't return. I looked up at the paste clumps. Another battle lost.

"So you've come back . . . finally."

The deep voice made me jump. Jeremy stood in the doorway. Since I'd last seen him, he'd grown a close-clipped beard, something that usually happened when he got too distracted to shave, then couldn't be bothered undoing the damage. It made him look older, though still nowhere near his true age of fifty-one. We age slowly. Jeremy could pass for mid-thirties: his hairstyle furthering the illusion of youth, shoulder-length and tied at the nape of his neck. It was a style adopted not out of fashion but because it meant fewer haircuts. Trips to a public barber were intolerable for Jeremy, so Clay or I cut his hair, which wasn't an experience to be endured more than a few times a year. When he stepped into the room, his bangs fell into his eyes, shattering the austerity of his face. He shoved them back, a gesture so familiar it made my throat ache.

He looked around. "Where's Clay?"

Typical. First, he gets after me for being late. Then he asks about Clay. A twinge of hurt darted through me, but I pushed it away. It wasn't like I expected him to welcome me back with hugs and kisses. That wasn't Jeremy's way, though a "good to see you" or "how was your flight?" would have been nice.

"We heard shots in the back forest," I said. "He mumbled something about shallow graves and took off."

"I've been trying to contact you for three days."

"I was busy."

His cheek twitched. With Jeremy, this was the equivalent of an emotional outburst. "When I call, you call me back," he said, his voice deceptively soft. "I wouldn't call you if it wasn't important. If I do call, you answer. That was the arrangement."

"Correct, that *was* the arrangement. Past tense. Our arrangement ended when I left the Pack."

"When you left the Pack? And when did this happen? Forgive me if I missed something, but I don't recall any such conversation, Elena."

"I thought it was understood."

Clay walked in the room carrying a tray of cold cuts and cheese. He laid it on the desk and looked from me to Jeremy.

Jeremy continued. "So you're no longer part of the Pack now?"

"Correct."

"Then you're one of them—a mutt?"

"Of course not, Jer," Clay said, thumping down beside me on the couch.

I moved to the fireplace.

"Well, which is it?" Jeremy asked, his gaze skewering mine. "Pack or not?"

"Come on, Jer," Clay said. "You know she doesn't mean it."

"We had an arrangement, Elena. I wouldn't contact you unless I needed you. Well, I need you and now you're sulking and fuming because I had the gall to remind you of your responsibilities."

"You need me for what? To take care of a trespassing mutt? That's Clay's job."

Jeremy shook his head. "You don't use a wrecking ball to exterminate one mouse. Clay has his strengths. Subtlety is not one of them."

Clay grinned at me and shrugged. I looked away.

"So what's going on that's so damned important you need me?" I asked.

Jeremy turned and headed for the door. "It's late. I've called a Meet for tomorrow. I'll tell you everything then. Hopefully you'll feel less confrontational after a good sleep."

"Whoa!" I said, stepping out to block his path. "I dropped everything to come here. I skipped out of work, paid for an airline ticket, and raced here as fast as I could because no one was answering the damned phone. I want to know why I'm here and I want to know now. If you walk out that door, I'm not going to promise you'll still find me here in the morning."

"So be it," Jeremy said, his voice so cool I shivered in the draft. "If you decide to leave, have Clay drive you to Syracuse."

"Yeah, right," I said. "I'd be more likely to get to the airport by thumbing a ride with the local psychopath."

Clay grinned. "You forget, darling. I am the local psychopath."

I muttered my complete and heartfelt agreement. Jeremy said nothing, just stood there and waited for me to step aside. I did. Old habits are hard to break. Jeremy left the room. A minute later, his bedroom door closed upstairs.

"Arrogant son-of-a-bitch," I muttered.

Clay only shrugged. He was leaning back in his seat, eyes watching me, lips curved in a pensive smile that set my teeth on edge.

"What the hell do you want?" I said.

His smile turned to a grin, white teeth flashing. "You. What else?"

"Where? Right here? On the floor?"

"Nah. Not that. Not yet. Just the same old thing I always want. You. Here. For good."

I wished he'd stuck with my interpretation. He caught my eye.

"I'm glad you're home, darling. I missed you."

I nearly tripped over my feet running from the room.

Meet

NO MATTER WHAT JEREMY HAD SAID, I KNEW BETTER THAN TO leave. He might pretend not to care what I did, but he'd stop me if I tried to leave before he'd told me whatever he'd wanted to tell me. I had three choices. First, I could call him on it and walk out. Second, I could storm to his room and demand he tell me what was going on. Third, I could go to my old bedroom, sleep, and find out what he wanted in the morning. I weighed the options. Getting a cab back to Syracuse would be impossible now, since the local taxi service shut down over an hour ago. I could take one of the cars and ditch it at the airport, but my chances of catching a flight to Toronto at three A.M. were next to none and I didn't relish sleeping in the airport. Nor did I relish the idea of fighting with Jeremy. One didn't fight with Jeremy Danvers; one shouted and raged and cursed him while he stood there with an inscrutable look on his face, waited until you'd exhausted yourself, then calmly refused to discuss the matter. I'd learned ways of getting under his skin, but I was out of practice. No, tonight I'd fight back by refusing to play their games. I'd go to bed, get a good sleep, settle this in the morning, and leave. Simple as that.

I grabbed my overnight bag and went upstairs to my old room, ignoring the fact that—although supposedly no one knew I was coming—the bedroom was aired out, window cracked open, fresh bedding on, and covers turned back. I took the cell phone from my bag and called Philip. With each unanswered ring, I felt a stab of disappointment. He was probably in bed already. When the machine clicked on. I thought of hanging up, calling back, and hoping the additional ringing would wake him, but I knew I was being selfish, wanting to talk to him to reestablish my link with the outside world. So I settled for leaving a brief message to let him know I'd arrived safely and I'd call again before I left the next day.

The silence of the house woke me the next morning. I'd become accustomed to waking in the city, cursing the sounds of traffic. When nothing conspired to get me up this morning, I bolted awake at ten, half expecting to see the world had ended. Then I realized I was at Stonehaven. I can't say I was relieved.

I struggled up from the embroidered bed sheets and thick feather pillows and pushed back the curtains from my canopy bed. Waking up in my room at Stonehaven was like awakening into a Victorian romance nightmare. The canopied bed alone was bad enough, something straight out of the Princess and the Pea, and it only got worse. A Hepplewhite cedar chest at the foot of my bed held wood-scented down comforters, just in case the two Egyptian cotton duvets on my bed weren't enough. Layers of opulent lace billowed around the window, streaming over a satin-covered window seat. The walls were pale pink, adorned with watercolors of flowers and sunsets. Across the room was a huge carved oak vanity, with a floor-length gilt mirror and silver vanity set. Even the top of the dresser was cluttered with Dresden figurines. Scarlett would have felt right at home.

The window seat was the reason Jeremy had picked this room for me, that and the cherry trees that had been blossoming just below the window. It had seemed appropriately pretty and feminine. The truth is, Jeremy had known squat about women and expecting me to go gaga over cherry blossoms had been the first of many mistakes. In Jeremy's defense, he couldn't be expected to know any better. Women played the most insignificant of roles in the world of werewolves. A werewolf's only reason for delving into the mind of a woman is to find the best way to get her in bed. Most of them can't even be bothered learning that. If you're ten times stronger than the gorgeous redhead standing at the bar, why waste your money buying her a drink? At least, that's the mutt point of view. Pack werewolves have developed more finesse. If a werewolf wants to live in one place, he can't make a habit of raping a woman every time the urge strikes. Pack werewolves even have mistresses and girlfriends, although they never form what humans would call close relationships. They certainly never marry. Nor do they let women raise their sons. As I've said, only sons inherit the werewolf gene. So, while daughters were ignored, it was a law of the Pack that all male children must be taken from their mothers in infancy and all ties with the mother must be severed. Jeremy couldn't be expected to know much about the opposite sex, having grown up in a world where mothers, sisters, and aunts were only words in a dictionary. And there were no female werewolves. Except me, of course. When I'd been bitten, Jeremy had expected a docile childlike creature who would meekly accept her fate and be happy with a pretty room and nice clothes. If he'd foreseen the future, he might have tossed me out the door . . . or worse.

The person who bit me had betrayed me in the worst possible way. I'd loved him, trusted him, and he'd turned me into a monster then left me with Jeremy. To say I reacted badly is an understatement. The bedroom arrangement didn't last. Within a week, Jeremy had to lock me in the cage. My Changes became as uncontrolled as my rages, and nothing Jeremy could say would make me listen. I despised him. He was my captor, the only one around upon whom I could heap the blame for every torment, physical and emotional, I was undergoing. If the cage was my hell, Jeremy was my Satan.

Finally, I'd escaped. I'd hitched rides back to Toronto, trading in the only commodity I had—my body. But within days of my arrival, I'd realized my assessment of the cage had been horribly inaccurate. It was not hell. It was only a way station on the voyage. Living unrestrained and being unable to control my Changes was the ninth circle of the inferno.

I started by killing animals to stay alive, rabbits, raccoons, dogs and even rats. Before long I lost all illusion of control and sunk into madness. Unable to reason, barely able to think, I'd been driven entirely by the needs of my stomach. The rabbits and raccoons weren't enough. I killed people. After the second one, Jeremy found me, took me home, and trained me. I never tried to escape again. I'd learned my lesson. There were worse things than Stonehaven.

After struggling out of bed, I trotted across the cold hardwood floor to the throw rug. The dresser and closet were stuffed with clothing I'd accumulated over the years. I found jeans and a shirt and yanked them on. Too lazy to comb my hair, I raked my fingers though it and tied it into a loose braid.

Once semi-presentable I opened the bedroom door and glanced across the hall. As Clay's deep snores reverberated from his bedroom, some tension eased out of my shoulders. That was one problem I could avoid this morning.

I slipped out into the hall and past his closed door. With an uncanny abruptness, the snoring stopped. Cursing under my breath I hurried down the first few stairs. Clay's door creaked open, followed by the padding of bare feet on hardwood. Don't stop, I warned myself, and don't turn around. Then I stopped and, of course, turned around.

He stood at the top of the stairs looking exhausted enough to tumble down them at the slightest touch. His close-cropped gold curls were an unruly mess, rumpled and plastered down by sweaty sleep. Sandy blond beard shadow covered his cheeks and square chin. His eyes were half-lidded, struggling to focus. He was dressed only in the white boxer shorts with black paw prints that I'd bought him as a joke during one of our better periods. With a yawn, he stretched and rolled his shoulders, rippling muscles down his chest.

"Rough night guarding my escape routes?" I asked.

He shrugged. Whenever I had a bad day at Stonehaven, Clay spent the night staking out my possible escape venues. Like I'd ever be so cowardly as to sneak off in the night. Well, okay, I'd done it before, but that wasn't the point.

"How 'bout some company for breakfast?" he asked.

"No."

Another drowsy shrug of his shoulders. Let a few more hours pass and he'd never take the rebuff without a fight. Hell, in a few hours, he wouldn't bother *asking* if he could join me. I started back down the stairs. I got exactly three steps when he jolted awake, trotted down the stairs after me, and grabbed my elbow.

"Let me get your breakfast," he said. "I'll meet you in the sunroom. I want to talk to you."

"I don't have anything to say to you, Clayton."

"Give me five minutes."

Before I could answer, he'd jogged up the stairs and vanished into his room. I could have gone after him, but that would have meant following him into his bedroom. Definitely not a good idea.

At the bottom of the stairs, a smell stopped me in my tracks. Honeyed ham and pancakes, my favorite breakfast. I stepped into the sunroom and checked the table. Yes, stacks of ham and pancakes were waiting on a steaming platter. They hadn't materialized on their own, but I might have been less surprised to find that they had. The only person who could have made them was Jeremy, but Jeremy didn't cook. Not couldn't—didn't. That isn't to say he expected Clay or me to serve him, but when he did fix breakfast for us the only thing that steamed was the coffee. The rest was always a hodgepodge of breads, cheeses, cold meats, fruits, and anything else requiring minimal preparation.

Jeremy walked behind me into the sunroom. "It's getting cold. Sit and eat."

I said nothing about the breakfast. When Jeremy made a gesture he didn't like it recognized, much less thanked. For a moment I was sure this was Jeremy's way of welcoming me back. Then the old doubts resurfaced. Maybe he'd only fixed breakfast to placate me. With Jeremy, I could never read his intentions, even after all these years. Sometimes I was certain he wanted me at Stonehaven. Other times I was convinced he only accepted me because he had no choice, because I'd been thrust into his life and keeping me calm and under control was in the best interests of his Pack. I knew I spent too much time dwelling on this, struggling to interpret his every gesture, far too eager to see some sign of approval. Maybe I was still stuck in the old patterns of childhood, wanting a father more than I'd admit. I hoped not. Needy waif wasn't exactly an image I cared to project.

I sat down and dug in. The pancakes came from a mix, but I wasn't complaining. They were hot and filling, and came with butter and maple syrup—the real stuff, not the imitation junk I always bought to save a few bucks. I gulped down the first stack and reached for a second. Jeremy didn't so much as raise his eyebrows. One good thing about Stonehaven: I could eat as much as I wanted without anyone commenting or even noticing.

While Clay had staked out my bedroom window last night, it looked like Jeremy had been lying in wait for me here this morning. His easel was set up between his chair and the window. On it was a fresh sheet of paper with a few unconnected lines. He hadn't got far on the new sketch. The few lines he had drawn had obviously been erased and redrawn several times. One spot of paper was threatening to break through to the easel behind.

"Are you going to tell me what's going on?" I asked.

"Are you going to listen? Or are you trying to pick another fight?"

He drew a new line over the ghost of the last, then erased it. The brown of the easel peeked through the hole.

"It hasn't gone away, has it?" I said. "The reason I left. You're still angry."

He didn't look up from his sketch. Damn it, why didn't he look up?

"I was never angry with you, Elena. You were angry with yourself. That's why you left. You didn't like what you did. It frightened you, and you thought you could make it go away by leaving. Has it gone away?"

I said nothing.

Sixteen months ago, I'd gone to investigate a report of someone selling werewolf information. Now, the Pack doesn't chase down every joe who says he has proof of werewolves. That would be a full-time job for every living werewolf in and out of the Pack. We do keep an eye on stories that sound legitimate, excluding anything with keywords like silver bullet, baby killing, and ravaging half man–half beast creatures. What's left is a part-time job for two people: Clay and me. If an outside werewolf was causing trouble and Jeremy wanted to make an example of him, he sent Clay. If the trouble had gone beyond the point of a quick fix—or if it involved a human—then it needed caution and finesse. For those, he sent me. The case of Jose Carter required my brand of troubleshooting.

Jose Carter was a small-time con man who specialized in paranormal phenomena. He'd spent his life bilking the gullible and vulnerable with tales of loved ones trying to make contact from the beyond. Then, two years ago, while working in South America, he came across a small town that claimed a werewolf was preying on their village. Never one to miss an opportunity, Carter moved in and started gathering what he assumed would be phony evidence that he could sell in the United States. Trouble was, it wasn't phony. One of the mutts had been touring across Ecuador, hitting village after village and leaving a trail of dead bodies. The mutt thought he had the perfect gig, raiding villages so remote that no one would see the pattern. He hadn't counted on Jose Carter. And Carter hadn't counted on ever finding the real thing, but he was quick to recognize it when he did. He left Ecuador with eyewitness reports, hair samples, plaster paw-print casts, and photographs. Returning to the United States, he'd contacted several paranormal societies and tried to sell the information. He'd been so certain of his find that he'd offered to accompany the highest bidder back to South America to track the beast.

I'd caught up with Jose Carter at his "information auction" in Dallas. I'd tried to discredit him. I'd tried to steal the evidence. When nothing worked, I'd taken the only route left. I'd killed him. I did it on my own; without orders from Jeremy and without even contacting Jeremy. Afterward, I'd gone back to my hotel, cleaned up, and enjoyed a good sleep. When I awoke, the full impact of what I'd done hit me. No, not so much *what* I'd done, but how I'd done it, how easily I'd done it. I'd killed a man with as much moral compunction as I would have swatted a fly.

On the way back to New York, I'd prepared my argument for Jeremy, to explain why I'd acted without consulting him. Carter had been a clear threat. I'd done everything I could to stop him. Time had been running out. Had I called Jeremy, he would have wanted me to do the same thing, so I'd saved a step and taken care of matters myself. Before I'd reached Stonehaven, I'd realized the truth. It wasn't Jeremy I was trying to convince. It was myself. I'd crossed the line. I'd acted with the single-minded purpose of protecting my Pack, devoid of even a drop of compassion or mercy. I'd acted like Clay. That scared me, scared me so bad I'd run and sworn I'd never go back to that life again.

Had it gone away? Did I once again feel in complete control of my instincts and impulses? I didn't know. For over a year, I hadn't done anything so blatantly wrong, but nor had I been in a position where the opportunity arose. One more reason why I hadn't wanted to come back to Stonehaven. I didn't know if it was gone and I wasn't sure I wanted to find out.

A commotion at the front door snapped me out of my memories. As I glanced up, a tall, dark-haired figure burst into the sunroom. Nick caught sight of me, covered the room in three running steps, and swung me up off my seat. My heel caught the edge of my chair and toppled it over. He gave a mock growl as he squeezed me.

"You were gone too long, little sister. Much too long."

Lifting me up, Nick kissed me. Whatever his greeting, the kiss was definitely not fraternal, but a deep kiss that left me gasping. .Anyone else would have gotten smacked for it, but anyone else wouldn't have kissed with half of Nick's expertise, so I overlooked the indiscretion.

"Well, just make yourself at home," Clay drawled from the doorway.

Nick turned to Clay and grinned. Still holding me captive in one arm, he strode across the floor and thumped Clay on the back. Clay's arm flew up and grabbed Nick in a headlock. He pulled me free and shoved Nick away. Nick regained his balance and his grin, and bounced back to us.

"When did you get in?" he asked me, then poked Clay in the ribs. "And why didn't you tell me she was coming?"

From behind, someone grabbed me in a bear hug and lifted me off the ground.

"The prodigal has returned."

I twisted to see a face as familiar as Nick's. "You're as bad as your son," I said, wriggling out of his grasp. "Can't you guys just shake hands?"

Antonio laughed and let me down. "I should squeeze harder. Maybe that would teach you to stay home for a while."

Antonio Sorrentino shared his son's wavy dark hair and heart-stopping brown eyes. They usually passed themselves off as brothers. Antonio was fifty-three and looked half that, which owed as much to his passion for healthy living as to being a werewolf. He was shorter and sturdier than his son, with broad shoulders and bulging biceps that made Clay look like a featherweight.

"Has Peter arrived yet?" Antonio said, pulling out the chair beside Jeremy, who was sipping his second cup of coffee, undisturbed by the uproar.

Jeremy shook his head.

"So everyone's coming?" I asked.

"Finish your breakfast." Jeremy said, giving me the critical once-over. "You've lost weight. You can't do that. If you don't get enough energy, your control will start to slip. I've warned you before."

Finally pushing his easel aside, Jeremy turned to talk to Antonio. Clay reached over my shoulder, snatched a hunk of ham, and downed it in one gulp. When I glared at him, he gave me a disarming "just trying to help" shrug.

"Keep your fingers off her plate," Jeremy said without turning around. "Yours is in the kitchen. There's enough for everyone."

Antonio was first out the door. When Nick went to follow, Clay grabbed his arm. He didn't say a word. He didn't need to. Nick nodded and bounded off to fill two plates while Clay took the seat beside me.

"Bully," I muttered.

Clay lifted his eyebrows, blue eyes flashing innocently. His fingers darted out to snag another piece of ham off my plate. Grabbing my fork, I stabbed the back of his hand hard enough to make him yelp. Jeremy sipped his coffee and ignored us.

Antonio came back into the sunroom, plate piled so high I expected the pancakes to slide to the floor at any second, especially since he was holding the plate with only one hand. His other hand was busy forking a pancake toward his mouth. Nick followed his father and dropped Clay's plate in front of him, then pulled up a fifth chair, turned it backward, and straddled it. For a few minutes, there was blessed silence. Werewolves weren't much for mealtime conversation. The task of filling their stomachs demanded full concentration.

The quiet might have lasted even longer if the doorbell hadn't shattered the silence. Nick went to answer it and came back with Peter Myers. Peter was short and wiry with an easy grin and wild red hair that always looked as if he'd forgotten to comb it. Once again, we went through the rituals of bear hugging, back thumping, and mock punching. Greetings amongst the Pack were as exuberant as they were physical, often leaving as many bruises as a few rounds of roughhousing.

"When's Logan coming?" I asked as everyone settled back to the business of eating.

"He's not," Jeremy said. "He had to fly to Los Angeles for a court case. Last-minute legal substitution. I contacted him last night and let him know what's going on."

"Which reminds me," Clay said, turning to me. "Last time I talked to Logan, he let something slip about speaking to you. 'Course, that's not possible, since you cut off all contact with the Pack, right?"

I looked at Clay, but didn't answer. I didn't need to. He could see my reply in my eyes. His face flushed with anger and he stabbed a slice of ham hard enough to rock the table. I'd spoken to Logan at least once a week since I'd left, telling myself that so long as I didn't go see him, I wasn't exactly breaking my vow. Besides, Logan was more than my Pack brother; he was my friend, maybe the only true friend I'd ever had. Although we were the same age, we shared more in common than being able to name both members of WHAM! . . . Logan understood the allure of the outside world. He enjoyed the protection and companionship the Pack offered, but he was equally at home in the human world, where he had an apartment in Albany, a long-term girlfriend, and a flourishing legal career. As soon as I realized that Jeremy had called a Meet, my first thought had been, Great, Logan's coming. Now I wouldn't even have that compensation for this unwanted visit.

A few minutes later, Jeremy and Antonio went out to the back porch to talk. As Jeremy's closest and oldest friend, Antonio often served as a sounding board for Jeremy's ideas and plans, a court adviser of sorts. Antonio and Jeremy had grown up together, sons of the Pack's two most distinguished families. Antonio's father had been Pack Alpha before Jeremy. When Dominic died, many in the Pack had assumed Antonio would take over the role, even though Pack leadership was not hereditary. As with real wolves, the Alpha of the Pack was traditionally the best fighter. Before Clay grew up, Antonio was the Pack's top warrior. Moreover, he had brains and more common sense than a dozen normal werewolves. Yet, on his father's death, Antonio had backed Jeremy, recognizing in him strengths that would save the Pack. With Antonio's help, Jeremy had been able to squash any objection to his succession. No one had challenged him since. The only werewolf with the power to contest Jeremy's position was Clay, and Clay would sooner cut off his right arm than challenge the man who had rescued and raised him.

When Jeremy was twenty-one, his father had returned from a trip with a strange story. He'd been passing through Louisiana when he'd scented a werewolf. He'd tracked it and discovered a preadolescent werewolf living like an animal in the swamps. To Malcolm Danvers, this had been nothing more than an intriguing dinner tale, since no one had ever heard of a child werewolf. While hereditary werewolves didn't experience their first Change until adulthood, usually between the ages of eighteen and twenty-one, a human bitten by a werewolf was a werewolf immediately, regardless of his age. The youngest person known to have become a werewolf was fifteen. It was assumed that if a child was bitten, he would die, if not of the bite, then surely from the shock. Even if he miraculously survived the attack, a child couldn't have the fortitude to survive the first Change. This boy in Louisiana looked no more than seven or eight, but Malcolm had seen him in both forms, so he was clearly a full-fledged bitten werewolf. The Pack chalked up his survival to sheer luck, a fluke of nature having nothing to do with strength or willpower. The wolf-child may have lived this long, but he certainly couldn't survive much longer. The next time Malcolm visited Louisiana, he expected to find the boy long dead. He even laid a few hefty wagers on this with his Pack brothers.

The next day, Jeremy caught a flight to Baton Rouge where he'd found the boy, who had no idea what had happened to him or how long he'd been a werewolf. He'd been living in the swamps and tenements, eking out an existence killing rats and dogs and children. At such an early age his Changes were uncontrollable and he vacillated continually between forms, reason having almost given way to madness. The boy had looked like an animal even in human form, naked with matted hair and nails like talons.

Jeremy had brought the boy home and tried to civilize him. As it turned out, the task was as impossible as civilizing a wild animal. The best you can hope for is to tame it. Clay had lived on his own as a werewolf for so long that he no longer remembered being human. He had become a wolf, more of a true wolf than any normal werewolf could be, governed by the simplest of instincts, the need to hunt for food, to defend his territory, and to protect his family. If Jeremy had questioned this, Clay's first encounter with Nicholas had banished any doubts.

As a boy, Clay would have nothing to do with human children, so Jeremy decided he should meet one of the Pack sons, thinking Clay might be more willing to accept a playmate, who, while not a werewolf yet, at least had the blood in his veins. As I've said, sons of the Pack were taken from their mothers and raised by their fathers. More than that, they were raised by the Pack itself. The boys were indulged and cherished by the whole Pack, maybe to compensate for a difficult life to come, more likely to foster the bonds necessary for a strong Pack. The children would often pass their summer holidays moving from one house to another, spending as much time as possible with the "uncles" and "cousins" who would become their Pack brothers. Since the Pack was never large, there were usually no more than two boys of a similar age. When Clay came to live with Jeremy there were only two Pack sons under ten: Nick, who'd been eight and Daniel Santos, who'd been almost seven—the age Jeremy decided Clay would officially be. Of the two, Nick would be Clay's first playmate. Maybe Jeremy picked Nick because he was the son of his best friend. Or maybe he already saw something in Daniel that made him decide he'd make an unsuitable playmate. Whatever the reason, Jeremy's choice was one that would resonate throughout the lives of the three boys. But that's another story.

At their first meeting, Antonio brought Nick to Stonehaven and introduced him to Clay, fully expecting the two boys to run off and play a good old-fashioned game of cops and robbers. As Antonio tells the story, Clay stood there for a moment, sized up the older and taller boy, then sprang, pinning Nick to the ground with his arm on his throat, whereupon Nick promptly pissed his pants. Disgusted at his adversary's lack of worthiness, Clay decided to let him live and soon found Nick had his uses . . . as a wrestling dummy, an errand boy, and a devoted follower. Which isn't to say the two never engaged in a good old-fashioned game of cops and robbers, but whenever they did, no matter which role Nick was given, he always ended up being the one gagged, bound to a tree, and sometimes abandoned.

Clay eventually learned better instinct control, but even now it was a struggle against his nature. For Clay, instinct ruled. He'd learned tricks he could employ if he had advance notice, such as hearing hunters on the property in the distance. But without such warning, his temper took over and he'd explode, sometimes endangering the Pack. No matter how smart he was—his IQ was once measured at 160—he couldn't control his instincts. Sometimes I thought this made it harder, having the brains to know he was screwing up and being unable to stop himself. Other times I figured if he was so smart, he should be able to control it. Maybe he just didn't try hard enough. I liked that explanation better.

Jeremy and Antonio returned from their talk and we all moved to the study, where Jeremy explained the situation. There was a werewolf in Bear Valley. The wild dog story was a plausible explanation devised by locals desperate for an answer. There had been canine tracks around the body. The kill itself was canine, throat ripped out and body partly devoured. Of course, no one could explain how the young woman had come to be wandering around the forest at night in the first place, particularly in a skirt and high heels. It looked like a dog kill, so the locals had decided it was. We knew better.

The killer was a werewolf. All the signs were there. The surprise was that he was still in Bear Valley, even that he'd arrived there at all. How had one of the mutts gotten so close to Stonehaven? How had he killed a local woman before Jeremy and Clay had even figured out he was there? The answer was simple: complacency. After twenty years of not seeing a werewolf set foot north of New York City, Clay had relaxed his guard. Jeremy had continued to monitor the papers, but he'd paid more attention to events in other parts of the Pack territory. If he expected trouble, he expected it elsewhere, maybe in Toronto, or Albany where Logan kept an apartment, or the Catskills, where the Sorrentinos' estate was, or across the border in Vermont where Peter lived. But not near Stonehaven. Never near Stonehaven.

When the dead woman had disappeared Jeremy knew about it but paid little attention. Humans went missing all the time. There had been no suggestion that the disappearance had anything to do with a werewolf. Three days ago the woman's body had been found, but by then it was too late. The window of opportunity for quickly and safely dispatching the trespasser had passed. The townsfolk were up in arms over the killing. Within hours hunters were combing the woods looking for predators, human or canine. As much as Jeremy was respected in the community, he was still an outsider—someone who lived there but held himself apart from the community. For years people in and around Bear Valley had granted the Danvers their privacy, prompted in part by the large checks that came from Stonehaven each Christmas earmarked for school improvements or a new library or whatever else city council was struggling to pay for. When danger came calling, though, it was human nature to look to the outsider. It wouldn't be long before someone looked toward Stonehaven and its generous yet mysterious inhabitants and said, "You know, we don't really know them, do we?"

"What we need to do first is find this mutt," Jeremy said. "Elena has the best sense of smell, so she'll be—"

"I'm not staying," I said.

The room went silent. Everyone turned to look at me, Jeremy's expression inscrutable, Clay's jaw setting for a fight, Antonio and Peter looking shocked, and Nick staring at me in confusion. I cursed myself for having let things get this far. The middle of a meeting was not the time to assert my independence from the Pack. I'd tried to tell Jeremy the night before, but he'd obviously chosen to ignore it and hope it went away with a good night's sleep. I should have taken him aside this morning and explained it, instead of sitting down for breakfast and letting the others think everything was back to normal. But that's the way Stonehaven worked. I came back, got caught up in it—running with Clay, arguing with Jeremy, sleeping in my room, reuniting with the others—and I forgot everything else. Now, as Jeremy began to make plans for me, my memory improved.

"I thought you came back," Nick said, breaking the silence. "You're here. I don't understand."

"I'm here because Jeremy left me an urgent message to call him. I tried calling, but no one answered, so I came out to see what was wrong."

I realized this sounded lame even as the words left my mouth.

"I called," I said. "And called and called and called. I was worried, okay? So I came to find out what Jeremy wanted. I asked him last night, but he wouldn't tell me."

"So now that you know, you're leaving. Again," Clay said, his voice low but hard.

I turned on him. "I told you last night—"

"Jeremy called you for a reason, Elena," Antonio said, stepping between Clay and me. "We need to find out who this mutt is. You keep the dossiers. You know them. That's your job."

"That *was* my job."

Nick straightened up, confusion now mixed with alarm. "What does that mean?"

Clay started getting to his feet.

"It means Elena and I have something to discuss in private," Jeremy said. "We'll continue this meeting later."

Legacy

PETER AND ANTONIO CLEARED THE ROOM QUICKLY. NICK LINgered trying to catch my eye. When I looked away, he hesitated, then followed his father. Clay thumped back into his seat.

"Clayton," Jeremy said.

"I'm staying. This has as much to do with me as it does you. Probably more. If Elena thinks she can show up, then walk right back out, after I've been waiting for over a year—"

"You'll do what?" I said, stepping toward him. "Kidnap me and lock me in a hotel room again?"

"That was six years ago. And I was only trying to convince you to talk to me before you left."

"Convince? Hah. I'd probably still be there if I hadn't *convinced* you to set me free by hanging you off the balcony by your ankles. If I'd had any sense, I'd have let go while I had the chance."

"Wouldn't have done any good, darling. I bounce. You can't get rid of me that easily."

"I'm getting rid of you now," Jeremy said. "Out. That's an order."

Clay paused, then sighed, hauled himself to his feet, left the room, and closed the door. That didn't mean he was gone, though. No footsteps receded down the hall. The floor thudded as he dropped down to sit outside and eavesdrop. Jeremy chose to ignore it.

"We need your help," Jeremy said, turning back to me. "You've researched the mutts. You took that on as a job. You know more about them than any of us."

"I took on the job when I was part of the Pack. I told you—"

"We need your nose to find him and your knowledge to identify him. Then we need your help to get rid of him. It's a tricky situation, Elena. Clay's not the one to handle this. We need to proceed with absolute caution. This mutt has killed on our territory and he's insinuated himself into our town. We need to lure him out without calling attention to ourselves or making him panic. You can do that. Only you."

"I'm sorry, Jer, but this isn't my problem. I don't live here anymore. I'm not supposed to be looking for mutts. It's not my job."

"It's my job, I know. This should never have happened. I wasn't paying enough attention. But that doesn't change the fact that it's happened and we're all in danger because of it—even you. If this mutt continues making trouble, he runs the risk of being caught. If he's caught, what will prevent him from telling the authorities about us?"

"But I—"

"All I want is your help dealing with this problem. Once it's cleared up, you can do as you wish."

"And if I wish to leave the Pack? Did you mean what you said last night? That the choice is mine?"

Something flitted across Jeremy's face. He brushed his bangs back and the expression was gone. "I was angry last night. There's no reason to be in such a rush to make this decision, Elena. I said I'd let you go and live your own life and I'd only call you back if it was urgent. This is urgent. I haven't phoned you for anything else. I haven't let Clay contact you. I haven't summoned you back for the other Meets. I haven't expected you to maintain the dossiers or anything else you normally do for us. No one else would get that kind of treatment. You get it because I want to give you all the freedom you need to make the right decision."

"You're hoping I'll grow out of it."

"Adjusting to this has been more difficult for you than anyone else. You didn't grow up knowing you'd become a werewolf. Being bitten would have been bad enough, but the way it happened, the circumstances under which it happened, make it ten times harder. It's in your nature to fight something you didn't choose. When you make your choice, I want it to be because you've spent enough time out there to know that it's what you want, not because you're stubborn and want to assert your right to self-determination here and now."

"In other words, you're hoping I'll grow out of it."

"I'm asking for your help, Elena. Asking, not demanding. Help me solve this problem and you can go back to Toronto. No one will stop you." He glanced toward the door, listening for Clay's protest, but only silence returned. "I'll give you some time to think about it. Come see me when you're ready."

I stayed in the study for over an hour. Part of me cursed myself for coming back, cursed Jeremy for putting this on me, cursed Clay for . . . well, for everything else. I wanted to stomp my feet in a two-year-old's tantrum and shout that it wasn't fair. But it was fair. Jeremy was being perfectly reasonable. That was the worst of it.

I owed the Pack a debt I hadn't finished paying. I owed Antonio and Peter and Nick and Logan for their friendship and their protection and, even if they were inclined to treat me like a kid sister, someone to pet and coddle and tease, they'd accepted me and looked after me when I couldn't look after myself. Most of all, though, I owed Jeremy. As much as I railed at his demands and tyrannical authority, I never forgot how much I owed him.

When I'd been bitten, Jeremy had taken me in, sheltered me, fed me, and taught me how to control my Changes, rein in my impulses, and fit into the outside world. The Pack often jokes that raising Clay was Jeremy's greatest challenge, the seven labors of Hercules all rolled into one. If they knew what Jeremy had gone through with me they might change their minds. I put him through hell for one solid year. When he'd brought food, I'd thrown it at him. When he'd talked to me, I'd cursed and spat at him. When he'd come near me, I'd attacked him. Later, when I'd escaped, I'd put the entire Pack at risk. Any other werewolf would have given up, hunted me down, and killed me. Jeremy hunted me down, brought me back to Stonehaven, and started all over again.

When I was well again he'd encouraged me to finish my university degree, footing the bill for tuition, an apartment, and anything else I needed. When I'd finished school and started doing freelance journalism he'd encouraged and supported me. When I'd announced I wanted to try living on my own he'd disagreed, but he'd let me go and watched over me. It didn't matter whether he did these things because he was fond of me or, as I feared, only because it was in the best interests of the Pack to keep me safe and under their control. It only mattered that he'd done it. Now I cursed him for interfering with my new life. The truth was that without Jeremy's help I wouldn't have a new life. If I'd survived at all, I'd be like the mutts, barely able to control my Changes, completely unable to control my impulses, killing humans, moving from place to place one step ahead of suspicions, no job, no apartment, no friends, no lover, no future.

Now he asked something of me. One favor, not even phrased as such. Just a request for help.

I couldn't refuse.

I told Jeremy I'd stay long enough to help them find and kill this mutt on the condition that, when it was over, I could leave without him or Clay trying to stop me. Jeremy agreed. Then he went to tell the others, taking Clay out back for an extended explanation. When Clay returned, he was in high spirits, joking with Peter, mock wrestling with Nick, chatting with Antonio, and offering me the couch when we went back to the study to resume the meeting. Since Jeremy wouldn't have sugarcoated my arrangement, Clay had obviously reinterpreted the facts through his own filter of logic, a logic as indecipherable as his code of behavior and ethics. I'd straighten him out soon enough.

As expected, the plan was to hunt down and kill the mutt. Given the dicey nature of the affair, this would take place in one or two phases. Tonight, the five of us, excluding Jeremy, would go into town to track the mutt down. We'd split into two groups, Antonio and Peter in one, the rest of us in the other. If we found the mutt's lair, Antonio or I would determine whether or not the mutt could be killed safely. If it wasn't a safe kill, we'd gather information to plot the killing for another night. After the Jose Carter fiasco I was surprised Jeremy was willing to give me the responsibility of making such a decision, but no one else questioned it, so I kept quiet.

Before lunch I went to my room and called Philip. Downstairs, Peter and Antonio were loudly debating some fine point of high finance. Drawers in the kitchen banged open and shut and the smell of roasting lamb wafted up to me as Clay and Nick made lunch. Although I couldn't hear Jeremy I knew he was still where we'd left him, in the study poring over maps of Bear Valley to determine the best areas of town for our search that night.

Once in my room I walked to my bed, pushing back the canopy, crawled inside with my cell phone, and let the curtain swing closed, cutting off the outside view. When Philip didn't answer his office number, I tried his cell phone. He picked up on the third ring. As his voice crackled down the line, all noise from downstairs seemed to stop and I was transported to another world, where planning to hunt down a werewolf was only a B movie plotline.

"It's me," I said. "Are you busy?"

"Heading off for lunch with a client. Potential client. I got your message. I went downstairs for a thirty-minute workout and missed your call. Can I get your number there? Hold on while I find some paper."

"I've got my cell phone."

"Okay, I'm an idiot. Of course you do. So if I need you, I can call your cell, right?"

"I can't take it in the hospital. Against the rules. I'll check for messages though."

"Hospital? Damn it. I'm sorry. Five minutes into the conversation and I haven't even asked what happened to your cousin. An accident?"

"His wife actually. I used to come down here in the summers and a bunch of us hung out together, Jeremy, his brothers, Celia—that's his wife." Philip knew my parents were dead but I'd told him none of the gory details, such as how young I was when it happened, so I was free to improvise. "Anyway, Celia was in a car accident. Touch-and-go for a while, when Jeremy called me. She's off the critical list now."

"Thank God. Geez, that's awful. How's everyone holding up?"

"Okay. The problem is the kids. Three of them. Jeremy's really at loose ends here, trying to look after the little ones and worrying about Celia. I offered to stay for a few days, at least until Celia's parents get back from Europe. Everyone's pretty shaken up right now."

"I can imagine. Hold on." Static buzzed down the line. "Good. I'm off the expressway. Sorry about that. So you're staying to help out?"

"Until after the weekend. Is that okay?"

"Sure. Absolutely. If I wasn't so tied up with work this week I'd come down to help out myself. Do you need anything?"

"Got my credit card."

He chuckled. "That's all anyone needs these days. If you max out, give me a shout and I'll transfer some money from my account. Damn—passed my turn."

"I'll let you go."

"Sorry. Call me tonight if you get a chance, though I expect you'll be pretty busy. Three kids. How old?"

"All under five."

"Ouch. You will be busy. I'll miss you."

"It'll only be a couple days."

"Good. Talk to you soon. Love you."

"You too. Bye."

As I hung up, I closed my eyes and exhaled. See? Not so bad. Philip was still Philip. Nothing had changed. Philip and my new life were out there, waiting for me to return. Only a few more days and I could go back to them.

After lunch, I went to the study to check my dossiers, hoping to find something that might help me figure out which mutt was causing trouble in Bear Valley. One of my jobs with the Pack was to keep tabs on non-Pack werewolves. I'd built a dossier of them, complete with photos and behavioral sketches. I could recite over two dozen names and last known locations, and separate the list into the good, the bad, and the ugly—those who could suppress the urge to kill, those who couldn't, and those who didn't bother trying. Judging by this mutt's behavior, he fell into the last category. That narrowed it down from twenty-seven to about twenty.

I turned to the cupboards below the bookshelf. Opening the second one, I cleared a path through the brandy glasses and felt around the back panel for an exposed wooden nail. When I found it, I twisted the nail and the rear panel sprung open. Inside the secret compartment we kept the only two condemning articles in Stonehaven, the only things that could link us to what we were. One was my book of dossiers. When I looked, though, it wasn't there. I sighed. Only Jeremy would have taken it out and he'd left for a walk an hour ago. Though I could always go looking for him, I knew he wasn't just taking in exercise but was finalizing the plans for our mutt hunt that night. Interruptions were not appreciated.

As I was closing the compartment I saw the second book lying there and, on a whim, pulled it out and opened it, though I'd read it so many times before I could recite most of it from memory. When Jeremy first told me about the Legacy I expected some musty, stinking, half-rotted tome. But the centuries-old book was in better shape than my college texts. Naturally the pages were yellowed and fragile, but each Pack Alpha had kept it in a special compartment, free from dust, mildew, light, and any of the other elements that could kill a book.

The Legacy purported to tell the history of werewolves, particularly of the Pack, yet it wasn't a straightforward account of dates and events. Instead, every Pack Alpha had added what he considered important, making it a mishmash of history, genealogy, and lore.

One section dealt entirely with scientific experimentation on the nature and boundaries of the werewolf condition. A Pack Alpha during the Renaissance had been particularly fascinated with legends of werewolf immortality. He'd detailed every one, from the stories of werewolves becoming immortal by drinking the blood of infants to the tales of werewolves becoming vampires after death. Then he'd proceeded with well-controlled experiments, all involving mutts that he'd capture, work on, then kill and wait for their resurrection. None of his experiments worked, but he'd been remarkably successful at decreasing the European mutt population.

A century later, a Pack Alpha became obsessed with the pursuit of better sex—the only surprising part of this being that it took several hundred years for someone to do it. He'd started with the hypothesis that human-werewolf sex was inherently dissatisfying because it involved two different species. So he bit a few women. When they didn't survive, he concluded that rumors of female werewolves throughout the ages were false and such a thing was biologically impossible. Moving right along, he tried variations on sex in both forms—as a wolf and as a human with both normal wolves and humans. None approached being in good old-fashioned human form having human sex, so he went back to women and started experimenting with variations on positions, acts, locales, et cetera. Finally, he found the ultimate act of sexual satisfaction—waiting until the first notes of climax struck, then slashing his partner's throat. He described his formula in vivid detail, with all the flowery emoting of a new religious convert. Fortunately, his practice never gained popularity among the Pack, probably because the Alpha was burned at the stake a few months later, after having depleted his village's entire supply of eligible young women.

On the less factual side, the Legacy contained countless stories of werewolves through the ages. Most of these were "my father told me this when I was a child" sort of yarns, many dating back to before the first edition of the Legacy was written. There were tales of werewolves who'd lived their lives in reverse, staying wolves most of the time and changing to humans only when the physical need demanded. There were stories of knights and soldiers and bandits and marauders who'd supposedly been werewolves. Most of these names had vanished from history, but one was still known, even by those who'd never cracked open a history book in their lives. Human history tells of the legend that Genghis Khan's family tree started with a wolf and a doe. According to the Legacy, that was more truth than allegory, the wolf being a werewolf and the doe being a symbol for a human mother. According to that line of reasoning, Genghis Khan himself would have been a werewolf, which explained his lust for blood and his near-supernatural abilities in war. It likely wasn't any truer than the countless human genealogies that include Napoleon and Cleopatra in their family tree. Still, it made a good story.

An equally good tale is one that was also found in human werewolf mythology. A newlywed nobleman's village was plagued by a werewolf. One night, while staking out the beast, the nobleman hears a noise in the bushes and sees a monstrous wolf. He jumps from his saddle and gives chase through the woods on foot. The beast flees from him. At one point, he gets close enough to swing his sword and lops off one of the wolf's front paws. The creature escapes, but when the nobleman goes back to retrieve the paw, it's turned into a woman's hand. Exhausted, he returns to his home to tell his wife what happened. He finds his wife hiding in the back rooms, binding the bloody stump where her hand used to be. Realizing the truth, he kills her. Now, the human version of the story ends there, but the Legacy goes further, giving the ending a pro-werewolf twist. In the Legacy tale, the nobleman kills his new wife by slicing open her stomach. When he does so, out tumbles a litter of wolf pups, his own children. The sight drives the nobleman mad and he kills himself with his sword. Now, as a female werewolf, I'm not particularly keen on the thought of a bellyful of puppies. I prefer to interpret the pups as an allegorical symbol of the nobleman's guilt. When he realizes he's killed his wife without giving her a chance to explain, he goes mad and kills himself. A much more fitting end.

In addition to these stories and musings, each Alpha chronicled the genealogy of the Pack during his reign. This included not only family trees, but brief descriptions of each person's history and life story. Most family trees were long and convoluted. In the current Pack, though, there were three blips, one name with no others before or after it. Clay and I were two. Logan was the third. Unlike Clay and me, Logan was a hereditary werewolf. No one knew who Logan's father was. He'd been put up for adoption as an infant. The only thing that came with him was an envelope to be opened on his sixteenth birthday. Inside the envelope was a slip of paper with two surnames and two addresses, that of the Danvers at Stonehaven and the Sorrentinos at their estate outside New York City. It was unlikely that Logan's father was Pack, since no Pack member would put a son up for adoption. Yet his father had known that the Pack wouldn't turn a sixteen-year-old werewolf away, whatever his parentage, so he'd directed his son to them, ensuring Logan would find out what he was before his first Change and, in doing so, have the chance to start his new life with training and protection. Maybe this proved that not all mutts were lousy fathers, or maybe only that anomalies were possible anywhere in life.

Most other Pack family trees had plenty of branches. Like the Danvers, the Sorrentino family could trace its roots to the beginning of the Legacy. Antonio's father, Dominic, had been Alpha until his death. He'd had three sons, Gregory, who was dead, Benedict, who'd left the Pack before I arrived, and Antonio, the youngest. Antonio's only son was Nick. In the Legacy, the annotation LKB was marked in parentheses beside Nick's initials. Nick didn't know what it meant. As far as I knew, he'd never asked. If he'd even read the Legacy, which I doubted, he'd have figured that if no one had explained the notation to him it must not be important. Nick was like that, totally accepting. The letters were important, but there was no sense telling Nick what they stood for, stirring up questions that couldn't be answered and emotions that couldn't be satisfied. LKB were Nick's mother's initials. It was the only place in the Legacy where a mother was memorialized. Jeremy had added it. Neither Jeremy nor Antonio had explained this to me. It was Peter who'd told me the story years ago.

When Antonio was sixteen, attending a posh private school outside New York City, he'd fallen in love with a local girl. He'd known better than to tell his father, but had let his best friend, fourteen-year-old Jeremy, in on the secret and the two had conspired to keep the relationship hidden from the Pack. It worked for a year. Then the girl became pregnant. On Jeremy's advice, Antonio told his father. Apparently, Jeremy had thought Dominic would see that his son was in love and break Pack law to help him. I guess everyone is young once. Young, romantic, and very naive. Even Jeremy. Things didn't exactly work as Jeremy had envisioned. Big surprise there. Dominic yanked Antonio out of school and put him under house arrest while the Pack waited for the baby to be born.

With Jeremy's help, Antonio had escaped, gone back to the girl, and declared his independence from the Pack. From there, things got really ugly. Peter glossed over the details, saying only that Antonio and his girlfriend had gone into hiding while Jeremy ran interference between father and son, desperate for a reconciliation. Somewhere in the midst of this, Nick was born.

Three months later, Antonio had his first Change. Over the next six months, he'd realized that his father was right. No matter how much he loved Nick's mother, it wouldn't work. Not only would he ruin her life, but he'd ruin his son's, sentencing him to a life as a mutt. One night he took Nick, left an envelope of money on the table, and walked out. He delivered Nick to Jeremy and told him to take the child to Dominic. Then he vanished. For three months, Antonio was gone, not even Jeremy knew where. Just as abruptly, he returned. He took Nick to raise and never mentioned the girl again. Everyone thought that was the end of it. Years later, though, Peter came to visit Antonio and tracked him to a suburb, where he'd found Antonio sitting in his car outside a playground, watching a young woman playing with a toddler. I wondered how often he'd done that, wondered if he ever did it now, checking up on Nick's mother, maybe watching her playing with her grandchildren. When I look at Antonio—boisterous, loud, self-assured Antonio—I can't imagine him holding a torch for a lost love, but in all the years I've known him, I've never heard him mention any woman in his life. Oh, there are women in his life, but they come and go, never staying long enough to make it into even the most idle conversation.

At the time, I wondered why Peter told me that story, a chapter of Pack history that would never make it into the Legacy. Later I came to realize that he'd thought letting me in on a harmless Pack secret might make me feel more part of the Pack, might help me better understand my Pack brothers. Peter did a lot of that. Not to say that the others shut me out or made me feel unwelcome. Nothing of the sort. The only person whose acceptance I'd ever doubted was Jeremy's and maybe that was more my problem than his. I'd met Logan and Nick, through

Clay, before I became a werewolf. After I was bitten, they'd both been there and, when I was ready to accept their help, they'd done whatever they could to cheer me up—as much as you could cheer up someone who's just learned that life as she's known it is over. When I met Antonio at my first Pack meeting, he'd flattered and teased and engaged me in conversation as easily as if he'd known me for years. But Peter had been different. Acceptance wasn't enough. He always went that extra step. He'd been the first to tell me his background, like a newfound uncle filling me in on family history.

Peter had been raised in the Pack but, at twenty-two, decided to leave. No major argument or rebellion precipitated his departure. He'd simply decided to try life from the other side, more an experiment in alternate lifestyles than a revolt against the Pack. As Peter put it, Dominic saw him neither as a dangerous non-Pack liability nor as a necessary Pack asset, so he let him leave. With a college degree in audiovisual technology Peter had gone after the most glamorous work he could imagine, as a sound technician for rock bands. He'd started with bar bands and, within five years, had worked his way up to big concert venues. That was when his thirst for new experiences got dangerous, as he'd lapped up the whole rock band lifestyle—drugs, booze, and parties past dawn. Then something happened. Something bad. Peter didn't elaborate, but said it was bad enough to warrant the death sentence if the Pack found out. He could have run, hid, and hoped. But he didn't. Instead, he'd looked at his life and what he'd done and realized it wouldn't get any better if he ran. He'd only screw up again. He decided to throw himself on the mercy of the Pack. If Dominic ordered his execution, at least his first mistake would be his last. He hoped, though, that Dominic would grant him absolution and let him return to the Pack, where he could get help regaining control over his life. To improve his chances, he appealed to the one Pack brother he trusted to plead his case with Dominic. He'd called Jeremy. Instead of going to Dominic, Jeremy flew to Los Angeles, bringing ten-year-old Clay. While Peter baby-sat Clay, Jeremy spent a week erasing all traces of Peter's mistake. Then he took Peter back to New York and orchestrated his return to the Pack with nary a word about his misstep in California. Today no one would guess Peter had ever made such a mistake or had ever left the Pack. He was as devoted to Jeremy as Clay and Antonio, though in his own way, quiet and accepting, never arguing or offering so much as a dissenting opinion. The only trace of Peter's wild years was his job. He still worked as a sound technician, one of the best in the business. He routinely took off on long tours, but Jeremy never worried about him or doubted that he was anything but absolutely circumspect in his outside life. Jeremy had even let me take off with Peter for a few weeks back when I was still getting my bearings as a werewolf. Peter had invited me along on the Canadian leg of a U2 tour. It had been the experience of a lifetime, making me forget all the problems of my new life, which was exactly what Peter had intended.

As I was thinking this, a pair of hands grabbed me under the armpits and hoisted me off my chair.

"Wake up!" Antonio said, tickling me, then dropping me back onto the chair. He leaned over my shoulder and picked up the Legacy. "Just in time, Pete. Five more minutes of reading this and she'd have been in a coma."

Peter walked in front of me, took the book from Antonio, and made a face. "Are we such bad company that you'd rather hide out in here reading that old thing?"

Antonio grinned. "I'd guess it's not us she's avoiding, but a certain blond-haired tornado. Jeremy sent him to the store with Nicky, so you can come out of hiding now."

"We came to ask if you felt like taking a walk," Peter said. "Stretch our legs, get caught up."

"Actually, I was—" I began.

Antonio lifted me by the armpits again, this time putting me on my feet. "Actually, she was just going to come find us and tell us how much she missed us and is dying to get caught up."

"I was—"

Peter grabbed my wrists and tugged me toward the door. I dug in my heels.

"I'll go," I said. "I was just going to say that I came in here to read the dossiers, but Jeremy must have them. I was hoping maybe they'd help me figure out who could be behind this. Do you guys have any ideas?"

"Plenty," Antonio said. "Now come for a walk and we'll tell you."

When we'd left the backyard and headed into the forest, Antonio began.

"My money's on Daniel," he said

"Daniel?" Peter frowned. "How'd you figure that?"

Antonio lifted a hand and started counting off reasons on his fingers. "One, he used to be Pack so he knows how dangerous this kind of killing on our territory is, that we can't—and won't—leave town. Two, he hates Clay. Three, he hates Jeremy. Four, he hates all of us—with the exception of our dear Elena, who, conveniently, wasn't at Stonehaven to be affected by the mess, which I'm sure Daniel knew. Five, he really hates Clay. Six—oh, wait, other hand—six, he's a murderous cannibalizing bastard. Seven, did I mention he chose to strike when Elena wasn't around? Eight, if he caused enough havoc, Elena might be in the market for a new partner. Nine, he really, really, REALLY hates Clay. Ten, he's sworn undying revenge against the entire Pack, particularly those two members who happen to be currently living at Stonehaven. I'm out of fingers here, buddy. How many more reasons do you need?"

"How about one that involves utter suicidal stupidity. Daniel doesn't meet that qualification. No offense, Tonio, but I think you're seeing Daniel in this because you want to see him in it. He makes a convenient fall guy—not that I wouldn't like to help him with that final fall. But if you're placing wagers—small wagers, please, I don't have your capital to blow—I'd go with Zachary Cain. Definitely dumb enough. Big brute probably woke up one morning, thought, Hey, why don't I kill some girl on Pack territory for a kick. Probably wondered why he hadn't thought of it before. Because it's stupid, stupid."

"It could be someone minor," I said. "One of the bit players tired of being banished to the wings. Any mutts been making a ruckus lately?"

"Petty stuff," Antonio said. "None of the minor leagues making any major plays. Of the big four, Daniel, Cain, and Jimmy Koenig have been quiet. Karl Marsten killed a mutt in Miami last winter, but I don't think this Bear Valley problem could be him. Not his m.o., unless he's taken up not only killing humans but eating them. Unlikely."

"Who'd he kill?" I asked.

"Ethan Ritter," Peter said. "Range dispute. Clean kill. Thorough disposal. Typical Marsten stuff. We only know about it because I was passing through Florida earlier this spring on a tour. Marsten caught up with me, took me to dinner, told me he'd offed Ritter so you could strike his name from your dossiers. Had a nice little chat, rang up an astronomic bill, which he paid for in cash. He asked if we'd heard from you, sent his regards to everyone."

"I'm surprised he doesn't send Christmas cards," Antonio said. "I can see them now. Tasteful, embossed vellum cards, the best he can steal. Little notes in perfect penmanship, 'Happy holidays. Hope everyone is well. I sliced up Ethan Ritter in Miami and scattered his remains in the Atlantic. Best wishes for the New Year. Karl.'"

Peter laughed. "That guy has never figured out which side of our fence he's on."

"Oh, he's figured it out," I said. "That's exactly why he takes us out to fancy dinners and updates us on his mutt kills. He's hoping *we'll* forget which side of the fence he's on."

"Not likely," Antonio said. "A mutt is a mutt and Karl Marsten is definitely a mutt. A dangerous mutt."

I nodded. "But, as you said, not likely to be eating humans in Bear Valley. I'm as biased as you, but I really like the idea of Daniel. Do we have his last known whereabouts?"

There was a moment of silence. More than a moment. Much more.

"No one's been keeping track," Peter said at last.

"Not a big deal," Antonio said, breaking into a grin, grabbing me and swinging me in the air. "Forget Pack business. Tell us what you've been up to. We missed you."

It was a big deal. I knew why they were making light of it. Because the big deal was my fault. Tracking mutts was my job. If I'd told Jeremy I was leaving the Pack last year, he'd have found someone else to do it. If I'd called at any point and said I wasn't coming back, he'd have found someone else to do it. But I'd left my departure open-ended. I always did. I'd left Stonehaven before, getting into a fight with Clay and storming out for a much-needed rest. Days, maybe weeks later, I'd return. This time, the weeks had turned to months, then to a year. I thought they'd figure it out, know I wasn't coming back, but maybe they hadn't, maybe they'd still been waiting, like Clay waiting all day at the front gate, confident that I'd eventually return because I always did and because I hadn't said I wouldn't. I wondered how long they would have waited.

After dinner, I was heading to my room when Nicholas pounced out of Clay's room, grabbed me around the waist, and dragged me inside. Clay's bedroom was opposite mine, both in location and decor. The color scheme was black and white. The thick carpet was snow white. Jeremy had painted the walls white with bold, geometric black shapes. Clay's bed was king-size and brass, covered with a black-and-white bedspread embroidered with symbols from some obscure religion. Along the west wall was a top-of-the-line entertainment system, complete with the only stereo, VCR, and television in the house. The far wall was covered with pictures of me—a montage of photographs and sketches that reminded me of the "altars" found in the homes of obsessed psychopaths, which, all things considered, wasn't such a bad description of Clay.

Nick threw me onto the bed and jumped on top of me, pulling my shirt from my jeans to tickle my stomach. He grinned suggestively, white teeth glinting beneath his dark mustache.

"Looking forward to tonight?" he asked, running his fingers from my belly button farther under my shirt. I slapped his hand back down to my stomach.

"We aren't supposed to have fun," I said. "This is a serious matter, requiring a serious attitude."

A whoop of laughter exploded from the bathroom. Clay came out, wiping his hands on a towel. "You can almost say that with a straight face, darling. I'm impressed."

I rolled my eyes and said nothing.

Clay thudded down beside me, making the bedsprings groan. "Come on. Admit it. You're looking forward to it."

I shrugged.

"Liar. You are. How often do we get to run in town? An officially sanctioned mutt hunt."

Clay's eyes glinted. He reached down to stroke the inside of my forearm and I shivered. Nervous anticipation twirled in my stomach. Turning his head to the side, Clay looked out the window at the gathering dusk. His fingertips tickled against the inside of my elbow. My gaze swept over his face, taking in the line of his jaw, the tendons on his neck, the dark blond shadow on his chin, and the curve of his lips. Heat started in the pit of my stomach and radiated down. He swiveled back to face me. His pupils were dilated and I could smell his excitement. He gave a hoarse chuckle, leaned toward me, and whispered those three magical little words.

"Time to hunt."

Hunt

BEAR VALLEY WAS A BLUE-COLLAR TOWN OF EIGHT THOUSAND that had got its start in the heyday of industrialization and boomed during the forties and fifties. But three recessions and downsizing had taken their toll. There was a tractor factory to the east and paper plant to the north and most people worked in one of these two behemoths. Bear Valley was a place that prided itself on hometown values, where people worked hard, played hard, and filled the baseball stadium regardless of whether the local team was first or last in the league. In Bear Valley, the bars closed at midnight on weekdays, the annual PTA jumble sale was a major social event, and gun control meant not letting your kids shoot with anything bigger than a twenty-gauge. At night, young women walked the streets of Bear Valley fearing little more than catcalls whistled from passing pickups by guys they'd known since childhood. They did not get murdered by strangers and they certainly did not get dragged off, slaughtered, and eaten by mad dogs.

We split up for the drive. Antonio and Peter headed for the west side of town, where there were a couple of three-story walk-ups and two highway-side motels. This meant that they had the better sector, since the mutt was more likely to be found in less permanent housing, but the downside was that Jeremy had decided they'd have to search in human form, since they couldn't exactly roam an apartment complex as wolves.

Clay, Nick, and I were to canvass the east end, where we hoped to find the mutt renting or boarding. We took my car, an old Camaro that I always found some excuse for leaving at Stonehaven. Clay was driving. It was my fault, really—he'd challenged me in a race to the garage. My ego accepted and my feet lost. We arrived in the city just past nine-thirty. Clay dropped me off behind a medical clinic that had closed at five. I Changed between two Dumpsters that reeked of disinfectant.

Changing forms is much like any other bodily function in that it comes most easily when the body needs to do it. An uncontrolled werewolf undergoes the transformation under two circumstances: when he is threatened and when his internal cycle dictates the need. The need is roughly lunar based, though it has little to do with the full moon. Our natural cycles are usually weekly. As the time approached, we could feel the symptoms: the restlessness, the itchy skin, the internal cramps and pangs, the overwhelming sensation that something needed to be done and the body and mind wouldn't rest until that need had been satisfied. The signals became as recognizable as the signs of hunger, and like hunger, we could put off dealing with it, but before long the body would take over and force a Change. Also like hunger, we could anticipate the symptoms and satisfy the need beforehand. Or we could forgo the natural cycle completely and learn how to transform ourselves as often as we liked. That is what the Pack taught us to do, to Change more often to improve our control and ensure we didn't wait too long, since waiting could lead to nasty side effects like our hands turning to paws in the middle of grocery shopping, or once a wolf, being overcome by frustrated rage and bloodlust. In Toronto I'd ignored Jeremy's teachings and given in to my need only when necessary, partly to distance myself from my "curse" and partly because in the city it was a major production requiring so much planning and caution that I was left too exhausted to repeat the experience more than once a week. So once again, I was out of practice. I'd Changed only *yesterday* and I knew doing it again less than twenty-four hours later would be hell. Like having sex without foreplay, it was either going to be extremely painful or I wasn't going to be able to perform at all. I should have told Jeremy this when he said we had to become wolves for the hunt, but I couldn't. I was, well, I was embarrassed. In Toronto, I'd done it as little as possible because I was ashamed. Two days later I was at Stonehaven refusing to admit that I couldn't do it as often as the others because I was ashamed. One more thing to send my brain spinning into permanent confusion.

It took over a half hour to complete the process, triple the normal amount of time. Did it hurt? Well, I don't have a lot of experience with non-shapechanging pain, but I feel safe in saying that being drawn and quartered might have hurt a bit less. When it was over, I rested for another twenty minutes, thankful I'd been able to do it at all. Given the choice between the agony of the Change and admitting to Clay and the others that I could no longer do it on demand, I'd pick drawing and quartering any day. Physical pain fades faster than wounded pride.

I started in a subdivision of old row houses that hadn't been converted to condos and probably never would be. It was past ten o'clock, but the streets were already deserted. Children had been yanked from the playground hours ago by anxious parents. Even adults had taken cover when the sun went down. Despite the warm May night, no one sat on their porches or shot hoops in their driveway. The wavering blue light of television flashed against drawn curtains. Sitcom laugh tracks screeched through the still night, offering escapism for the nervous. Bear Valley was afraid.

I stole along the front of the town houses, hidden between the brickwork and foundation shrubbery. At each doorway, I stuck my muzzle out and sniffed, then scampered across to the safety of the next string of bushes. Every flash of car lights made me freeze. My heart thudded, tripping with nervous excitement. There was little fun in this, but the danger added an element I hadn't experienced in years. If I was seen, even for a second, I was in trouble. I was a wolf skulking around a town in the throes of a collective nightmare about wild dogs. A flash of my shape silhouetted against a drawn blind would bring out the shotguns.

Over an hour later, I was midway through my fourth lane of row houses when a click-clicking stopped me cold. I pressed myself against the cool brick of the house and listened. Someone was coming down the sidewalk, clicking with each step. Clay? He'd better not. Even if hunting together might be more fun, Jeremy had instructed us to work separately to cover more ground. I stopped between the boughs of a cedar, peered out, and saw a woman hurrying up the sidewalk, heels clacking against the concrete. She wore a uniform of some kind, polyester skirt barely covering ample hips. Clutching an imitation leather handbag, she was moving as fast as her two-inch heels would allow. With every few steps she glanced over her shoulder. I sniffed the air and caught a faint whiff of Obsession cologne overladen with the stink of grease and cigarette smoke. A diner waitress coming home after her shift, not expecting darkness to have fallen so completely. As she drew closer, I smelled something else. Fear. Untainted, unmistakable fear. I prayed she wouldn't run. She didn't. With one final, fearful glance back at the street she scurried into her house and locked the door. I went back to work.

A few minutes later, a howl rang out. Clay. He didn't use the distinctive wolf howl, which would have certainly roused attention, but instead mimicked the cry of a lonely dog. He'd found something. I waited. When a second howl came, I used it to pinpoint his location, then started to run. I kept to the gutters, but didn't worry so much about staying out of sight. At this pace, anyone spotting me would see only a flash of pale fur.

I ran into an obstacle when I hit the main road and realized I had to cross it. While not many locals were still out, the main road was also a state highway meaning truckers sped through every few minutes. I waited for a big enough gap between semis and darted across. On the other side was Clay's assigned district, a subdivision of aging wartime houses and duplexes. As I tried to find his scent, I caught another, one that made me skid to a halt, my rear legs sliding forward and tumbling me backward. I shook myself, cursing my clumsiness, then retraced my steps. There, at the junction of two streets, I smelled a werewolf, someone I didn't recognize. The trail was old, but clear. He'd passed this way more than once. I gazed down the street. It was still in the general direction of where I'd heard Clay, so I changed course and followed the mutt's trail.

The scent led to a single-level brick house with aluminum-sided additions on the back. The yard was small and freshly cut, but creeping weeds competed for space with the grass. Garbage was piled next to a gatepost and the odor made me wince. Judging by the three mailboxes out front, there were three apartments. The house was dark. I snuffled along the sidewalk. It was inundated with werewolf scent and I couldn't tell where one trail ended and the next began. The distinguishing factor was age. He'd been past here regularly for several days.

In my excitement at finding the mutt's apartment, I didn't see a shadow slip beside me. I swung my head up to see Clay, in human form. He reached down and ran his hand through the fur behind my head. I snapped at him and dove into the bushes. After Changing to human form, I stepped out.

"You know I hate that," I muttered, raking my fingers through my tangled hair. "When I'm Changed, either you stay Changed or you respect my privacy. Petting me doesn't help."

"I wasn't 'petting' you, Elena. Christ, even the smallest gesture—" He stopped himself, inhaled and started again. "This is the mutt's place, the rear apartment, but he isn't here."

"You've been inside?"

"I was checking things out and waiting for you."

I looked down at his naked body, then at my own. "I don't suppose you thought to get clothing while you were standing around."

"You expect me to find something on a clothesline at this hour? Sorry, darling. Anyway, this has its advantages. If someone comes out, I'm sure you can convince him not to call the cops on us."

I snorted and walked around to the rear apartment door. It was secured only with a key lock. A sharp twist on the handle broke that. I'd barely pushed the door open a crack when the fetid odor of rotting meat hit me. I gagged and swallowed back the urge to cough. The place smelled like a charnel house. At least, it did to me. A human probably wouldn't have smelled a thing.

The door opened into a living room that looked like a stereotypical bachelor's place: unwashed clothing strewn across the threadbare sofa set and empty beer cans stacked like a house of cards in the corner.

Boxes with pizza crusts littered the corner table. But that wasn't the source of the stink. The mutt had killed here. There was no sign of a body, but the overpowering smell of blood and rotted flesh gave it away. He'd brought someone back to his apartment, killed her, and kept her around a day or two before dumping the remains.

I started in the main room, checking in closets and under furniture for any clue to the mutt's identity. Although I didn't recognize his scent, I might be able to figure out who he was with a few hints. When I didn't find anything, I went into the bedroom where Clay was on the floor, looking under the bed. As I walked in, he pulled out a hank of hair with the scalp still attached, tossed it aside, and kept searching for something more interesting. I stared at the bloody clump, feeling my gorge rise. Clay paid as much attention to it as he'd pay to a dirty tissue, more concerned with soiling his hands than anything else. As brilliant as Clay was, he couldn't understand why killing humans was taboo. He didn't slaughter innocent people, any more than the average person would swerve his car to intentionally hit an animal. But if a human posed a threat, his instincts told him to take whatever action was necessary. Jeremy forbade him to kill humans, so he avoided it for that reason and no other.

"Nothing," he said, his voice muffled. He backed out. "How about you?"

"Same. He knows enough to keep his place clear of ID."

"But not enough to keep his hands off the locals."

"Hereditary, but young," I said. "He smells new, but no new bitten werewolf could have that kind of experience so he must be young. Young and cocky. Daddy's taught him the basics, but he hasn't got enough experience to keep his nose clean or stay off Pack territory."

"Well, he's not going to live long enough to gain that experience. His first screwup was his last."

We were doing a last sweep of the apartment when Nick swung though the door, panting.

"I heard you call," he said. "You found his apartment? Is he here?"

"No," I said.

"Can we wait?" Nick asked, eyes hopeful.

I hesitated, then shook my head. "He'd smell us before he even got to the door. Jeremy said to kill only if we can do it safely. We can't. Unless he's a complete novice, he'll pick up our scents when he gets back. With any luck, he'll take a hint and get out of town. If so, we can hunt him later and kill him off Pack territory. Definitely safer."

Clay reached over to the nightstand, where he'd put things that he'd pulled from under the bed. He handed me two matchbooks.

"Bet I can guess where the mutt spends his evenings," Clay said. "If he's too dumb to blow town before we come after him tomorrow night, we can probably find him scouting for dinner at the local meat markets."

I looked at the matchbooks. The first was for *Rick's Tavern,* one of only three licensed establishments in the area. The second was a cheap brown matchbook with an address rubber-stamped on the back. I memorized the address, since we couldn't take anything with us, being a bit short of pocket space at the time.

"Back to get our clothes," Clay said. "Nick and I left ours across Main near where we dropped you off, so we can run together most of the way. You want to Change in the bedroom? We'll stay in here."

My heart started to hammer. "Change?"

"Yeah, Change. You planning to jog back to the car naked, darling? Not that I mind, so long as no one else gets an eyeful. But it might get a bit tricky, streaking across the highway."

"There's clothing here."

Clay snorted. "I'd rather be caught naked than wearing some mutt's clothes." When I didn't reply, he frowned. "Something wrong, darling?"

"No, I just— No. Nothing's wrong."

I walked into the bedroom, shutting the door all but a crack, so I could get out when—or if—my Change was successful. Thankfully, no one thought it odd that I wanted privacy. As close as the Pack was, most liked to make their transformations in private. As always, Clay was the exception. He didn't care who saw him Change. To him, it was a natural state and therefore nothing to be ashamed of, even if the midpoint of a Change turned you into something fit only for a freak show. For Clay, vanity was yet another bizarre and foreign human concept. Nothing natural should need to be hidden. The bathroom locks at Stonehaven had been broken for over twenty years. No one bothered to fix them. Some things weren't worth the effort of fighting Clay's nature. We drew the line, though, when it came to Changing together.

I crossed to the other side of the bed so Clay and Nick couldn't see me through the door. Then I sunk to all fours, concentrated and hoped. For five long minutes, nothing happened. I started to sweat and tried harder. Several more minutes passed. I thought I felt my hands changing into claws, but when I looked down, it was only my very human fingers digging into the carpet.

Out of the corner of my eye, I saw the door move. A black nose poked into the room. A golden muzzle followed. Jumping forward, I slammed the door shut before Clay saw me. He gave a questioning whine. I grunted, hoping the noise sounded sufficiently canine. Clay grunted back and padded away from the door. A respite, but a brief one. In less than five minutes he'd try again. Clay wasn't known for his patience.

Creeping across the carpet, I eased the door back open a crack so I could prod it open if—when, please when—I Changed. Just in case, I thought of backup plans. Grab some clothing and break out the window? As I was sizing up the tiny window, my skin started to tingle and stretch. I glanced down to see my fingernails thickening, my fingers shortening. Giving a deep sigh of relief, I closed my eyes and let the transformation take over.

We crept through the yard behind the house and came out on the north side of Bear Valley's fast-food strip, a gauntlet of every known chain restaurant with a drive-thru. After sneaking through the rear parking lots, we headed into a maze of alleys wending through a block of storage units. Finally out from under the floodlights, we began to run.

Before long, Clay and I started to race. It was more of an obstacle course than a flat-out race, slipping in the puddles and stumbling over garbage bags. I'd taken the lead when a garbage can crashed at the end of the alley. All three of us skidded to a halt.

"What the fuck are you doing?" said a young male voice. "Watch where you're going and get your ass in gear. If my old man finds I snuck out, he'll nail my hide to the woodshed door."

Another male voice only gave a drunken giggle in reply. The garbage can scraped along the gravel, then two heads came into view, moving into the alley. I inched into the shadows until my rump hit the brick wall. I was sandwiched between a pile of garbage and a stack of boxes. Across from me, Clay and Nick retreated into a doorway and disappeared into the darkness, leaving only Clay's glowing blue eyes. He looked from me to the approaching boys, telling me that the shadows weren't doing their job and I was exposed. It was too late to move. I could only hope the boys were too drunk to pay attention as they stumbled past.

The boys were chattering about something, but the words passed through my ears as white noise. To understand human speech in this form, I had to concentrate, much like I would to understand someone speaking French. I couldn't bother with that now. I was too busy watching their feet as they drew closer.

As they came alongside the garbage pile, I crouched, flattening myself to the ground. Their boots took three more steps, propelling them just past my hiding spot. I forced myself not to listen, instead looking up at their faces and taking my cue from there. They were no more than seventeen years old. One was tall, dark haired, wearing a leather jacket, ripped jeans, and combat boots, with a tattoo around his neck, and studs through his lips and nose. His red-haired companion wore a similar outfit, but without the tattoo and piercings, lacking the courage—or the idiocy—to turn a fashion statement into permanent disfigurement.

They continued to jabber as they walked away. Then the dark-haired kid tripped. Falling, he twisted, grabbed the side of a garbage bin, and saw me. He blinked once. Then he tugged his friend's jacket sleeve and pointed. Instinct goaded me to counter threat with attack. Reason forced me to wait. Ten years ago, I'd have killed the boys the moment they entered the alley. Five years ago, I'd have leapt as soon as one noticed me. Even today I could feel the struggle deep in my gut, a twisting fear that made my muscles twitch in readiness for the attack. It was this—the battle for control of my body—that I hated more than anything else.

A low rumble echoed through the alley. Feeling the vibrations in my throat, I realized I was growling. My ears were plastered against my head. For one second, my brain tried to override instinct, then saw the advantage in surrendering, in letting the boys see how close they stood to death.

I curled back my lips and snarled. Both boys jumped backward. The redhead turned and ran down the alley, tripping and stumbling through the trash. The other boy's eyes followed his friend. Then, instead of bolting after him, his hand shot out into the garbage pile. When he pulled back, the moonlight glinted off something in his hand. He turned to me, holding a broken bottle, the fear on his face replaced by a grin of power. Motion blurred behind him and I glanced up to see Clay in a crouch. The muscles in his shoulders bunched. I looked back at the boy, then sprang. Clay leapt. In midair, I twisted away from the boy and caught Clay full in the chest. We tumbled through the air together and hit the ground running, Nick at our heels. We ran the rest of the way back to our clothes.

We got to Stonehaven after two. Antonio and Peter were still out. There hadn't been any safe way to find them and tell them we'd already discovered where the mutt was staying. The house was silent and dark. Jeremy hadn't waited up. He knew if anything had happened, we'd wake him. Clay and I raced for the steps, jostling to be the first one up, bickering as we ran. Behind us, Nick mimicked our fight, but kept on our heels. We hit the top of the stairs and raced for Jeremy's room at the end of the hall. Before we could get there, the door creaked open.

"Did you find him?" Jeremy asked, a disembodied voice from the darkness.

"We found where he's staying," I said. "He's—"

"Did you kill him?"

"Nah," Clay said. "Too risky. But we'll—"

"Good. Tell me the rest in the morning."

The door closed. Clay and I looked at each other. Then I shrugged and headed back down the hall.

"I'll just have to beat you to it tomorrow," I said.

Clay pounced, knocking me onto the hardwood floor. He stayed on top of me, pinning my arms to the floor and grinning down, the excitement of the hunt still shining in his eyes. "You think so? How about we play for it? You name the game."

"Poker," Nick said.

Clay twisted to look up at him. "And what stakes are you playing for?"

Nick grinned. "The usual. It's been a long time."

Clay laughed, got up, and lifted me into his arms. When we got to his room, he tossed me onto the bed, then headed to the bar to mix drinks. Nick jumped on top of me. I threw him off and struggled up.

"What makes you think I'm going to play at all?" I asked.

"You missed us," Nick said.

He made a show of unbuttoning his shirt and shrugging it off, making sure I saw a good display of his muscles. Undressing was like some damned mating ritual with these guys. They seemed to think that the sight of a handsome face, muscular biceps, and a flat stomach would turn me into a helpless mass of hormones, willing to play their juvenile games. It usually worked, but that wasn't the point.

"Whiskey and soda?" Clay called from across the room.

"Perfect," Nick said.

Clay didn't ask what I wanted. Nick took the clip from my hair and nibbled my ear, warm breath smelling faintly of dinner. I relaxed on the bed. As his lips moved down my neck, I twisted my face, nuzzling his neck and inhaling the musky smell of him. I moved to the hollow in his collarbone and felt his heartbeat leap.

Nick jumped. I looked up to see Clay pressing a cold glass against Nick's back. He grabbed Nick's shoulder and yanked him off me.

"Go find the cards," he said.

"Where are they?" Nick asked.

"Look. That'll keep you busy for a while."

Clay sat down next to my head and handed me a drink. I took a sip. Rum and Coke. He gulped his own, then leaned over me.

"Perfect night, wasn't it?"

"It could have been." I smiled up at him. "But you were there."

"Which means it was only the beginning of a perfect night."

As he leaned over me, his fingers brushed against my thigh and slid over my hip. The thick, almost palpable smell of him sent a slow burn radiating down from my stomach.

"You had fun," he said. "Admit it."

"Maybe."

Nick jumped back onto the bed. "Playtime. Are you guys sticking to your stakes? Winner tells Jeremy what happened tonight?"

Clay's lips curved in a slow smile. "Nah. I'm going for something else. If I win, Elena comes outside with me, to the woods."

"For what?" I asked.

The smile widened to show perfect white teeth. "Does it matter?"

"And if I win, what do I get?" I asked.

"Whatever you want. If you win, you choose your prize. You can tell Jeremy what happened, or you can take the kill tomorrow, or anything else you'd like."

"I can take the kill?"

He threw his head back and laughed. "I knew you'd like that one. Sure, darling. You win and the mutt is yours."

That was an offer I couldn't resist. So we played.

Clay won.

Blame

I FOLLOWED CLAY TO THE WOODS. NICK HAD TRIED TO COME WITH us, but at one look from Clay, he'd stayed in the bedroom. When we got to a clearing, Clay stopped, turned around, and looked at me, saying nothing.

"We can't," I shivered in the night air.

He didn't answer. How many times had we replayed this scene? Didn't I ever learn? I knew how this would end when I picked up the cards—I'd been thinking of nothing else throughout the game.

He kissed me. I could feel the heat from his body, so familiar I could drown in it. The rich scent of him wafted through my brain, as intoxicating as peyote smoke. I felt myself succumbing to the smell, but a part of my brain that could still think sounded the alarm. Been here. Done this. Remember how it turns out?

I moved back, more testing his reaction than seriously resisting. He pushed me against a tree, hands sliding to my hips and gripping hard. His lips went back to mine, kisses deepening. I started to struggle in earnest. He pinned me between his body and the tree. I kicked out at him and he pulled back, shaking his head. I scrambled to catch my breath and looked around. The clearing was empty. Clay was gone. As my fogged brain struggled to process this, my arms were yanked behind my head, toppling me to my knees.

"What the—"

"Hold still," Clay said from behind me. "I'm helping."

"Helping? Helping what?"

I tried to pull my arms down, but he held them tight. Something soft slipped around my wrists. A sapling swayed overhead. Then Clay let go. I jerked my arms but only moved a couple of inches before the cloth around my wrists snapped tight. Once I was secured, he walked around and knelt over me, obviously far too pleased with what he was seeing.

"This isn't funny," I said. "Untie me. Now."

Still grinning, he took hold of the top of my T-shirt and ripped it down the middle. Then he undid my bra. I started to say something, then stopped, inhaling sharply. He'd taken my breast in his mouth and was teasing the nipple with his teeth. He flicked his tongue and it sprung up, hard. A dart of lust fogged my brain. I gasped. He chuckled and the vibration sent a shivering tickle through me.

"Is that better?" he whispered. "Since you can't fight me, you can't be expected to stop me. It's out of your control."

His hand moved from my breast and stroked my stomach, moving lower with frustrating slowness. I had an unbidden image of his naked body over me. The lust flared. He shifted around. I could feel his erection slide up my thigh. I spread my legs a bit and felt the roughness of his jeans brush against me. Then he pulled back.

"Can you still feel tonight?" he whispered, bending to my ear. "The hunt. The chase. Running through the city."

I shivered.

"Where do you feel it?" Clay asked, his voice deepening, eyes burning phosphorescent blue.

His hands slid to my jeans, unbuttoning them and sliding them over my hips. He touched the inside of my thigh, holding his fingers there just long enough to make my heart skip.

"Do you feel it here?"

He slid his hand down to the inside of my knees, tracing the path of the chills coursing through me. I closed my eyes and let the images of the night flow through my brain, the locked doors, the silent streets, the scent of fear. I remembered Clay's hand running through my fur, the spark of hunger in his eyes as he entered the apartment, the joy of racing through the city. I remembered the danger in the alley, watching the two boys, waiting, hearing Clay's roar as he lunged at them. The excitement was still there, pulsing through every part of my body.

"Can you feel it?" he asked, face coming to mine.

I started to close my eyes.

"Don't," he whispered. "Watch me."

His fingers traced up my thigh, slowly. He toyed with the edge of my panties for a moment, then plunged his fingers into me. I let out a gasp. His fingers moved inside of me, finding the center of my excitement. I bit my lip to keep from crying out. Just as I could feel the waves of climax building, my brain kicked in and I realized what I was doing. I struggled to pull back from his hand, but he kept it tight against me, fingers moving in me. The climax started to crest again, but I fought it, not wanting to give him that. I closed my eyes tight against him and jerked my arms hard against their bindings. The tree groaned, but the bindings held. Suddenly, his hand stopped and moved away. The metallic whir of a zipper cut through the night air.

My eyes flew open to see him pulling his jeans down over his hips. As I saw the hunger in his eyes and his body, my hips moved up unbidden to meet him. I shook my head sharply, trying to clear it. I twisted away. Clay bent down, his face coming to mine.

"I won't force you, Elena. You like to pretend I would, but you know I won't. All you have to do is tell me no. Tell me to stop. Tell me to untie you. I will."

His hand slipped between my thighs, parting them before I could clench them shut. Heat and wetness rushed out to meet him, my body betraying me. I felt the tip of him brush against me, but he didn't go any further.

"Tell me to stop," he whispered. "Just tell me."

I glared at him, but the words wouldn't come to my lips. We lay there a moment, eyes locked. Then he grabbed me under the arms and pushed into me. My body convulsed. For one long second, he didn't move. I could feel him inside me, his hips pressed against mine. He pulled back slowly and my body protested, moving involuntarily against him, trying to keep him. I felt his arms go over my head. My bindings jerked once, then broke in his hands. He thrust into me and my resistance snapped. I grabbed him, hands entwining in his hair, legs wrapping around him. He released my arms and kissed me, deep kisses that devoured me as he moved inside me. So long. It had been so long and I'd missed him so much.

When it was over we collapsed on the grass, panting as if we'd run a marathon. We lay there still entwined around each other. Clay buried his face in my hair, told me that he loved me, and nodded off. I lay in a drowsy haze. Finally I turned my head and looked down at him. My demon lover. Eleven years ago, I'd given him everything. But it hadn't been enough.

"You bit me," I whispered.

Clay bit me in the study at Stonehaven. I'd been alone with Jeremy, who'd been trying to figure out a way to get rid of me, though I didn't know that at the time. He seemed to be asking simple, benign questions, the sort a concerned father might ask of the young woman his son planned to marry. Clay and I were engaged. He'd already introduced me to his best friends, Nicholas and Logan. Now he'd brought me to Stonehaven to introduce me to Jeremy.

While Jeremy was interrogating me, I thought I heard Clay's footsteps, but they'd stopped. Either I'd imagined it or he'd gone someplace else. Jeremy was standing by the window, quarter profile toward me. He looked out over the backyard.

"By the time you marry, Clayton's term at the university will have ended," Jeremy said. "What if he finds work elsewhere? Are you prepared to abandon your studies?"

Before I could formulate a reply, the door opened. I wish I could say it creaked open or something equally ominous. But it didn't. It simply opened. Seeing it move, I turned. A dog slipped in, head low as if expecting a reprimand for being in the wrong part of the house. It was huge, nearly as tall as a Great Dane, but as solid as a well-muscled shepherd. The gold of its fur sparkled. As it came in the room, it turned to look at me with eyes of the brightest blue. The dog looked up at me, mouth falling open. I smiled back. Despite its size, I knew I had nothing to fear. I felt that clearly.

"Wow," I said. "He's gorgeous. Or is it a she?"

Jeremy turned. His eyes widened and he blanched. He stepped forward, then stopped and shouted for Clay.

"Did Clay let him out?" I said. "It's okay. I don't mind."

I dangled my fingers, enticing the dog over.

"Don't move," Jeremy said, his voice low. "Take your hand away."

"It's okay. I'm letting him smell me. You're supposed to do that with a strange dog before you pet them. I had some dogs growing up. Well, my foster families did, at least. See his posture? Ears forward, mouth open, tail wagging? That means he's calm and curious."

"Pull your hand back now."

I glanced over at Jeremy. He was tensed, as if ready to jump at the dog if it attacked me. He called for Clay again.

"Really, it's okay," I said, getting annoyed now. "If he's skittish, you're only going to scare him by yelling. Trust me. I was bitten by a dog once. Yappy little Chihuahua, but it hurt like hell. I've still got the scar. This guy's a big brute, but he's friendly enough. Big dogs usually are. It's the little buggers you have to watch."

The dog had crept closer. One eye was on Jeremy, wary, watching his body language as if expecting a beating. Anger surged through me. Was the dog abused? Jeremy didn't seem the type, but I'd barely met him. I turned from Jeremy and reached out farther.

"Hey, boy," I whispered. "You're a pretty one, aren't you?"

The dog stepped toward me, moving slowly and carefully, as if we were both afraid of startling each other. Its muzzle came toward my hand. As it lifted its nose to sniff my fingers, it suddenly jerked up, grabbing my hand and nipping. I yelped, more in surprise than in pain. The dog began to lick my hand. Jeremy sprang across the room. The dog ducked and bolted out the door. Jeremy started after him.

"Don't," I said, leaping to my feet. "He didn't mean it. He was just playing."

Jeremy strode over to me and grabbed my hand, inspecting the bite.

Two teeth had broken through the skin, leaving tiny puncture wounds that only trickled a few drops of blood.

"He barely broke the skin," I said. "A love bite. See?"

Several minutes passed while Jeremy examined my wound. Then there was a commotion at the door. I looked up, expecting to see the dog again. Instead, Clay swung through. I couldn't see his expression. Jeremy was between us, obstructing my view.

"The dog nipped me," I said. "No big deal."

Jeremy turned on Clay. "Get out," he said, his voice so low I barely heard it.

Clay stood frozen in the doorway.

"Get out!" Jeremy shouted.

"It's not *his* fault," I said. "Maybe he let the dog in, but—"

I stopped. My hand started to burn. The twin punctures had turned an angry red. I gave my hand a sharp shake and looked over at Jeremy.

"I should clean this," I said. "Do you have Bactine or something?"

As I stepped forward, my legs gave out. The last thing I saw was Jeremy and Clay both grabbing for me. Then everything went black.

After Clay bit me, I didn't regain consciousness for two days, though at the time I thought only hours had passed. I awoke in one of the guest rooms, the one that would later become my bedroom. Opening my eyes required major effort. The lids felt hot and swollen. My throat ached, my ears ached, my head ached. Hell, even my teeth hurt. I blinked a few times. The room dipped and swayed, then came into focus. Jeremy was sitting in a chair by the bed. I lifted my head. Pain exploded behind my eyes. My head fell back to the pillow and I groaned. I heard Jeremy stand, then saw him looking down at me.

"Where's Clay?" I asked. It sounded more like "whaaaclaaa," as if I were speaking through a mouthful of marshmallows. I swallowed, wincing at the pain. "Where's Clay?"

"You're sick," Jeremy said.

"Really? I couldn't tell." The retort cost me too much. I had to close my eyes and swallow again before continuing. "What happened?"

"He bit you."

The memory flashed back. I could feel my hand throbbing now. I struggled to lift it. The two puncture wounds had swollen to the size of robin's eggs. Heat radiated off them. There was no sign of pus or infection, but something was definitely wrong. A lick of fear raced through me. Was the dog rabid? What were the symptoms of rabies? What else could you contract from a dog bite? Distemper?

"Hospital," I croaked. "I should go to the hospital."

"Drink this."

A glass appeared. It looked like water. Jeremy slid his hand behind my neck and lifted my head so I could drink. I jerked away, striking the glass with my chin and toppling it onto the bed. Jeremy swore and pulled the soaked coverlet back.

"Where's Clay?"

"You have to drink," he said.

He lifted a fresh coverlet from the foot of the bed, shook it, and laid it over me. I squirmed from under it.

"Where's Clay?"

"He bit you."

"I know the damned dog bit me." I jerked back as Jeremy put his hand on my forehead. "Answer my question. Where's Clay?"

"He bit you. Clay bit you."

I stopped struggling and blinked. I thought I'd heard wrong.

"Clay bit me?" I said slowly.

Jeremy didn't correct me. He stood there, looking down at me, waiting.

"The dog bit me," I said.

"It wasn't a dog. It was Clay. He . . . he changed form."

"Changed form," I repeated.

I stared at Jeremy, then twisted from side to side, trying to get up. Jeremy grabbed my shoulders and held me down. Panic ignited in me. I fought with more strength than I thought I had, flailing and kicking. He pinned me to the bed with as much effort as he might use to restrain a two-year-old.

"Stop it, Elena." My name came off his tongue awkwardly, like a foreign word.

"Where's Clay?" I shouted, ignoring the pain searing down my throat. "Where's Clay?"

"He's gone. I made him leave after he . . . bit you."

Jeremy seized both my arms and held them fast, pinning me so securely I couldn't move. He inhaled and started again.

"He's a . . ." He faltered, then shook his head. "I don't need to tell you what he is, Elena. You saw him change forms. You saw him become a wolf."

"No!" I kicked up, my legs striking only air. "You're crazy. Fucking crazy. I saw a dog. Let me go! Clay!"

"He bit you, Elena. That means . . . it means you're the same thing. You're becoming the same thing. That's why you're sick. You need to let me help you."

I closed my eyes and screamed, drowning his words. Where was Clay? Why had he left me with this madman? Why had he abandoned me? He loved me. I knew he loved me.

"I know you don't believe it, Elena. But watch me. Just watch."

I wrenched my head sideways, so I wasn't looking at him. I could see only his arm holding mine to the bed. After a moment, his forearm seemed to shimmer and contract. I shook my head sharply, feeling the pain inside it bounce around like a red-hot coal. My vision blurred, then cleared. Jeremy's arm convulsed, the wrist narrowing, the hand twisting and contorting into a knot. I wanted to close my eyes, but I couldn't. I was transfixed by the sight before me. The black hairs on his arm thickened. More hairs sprouted, shooting out from his skin and growing longer and longer. The pressure of his fingers relaxed. I looked down. There were no fingers there. A black paw rested on my arm. I shut my eyes then and screamed until the world went dark.

It took over a year for me to truly comprehend what I'd become, that it wasn't a nightmare or a delusion, and that it would never end, that there was no cure. Jeremy allowed Clay back eighteen months later, but it would never be the same between us again. It couldn't be. There are some things you cannot forgive.

I awoke several hours later, feeling Clay's arms around me, my back pressed against him. A slow wave of peace started lulling me back to sleep. Then I jerked awake. Clay's arms around me. My back pressed against him. Lying together in the grass. Naked. Oh, shit.

I extricated myself from his grasp without waking him, then slipped from the clearing and hurried to the house. Jeremy was on the back porch, reading *The New York Times* in the first blush of sunrise. When I saw him I stopped, but it was too late. He'd seen me. Yes, I was naked, but that wasn't why I would have rather avoided Jeremy. Years of Pack life had stripped me of my modesty—no pun intended. Whenever we ran, we finished naked and often far from our clothing. Disconcerting at first, waking from a post-run sleep to find yourself lying in a grotto with three or four naked guys. Disconcerting, though not an altogether unpleasant experience, given that these guys were all werewolves, hence in excellent physical condition and didn't look too shabby au natural. But I digress. The point is that Jeremy had been seeing my naked body for years. When I stepped from the trees sans clothing, he didn't even notice the lack.

He folded the paper, got up from his lounge chair, and waited. Lifting my chin, I made the journey to the porch. He would smell Clay on me. There was no way I could escape that.

"I'm tired," I said, trying to brush past him. "It's been a long night. I'm going back to bed."

"I'd like to hear what you found last night."

His voice was soft. A request, not a command. It would've been easier to ignore a direct order. As I stood there, the thought of going to bed, being alone with my thoughts, was suddenly too much. Jeremy was offering a distraction. I decided to take it. Sinking onto a chair, I told him the whole story. Okay, it wasn't the whole story, but I told him about finding the mutt's apartment, leaving out the aftermath with the boys in the alley and definitely excluding anything that happened after we got back. Jeremy listened and said little. As I finished, I caught a flicker of movement in the backyard. Clay strode from out of the forest, shoulders rigid, mouth set in a hard line.

"Go inside," Jeremy said. "Get some sleep. I'll look after him."

I escaped into the house.

Up in my room, I took my cell phone from my bag and called Toronto. I didn't call Philip, but it wasn't because I felt guilty. I didn't call him because I knew I should feel guilty and, since I couldn't, it didn't seem right to call. Does that make sense? Probably not.

If I'd had sex with anyone other than Clay, I would have felt guilty. On the other hand, the chances of me cheating on Philip with anyone other than Clay were so infinitesimal that the point was moot. I was loyal by nature, whether I wanted to be or not. Yet what I had with Clay was so old, so complex, that sleeping with him couldn't be compared to normal sex. It was giving in to something I felt so deeply that all the anger and hurt and hate in the world couldn't stop me from going back to him. Being a werewolf, being at Stonehaven, and being with Clay were so tightly interwoven that I couldn't separate the strands. Surrender to one meant surrender to all. Giving myself to Clay wasn't betraying Philip, it was betraying myself. That terrified me. Even as I sat on my bed, clutching the phone in one hand, I felt myself slipping. The barrier between my worlds was solidifying and I was trapped on the wrong side.

I sat there, staring at the phone, trying to decide who to call, what contact in my human life had the power to pull me back. For a second, I thought of calling Anne or Diane. I rejected the idea immediately then wondered why I'd thought of it at all. If talking to Philip wouldn't help me, why would I ever consider calling his mother or sister? I chased the thought a moment, but something in it scared me off. After a brief pause, my fingers hit buttons of their own accord. As the phone rang, I numbly wondered who I'd called. Then the voice mail clicked on. "Hi, you've reached Elena Michaels at *Focus Toronto*. I'm not in the office right now, but if you'll leave your name and number at the sound of the tone, I'll return your call as soon as possible." I hung up, pulled back the covers, crawled into bed, then reached for the phone and hit REDIAL.

By the fifth call, I was asleep.

It was nearly noon by the time I awoke. As I dressed, footsteps in the hallway stopped me cold.

"Elena?"

Clay rattled the door handle. It was locked. The only lock in the house Clay didn't dare break.

"I heard you get up," he said. "Let me in. I want to talk to you."

I finished tugging on my jeans.

"Elena? Come on." The door rattled harder. "Let me in. We need to talk."

Pulling my hair back, I clipped it at the nape of my neck. Then I walked across the room, opened the window, and swung out, hitting the ground below with a thud. Pricks of shock raced up my calves, but I wasn't hurt. A two-story jump wasn't dangerous for a werewolf.

Above me, Clay pounded at my door. I headed around the house and went in the front. Jeremy and Antonio were walking down the hall when I stepped in. Jeremy stopped and raised one eyebrow.

"The stairs aren't challenging enough anymore?" he asked.

Antonio laughed. "Challenge has nothing to do with it, Jer. I'd say it's the big bad wolf huffing and puffing at her door up there." He leaned around the corner and shouted up the stairs. "You can stop shaking the house apart now, Clayton. You've been outmaneuvered. She's down here."

Jeremy shook his head and steered me toward the kitchen. By the time Clay came down, I was halfway through breakfast. Jeremy directed him to a seat at the opposite end of the table. He grumbled, but obeyed. Nick and Peter arrived shortly after and, in the ensuing chaos of breakfast, I relaxed and was able to ignore Clay. When we were done eating, I told the others what we'd found the night before. As I talked, Jeremy scanned the newspapers. I was wrapping up when Jeremy put down the paper and looked at me.

"Is that everything?" he asked.

Something in his voice dared me to say it was. I hesitated, then nodded.

"Are you quite certain?" he asked.

"Uh—yes. I think so."

He folded the paper with maximum bustle and delay, then laid it in front of me. Front page of the *Bear Valley Post.* Top headline. WILD DOGS SPOTTED IN CITY.

"Oh," I said. "Whoops."

Jeremy made a noise in his throat that could have been interpreted as a growl. I read the article. The two boys we'd seen in the alley had woken their parents with the story, who'd in turn woken the newspaper editor. The boys claimed to have seen the killers. Two, maybe three, huge shepherdlike dogs lurking within the very heart of town.

"Three," Jeremy said, his voice low. "All three of you. Together."

Peter and Antonio slipped from the table. Clay looked at Nick and jerked his chin, telling Nick he was free to leave, too. No one would blame Nick for this. Jeremy knew the instigators from the followers. Nick shook his head and stayed put. He'd take his share.

"We were returning from the mutt's apartment," I said. "The kids walked into the alley. They saw me."

"Elena didn't have enough room to hide," Clay interjected. "One of them grabbed a broken bottle. I lost it. I leapt at them. Elena stopped me and we took off. No one got hurt."

"We all got hurt," Jeremy said. "I told you to split up."

"We did," I said. "Like I said, this was after we found the apartment."

"I told you to Change to human after you found him."

"And do what? Walk to the car butt-naked?"

Jeremy's mouth twitched. A full minute of silence followed. Then Jeremy got to his feet, motioned for me to follow, and walked from the room. Clay and Nick looked at me, but I shook my head. This was a private invitation, as much as I'd love to share it. I followed Jeremy out of the house.

———

Jeremy led me into the woods, taking the walking paths. We'd gone nearly a half-mile before he said anything. Even then, he didn't turn around, just kept walking in front of me.

"You know we're in danger," he said.

"We all know—"

"I'm not sure you do. Maybe you've been away from the Pack too long, Elena. Or maybe you think because you've moved to Toronto this doesn't affect you."

"Are you suggesting I'd purposely sabotage—"

"Of course not. I'm saying that maybe you need to be reminded how important this is to all of us, no matter where we live. People in Bear Valley are looking for a killer, Elena. That killer is a werewolf. We are werewolves. If he's caught, how long do you think it'll be before the town comes knocking at our door? If they find this mutt alive and figure out what he is, he'll talk. He's not in Bear Valley by accident, Elena. Any mutt with a father knows we live around here. If this one is discovered, he'll lead the authorities here, to Clayton and me and, through us, to the rest of the Pack, and eventually, to every werewolf, including any who are trying to deny any connection with the Pack."

"Do you think I don't realize that?"

"I trusted you to set the tone last night, Elena."

Ouch. That hurt. More than I liked to admit, so I hid it in my usual way.

"Then that was your mistake," I snapped. "I didn't ask for your trust. Look what happened with Carter. You trusted me with that, didn't you? Once burned . . ."

"As far as I'm concerned, your only mistake with Carter was not contacting me before you acted. I know it has more meaning for you, but that's exactly why you're supposed to contact me, so I give the order. I take the responsibility for the decision. For the death. I know you—"

"I don't want to talk about it."

"Of course not."

We walked in silence. I felt the words jammed up in my throat, desperate for release, for the chance to talk about what I'd done and what I'd felt. As I walked, a smell hit me and, with it, the words dissolved.

"Do you smell that?" I asked.

Jeremy sighed. "Elena. I wish you would—"

"There. Sorry. I didn't mean to interrupt, but"—my nose twitched, picking up the smell in the breeze—"that scent. Do you smell it?"

Jeremy's nostrils flared. He sniffed the breeze impatiently as if he didn't expect to find anything. Then he blinked. That smallest, most benign reaction was enough. He'd smelled it, too. Blood. Human blood.

Trespass

I TRACKED THE SCENT OF BLOOD TO THE EAST FENCE LINE. AS WE got closer, something else overpowered the smell of blood. Something worse. Decomposing flesh.

We came to a low wooden bridge that crossed a stream. Once on the other side, I stopped. The smell was gone. I sniffed the east wind again. There were traces of rot in the air, but the overwhelming stench had vanished. I turned and looked down at the stream. Something pale protruded from under the bridge. It was a bare foot, bloated, gray toes pointing at the sky. I jogged down the incline and waded into the stream. Jeremy leaned over the bridge, saw the foot, then pulled back and waited for me to investigate.

Grabbing the side of the bridge, I knelt in the icy water of the stream, drenching my jeans from ankle to knee. The bare foot was attached to a slender calf. The stench was overwhelming. As I switched to breathing through my mouth, my stomach lurched. Now I could taste the rot as well as smell it. I went back to breathing through my nose. The calf led to a knee, then fell away into shredded skin and muscle with bone shining through, leaving the femur looking like a big ham bone gnawed by a dog with more appetite for destruction than dinner. The other thigh was a maggot-infested stump, the bone snapped by powerful jaws. When I peered under the bridge, I saw the rest of the second leg, or pieces of it, strewn around, like someone shaking the last bits of garbage from the bag. Above the thighs, the torso was an indistinguishable mass of mangled flesh. If the arms were still attached, I didn't see them. Likely they were some of the bits scattered farther back. The head was twisted backward, the neck almost bitten through. I didn't want to look at the face. It's easier if you don't see the face, if you can dismiss a rotting corpse as a prop from a B horror movie. Still, easier isn't always better. This wasn't a movie prop and she didn't deserve to be dismissed as one. I assumed it was a she because of the size and slenderness but, as I shifted the head, I realized my mistake. It was a young man, little more than a boy. His eyes were wide, crusted with dirt, as dull as scuffed marbles. Otherwise, his face was unmarred: smooth-skinned, well fed, and very, very young.

It was another werewolf kill. Even if I couldn't smell the mutt through the rot and the blood, I knew it by the rough tearing of the throat, the gaping chew marks on the torso. The mutt had brought the body here. To Stonehaven. He hadn't killed the boy here. There was no sign of blood, but the caked dirt indicated he'd been buried and dug up. Last night, while we were ransacking the mutt's apartment, he'd been taking the body to Stonehaven, where we would find it. The insult sent tremors of fury through me.

"We'll have to dispose of it," Jeremy said. "Leave it for now. We'll go back to the house—"

A crash in the bushes stopped him short. I yanked my head from under the bridge. Someone was trampling through the undergrowth like a bull rhino. Humans. I quickly bent, rinsed my hands in the stream and scrambled up the bank. I was barely at the top when two men in bright orange hunting vests burst from the forest.

"This is private property," Jeremy said, his quiet voice cutting through the silence of the clearing.

The two men jumped and spun around. Jeremy stayed on the bridge and reached one hand behind his back, pulling me to him.

"I said, this is private property," he repeated.

One man, a stout kid in his late teens, stepped forward. "Yeah, then what are you doing here, buddy?"

The older man grabbed the kid's elbow and pulled him back. "Excuse my son's manners, sir. I'm assuming you're . . ." He trailed off, searching for a name and coming up blank.

"I own the property, yes," Jeremy said, voice still soft.

A man and a woman came up behind the two, nearly bowling them over. They stopped short and looked at us as if seeing apparitions. The older man whispered something to them, then turned back to Jeremy and cleared his throat.

"Yes, sir. I understand you own this land, but you see, we've got ourselves a bit of a situation. I'm sure you heard about that girl that got killed a few days ago. Well, it's dogs, sir. Wild dogs. Big ones. Two of our boys from town saw them last night. Then we got a call this morning, saying something had been spotted on the far side of the woods out here around midnight."

"So you're conducting a search."

The man straightened. "Right, sir. So, if you don't mind—"

"I do mind."

The man blinked. "Yes, but you see, we've got to check things out and—"

"Did you stop at the house to ask permission?"

"No, but—"

"Did you phone the house to ask permission?"

"No, but—"

The man's voice had gone up an octave and the boy behind him was fidgeting and mumbling. Jeremy continued in the same unruffled tone.

"Then I'd suggest you go back the way you came and wait for me at the house. If you want to search these woods, you need permission. Under the circumstances, I certainly don't mind granting that permission, but I don't want to worry about running into armed men when I'm taking a walk on my own property."

"We're looking for wild dogs," the woman said. "Not people."

"In the excitement of the hunt, any mistake is possible. Since this is my land, I choose not to take that chance. I use these woods. My family and my guests use these woods. That's why I don't allow hunters up here. Now, if you'll go around to the house, I'll finish my walk and meet you there. I can provide you with maps of the property and warn my guests to stay out of the forest while you're here. Does that sound reasonable?"

The couple had joined the boy in his grumbling, but the older man seemed to be considering it, weighing inconvenience with propriety. Just as he appeared ready to relent, a voice rang out from behind them.

"What the hell is going on here?!"

Clay barreled out from the forest. I winced and thought I saw Jeremy do the same, although it might have been a trick of the sunlight through the trees. Clay stopped at the edge of the clearing and looked from the search party to us and back again.

"What the hell are you doing here?" he said, stepping up to the group of searchers.

"They're looking for wild dogs," Jeremy said softly.

Clay's hands clenched at his sides. The heat of his fury scorched all the way across the clearing. The other day when we'd heard the hunters on the property, Clay had been furious. His territory had been invaded. Yet he'd been able to control it because he hadn't seen the trespassers, had been forbidden to get close enough to them to see them and smell them and react as his instincts demanded. Even if he'd come upon them, he would have had enough advance warning to get his temper under control. This was different. He'd come looking for us and hadn't smelled them until it was too late to prepare. The trespassers were no longer unseen guns firing in the dark, but actual humans, standing right in front of him, live targets for his rage.

"Did you miss the fucking signs on the way in?" he snarled, turning on the younger man, the strongest of the group. "Or is trespassing too goddamned many syllables for you?"

"Clayton," Jeremy warned.

Clay didn't hear him. I knew that. All he could hear was the blood pounding in his ears, the need to defend his territory screaming through his brain. He stepped closer to the young man. The boy inched back against a tree.

"This is private property," Clay said. "Do you understand what that means?"

Jeremy started down from the bridge with me at his heels. We were halfway across the clearing when a sound trumpeted from the woods. A baying hound. A dog on a scent. I looked from Jeremy to Clay. They'd both stopped and were listening, trying to pinpoint the direction of the noise. I stepped back toward the bridge. With every second, the hound's song drew closer, the tempo rising, infused with the joy of triumph. It smelled the body under the bridge.

I took another step backward. Before I could think, the dog flew from the forest. It was heading straight for me, eyes unseeing, brain bound up with the smell. It got within a yard of me, then skidded to a halt. Now it smelled something else. Me.

The dog looked at me. It was a big crossbreed, something between a shepherd and a redbone hound. It dipped its muzzle and blinked in confusion. Then it lifted its head and pulled back its lips in a deep growl. It didn't know what I was, but it sure as hell didn't like me. One of the men shouted. The dog ignored it. It growled another warning. The older man ran at the dog. Seeing my window of opportunity evaporating, I met the dog's eyes and bared my teeth. Come and get me. It did.

The dog leapt. Its teeth clamped around my forearm. I fell to the ground, lifting my arms over my face as if protecting myself. The dog held on tight. As its teeth sunk into my arm, I let out a wail of pain and fear. I kicked feebly at the beast, my blows barely connecting with its stomach. Over my head, I heard an uproar. Someone tore the dog away, jerking my arm with it. Then the dog went limp. Its teeth fell from my arm. I looked up to see Clay standing over me, hands still wrapped around the dead dog's throat. He threw the corpse aside and dropped to his knees. I buried my head in my arms and started to sob.

"There, there," he said, pulling me close and stroking my hair. "It's all over."

He was trying hard not to laugh, his body shaking with the effort. I resisted the urge to pinch him and continued wailing. Jeremy demanded to know who owned the dog and whether its shots were up to date. The searchers' voices drowned out one another as they babbled apologies. Someone tore off to find the dog's owner. Clay and I stayed on the ground as I sobbed and he comforted me. He was enjoying this far too much, but I didn't dare stand for fear the searchers would notice that my eyes were dry and I looked remarkably composed for a woman savaged by a vicious beast.

After a few minutes, the dog's owner arrived and was none too pleased to find his prized hound lying dead in the grass. He shut up when he found out what had happened and started promising to pay for medical bills, probably fearing a lawsuit. Jeremy gave him a dressing-down over letting his dog run unleashed on private property. When Jeremy finished, the man assured him that the dog had all its shots, then quietly hauled away the carcass with the help of the younger man. This time, when Jeremy asked them all to leave the property, no one argued. When the chaos finally fell to silence, I shoved Clay off me and got to my feet.

"How's the arm?" Jeremy asked, walking toward me.

I examined the injury. There were four deep puncture wounds, still seeping blood, but the tearing was minimal. I clenched and unclenched my fist. It hurt like hell, but everything appeared to be in working order. I wasn't too concerned. Werewolves heal quickly, which is probably the reason we inflict injury on one another with such abandon.

"The first war wound," I said.

"Hopefully the last," Jeremy said dryly, taking my arm to examine the damage. "It could have been worse, I suppose."

"She did a great job," Clay said.

I glared at him. "I wouldn't have had to if you hadn't charged in ranting and raving like a lunatic. Jeremy had almost got rid of them when you showed up."

Jeremy shifted to the left, blocking my view of Clay, as if we were Siamese fighting fish that wouldn't attack if we couldn't see each other. "Come with me to the house and we'll get your arm cleaned up. Clay, there's a body under the bridge. Put it in the shed and we'll dispose of it in town tonight."

"A body?"

"A boy. Probably a runaway."

"You mean that mutt brought a body—"

"Just get it out of here before they decide to come back."

Jeremy took my good arm and led me away before Clay could argue.

On the way back to the house, we talked. Or, I should say, Jeremy talked, I listened. The danger seemed to be escalating with each passing hour. First we'd been spotted in the city. Next we'd found a body on the property. Then we'd had a confrontation with the locals, calling attention to ourselves and probably raising suspicion. All in twelve hours. The mutt had to die. Tonight.

When Clay came back to the house, he wanted to talk to Jeremy and me. I found an excuse and hightailed it up to my room. I knew what he wanted to say, to apologize for screwing up, for confronting the searchers and causing trouble. Let Jeremy absolve him. That was his job, not mine.

After Jeremy and Clay had finished their talk, Jeremy took the others into the study to explain what had happened. Since I didn't need the instant replay, I stayed in my room and called Philip. He talked about an ad campaign he was trying to snag, something about lakefront condos. I admit I wasn't paying much attention to his words. Instead, I listened to his voice, closing my eyes and imagining I was there beside him, in a place where dead bodies in the backyard would have been cause for indescribable horror, not quick cleanup plans. I tried to think as Philip would, to feel compassion and grief for that dead boy, a life as full as my own cut short.

As Philip talked, my thoughts wandered to my night with Clay. I didn't have to work very hard to guess how Philip would feel about that. What the hell had I been thinking? I hadn't been thinking—that was the trouble. If I hadn't felt guilt a few hours ago, I felt it now, listening to Philip and picturing how he would react if he knew where I'd spent the night. I was a fool. Here I had a wonderful man who cared for me and I was screwing around with a self-absorbed, conniving monster who'd betrayed me in the worst possible way. It was a mistake I swore not to repeat.

After a late lunch, Jeremy took Clay for a walk to give him instructions for that night. I'd already received mine. Clay and I were going after the mutt together—I didn't have a choice in the matter, but I'd still argued. I would find the mutt and lure him out to a safe place where Clay would finish him off. It was an old routine and, as much as I hated to admit it, one that worked.

While the others were cleaning up the dishes, I slipped away. I wandered through the house and ended up in Jeremy's studio. The midafternoon sun danced through the leaves of the chestnut tree outside, casting pirouetting shadows on the floor.

I thumbed through a stack of canvases leaning against the wall, scenes of wolves playing and singing and sleeping together, curled up in heaps of intertwining limbs and varicolored fur. Juxtaposed with these were pictures of wolves in city alleys, watching passersby, wolves allowing children to touch them while mothers looked the other way. When Jeremy did agree to sell one of his paintings, it was the second style that earned him the big bucks. The scenes were enigmatic and surreal, painted in reds, greens, and purples so dark they looked like shades of black. Bold splashes of yellows and oranges electrified the darkness in incongruous places, like the reflection of the moon in a puddle. A dangerous subject, but Jeremy was careful, selling them under an assumed name and never making public appearances. No one outside the Pack ever came to Stonehaven, except chaperoned service people, so his paintings were safe displayed here in his studio.

Jeremy painted human models too, though only members of the Pack. One of his favorites was on the wall by the window. In it, I was standing on the edge of a cliff, naked, with my back to the viewer. Clay was sitting on the ground beside me, his arm wrapped around my leg. Below the cliff, a pack of wolves played in a forest clearing. The title was scrawled in the bottom corner: *Eden.*

On the opposite was hung two portraits. The first showed Clay in his late teens. He was sitting out back in a white wicker chair, with a wistful half smile on his face as his gaze focused on something above the painter. He looked like Michelangelo's *David* come to life, youthful perfection all innocence and dreaminess. On a good day, I saw the portrait as Jeremy's wishful thinking. On a bad day, it smacked of outright delusion.

The portrait that hung next to it was equally unsettling. It was me. I was sitting with my back to the painter, twisting to give a view of my full face and upper body. My hair was loose, falling in tangled curls and hiding my breasts. Like Clay's picture, though, the expression was the focal point. My dark blue eyes looked clearer and sharper than normal, giving them an animal-like glint. I was smiling with my lips parted and teeth showing. The impact was one of feral sensuality, with a dangerous edge that I didn't see when I looked in the mirror.

"Ah-ha," Nick called from the doorway. "So this is where you're hiding. Phone call for you. It's Logan."

I was out the door so fast I nearly knocked over a pile of paintings. Nick followed and pointed me to the phone in the study. As I was heading down the hall, Clay walked through the back door. He didn't see me. I slipped into the study and shut the door as I heard Clay asking Nick where I was. Nick made some noncommittal answer, not daring to risk Clay's anger by admitting the truth. Clay was still pissed off over me contacting Logan during my absence. He didn't suspect I was screwing around with Logan or anything so banal. He knew the truth—that Logan and I were friends, very good friends, but that was enough to ignite his jealousy, not of my body, but of my time and my attention.

I picked up the phone and said hello.

"Ellie!" Logan's voice boomed through a blanket of static. "I can't believe you're actually there. How's it going? Still alive?"

"So far, but it's only been two days. The line buzzed, went silent for a second, then hissed back to life. "Either L.A. has worse phone service than Tibet or you're on a cell phone. Where are you?"

"Driving to the courthouse. Listen, things here are wrapping up fast. We got a settlement. That's why I called."

"You're coming back?"

His laugh sizzled across the line. "Eager to see me? I'd be flattered if I didn't suspect you just want a buffer against Clayton. Yes, I'm coming back. I'm not sure exactly when, but it should be tonight or tomorrow morning. We've got to finish up work here and I'll catch the next plane out."

"Great. I can't wait to see you."

"Likewise, though I'm still miffed you wouldn't let me come to Toronto at Christmas. I was looking forward to burnt gingerbread. Another great holiday tradition lost."

"Maybe this year."

"Definitely this year." The phone crackled and went silent, then clicked back. "—lo?"

"I'm still here."

"I'd better sign off before I lose you. Don't wait up for me. I'll see you tomorrow and I'll whisk you away to lunch so you can relax for a while, catch your breath. Okay?"

"Definitely okay. I'll see you then."

He said good-bye and hung up. As I put the receiver back in the cradle, I could hear Nick in the hall, rounding up players for a game of touch football. He stopped outside the study door and tapped.

"I'm in," I said. "I'll meet you out there."

I looked back at the phone. Logan was coming. That was enough to make me forget all the problems and annoyances of the day. I smiled to myself and hurried out the door, suddenly eager for a good roughhousing before the excitement of the mutt hunt.

Predator

AFTER DINNER, I PREPARED FOR THE EVENING. THE CHOICE OF clothing posed a problem. If I was going to hook this mutt, I needed to pull on the mask that worked best with werewolves: Elena the sexual predator. This didn't mean miniskirts, fishnets, and see-through blouses, namely because I didn't own any. And I didn't own any because they looked ridiculous on me. Skimpy tops, stiletto heels, and barely there bottoms made me look like a coltish fourteen-year-old playing dress up. Nature didn't bless me with curves and my lifestyle didn't let me develop extra padding. I was too tall, too thin, and too athletic to be any guy's idea of centerfold fodder.

When I'd started living at Stonehaven, my wardrobe was strictly thrift-shop casual, no matter how much money Jeremy gave me for shopping. I didn't know what else to buy. When Antonio had bought us seats to a Broadway opening, I'd panicked. There were no women around to ask for help in choosing a dress and I didn't dare ask Jeremy for fear I'd end up in some taffeta and lace monstrosity fit only for a high school prom. I'd gone to a row of upscale shops in New York, but I got lost, literally and figuratively. My savior had appeared in a most unlikely form: Nicholas. Nick spent more time around women, particularly beautiful, rich young women, than any man outside of a James Bond film. His taste was impeccable, favoring classic designs, simple fabrics, and smooth lines that somehow turned my height and lack of curves into assets. All of my dress-up clothes had been bought with

Nick in tow. Not only didn't he mind spending an entire day touring Fifth Avenue, but he'd have his credit card on the counter before I could fish mine from my wallet. Little wonder he was so popular with the ladies.

I picked out a dress for that night, one that Nick had actually bought me for my birthday two years ago. It was gorgeous indigo silk, knee length with no fancy trim or other adornment. Simple, yet elegant. To keep it casual, I decided to forgo nylons and wear sandals.

As I was putting on my makeup, Clay walked in and gave my outfit the once-over. "Looks good," he said. Then he glanced around at my princess bedroom and grinned. "'Course, it doesn't really suit the setting. It needs a little something. Maybe a lace shawl from the curtains. Or a sprig of cherry blossoms."

I snarled at him through the mirror and went back to my makeup, studying a jar of pink stuff and trying to remember whether it was for my lips or my cheeks. Behind me, Clay bounced on the bed, fluffing the overstuffed pillows and laughing. He'd changed into baggy Dockers, a white T-shirt, and a loose linen jacket. The outfit hid his build and gave him a collegiate, clean-cut look, the message here being as nonthreatening as possible. Nick must have helped him pick his clothes. Clay didn't know the meaning of nonthreatening.

At nine we left, taking Jeremy's Explorer. Clay loathed the bulky SUV, but we needed the cargo space if we managed to capture and kill this mutt. Later that night, Antonio and Nicholas would dispose of the young boy's body at the local dump. We could have saved them a trip and taken it ourselves, but eau de decomposing flesh wasn't a good perfume choice when mingling with humans.

Although I hated the idea of spending the evening with Clay after what had happened between us, I soon relaxed. He didn't mention the previous night or say anything about Logan's call. By the time we got to town, we were carrying on a perfectly normal conversation about South American jaguar cults. If I didn't know him better, I'd almost think he was making a conscious effort to play nice. But I knew him better. Whatever his motivation, I went along with it. We had a job to do and we had to be together all evening to do it. Duty came first.

Our first stop was the mutt's apartment. I parked at the McDonald's behind the house, then we circled the block. The apartment was dark. The mutt was out. We could only hope he was at one of the bars.

All three bars were a bust. The fourth place on our list was the one without a name, only the address I'd memorized from the matchbook. The address led us behind the paper plant to an abandoned warehouse. Judging by the music booming from within, it wasn't "abandoned" tonight.

"What's up with this?" Clay asked.

"It's a rave. Not quite a bar, not quite a private party."

"Huh. Can you get in?"

"Probably."

"Go on then. I'll take up my post at a window."

I went around to the back of the building. The entrance was a basement door down a flight of steps. A sliver of light illuminated the edges. When I knocked, a bald man opened the door. A tilt of my head and a promise in my smile and I was in with a handful of free drink tickets. I'd hoped it would be more of a challenge.

The hallway led to a massive open room, roughly rectangular. A second-story catwalk had been converted into a narrow balcony with a makeshift set of stairs and no second-level railing. With no railing to stop them, people were sitting on the edge of the balcony, tossing beer caps onto the crowd below. Dusty warehouse boxes and old boards served as a bar along the left wall. Scattered in front of the bar were rusty tables and chairs, the sort of folding furniture you'd find in yard sales and pass over if your tetanus shots weren't up to date.

I'd been worried this would be like a Toronto rave, where the average patron spent more time worrying about midterms than mortgage payments. Definitely not a party where I could pass unnoticed. I looked young, but I was definitely past the zit cream and orthodontics stage of life. I needn't have worried. Bear Valley wasn't the big city. There were some underage kids here at this rave, but they were outnumbered by young and not-so-young adults, most sticking to Millers and marijuana but a few shooting heroin as openly as they downed their drinks. This was the side of Bear Valley the town councillors liked to ignore. If a local politician had wandered in here, he would have convinced himself they were all out-of-towners, probably from Syracuse.

The right side of the room was the dance floor, a.k.a. an unfurnished expanse of space where people were either dancing or suffering in the throes of a mass epileptic fit. The music was deafening, which I wouldn't have minded so much if the tunes didn't sound like something the bouncers had recorded in the back room. The smell of cheap booze and cheaper perfume pirouetted in my stomach. I stifled my nausea and began to search.

The mutt was there.

I picked up his scent on my second tour of the room. Weaving in and out of the crowd, I followed the smell until it led to a person. When I saw the person that the trail led to, I doubted my nose and circled back to double check. Yes, the guy at the table was definitely our mutt. And a less prepossessing werewolf, I had yet to meet. Even *I* looked scarier than this guy. He had acorn brown hair, a slender build, and a scrubbed, wholesome face—the quintessential college kid, right down to the Doc Martens and chinos. He looked familiar, but I hadn't committed all the photos in the Pack's dossiers to memory. It didn't matter who he was. It only mattered that he was here. A flash of rage burst inside me. This was the mutt causing all the trouble? This baby-faced brat had the Pack all in a panic, looking over our shoulders for guns and racing around Bear Valley to find him? I had to stop myself from marching over, grabbing him by the collar, and tossing him outside to Clay.

I resisted the urge even to go to him. Let him find me. He'd pick up my scent soon enough and he'd know who I was. All mutts knew who I was. Remember, I was the only one of my kind. From my scent, a mutt could tell that I was both werewolf and female. Not exactly a Sherlockian feat of deduction to figure out who I was. I passed twenty feet from this mutt's table and he didn't pick up my scent. Either the smells in the room were too overpowering or he was too dumb to use his nose. Probably the latter.

Knowing he'd smell me eventually, I turned in a drink ticket for a rum and Coke, found a table near the dance floor, and waited. As I scanned the crowd, I found the mutt again easily. With his short hair, polo shirt, and clean-shaven face, he stuck out like a Yanni fan at an Iron Maiden concert. He was sitting by himself, scanning the crowd with a hunger that stole the innocence from his eyes.

I took a few sips of my drink, then glanced back at the mutt's table. He was gone.

"Elena."

Not turning, I inhaled his scent. It was the mutt. I settled into my chair, took another sip of my drink and continued watching the dance floor. He moved around the table, looked at me, and smiled. Then he pulled out a chair.

"May I sit?" he asked.

"No."

He started to sit.

I looked up at him. "I said no, didn't I?"

He hesitated, grinning as he waited for some sign that I was kidding. I hooked the chair with my foot and yanked it into the table. He stopped grinning.

"I'm Scott," he said. "Scott Brandon."

The name tickled the back of my mind. I mentally tried to pull forward his page from the Pack's dossier, but couldn't. It had been too long. I should have done my homework before I left.

He stepped toward me. When I glared, he backed off. I sipped my drink again, then looked at him over the rim.

"Do you have any idea what happens to mutts who trespass on Pack territory?" I asked.

"Should I?"

I snorted and shook my head. Young and cocky. A bad combination, but more annoying than dangerous. Obviously this mutt's daddy hadn't told him bedtime stories about Clay. A serious educational oversight, but one that would soon be resolved. I almost smiled at the thought.

"So, what brings you to Bear Valley?" I said, feigning bored interest. "The paper mill hasn't been hiring in years, so I hope you're not looking for work."

"Work?" A nasty smile lit his eyes. "Nah, I'm not much for work. I'm looking for fun. Our kind of fun."

I stared at him for a long minute, then got to my feet and walked away. Brandon came after me. I made it to the far wall before Brandon grabbed my elbow. His fingers dug into the bone. I yanked away and whirled to face him. The smile was gone from his face, replaced by a hard edge mingled with the petulant ill-humor of a spoiled child. Good. Very good. Now all I had to do was break away and let him follow me outside. By then he'd be in enough of a temper that he wouldn't see Clay until it was too late.

"I was talking to you, Elena."

"So?"

He grabbed me by both arms and slammed me back against the wall. My arms flew up to throw him off, but I stopped myself. I couldn't afford a scene, and somehow the sight of a woman brawling with a man is always an attention-grabber, particularly if she can pitch him across the room.

As Brandon leaned toward me, an ugly smile contorted his features. He reached up and stroked one finger down my cheek.

"You are so beautiful, Elena. And do you know what you smell like to me?" He inhaled and closed his eyes. "A bitch in heat." He pressed into me, letting me feel his erection. "You and I could have a lot of fun together."

"I don't think you'd like my kind of fun."

His smile turned predatory. "I've heard you don't get a lot of fun in your life. You've got this Pack breathing down your neck, smothering you with all their stupid rules and laws. A woman like you deserves better. You need someone to teach you what it's like to kill, really kill, not bring down some mindless rabbit or deer, but a human. A thinking, breathing, conscious human."

He paused, then continued, "Have you ever seen someone's eyes when they know they are about to die, at that moment when they realize you *are* death." He inhaled, then exhaled slowly, the tip of his tongue showing through his teeth, eyes flooded with lust. "That's power, Elena. True power. I can show you that tonight."

Keeping hold of my arms, he moved aside to show me the crowd.

"Pick someone, Elena. Pick anyone. Tonight they die. Tonight they're yours. How does that make you feel?"

I said nothing.

Brandon continued, "Pick someone and imagine it. Close your eyes. See yourself leading them out, taking them into the woods, and ripping out their throat." A shudder ran through him. "Can you see their eyes? Can you smell their blood? Can you feel the blood, everywhere, soaking you, the power of life flowing out at your feet? It won't be enough. It never is. But I'll be there. I'll make it enough. I'll fuck you right there, in the pool of their blood. Can you imagine that?"

I smiled up at him and said nothing. Instead, I slid a finger down his chest and over his stomach. For a moment, I toyed with the button on his fly, then slowly slid my hand under his shirt and stroked his stomach, tracing circles around his belly button. As I concentrated, I could feel my hand thickening, the nails lengthening. This was something Clay had taught me, a trick few other werewolves could do, changing only part of the body. When my nails became claws, I scraped them over Brandon's stomach.

"Can you feel that?" I whispered in his ear, pressing myself against him. "If you don't step away right now, I'm going to rip out your guts and feed them to you. That's my kind of fun."

Brandon jerked back. I held him tight with my free hand. He slammed me against the wall. I dug my half-formed talons into his stomach, feeling them pop through skin. His eyes widened and he yelped, but the roaring music swallowed his cry. I looked around, making sure no one was paying attention to the young couple embracing in the corner. When I turned back to Brandon, I realized I'd let the game stretch one period too long. His face contorted, jaw stiffening as the veins in his neck bulged. His face shimmered and rippled like a reflection in a barely flowing stream. His brow thickened and his cheeks sloped upward to meet his nose. The classic fear reflex of an untrained werewolf: Change.

I grabbed Brandon by the arm and dragged him into the nearest corridor. As I searched for an exit, I could feel his arm changing beneath my grip, his shirtsleeve ripping, his forearm pulsing and contracting. I was almost at the end of the hallway when I realized there wasn't an exit, only two bathroom doors. The men's room door opened and a man belched loudly. Another man laughed. I glanced back at Brandon, hoping his Change hadn't progressed beyond the point where it could be fluffed off as a physical deformity. No such luck—unless the bar's patrons were drunk enough to overlook someone whose face looked as if giant maggots were squirming under his skin. A man stepped from the bathroom. I spun Brandon around and saw a storage room door a few feet away. Shoving him ahead of me, I sprinted to the door, then snapped the lock, opened the door, and thrust Brandon inside.

As I leaned against the door, my mind raced for a solution. Could I get him out? Oh, sure, just slap a collar and leash on a 150-pound wolf and lead him to the door. No one would notice. I cursed myself. How had I let this happen? I'd had him. At the moment where he'd offered to show me how to kill a human, I'd had him. All I had to do was say yes. Pick some guy leaving the bar and tail him into the street. Brandon would have followed me and Clay would have been waiting outside. Game over. But no, that hadn't been enough. I had to push it, to see how far I could go.

"Shit, shit, shit," I muttered.

From behind the closed door, there was a deafening roar of pain, one that even the music down the hall couldn't drown out. Two passing women turned and stared.

"My boyfriend," I said, trying to smile. "He's sick. A bad batch. New dealer."

One of the women looked at the closed door. "Maybe you should get him to a hospital," she said, but continued walking, advice dispensed, duty done.

"Clayton," I whispered. "Where are you?"

I wasn't surprised that Clay hadn't busted down any doors when Brandon cornered me. Clay never underestimated my ability to defend myself. He'd only come to my rescue when I was in real danger. I wasn't in danger now, but I needed his help. Unfortunately, wherever he was hiding, he couldn't possibly see me in this hallway.

A crash echoed from inside the storage room. Brandon was done with his Change and was trying to get out. I had to stop him. And to stop him, I almost certainly had to kill him. Could I do that without causing a scene? Another crash resounded from the room, followed by the sound of splintering wood. Then silence.

I yanked open the door. Tattered scraps of clothing covered the floor. On the south wall was a second door leading back into the warehouse. In the middle of the cheap plywood was a gaping hole.

Chaos

I RACED INTO THE MAIN ROOM. THERE WASN'T ANY SCREAMING. Not right away. The first sounds I heard were voices, more annoyed than alarmed. "What the—" "Did you—" "Watch it—" When I rounded the corner, I saw a path of toppled chairs and tables looping a tipsy half circle from the storage room to the dance floor. People milled around the overturned tables, collecting coats and purses and broken drink glasses. A boy well under legal drinking age sat cross-legged on the floor, cradling a broken arm. A woman stood on a chair, thrusting an empty glass toward the swath Brandon had cut across the dance floor and demanding that the "damn bastard" pay for her spilled drink, having somehow failed to notice that the "damn bastard" had fangs, fur, and no obvious place to carry a wallet.

I was still making my way toward the dance floor when Brandon roared. Then came the first scream. Then the thunder of a hundred people stampeding for the exit.

The stampede really didn't help matters, especially when my goal lay in the exact opposite direction of the human flow. At first, I was polite. Really. I said "excuse me," tried to squeeze through gaps, even apologized for stepping on some toes. What can I say, I'm Canadian. After a few elbows to the chest and more than a few obscenities shouted in my ear, I gave up and cut my own path. When one hefty bruiser tried to shove me back, I grabbed him by the collar and showed him the express route to the door. Things got a bit better after that.

Although I was no longer in danger of being trampled, I was still progressing by inches. I couldn't see anything. I'm not short—5′10″ to be precise—but even an NBA superstar couldn't have seen over that seething mass of humanity. If there was a back door or emergency exit, no one knew about it. They were all heading for the main entrance and getting jammed in the narrow front corridor.

Not only couldn't I see, I couldn't hear anything but the sound of the crowd, curses and shouts and cries melding into a Babel's tower of noise, nothing clear except the universal language of panic. People shoved and hammered at one another, as if being one step closer to the door meant the difference between life and death. Others weren't moving of their own volition at all, but were carried along by the tide of the mob. I looked into faces and saw nothing there. They were as white and expressionless as plaster masks. Only the eyes held the truth, rolling and wild, the instinct for survival taking over. Most didn't even know what they were running from. It didn't matter. They could smell the fear rising from the crowd as well as any werewolf could and the scent of it seeped into their brains, infecting them with its power. They smelled it, they felt it, and they ran from it. They were giving Brandon exactly what he craved.

I was midway across the dance floor when I stumbled over a woman lying in a pool of blood. Blood still jetted from her neck in a fountain, spraying anyone who came close. People tripped over her and slid in her blood. Not one of them even looked down. I shouldn't have looked down either. But I did. Her eyes rolled, meeting mine for a second. Bloody froth trickled and bubbled from her lips. Her hand convulsed off the floor as if trying to reach up. Then it stopped in midair, paused, and fluttered down into the pool of blood. Her eyes died. The blood had stopped spurting and was now streaming. A man tripped over her, looked down, swore, and kicked her out of his way. I tore my gaze away and kept moving.

As I stepped over the body, glass shattered overhead. I looked up to see Clay's feet shooting through a high window near the bar. He swung in and dropped to the floor. It was a good twenty-foot fall, not something Jeremy encouraged us to do in front of a crowd, but considering no one was paying any attention to a dead body beneath their feet, surely no one was going to notice a man vaulting through a window behind them. Clay climbed onto the bar and surveyed the crowd. When he saw me, he waved me over. I pointed deeper into the throng, where I assumed Brandon was. Clay shook his head and motioned again. I picked an angle roughly in line with the crowd flow and made my way toward him.

"Love that entrance," I shouted over the din as I climbed onto the bar.

"Have you seen the front door, darling? I'd need a blowtorch to cut through the crowd. The only other exit is bricked over."

I looked above the crowd. "So Brandon's not back in that corner?"

"Who?"

"The mutt. Is he there?"

"Oh, he's there all right. But you're wasting your energy trying to get to him."

I spotted Brandon. As I suspected, he'd fully changed into a wolf. He seemed to be bouncing between the corner walls, leaping and pouncing and slashing at nothing. I was about to say that it looked as if the mutt had snapped. Then the crowd parted enough for me to see that he was attacking more than air. A man lay in crash position on the floor, back up, knees to his chest, head down, hands linked to protect the back of his neck. His clothing was shredded and drenched with blood. He was motionless, obviously dead, but Brandon wasn't leaving him alone. He leapt at the man, grabbed his foot, and spun him in a circle. Then he danced back, tail high. He crouched and mock-lunged, then feinted to the side. The man now lay twisted half on his side, letting me see more of his injuries than I wanted. His shirt was ripped open. His torso was streaked with blood, his stomach solid red. The end of his belt dangled to the floor. Then I realized it wasn't his belt, but a loop of intestine. As I was turning away, the body moved. The man rocked, as if trying to flip back on his stomach to protect himself.

"Oh god." I whispered. "He's not dead."

Brandon leapt at his prey again and sank his teeth into the man's scalp. He yanked him up, tossed him aside, and pranced away again.

"He's not even trying to kill him," I said.

"Why would he?" Clay said, curling back his lip. "He's having fun."

Disgust dripped from every word. This wasn't killing for food or killing for survival. That Clay could understand. This was, to him, a display of another incomprehensible human trait—killing for pleasure.

"While he's busy, I'll do some scouting," Clay continued. "Give me five minutes. When the crowd clears, make your move. Drive him toward that side hall. I'll be waiting."

Clay jumped off the bar and vanished into the mob. I looked back at Brandon torturing his prey. Again, I didn't want to look, didn't want to think about what was going on below me, that a man was dying horribly but was still alive and I wasn't doing a damned thing about it. I reminded myself that it was almost certainly too late to save him and, even if he did survive, he'd have to go to the hospital, which we couldn't allow because, having been bitten by Brandon, the man was now a werewolf himself. Although rationally I knew I couldn't risk going to him, I felt compelled to, if only to end his suffering. Sometimes I think it would be better if I could be like Clay, to acknowledge that what Brandon was doing was wrong but equally acknowledge that it wasn't in my power to right that wrong and to walk away without regret. But I don't ever want to be like that, that hard, that tough. Clay had an excuse. I didn't.

I tore my gaze away from Brandon and his prey. Sick bastard. No animal would do something like that. As I thought this, something clicked in my brain, a piece falling into place so hard the resonance made me jump. The room went suddenly silent, the drumming in my ears drowning out the crowd, giving me one moment of perfect clarity amidst the chaos.

I knew where I'd seen Brandon's face, heard his name, and it wasn't in the Pack's werewolf dossiers. Television. *Inside Scoop.* The piece on the killer in North Carolina. The tape of the police interview flipped through my head again, the grainy image sparking to life. "I wanted to watch someone die." Scott Brandon. I shook my head sharply. No, that couldn't be. That didn't make sense. A werewolf couldn't survive in prison without being discovered. Then I remembered Brandon's scent again, a nuance I'd picked up that night in his apartment. "He's new," I'd told Clay. I could smell it in his scent and I'd assumed it meant he was a hereditary werewolf recently come of age. But he wasn't. He'd been bitten.

Again, my brain rejected the idea. Brandon had only escaped from jail a few months ago. It took longer than that for a werewolf to recover from the shock of being turned. Or did it? Was it impossible that he'd recovered so quickly? I had to admit that it wasn't. My own recovery had been hampered by my refusal to accept what had happened to me. What if it wasn't like that? What if someone *wanted* to become a werewolf, was prepared for it, embraced it? That could make all the difference.

Yet there was still more that didn't make sense. What was Brandon doing here? If he was a hereditary werewolf, that would explain how he knew about Bear Valley, the Pack, and Stonehaven. How would a newly turned werewolf know that? But Brandon knew. He'd called me by name. He'd talked about the Pack, said he'd heard things about me. From who? Another werewolf, of course. An experienced werewolf. But mutts didn't do that. They didn't allow bitten werewolves to live, let alone help them. It was impossible. No, I corrected. Not impossible. Just so incredibly unlikely that my brain refused to consider the implications.

I couldn't deal with this now. We had a more serious problem on our hands than sorting out the whys and wherefores of Brandon's existence. The fact of his existence was enough. Ending that existence wouldn't be as simple as I'd thought. He wasn't a careless punk kid, but something far more dangerous: a true killer. I looked for Clay, wanting to warn him. Then I realized it wouldn't do any good. Brandon was a killer from the human world. I could tell Clay that Brandon was a chartered accountant and it would have the same impact. He wouldn't understand.

I hopped from the bar and eased through the last scattering of the crowd. In the back corner, Brandon was still playing with his food, which gave the occasional twitch of life. The crowd was almost out of the main room, now jammed in the hallway. I kept moving. Brandon skirted his prey, then leapt in for a pounce and grab. He had his fangs around the man's forearm and was shaking it like a chew toy when he noticed me. He growled uncertainly, his blood-fogged brain taking time to recognize me.

I stopped. We stared at each other. I thought about how dangerous it was to face him down in this form. I thought of Brandon's eyes gleaming with near-carnal bloodlust as he talked about killing. I thought of what he could do to me before Clay could come to my aid. It worked. Fear seeped from me like sweat. That got Brandon's attention. He dropped his prey and lunged at me. I waited until he was in mid-jump, then I turned and ran. Of course he followed. Fleeing prey is so much more fun than the near-comatose variety.

I circled toward the back wall to keep Brandon away from the clogged exit. Running behind the bar, I headed for the balcony stairs. As I stepped onto the first riser, I veered and dashed toward the bathroom hall. Clay was there. I passed him and slid to a stop. Behind me, Brandon did the same, nails careering over the linoleum. He stopped in front of Clay. His nostrils flared, again uncertain. His nose told him Clay was a werewolf and some dimly functioning part of his brain realized this was cause for concern. He growled experimentally. Clay's foot shot out, caught him under the muzzle, and knocked him flying onto his backside. Brandon scrambled to his feet, wheeled, and bolted. Clay ran after him. They disappeared into the main room. By the time I got there, Clay had driven Brandon onto the balcony.

I was almost to the top of the balcony stairs when Brandon leapt over the edge, followed by Clay's resounding "Fuck!" Before I could turn, Clay was jumping to the floor. I rushed down the stairs and ran to the exit to head Brandon off if he tried to escape. The front half of the hall was still clogged with people. No one was getting in or out.

Brandon didn't head for the door. Instead, he circled back to the rear corner of the room. Clay was right behind him. I staked out my post by the exit. Brandon ran for the corner, maybe because it held some vague sense of familiarity. When he got there, he nearly collided with the wall. He turned sharply and veered in a tight circle, tripping over the body on the floor. This time, the man didn't move. His dead eyes stared up at the ceiling. Recovering from his stumble, Brandon headed back toward the corner as if expecting a door to materialize there. Finally, he realized he was trapped and turned to face Clay.

For several long seconds, Clay and Brandon stared at each other. The first flicker of real anxiety sparked in me. Not even Clay was safe against a werewolf in wolf form. As I watched them, I could feel the tension thrumming through me, instinct telling me to protect Clay while common sense told me to guard the exit.

Brandon broke the standoff. He growled and hunkered down, hackles rising. Clay didn't move. Brandon growled again as if giving fair warning. Then he leapt. Clay dropped and rolled to the side. Brandon crashed and slid on the linoleum. Before Brandon could recover, Clay was on him. He grabbed Brandon by the loose skin at the back of his neck and threw his leg over Brandon's back. Then he shoved Brandon's head to the floor, pinning him.

Brandon struggled wildly. His claws skittered along the floor, unable to get a grip. He snarled and growled, snapping from side to side, trying to bite Clay's hands. Clay put his left knee on Brandon's back and wrapped his hands around Brandon's throat. As Clay squeezed, Brandon gave one last tremendous buck. Clay's right foot bounced off the ground just enough to make him shift position. As his foot came back down, it headed for a puddle of the dead man's blood.

"Clay!" I shouted.

Too late. His shoe hit the blood and his ankle twisted, shooting out from under him. Brandon threw himself forward at exactly the right second. Clay tumbled off his back. The second Brandon was free, he saw the exit and made a beeline for it.

I didn't bother blocking the hallway. He could have plowed through me as if I weren't there. Instead, as he passed, I dove at him and grabbed two handfuls of fur. We toppled over together. As we rolled, he snapped at my arm. I twisted it away, but not quite fast enough. One of his canines caught the skin under my forearm, ripping a path to my elbow and tearing through my injuries from that morning. I gasped. I didn't let go, but I did loosen my grip. It was enough. Brandon wrenched free. Clay arrived one second too late. Brandon was already tearing down the hall. The far end of it was still congested with people, but they somehow found a way to clear out when they saw Brandon coming.

Clay started going after Brandon, but I grabbed the back of his shirt.

"We shouldn't go out together," I said.

"Right. You follow him. I'll go back through the window."

I wasn't sure how this was possible, unless he'd developed the ability to scale walls, but there wasn't time to debate the matter. I nodded and ran down the rest of the hallway. I burst through the door to find myself in the midst of a chaos twice as bad as that inside the warehouse earlier. The crowd had got itself outside the door and stopped. Some people looked like they were in shock. The rest weren't moving because they didn't want to miss anything. Added to that, the entire Bear Valley police force and a battalion of state troopers had arrived. Most of the police were still half asleep, milling around in dazed confusion. Sirens howled. Cops barked orders. Nobody listened. Brandon was gone.

I paused to get my bearings. Finally, I was able to filter out the garbage and zero in on the clues. To my left, a barricade had been toppled over. One of the partygoers was waving toward the road. Three cops were jogging over to him. I followed. When I slipped past the fallen barricade, I found that another group of cops was in pursuit, fanned across the roadway, shouting instructions and motioning at an alleyway. When two officers started to run forward, someone stopped them, yelling that there was no need to rush, it was a blind alley. Brandon was trapped.

I scouted the area, trying to determine the likelihood of getting to Brandon before the cops did, and preferably without intercepting any stray bullets. As I stepped off the curb, someone grabbed my arm. I turned to see a middle-aged state trooper.

"Back behind the line, miss. There's nothing to see."

As he tugged me onto the curb, he looked down. The blood from my cut arm trickled over his fingers.

"Thank God," I gasped. "I've been trying to find someone. No one's paying attention—everyone's—" I stopped and gulped air. "Inside. There's people. They're still in there. There was this dog, this huge dog—They're hurt. My boyfriend—"

The officer swore and dropped my arm. He turned to a group of cops heading out onto the roadway.

"There's still people in there!" he yelled. "Has anyone checked inside?"

One of the cops said something I didn't catch. I inched backward as the two officers yelled and gestured. Apparently, neither one knew who was in charge or whether ambulances had been summoned or whether anyone had gone inside yet. Several ran off toward the warehouse. More decided their time and energy was better spent arguing. I slipped across the street. No one noticed.

There were still enough cops guarding the alleyway that I couldn't waltz down there and confront Brandon. I looked for a back way. As I creeped down a nearby alley, garbage cans clanged ahead. In the distance, something flashed against the moonlight. A four-legged figure appeared atop a brick wall. It crouched, then jumped. Obviously the alley wasn't as well blocked as the cops thought—although, to their credit, they wouldn't expect an animal to leap onto an eight-foot wall.

I ran toward the wall, then realized Brandon was making his escape in the opposite direction and heading straight for me. So I waited. He raced straight at me, too panicked to take in his surroundings. As he approached, I broke into a running leap and vaulted over his back, dropping to the ground behind him, rolling in a somersault, and landing in a runner's crouch. It was an absolutely perfect move, one that I couldn't duplicate for a million bucks. Of course, no one was there to appreciate it. I started to run. I'd calculated correctly. Brandon's love of the chase outweighed his instinct for survival. When I turned a corner, he followed. I weaved through the alleys, leading him away from the blockaded street and the police. Once or twice, I caught Clay's scent. He was close by, waiting for the ambush, but the location wasn't right. Finally, I glanced down a connecting alley and saw the highway. On the other side, the industrial section gave way to wooded parkland. Perfect. A place for us to Change and safely ambush Brandon, then smuggle his body out.

I sprinted for the road. Unfortunately, I forgot that most basic of kindergarten rules: I didn't look both ways before crossing. I ran in front of a semi, so close that the draft knocked me off my feet. I rolled to the roadside and leapt to my feet. As I spun around, a gunshot shattered the night air. Brandon was running across the road when the shot struck him. The top of his head burst in an explosion of blood and brain. The force of the blast knocked him sideways into a path of an oncoming pickup. The truck hit him with a sickening splat, then careered out of control. It spun past me, Brandon's body on the front grill, most of his head gone, other assorted body bits flying free as the truck did a 360. With the force of the spin, Brandon's body flew free and jettisoned across the roadway. Most of his body, at least. As the driver got the truck under control and stopped, I could see swaths of fur, blood, and skin still embedded in the grill. It was enough to make me wish the legends were true, that ordinary methods couldn't kill a werewolf, and somewhere in that mangled heap of blood and gore on the roadway Scott Brandon was still alive, conscious and unable to scream. A fitting end for a sadist. Unfortunately, he'd been dead as soon as the first shot hit him. Silver bullets made a nice gothic touch, but they weren't necessary for killing a werewolf. Anything that could kill a human or a wolf could polish us off just as neatly.

A crowd was gathering around Brandon's remains. All they would see was a very large, very dead, brown canine. He wouldn't change back into a human. That was another falsehood about werewolves. According to myth, werewolves are supposed to turn back into humans when wounded. There's a zillion legends where a farmer or hunter shoots a wolf, but when he goes to track the wounded beast he finds—egad!—bloody human footprints instead. Nice trick, but it didn't work that way. Which was really good for us, or we'd be changing shape every time a Pack brother nipped us too hard. Damned inconvenient, really. Truth is, die a wolf and you'd better forget those plans for an open-casket funeral. Brandon's remains would be hauled off to the Bear Valley Humane Society and disposed of without ceremony or autopsy. Scott Brandon, the escaped killer from North Carolina, would never be found.

"Damn, I do hope he gets a proper burial," a voice drawled behind me. "Poor misguided bastard deserves one, don't you think?"

I turned to Clay and shook my head. "I screwed up."

"Nah. He's dead. That was the point of the evening. You did just fine, darling."

He put his arm around my waist and leaned down to kiss me. I squirmed out of his grasp.

"We should go," I said. "Jeremy wouldn't like us hanging around."

Clay reached for me again, mouth opening to say something. I turned away fast and headed down the street. After a few steps he jogged up beside me. The walk back to the parking lot was a quiet one.

We rounded the corner beside the grocery, where I'd left the Explorer. The parking lot was dark, the overhead lights turned out when the store closed for the night, Bear Valley being the kind of place where lighting was still used for customer convenience rather than security. We'd left the Explorer at the rear of the lot, beside a chain-link fence. There had been a few other cars when we'd arrived, but they were gone now, the legal bars having closed long ago. I took the car keys from my purse. They jangled harshly in the silence.

"Son of a bitch," Clay muttered.

I turned, thinking the sound of the keys had startled him, but he was staring at the Explorer. He slowed and shook his head.

"Looks like someone caught a flight tonight after all," he said.

I followed his gaze. A fair-haired, bearded man sat on the asphalt, leaning back against the Explorer's front tire, ankles crossed. An overnight bag lay by his side. Logan. I grinned and started to run. Behind me, Clay shouted. I ignored him. I'd been waiting a year to see Logan. Clay could stick his jealousy up his ass. Better yet, he could rant and rave to himself as he walked all the way back to Stonehaven. After all, I was the one with the keys.

"Hey!" I called. "You're an hour too late. You missed all the excitement."

Clay was running now, still calling my name. I stopped in front of Logan and grinned down at him.

"Are you just going to sit there or—"

I stopped. Logan's eyes stared out across the parking lot. Blank. Unseeing. Dead.

"No," I whispered. "No."

Dimly, I heard Clay run up behind me, felt his arms going around me, catching me as I stumbled back. A deafening howl split open the quiet of the night. Someone howling. Me.

Grief

I DON'T REMEMBER HOW I GOT BACK TO STONEHAVEN. I ASSUME Clay bundled me into the Explorer, then got Logan's body into the rear compartment and drove us home. I vaguely recall walking through the garage door into the house, Jeremy appearing in the hall and starting to ask what happened with the mutt. He must have seen my face because he didn't finish the question. I brushed past him. Behind me, I heard Clay say something, heard Jeremy's oath, heard running footsteps as the others overheard and appeared from wherever they'd been waiting for us. I kept walking to the stairs. No one tried to stop me. Or maybe they did and I just don't remember it. I went to my room, closed the door behind me, pulled back the canopy from my bed, and crawled into its sanctuary.

I don't know how long passed. Maybe hours. Probably minutes, just long enough for Clay to explain things to the others. Then I heard his footfalls on the stairs. He stopped outside my door and rapped on it. When I didn't answer, he knocked louder.

"Elena?" he called.

"Go away."

The door groaned, as if he were leaning against it. "I want to see you."

"No."

"Let me come in and talk to you. I know how much you're hurting—"

I scrambled up and snarled toward the door, "You don't have any idea how much I'm hurting. Why should you? You're probably glad he's gone. One less obstacle to my attention."

He inhaled sharply. "That's not true. You know it isn't. He was my brother." The door groaned again. "Let me in, darling. I want to be with you."

"No."

"Elena, please. I want to—"

"No!"

He was quiet for a moment. I listened to his breathing, heard it catch as he swallowed. Then he made a low noise of anguish that crescendoed in a growl of grief. His shoes squealed as he turned suddenly, then slammed his fist against the far wall. A shower of plaster chunks pattered to the floor. His bedroom door slammed. Then another crash, something larger this time—a nightstand or a lamp hurling into the wall. In my head, I followed the path of his rampage, seeing each piece of furniture smash into bits and wishing I could do the same. I wanted to throw things, destroy things, feel the pain of my hand striking the wall, lash out at everything around me until my grief and rage were swallowed by exhaustion. But I couldn't do it. Some rational part of my brain stopped me, reminded me that there would be consequences. When I recovered my senses, I'd be ashamed of myself for losing control and leaving a swath of destruction that Jeremy would have to pay for. I looked up at the Dresden shepherdesses on my dresser and imagined smashing them on the hardwood, seeing their insipid faces shatter into razor-sharp shards of glass. It would feel wonderful, but I'd never do it. I'd remember how much time Jeremy had put into picking them out for me, how it would hurt him if I destroyed his gift. However much I wanted to explode, I couldn't bring myself to do it. I couldn't afford the luxury. And because Clay could, I hated him for it.

Having no way to vent my pain, I spent the next few hours curled atop my bedcovers, not moving even when my leg muscles seized up and begged me to shift position. I stared at the canopy curtains, my mind as blank as I could make it, afraid to think anything or feel anything. Hours later I was still lying like that when Jeremy tapped at my door. I didn't answer. The door opened, then closed, jamb clicking as it slid back in place. The canopy curtains whispered, then the mattress dipped as Jeremy sat behind me. His hand went to my shoulder, resting there. I closed my eyes as the warmth of his fingers seeped through my shirt. For several minutes, he said nothing. Then he reached over, pulled a strand of hair from my face and tucked it behind my ear.

I didn't deserve Jeremy's kindness. I knew that. I suppose that was why I always questioned his motivation. In the beginning, every time he'd done something nice for me, I'd searched for a glimpse of evil behind the kindness, some nefarious motivation. After all, he was a monster. He had to be evil. When I'd realized there was nothing bad in Jeremy, I'd latched on to another excuse: that he was good to me because he was stuck with me, because he was a decent guy and maybe even because he felt some responsibility for what his ward had done to me. If he took me to Broadway plays and expensive dinners for two, it was because he wanted to keep me quiet and happy, not because he enjoyed my company. I wanted him to enjoy my company, but couldn't believe in it because I didn't see much in myself to warrant it. Not that I thought I was unworthy of love and attention, but not from someone of Jeremy's moral caliber. I'd failed to win the affection of a dozen foster fathers, so I couldn't believe I'd won it now, from someone worth more than those men combined. Still, there were times when I let myself believe Jeremy truly cared for me, when I was hurting too much to deny myself the fantasy. Now was one of those times. I closed my eyes, felt his presence, and let myself believe.

For a while, we sat in silence, then he said softly, "We've buried him. Is there anything you'd like to do?"

I knew what he was asking: was there any human rite of burial that would make me feel better? I wished there was. I wished I could reach inside myself and find some reassuring ritual of death, but my early religious experiences hadn't allowed for reassurance or trust in the power of an almighty being. My most vivid memory of church was sitting in a pew between one set of foster parents, my foster mother leaning forward, straining to hear the pastor and to ignore the fact that her husband's hand was exploring the spiritual mysteries shrouded beneath my skirt. The only thing I'd ever prayed for was deliverance. God must have had more important things on his mind. He'd ignored me and I'd learned to return the snub.

Still, whatever my beliefs, I felt I should do something to mark Logan's passing, at least go to the burial site to pay my respects. When I told Jeremy this, he offered to accompany me, which I accepted with a nod. He helped me get up and put his hand under my elbow, gently guiding me down the stairs. Had it been anyone else or any other time, I would have shrugged off the assistance. But right then I was grateful for it. The floor swayed and dipped under my feet. I walked cautiously down the steps and into the back hall. The study door opened and Antonio looked out, a half-full brandy glass in his hand. He glanced at Jeremy. When Jeremy shook his head, Antonio nodded, then retreated into the room. As we passed the door, it opened again. Without looking I knew who was coming out. Jeremy glanced over his shoulder and held up a hand. I didn't hear the door close, nor did I hear Clay's footsteps following us. I imagined him in the hallway, watching us leave, and I walked a little faster.

They'd buried Logan in a grove just inside the woods behind the house. It was a pretty spot where the midday sun danced through the leaves onto the wildflowers below. I thought of this, then realized the absurdity of picking a pleasant place to bury the dead. Logan couldn't see it. He didn't care where he lay. The carefully chosen spot was only a comfort to the living. It didn't comfort me.

I bent to pick some tiny white flowers to lay on the overturned earth. Again, I didn't know why I was doing it. Logan wouldn't care. Another meaningless gesture intended to offer some small degree of comfort, the comfort of a ritual enacted over the bodies of the dead since humans first began to mourn their dead. As I stood over the grave, clutching my pathetic bunch of flowers, I remembered the last and only funeral I'd been to. My parents. My mother's best friend—the one who had tried to adopt me—had arranged a small funeral. Later I'd learned that my parents didn't have life insurance, so I'm sure my mother's friend must have paid for it. She took me to the funeral, stood beside me, and held my hand. It would be the last time I ever saw her. The foster system believed in clean breaks.

That day, I'd stood there, looking down at the graves and waiting. My parents were coming back. I knew that. Sure, I'd seen the coffins and had been allowed a glimpse of my mother's body inside one. I'd seen the men lower the boxes into the ground and cover them with dirt. That didn't matter. They were coming back. I had no experience with real death, only the loud, garish renderings of it on Saturday morning cartoons, where the coyote died and died again but always returned in time to plot one last silly scheme before the credits rolled. That was the way it worked. Death was temporary, lasting only long enough to provoke a laugh from kids in pajamas sitting cross-legged in front of the TV set, gorging themselves on handfuls of Froot Loops. I'd even seen this trick performed with real people when my father had taken me to a magic show at his office Christmas party. They'd put a woman in a box, cut her in half, and spun the box around. When they reopened the door, she'd jumped up, smiling and whole, to the cheers and laughs of the crowd. So too would my parents leap from their boxes, smiling and whole. It was a joke. A wonderful, terrifying joke. All I had to do was wait for it to be over. As I'd stood there, over my parents' graves, I'd started to giggle. The pastor turned on me then, fixing me with a glare that condemned me as an unfeeling brat. I didn't care. He wasn't in on the joke. I stood there, smiling to myself as I waited . . . and waited.

As I stared down at Logan's grave, I ached for that fantasy to return, to allow myself to pretend he was coming back, that death was only temporary. But I knew better now. Dead was dead. Buried was buried. Gone was gone. I fell to my knees, crushing the flowers in my fist. Something inside me snapped. I fell forward and started to sob. Once I started, I couldn't stop, the tears flowing until my eyes throbbed and my throat ached. Finally, a voice pierced my grief. Not Jeremy, who'd stood silently behind me, knowing not to interfere. This was the one who dared interfere.

"—now!" Clay was yelling. "I can't listen to her and not—"

Jeremy's voice, words muffled in a soft whisper.

"No!" Clay shouted. "They can't do this. Not to Logan. Not to her. I will not stand by—"

Another interrupting murmur.

"Christ! How can you—" Clay's voice choked off in rage.

I heard something, a rustling of branches, Jeremy pulling Clay off into the woods to talk to him, leaving me to my grief. As I knelt there, I listened. Clay wanted to go after Logan's killer—not tomorrow or even tonight, but right now. They'd picked up the scent of an unfamiliar werewolf on Logan's body. While we'd been chasing Brandon, another mutt had killed Logan. Jeremy was trying to dissuade Clay, telling him that it was still daytime, he was too angry, they needed to plan. It didn't matter what Jeremy said or how much sense he made. The storm of Clay's fury drowned all logic. I waited for Jeremy to forbid Clay to go after the mutt. I listened for the words. But they didn't come. Distracted by his own grief, Jeremy argued and tried to reason with Clay, but didn't expressly forbid him to take revenge. A fatal oversight. As I rubbed my dirt-streaked hands over my wet face, my grief was swallowed by fear. While they argued, I crept from the grove, and hurried to the house.

Ten minutes later, Clay yanked open the door of his Boxster and thumped onto the driver's seat.

"Where are we going?" I asked, my sore throat barely allowing me a whisper.

He jumped and turned to see me huddled in the passenger seat.

"You're going after him," I said before he could say anything. "I want to be there. I need to be there."

That was partly true. I did need some way to exorcise my grief and, like Clay, I only knew one way to do it. Revenge. When I thought of some mutt killing Logan, the rage that filled me was terrifying. It whipped through my body like some demonic snake, inciting every part of me to anger, moving so fast and out of control that I had to physically clench my fists and hold them rigid to keep from striking out. I'd known rages like this since childhood. Back then, I'd been frustrated at my inability to use them, to lash out in any meaningful way. Today I could use the anger more than I ever imagined possible. That only made the rages more frightening. Even I didn't know what would happen if I ever gave in to them. Knowing I was taking concrete action by going after the killer helped me rein in my fury.

There was another reason why I was going with Clay. I was afraid to let him leave by himself, afraid that if I wasn't there to watch over him something would happen to him and there would be another grave in the wildflower grove. The thought of that made me feel things I couldn't even admit to myself.

"Are you sure?" he asked, twisting to face me. "You don't need to come along."

"Yes, I do. Don't try to stop me or I'll tell Jeremy that you've gone. I'll make him forbid you to do this. If you're already gone, I'll lead him to you."

Clay reached to touch me, but I turned to look out the window. After a moment of silence, the automatic garage door squealed open and the car's engine roared to life. He backed down the driveway at neck-snapping speed and we were off to Bear Valley.

On the road to Bear Valley, the fog of grief and anger whirling through my brain parted with the prospect of action—clear, definitive action. I focused on that instead. Any impulse to fly into Bear Valley and madly search for Logan's killer dissipated under the cold weight of reality. If I wanted revenge, we needed a plan.

As we entered Bear Valley, we got caught in rush hour traffic and had to wait through an entire light change before making a left turn from Main onto Elm. As the second light turned red, Clay tore through anyway, ignoring the horn blasts around him.

"Do you know where you're going?" I asked.

"To park."

"And then . . . ?"

"To find the bastard who killed Logan."

"Great idea. Precision planning." I grabbed the door handle as Clay spun into the downtown core's only public parking lot. "We can't hunt for him now. It's still daytime. Even if we found the mutt, we couldn't do anything."

"So what do you suggest? Enjoy a leisurely dinner while Logan's killer runs free?"

Although I hadn't eaten since the previous evening, my stomach lurched at the thought of food. I wanted to start hunting Logan's killer as much as Clay did, but reason dictated caution. Not matter how I hated the thought of anything distracting us from avenging Logan, we had to do exactly that. Distract ourselves for a few hours.

"We should find out what happened last night."

Clay slammed into a parking space. "What?"

"Find out how the town is reacting to what happened at the rave last night. Assess the damage. Are they looking for more wild dogs? Are they doing anything with Brandon's body? Did anyone see you jumping through a second-story window? Did anyone see me leading the mutt away?"

"For Christ's sake, who gives a damn what they saw or what they think?"

"You don't? If they decide to submit what's left of Scott Brandon for testing and they find something a wee bit strange, you aren't concerned? This is your backyard, Clay. Your home. You can't afford not to care."

Clay made a noise between a sigh and a frustrated snarl. "Fine. What do you suggest?"

I paused, not having thought this far ahead yet. Thoughts of Logan still filled my numbed mind. I forced them aside and concentrated on our next steps. After a few minutes, I said, "We buy the paper, go to the coffee shop and read it while we listen to what people are talking about. Then we plan how we'll stalk this mutt. After dark, we do it."

"Reading a damn paper isn't going to help us find Logan's killer. We'd be better off having dinner."

"Are you hungry?"

He turned off the ignition and was quiet. "No, I'm not."

"Then unless you have a more productive way to kill a couple of hours, that's the plan."

Trail

AFTER BUYING A PAPER, I STOPPED AT A PAY PHONE TO CALL JERemy. Peter answered, so I didn't need to actually speak to Jeremy. I asked Peter to tell Jeremy that I was with Clay and I'd convinced him that now wasn't the time to go after Logan's killer. Instead, we were taking inventory of the damage from the night before. Of course, I didn't mention that we'd be tracking down Logan's killer *later*. It was all a matter of interpretation. I wasn't actually lying. Really.

Bear Valley had three coffee shops, but The Donut Hole was the only one that counted. The other two were reserved for out-of-towners, truckers, and anyone else pulling off the highway for a caffeine-and-sugar jolt. As we walked into the Hole, the cowbell over the door jangled. Everyone turned. A few people at the counter smiled, one lifted a hand in greeting. I may have looked vaguely familiar, but it was Clay they recognized. In a town of eight thousand, a guy who looked like Clay stood as much chance of going unnoticed as his Porsche Boxster did in the local parking lot. Clay hated the attention. To him, his curse was his face, not his werewolf blood. Clay wanted nothing more than to fade into the background of human life. I think he would even have gotten rid of the Boxster if he could, but like my bedroom, it was a gift from Jeremy, the latest in a string of sports cars bought to indulge Clay's love of fast driving and sharp curves.

Still, Clay was lucky in Bear Valley. Even if his sports car and good looks turned heads, no one bothered him as they would have in the city. He was exempted from undue female attention by the gold band he wore on the fourth finger of his left hand, Bear Valley being the kind of place where a wedding ring still meant you were off-limits to the opposite sex. The ring wasn't a ruse, either. Clay wouldn't lower himself to such a petty deception. His ring was one of a matching pair we'd bought ten years ago, before the small matter of a bite on my hand kiboshed the whole wedding bliss and happily ever after thing. The fact that no marriage took place didn't matter to Clay. The ceremony itself was irrelevant, a meaningless human ritual he'd been willing to undergo for my sake. The underlying commitment was what mattered to him—the idea of a life partner, something the wolf in him recognized, call it marriage or mating or what you will. So he wore the ring. *That* I could live with, dismissing it as another fantasy of his delusion-plagued brain. It was when he'd introduce me as his wife that things could get a bit ugly.

The Donut Hole was a typical, one-on-every-corner coffee shop, down to the cracked red vinyl booth seats and the lingering smell of burnt chicory. The smoking section was inescapable—even if you managed to find a booth without an ashtray, the smoke from nearby booths found you within seconds, ignoring the upward path to the undersized ventilation system. The staff were all middle-aged women who'd raised a family, decided to spend their empty-nest years earning some cash, and discovered this was the only job for which the world considered them qualified. At this time of day, most of the patrons were working people, grabbing a last cup of coffee before heading home or lingering here to avoid going home sooner than necessary.

While I picked a booth, Clay went to the counter and returned with two coffees and two slices of homemade apple pie. I pushed the food aside and spread the *Bear Valley Post* across the Formica tabletop. The incident at the rave party had made the front page. Of course, the paper didn't call it a rave, since most of their readership—and probably most of their staff—wouldn't have a clue about what a rave was. Instead, they described it as a large private party rife with "illicit activity," which made it sound a whole lot more fun than the real thing. Although the paper didn't say so explicitly, it implied that the majority of partygoers had come from outside Bear Valley. Naturally.

The details of the "incident" were sparse, due to a combination of mitigating factors, namely that most of the witnesses had been drunk or stoned and the perpetrator was a dead dog, making him doubly difficult to interview. What facts there were could be reduced to this: a large canine had slaughtered two people at a party before being killed by police. Not exactly a story to fill the front page, so the reporter had bulked it up with enough speculation to earn him a job with the tabloids. It was assumed the dead canine was a dog and everyone seemed content with that explanation, meaning the authorities had no intention of calling in wildlife experts or sending the remains off to an expensive city laboratory. What was left of Brandon had already been disposed of, read: incinerated at the local humane society. They'd even forgone rabies testing, probably deciding that anyone who'd been at the rave deserved a round of rabies shots. Further, the reporter assumed the dead dog was involved with the killing of the young woman the previous week, although police hadn't ruled out the possibility of more wild dogs roaming the forests, especially since those teenage boys had spotted at least two canines the night before. Finally, despite all the speculation, there was no mention of anyone spotting a blond man or woman who'd seemed unusually involved in the incident. As I'd hoped, Clay and I had been just two more bystanders lost amidst the chaos.

"Waste of time," Clay grumbled. He'd been scanning the article upside down as I'd read it. "There's nothing there."

"Good. That's what we hoped for, so it was hardly a waste of time making sure."

He snorted and jabbed his fork into his untouched pie, sending up an explosion of crust, then shoved it away without taking a bite.

"You're sure whoever you smelled on—on—" I inhaled against the surge of pain—"on Logan was someone you didn't recognize."

"Yeah." Clay's eyes clouded, then sparked with anger. "A mutt. A fucking mutt. Two in Bear Valley. Of all the—"

"We can't think about that now. Forget how and why. Focus on who."

"I didn't recognize the scent. Neither did anyone else. Meaning it's a mutt we haven't run into often enough to recognize the scent."

"Or he's new. Like Brandon."

Clay frowned. "Two new mutts? One's odd enough, but—"

"Skip it. You didn't recognize him. Let's leave it at that for now. See if you can hear anyone talking about last night."

Clay grumbled. Ignoring him, I leaned back in my seat to listen to the conversations around us while I pretended to sip my coffee. The experience was a depressing one, not because no one was discussing the "incident," but because what most of them *were* discussing didn't exactly provide an uplifting glimpse into ordinary human life. Complaints of unfair bosses, backstabbing coworkers, ungrateful kids, meddling neighbors, boring jobs and even more boring marriages ricocheted from every corner of the room. No one was happy. Maybe it wasn't as bad as it seemed. Maybe the impersonal relationships formed in coffee shops were perfect for venting the trivial frustrations of life that city folks would take to a therapist—and spend a lot more than a buck for coffee to unload.

As I listened, an old anger and resentment started to surface. Why did people always complain about jobs and spouses and children and extended family? Didn't they realize how lucky they were to have these things? Even as a child, I'd hated hearing kids complain about their parents and siblings. I wanted to shout at them: if you don't like your family, give it to me—I'll take it and I'll never whine about an early bedtime or an annoying little sister. Growing up, I'd been surrounded by images of family. All children are. It seems to be the focus of every book, every television show, every movie, every damned commercial. Mother, father, brother, sister, grandparents, pets, and home. Words so familiar to every two-year-old that any other sort of life would be unthinkable. Unthinkable and wrong, just wrong. When I grew out of the self-pity stage, I realized that missing these things in my childhood didn't mean I had to miss them forever. I could give myself a family when I grew up.

It didn't even have to be the traditional husband, three kids, a dog, and a cute little bungalow. Any variation would do. As an adult, I could provide myself with everything life had cheated me of. Then, on the very cusp of adulthood, I became a werewolf.

My plans for the future vanished in that moment. I could make a life for myself in the human world, but it would never be what I had imagined. No husband. Living with someone was risky enough, sharing my life with someone was impossible—there was too much of it that could never be shared. No children. There was no record of a female werewolf giving birth, but even if I was willing to take the risk, I could never subject a child to the possibility of life as a werewolf. No husband, no children, and without either, no hope for a family or a home. All of that stripped away, as far beyond my reach as they'd been when I was a child.

Clay was watching me, eyes troubled. "You okay?"

He reached out for me, not with a sympathetic hand or a pat on the knee or anything so obvious. Instead, he slid his leg forward, touching mine, and continued to study my face. I turned to look at him. As I met his eyes, I wanted to shout at him, say that I was not okay, that I'd never be okay, that he had made sure I would never be okay again. He'd stolen all my dreams and hopes of a family in one act of unforgivable selfishness. I yanked my leg from his and looked away.

"Elena?" he said, leaning over the table. "Are you okay?"

"No. I'm not okay."

I stopped myself. What good would it do to say more? We were here to hunt Logan's killer, not to hash out our personal problems. It wasn't the time. Part of me knew it would never be the time. If we talked about it, we might work it out. That was a risk I wasn't willing to take. I never wanted to forget and I never wanted to forgive. I wouldn't let myself.

Mending fences with Clay would mean surrender. It would mean he'd won, that biting me had been worth the trouble. He'd have his mate, the life partner of his choice, the realization of his own domestic dreams. Well, I had my own dreams, and Clay had no role in them. Werewolf or not, I couldn't bear to give them up, especially now when I'd finally caught a glimpse of the possibilities in my life with Philip. I had a good, decent man, someone who saw and encouraged my potential for goodness and normalcy, things Clay never saw, didn't care about, and certainly never encouraged. Maybe marriage, kids, and a house in the suburbs weren't in our future but, as I said, any variation would do. With Philip, I could envision a satisfying variation, with a partner, a home, and an extended family. My brass ring had come into sight. All I had to do was muddle through this mess with the Pack, get back to Toronto, and wait for the chance to grab it.

"No," I repeated. "I'm not okay. Logan's dead and his killer is out there and I'm stuck sitting in some stupid coffee shop with—" I bit back the rest. "We're supposed to be listening for rumors, remember? Be quiet and listen."

I forced my attention back to the conversations around us. People were still bitching about their lives, but I ignored that and concentrated on listening for what I wanted to hear. Adding to the general despair, customers here and there discussed the events of last night in the weary "what is the world coming to" tone that people have probably used since early man saw his neighbors starting to walk upright. While most people were just rehashing the newspaper article, a few were giving birth to rumors that would be buzzing about town by nightfall. A woman in the back corner said that she'd heard the dog wasn't a wild dog at all, but an escaped guard dog owned by some relative of the mayor, the police force having been bribed or threatened by the mayor into circulating the wild dog story. Some people even thought the dog hadn't been involved at all, that the drug-crazed partygoers had killed the two people themselves in some kind of mass hysteria, then the cops shot an innocent dog outside. People can be damned creative sometimes. One thing was for sure, no one was talking about impossibly big wolves or demanding an inquest to know why the beast had acted as it had. Everyone assumed that it was perfectly natural for a dog to go berserk and slaughter people in a crowded warehouse. As I'd been eavesdropping, Clay had been pretending to read the paper. I say pretending because he didn't give a shit about current affairs in Bear Valley or anyplace else in the world. Like me, he'd been listening for rumors, though he'd never admit it.

"Can we go now?" he asked finally.

I sipped my cold coffee. The mug was still three-quarters full. Clay hadn't even started his. Neither of us touched our pie. For once, hunger was a distant concern.

"I suppose," I said, glancing out the window. "It's far from dark, but we probably won't find the trail for a while. Should we start at the parking lot?"

I couldn't bring myself to say "the parking lot where we found Logan," but Clay knew which one I meant. He nodded, got up, and ushered me out the door without another word.

As we approached the grocery store, I stopped before rounding the corner so I wouldn't see the spot where we'd found Logan. My heart was tripping so fast I had to concentrate to breathe.

"I can do it," Clay said, putting his hand against my back. "Stay here. I'll pick up the trail and see which way it leads."

I moved away from his hand. "You can't. The scent was faint last night. It'll be worse now. You need my nose."

"I can try."

"No."

I stepped around the corner, hesitated, almost stopping, then propelled myself forward. When I saw the spot where the Explorer had been parked, I jerked my gaze away, but it was too late. My mind was already replaying the scene from the night before, me rushing forward, Clay calling my name and running after me. He'd realized what had happened before I had. That's why he'd been trying to stop me. I understood that now—not that his motive mattered at this moment. It was just a meaningless distraction that ran through my brain, preventing me from thinking of what had happened here last night.

During the day, the parking lot looked like a different place. People bustled from car to store and back again. Like the coffee shop, the lot was filled with working people, most in jeans, a few in suits, toting single grocery bags with tonight's dinner or extra milk or bread grabbed on the way home. No one paid attention to us as we crossed the lot to the back fence. The spot where we'd parked last night was empty, being too far from the store to get used on any but the busiest shopping days.

I stood on the right side, where the passenger door of the Explorer had been. Closing my eyes, I inhaled. The scent of Logan filled my head. My knees buckled. Clay grabbed my elbow. I steadied myself, then sniffed again, trying to block Logan's scent. It didn't work. His lingering odor shoved aside all less familiar scents. With my eyes closed, I could imagine him standing in front of me, close enough to touch. I opened my eyes. The bright light of day chased the fantasy back to the shadows of my brain.

"I'm—" I started. "I'm having some trouble."

"It's here," Clay said. "Faint, but I'm picking up something. Hold on a sec and I'll see if I can grab it."

He paced to the left, shook his head, then came back and started again in another direction. On his second round of the compass points, he turned to me.

"Got it," he said. "Entrance trail is east, but the mutt exited here."

There was nothing in a scent that could tell even the best tracker whether someone was coming or going. Clay knew the difference because the approaching trail would also carry traces of Logan's smell, though he didn't mention this.

"Come over here and try," he said.

Once I got away from the parking spot, I relaxed. Clay stood near a minivan. I walked to him and sniffed the air. Yes, the scent was there. An unfamiliar werewolf. The trail led across the parking lot, away from the grocery store and toward Jack's Hunting and Hardware. From there, it ran along the sidewalk heading west, then circled back toward the main street, where we followed it to the downtown core. If that sounds quick and easy, it wasn't. A straight walk from point A to point B would have taken fifteen minutes. We spent over an hour, constantly missing the trail, looping back, finding where the mutt had turned a corner, and starting again. Once or twice I lost the scent completely. Trailing as humans made it even more difficult, not only because I couldn't smell as well, but because I couldn't exactly put my nose to the ground and sniff the mutt out. Well, I *could,* but such actions are frowned upon in polite society and often lead to a complimentary ride to the nearest psychiatric ward. Even the sight of someone on a street corner twitching her nose or pacing in a circle raised eyebrows. So I had to be discreet. Even if I could convince Clay to wait until nightfall, we couldn't change into wolves. After everything that had happened in Bear Valley, that wouldn't be a challenge, it'd be suicide.

Downtown Bear Valley closed at five, allowing employees to make it home for dinner and ignoring the fact that the average person worked until five and needed to shop afterward. This oversight may have explained the vacancy rate that had spread through the core like a cancer, affecting one shop, then its neighbors, and their neighbors, until the block looked like a massive advertisement for Bear Valley Realty. By the time we got back downtown, it was past seven and even the most dedicated shelf stockers had left for the evening. The streets were bare. The town seemed to have shut down for a collective dinner hour. I was able to be less cautious with my sniffing and we covered the next half mile in twenty minutes. The trail stopped at a Burger King that had been ostracized from its fast-food buddies on the other side of town. Here the mutt had presumably stopped to refuel. After another twenty minutes of circling and retracing my steps, I picked up the trail again. Ten minutes later we were standing in the parking lot of the Big Bear Motor Lodge.

"Well, this was a no-brainer," I muttered as we looked out over the collection of pickup trucks and ten-year-old sedans. "Two hotels in town. He's staying at one. Duh."

"Hey, you're the one who insisted we start from the grocery store."

"I didn't hear you suggesting anything else."

"It's called survival, darling. I know when to keep my mouth shut."

"Since when have—" I stopped, noticing a woman standing in her hotel room doorway, making no effort to hide her eavesdropping. It's always nice to know you can provide entertainment when the afternoon soaps are over.

I walked behind a pickup truck and squinted up at the two-story building. "How many rooms by your count?"

"Thirty-eight," Clay said without missing a beat. "Nineteen each up and down. A main-floor entry for the bottom. A lobby entrance and emergency exit for the second floor."

"If it were me, I'd take a room on the first floor," I said. "Direct room access. Easier to come and go at all hours."

"But the second floor has balconies, darling. And a hell of a view."

I looked across the road into a vacant lot filled with overgrown weeds, crumbling concrete blocks, and enough litter to keep a Scout troop busy for an entire Earth Day.

"First floor," I said. "I'll start. Go hide somewhere."

"Uh-uh. We've played this game before. I hide. You never seek. I'm a bit slow on the uptake, but I'm beginning to sense a pattern."

"Go."

Clay grinned, grabbed me around the waist and kissed me, then ducked out of the way before I could retaliate. While it was nice to see his mood had improved, it would be even nicer if it didn't take the prospect of murder and mayhem to improve it. Over the past couple hours of tracking, the old resentment that had resurfaced in the coffee shop had faded into my subconscious, where it would wait, like a wound that never healed over, only needing a bump or prod to reignite the pain. We had work to do and I had to deal with Clay to do it. For Logan's sake, I couldn't afford to be distracted by my own problems. If I dwelled on my anger with Clay every second I was forced to spend in his company, I'd have turned into a bitter, waspish harpy long ago. Of course, some might argue that I'd crossed that threshold years ago, but that wasn't the point.

While Clay went off to find a suitable waiting place, I scanned the area for props. Near a corrosion-encrusted Chevy Impala I spotted a sheet of paper. It was a receipt for a new car stereo, which I hoped hadn't gone into the Impala, or the owner had spent more money on the sound system than on the car. I brushed a wet leaf from the corner of the sheet, flattened it, then folded it in half and headed for the sidewalk connecting the doors of the main-floor rooms. Starting by the emergency exit, I walked slowly down the sidewalk, pretending to study the sheet of paper and allowing for generous sniffing pauses in front of each door. The eavesdropping woman had gone back into her room. Two people came out of a room near the end, but they ignored the young woman having such difficulty finding the room number written on her scrap of paper. People make special allowances for the mental capacity of blondes.

When I got to the end, I picked up the scent of the werewolf, heading not into a room, but into the lobby. The trail was thick here, indicating he'd gone this way several times. A second-floor room, accessible only through the lobby. Maybe he liked waking up to the sunrise over a vacant lot. I looped back through the parking lot. Clay came out from behind the building before I could look for him.

"Upstairs," I said.

"See, darling? No one ever claimed mutts have brains."

I tossed the stereo receipt into the bushes and we headed for the front door. As we went into the lobby, Clay put his arm around my waist and started complaining about an imaginary dinner at a local restaurant. As he prattled, I saw the stairs to the left of the check-in desk and steered us there, nodding as he bitched about waiting twenty minutes for the dinner check. The show wasn't necessary. The desk clerk didn't even look up as we went by.

Upstairs, the trail stopped at the third door on the left. Clay grabbed the handle, twisted, and broke it with a muffled snap. As I kept an eye out for other motel guests, Clay waited to see if anyone inside the room responded to the sound of the lock breaking. When he heard nothing, he eased the door open. The curtains were drawn and the room was dark. A door down the hall opened. I pushed Clay forward and we slipped inside.

Clay checked the bathroom to make sure the mutt was gone, then pulled a quarter from his pocket. "Heads we lie in wait, tails we give chase."

"We should stay here," I said. "Check the place out, search for clues while we wait."

Clay rolled his eyes.

"Oh fine," I said. "Just flip the damned thing."

When it came up heads, I stuck my tongue out at him. His hand darted out to grab it, but I pulled it back in time.

"Next time you won't be so fast," he said, then looked around the room. "So what do you hope to find?"

"Anything to explain why we had two mutts in Bear Valley within a week. Aren't you the least bit concerned about that?"

"'Course I am, darling. But I'm sticking concern and curiosity on the back burner. Plenty of time to examine them both when the mutt's dead. I'm not waiting around for this bastard to go after you or the others while I try to find out what he's doing here."

"You think I'm stalling?"

"No, I think you're trying to make efficient use of time. That's fine. I'm just saying don't expect me to be too eager to riffle through dresser drawers while that mutt's roaming our streets."

"Then go watch out the balcony or something while I search."

Clay didn't do this, of course. He helped me look, having simply made it clear that his heart wasn't in it. Mine wasn't either, but I know better than to pass up an opportunity. Besides, looking through this mutt's junk kept my hands and mind busy, leaving me little time to dwell on *why* we were tracking him.

Clay started in the bathroom. He was gone maybe ten minutes before he called out, "Here's the scoop. The guy uses hotel shampoo and hotel soap. He hasn't broken the seal on the conditioner. There's a Bic razor and no sign of a toothbrush, toothpaste, or mouthwash. So we're looking for a guy with split ends and a serious breath problem. Any of this helping, darling?"

I gritted my teeth against a reply. The walls were too thin for arguing. Besides, my own search of the main room hadn't turned up much more. I'd found two pairs of jeans, three shirts, and assorted socks and underwear, all of it previously worn and dumped on a chair for reuse. The Gideon Bible in the nightstand had been defaced with pentagrams and inverted crosses. Lovely. Also terribly unoriginal. I mean, if you feel compelled to scribble Satanic symbols on a Bible, the least you can do is draw stuff not found in every edition of *Weekly World News*. A very uncreative and obviously uninformed werewolf. He'd be in for a disappointment when he discovered werewolves were more likely to know a good recipe for beef Wellington than the recipe for a Satanic rite. In ten years, the devil had never contacted me with special instructions or even to say hello. Then again, neither had God. Maybe that meant they didn't exist. More likely, it meant neither was willing to take responsibility for me.

"Christ, you should see the stuff in there, darling," Clay said as he walked from the bathroom. "Aftershave, cologne, and musk deodorant. If we couldn't tell the mutt was new by the way he smells, we'd know it by the *way* he smells."

No experienced werewolf would be caught dead wearing cologne, at least not if he had a functioning olfactory system. The very smell of himself would drown out all other scents, making his nose useless. I don't even use scented hand soap. Finding unscented women's toiletry products wasn't easy. The cosmetics industry seemed obsessed with making women smell like anything but themselves. And we piled the stuff on with no regard for achieving a uniform masking smell, layering herbal shampoo on baby powder deodorant on lilac soap on the latest fragrance from Calvin Klein. When I had the misfortune to get stuck in a full elevator early in the morning, the overpowering clash of scents could leave me with a headache until noon.

After checking out the window, Clay walked to where I was sifting through the bedside trash can.

"I'd offer to help," he said. "But you seem to have things under control."

"Thanks."

"Have you checked under the bed?"

"Can't. The frame's solid to the floor." I used the hotel pen to push aside a used Kleenex. I won't say what it had been used for, but werewolves don't contract cold and flu viruses.

"I'll check under the mattress," Clay said.

I'd forgotten that. Werewolves often carry fake ID and stash the real stuff someplace like under their mattress.

"No ID," Clay said. "Just this scrapbook. I don't suppose you want that."

I jumped up so fast I conked my head on the giraffe-neck lamp. Clay grinned and held a blue book out of my reach.

"Mine," he said, grin broadening. Holding it out of my range, he leafed through a few pages, then curled his lip and tossed the book on the bed. "On second thought, it's all yours. Happy reading, darling. I'll stand guard by the window. Give me a synopsis later."

I took the book and sat on the edge of the bed. It was a photo album, the type with plastic film you can pull back from the pages and stick pictures underneath. Instead of photos, the mutt had filled this album with newspaper clippings. Not random clippings, but ones following a specific theme: serial killers. I flipped past page after page of articles, seeing some faces that were familiar—Berkowitz, Dahmer, Bundy—and others I didn't know. Not only were all the clippings about serial killers, but they all contained one key element, something the mutt had highlighted—a number: the number of people murdered. He'd even color-coded the stats, yellow highlighter for the number of people the killer claimed to have killed, blue for the number of bodies found, and pink for the number the authorities believed he was responsible for. In the margins, the mutt had written notes, tallying and comparing numbers like a fan compiling stats for some macabre sporting event.

About halfway through the book, the articles stopped. I was about to close it when I realized there were more clippings near the back. I flipped through the blank pages and came to another article. Unlike the others, this one didn't deal with statistics. In fact, it didn't even name the killer. The article, dated November 18, 1995, from the *Chicago Tribune*, simply stated that the body of a young woman had been found. The next article gave more details, telling how she'd been missing for over a week and appeared to have been held captive during the intervening time, before being strangled and dumped behind an elementary school. I flipped through the next few pages. Three more women found, all following the same pattern. Then one escaped, telling a horrifying story of a weeklong ordeal of rape and torture, held captive in the basement of an abandoned house. The police had traced the house to Thomas LeBlanc, a thirty-three-year-old medical lab technician. However, when it came time for the woman to identify LeBlanc, she couldn't. Her attacker had only come to her in the dark and had never spoken. Furthermore, LeBlanc had been out of town on business the week the third woman went missing. In a newspaper photo, LeBlanc could have passed for Scott Brandon's older brother, not in any real physical resemblance but in the complete banality of his face, well-groomed, blandly handsome and completely unprepossessing, your quintessential Wall Street WASP, features stripped of any ethnicity or interest. The face of the serial killer next door.

Despite an extensive investigation, the police were unable to come up with enough evidence to charge LeBlanc. In the last *Tribune* article, LeBlanc had packed his bags and left Chicago. Even if the justice system hadn't been able to convict LeBlanc, the people of Illinois had. Although that was the last article from Chicago, the scrapbook didn't end there. I counted six more clippings from the past few years, tracing a path of missing women through the Midwest to California and looping back up the East Coast. Thomas LeBlanc had been on the move. The last clipping was dated eight months ago, from Boston.

"Shit," Clay said, making me jump. "No way. No fucking way. Drop the book, darling. You've got to see this."

I hurried to the window. Clay held the heavy curtain back just enough for me to look out. An Acura had pulled into a spot near the lobby doors. Three men were walking away from it. When I saw the man heading from the driver's side, I wasn't shocked to see the face that had stared out from the *Tribune* article—Thomas LeBlanc, looking not nearly as well-groomed as he had in his photo. Of course, Clay didn't recognize him or even know from this distance that he was a werewolf. It was the other men who'd caught his attention. Karl Marsten and Zachary Cain, two mutts we both knew very well.

"Marsten and Cain? What the hell are they doing together?" Clay said. "And who's the other guy? He must be the one."

"Logan's killer," I said. "Thomas LeBlanc. We have to get out of here."

"Whoa," Clay said, holding his ground as I tugged him toward the door. "We're not going anywhere. This is what we came for, darling."

"We came to kill one mutt. One inexperienced mutt. Three against two is bad enough but—"

"We can handle it."

"With no sleep or food in twenty-four hours?"

"We could—"

"I can't."

Clay stopped there. He was quiet for a moment.

"If you stay," I continued, "then I stay. But I'm in no shape for a fight. I'm exhausted and hungry and my arm is screwed up from the dog bite and Brandon."

I was hitting beneath the belt, but I didn't care. I'd say whatever it took to get us out of that room. Clay's expression changed, first uncertain, then resolute.

"Okay," he said. "We bolt. Is there still time . . . ?"

"The balcony. We'll have to lower ourselves down. No jumping."

"Your arm?" He looked down at the scabbed-over wound. We heal fast and it felt fine, but I wasn't about to admit that. Not now.

"I'll live," I said.

Clay strode to the balcony, shoved the drapes aside, and slid the door open. "I'll go first and catch you if your arm gives out."

He was over the railing before I got out the door. I swung one leg over the ledge, then looked back into the room and saw the photo album on the bed. I should have grabbed it. There would be more clues there, more to help me get to know Thomas LeBlanc. Rule one of hunting: know your prey.

"Be right back," I called to Clay over the railing.

"No!"

I grabbed the book from the bed just as a card key slid into the door lock.

"It's not working," an unfamiliar voice said through the door. "The green light should come on."

I lunged from the bed to the balcony, tripping over a pair of underwear and nearly flying headfirst out the sliding door. As I was swinging over the railing, someone tried the door, found it open, and gave it a shove. I dropped to the ground. Clay wasn't there to catch me. When I turned, I saw him racing to the lobby door. I started to shout his name, thought better of it, ran and tackled him instead. We tumbled to the concrete just outside the first room door. The photo album flew from my hands, knocking him hard under the chin.

"Whoops," I said. "Sorry."

"You almost sound like you mean it," he growled, holding the book aloft in one hand. "You went back for this? For this?"

"I needed it."

He muttered something under his breath. I couldn't hear what he said and probably didn't want to. We were still lying on the sidewalk, me atop him. I lifted my head to listen. Someone walked out onto the balcony in LeBlanc's room. I heard the railing groan as the person leaned over it, looking out across the parking lot. We were hidden beneath the balcony.

"Shhh," I whispered.

"I know," he mouthed.

He shifted under me, hands moving to rest on my rear. It wasn't an uncomfortable position to be in—not that I wanted to be there, given the choice, but . . . Oh, never mind.

"You gave me a scare," he whispered.

He moved one hand to the back of my head, pulled me down, and started to kiss me. I closed my eyes and kissed him back. After all, if we had to lie on the sidewalk outside a hotel, we should at least be doing something that might explain why we were lying on the sidewalk, right? After a moment, Clay's eyes flickered to the right and narrowed. As I pulled back, he slid from under me and focused his glare on something behind us. The woman who'd been watching us argue earlier was back in her doorway, this time drinking a Diet Coke as she took in the show.

"Would you like some popcorn with that?" Clay said, getting to his feet and brushing himself off.

"It's a free country," the woman replied.

Now, if Clay had little patience with humans in general, he had even less with humans who invaded his privacy and could only manage the lamest of comebacks. His jaw hardened and he stepped past me. He stopped, back to me, facing the woman. It only took a second. Her eyes widened, she stumbled back, and the door slammed, locks clicking into place. Clay hadn't said anything. He'd just given her "the look"—a stare of pure malevolence that never failed to send humans scurrying. I tried to perfect the look once. When I thought I had it down pat, I'd tested it on some jerk who'd been coming on to me in a bar. Instead of scaring him off, it'd only set his engines revving at full throttle. I learned my lesson. Women can't do malevolence.

By now, whoever had been on LeBlanc's balcony was gone. Their next step might be to come outside for a closer look, since Marsten and Cain would be able to smell that Clay and I had been in LeBlanc's room and would probably assume we hadn't been gone long. I prodded Clay forward. As we skirted along the sidewalk, staying close to the building, I crossed my fingers and hoped the mutts didn't come outside. Not that we couldn't get away. We could. But Clay wouldn't. If they came out and saw him, he wouldn't run.

We got around the building and slipped away without being seen. The walk to the car was a quick one. Less than twenty minutes later we were on our way back to Stonehaven for reinforcements.

Synchronous

"ABSOLUTELY NOT," JEREMY SAID, GETTING UP FROM HIS CHAIR TO walk to the fireplace.

We were all in the study. The others had been waiting for us. Clay and I sat on the couch, Clay perched on the edge ready to bolt the second Jeremy said we could go after the mutts. Nick stood beside Clay, fingers tapping against the sofa back, equally anxious, but taking his cues from Clay. Peter and Antonio sat across the room. Both looked angry at the news, but they remained composed, awaiting Jeremy's decision with the greater control of age and experience.

"I can't believe you're asking," Jeremy continued. "I made it clear that I didn't want this, but you took off anyway. Then Elena calls to say you're just scouting out news about last night and somehow you end up—"

"It wasn't intentional," I said. "We came across his trail. We couldn't pass up the opportunity."

Jeremy gave me a look that advised me to shut my mouth before I dug myself in deeper. I shut it.

Jeremy walked back to his chair, but didn't sit. "No one is going after these three tonight. We are all exhausted and upset after last night, especially you two. If I hadn't trusted Elena's word when she called, I would have been down there this afternoon hauling the two of you back here."

"But we didn't *do* anything," Clay said.

"Only for lack of opportunity."

"But—"

"Yesterday we had one mutt in town. Today, he's dead and three more have shown up. Not only that, but of those four, we have Karl Marsten and Zachary Cain, two mutts who would be enough of a problem individually."

"Are you absolutely sure it was Marsten and Cain?" Antonio asked. "Of any two mutts I could imagine ever teaming up, those two rank right at the bottom of the list. What could they possibly have in common?"

"They're both mutts," Clay said.

"My guess would be that they haven't teamed up," I said. "Marsten must have something over Cain. A definite leader-follower relationship. Karl wants territory. Has for years."

"If he wants territory, he has to join the Pack," Jeremy said.

"Fuck that," Clay spat. "Karl Marsten is a thieving, conniving son-of-a-whore who'd stab his father in the back to get what he wanted."

"Don't forget the new recruits," I said. "Brandon and LeBlanc are both killers. Human killers. Someone—probably Marsten—found them, bit them, and trained them. He's creating an army of mutts. Not just any mutts, but ones who already know how to hunt, to kill. Know it and like it."

Antonio shook his head. "I still can't picture Marsten behind this. Parts of it, yes. But this thing about creating new mutts, it lacks . . . finesse. And recruiting Cain? The man's an idiot. A first-rate heavy hitter, but an idiot. The chances of him screwing up are too high. Marsten would know that."

"Who the fuck cares!" Clay said, exploding from his seat. "We've got three mutts in town. One of them killed Logan. How can you sit around discussing motivation and—"

"Sit down, Clayton," Jeremy said, his voice low.

Clay started to sit, then stopped. For a moment, he hung there, twin instincts battling within him. Then his hands clenched at his sides. He straightened up, turned on his heel, and strode to the study door.

"If you go, don't come back." Jeremy's voice was barely above a whisper, but it stopped Clay cold. "If you can't control the urge, Clayton, then go downstairs to the cage. I'll lock you in until it passes. But if the problem is that you *won't* control it, and you leave, then you're not welcome back."

Jeremy didn't mean it. Well, yes, he meant it, but not as it sounded. If Clay took off and Jeremy had threatened banishment, he'd have to follow through with it. But he wouldn't let Clay go without a fight. The threat was the best way to prevent that. Clay stood there, jaw working as if chewing his anger, his hands clenched at his sides. But he didn't move. He wouldn't. Banishment for Clay would be death—not from outside forces, but from within, the slow death of severing himself from what he believed in most. He'd never leave Jeremy or the Pack. It was his life. Jeremy might as well threaten to kill him if he went after the mutts.

Slowly, deliberately, Clay turned to Jeremy. Their eyes locked. There was a long pause, the mantel clock ticking off seconds like a time bomb, then Clay turned and walked out the door, veering not toward the garage or front door but heading for the rear of the house. The back door opened and slammed shut. I looked at Jeremy, then went after Clay.

I followed Clay into the woods. He walked until we were out of sight and hearing of the house. Then he slammed his fist into the nearest tree, making it rock and groan in protest. Flecks of blood flew.

"We can't let Cain and Marsten get away with this," he said. "We can't let them think we're backing down. We have to act. Now."

I said nothing.

He whirled to face me. "He's wrong. I'm so sure he's wrong."

He closed his eyes and inhaled deeply, face spasming as if the words cut him. The very notion of questioning Jeremy pierced him like the worst possible betrayal.

"He's right," Clay continued after a moment. "We're not ready for this. But I can't stand around while Logan's killer is out there, knowing the next one those mutts might go after could be you or Jeremy. I can't do it. He's got to know that."

Still I said nothing, knowing he wasn't looking for an answer, that he was only trying to work things out in his own mind.

"Fuck!" he yelled into the forest. "Fuck! Fuck! Fuck!"

He slammed his fist into the tree again, then raked his hand through his curls, crimson scattering through the gold leaving a red smear on his forehead. His eyes closed, chest heaving as he inhaled deeply. Then he exhaled, shuddered, and looked at me. Frustrated rage shone from his eyes, mingled with touches of dread.

"I'm trying here, darling. You know how hard I'm trying. Everything in me screams to go after them, hunt them down, tear out their goddamned throats. But I can't disobey him. I can't do it."

"I know."

He stepped toward me, arms going around me, mouth coming down to mine. His lips touched mine lightly, tentatively, waiting to be shoved away. I could taste his panic, his fight to control the dueling instincts that raged stronger than anything I could imagine. I put my arms around him, hands going up and entwining in his hair, pulling him closer. A moan of relief shuddered through him. He let the mantle of control slide free and grabbed me, pushing me back against a tree trunk.

He ripped at my clothes, nails scraping against my skin as he tore my shirt and pants free. I fumbled with his jeans, fingers clumsy as the heat of his desperation caught me like a brushfire. He pushed his jeans down and flung them off.

His lips came back to mine, bruisingly rough. I twisted my hands in his hair, pulling him closer. He moaned hoarsely. His hands ran over my naked body, kneading, grabbing my hips, my waist, my breasts. The bark of the tree bit into my back. As his fingers came up to my face, I smelled the blood on his hand, felt it running fresh and streaking across my cheeks as he caressed my face. The blood dripped onto our lips and I tasted it, metallic and familiar.

Without warning, his hands dropped to my rear, jolting me off the ground onto him. He growled as he slid inside me. My feet were off the ground, leaving me dangling and putting him in control. He slammed against me. His eyes stayed locked with mine. From deep in his chest came a rhythmic growl of desperate lust. His teeth were clenched. As his fingers dug into my hips, I felt the edge of his wedding band cut into me. Then his eyes clouded. His focus wavered and his body shuddered convulsively. He gave a low, panting moan, then slowed, face burrowing into my collarbone and hands moving up to protect my battered back from the tree. He moved slowly in me, still hard. He hadn't climaxed yet. It was a release of another sort, a sudden abatement of the violence that had ripped through him.

His hands stroked my back and pulled me against him. Face still nuzzled against me, he whispered, "I love you, Elena. I love you so much."

I wrapped my hands around him, nuzzling his ear and murmuring wordless noises. Still moving in me, he eased me away from the tree and stepped back and lowered us down to the ground with me on top of him. I wrapped my legs around his hips, then rose into the air, picking up the pace again. I tilted my head back, closing my eyes and feeling the cool night air on my face. I could hear Clay's voice, as if from a great distance, repeating my name. I heard myself answer, my voice calling his name into the silent forest. The climax came slow, almost languid, each wave passing through me with glorious singularity. I felt his climax, equally slow and decadent, and groaned with sympathetic release.

He put his arms up and pulled me down onto his chest, tucking my head under his chin. For a long time, we didn't move. I stayed there, listening to his heartbeat and waiting for the dread moment when reality would return. It would happen. The fog of lovemaking would part and he'd say something, do something, demand something to send us snarling at each other's throats. I felt him swallow, knew words were coming, and wished I could stop up my ears against them.

"I'd like to run," he said softly.

I was quiet for a moment, not sure if I'd heard right, waiting for the punch line.

"Run?" I repeated.

"If you're not too tired."

"You still need to work it off?"

"No. I just want to run. To do something. Something with you."

I hesitated, then nodded. We lay there for a few minutes longer before getting up to find a place to Change.

I took my time and my Change came surprisingly easy. Afterward I stood in the clearing and stretched—turning my head, flicking my ears, stretching my hind legs, and moving my tail. It felt gloriously good, as if I hadn't Changed in weeks. I blinked, adjusting to the darkness. The air smelled delicious and I inhaled greedily, filling my lungs, then snorting it out and seeing the barest wisps of condensation trumpet from my nostrils.

I was about to go back to the clearing when a lead weight barreled into my side and sent me flying. I caught a flash of golden fur, then found myself alone again with only traces of Clay's scent for company. Getting to my feet, I took a few wary steps forward. Nothing happened. I cocked my head, sniffing. Still nothing. I took three more steps and got torpedoed again, this time crashing sideways into a bush and not seeing so much as a hair of my attacker.

I waited, got my breath back, then leapt to my feet and started to run. Behind me, Clay burst into the clearing again and yipped on finding his quarry vanished. I ran faster. Bushes crashed somewhere behind me. Rounding a corner, I dove headfirst into a patch of underbrush and dropped to the ground. A blur of gold raced by. I sprang to my feet and backtracked. It took Clay a few seconds to realize the trick, but soon I heard the pounding of running paws behind me.

The next time I leapt to the side of the path, I must have been a split second too slow, giving him a flash of my hind legs or tail. I'd just crouched behind a bush when two hundred pounds of muscle vaulted it and dropped onto me. We tussled for a few minutes, yelping and growling, nipping and kicking. I managed to get my muzzle under his throat and heaved him over backward, then scrambled to my feet. Sharp teeth clamped on my hind leg and twisted, flipping me over. Clay pounced and pinned me. He stood over me for a minute, blue eyes gloating. Then, without warning, he leapt off and ran back into the forest. Now I was "it."

I chased Clay for about a half mile. He veered off the path at one point and tried to lose me in the thick brush. The trick gave him a twenty-foot advantage, but no more. I was expecting another ruse when a small shadow bolted across the clearing ahead. The smell of rabbit drifted over on the breeze. Clay slowed, twisting to do a double take at the fleeing rabbit. I picked up speed, tensed, and sprang at his back, but I was too late. He was gone.

As I was regaining my balance, a high-pitched squeal sliced through the forest. Within seconds, Clay bounded back through the bushes, the dead rabbit dangling from his jaws. He looked at me and waggled the rabbit, his eyes conveying the message with his actions: "Want it?" As he shook the rabbit, blood splattered to the ground. The smell wafted up, mingling with the scent of warm meat. I stepped forward, sniffing. My stomach rumbled. Clay made a noise low in his throat, a half growl that almost sounded like a laugh, and yanked the rabbit out of my reach. "Tease," I glared. He feigned tossing the rabbit toward me, but didn't release it. With a growl, I lunged. He danced backward, holding the rabbit just close enough that the smell of it filled my brain and made my stomach twist. I gave him a baleful stare, then looked out at the forest. There was plenty more dinner where that rabbit came from.

As I was turning to leave, Clay tossed the rabbit at my feet. I looked from it to him, expecting another trick. Instead, he sat back on his haunches and waited. I gave him one final glance, then ripped into the rabbit, gulping the warm meat in mouthfuls. Clay walked over and rubbed against me, licking flecks of splattered blood from my muzzle and neck. I stopped eating long enough to thank him with a nuzzle. When I went back to feeding, he loped into the woods to catch his own meal.

When I awoke the next morning, I was lying alone in the dew-damp grass. I scrambled up and looked around for Clay. The last thing I remembered, we'd Changed back, curled up, and gone to sleep. I put out my hand and touched the dry spot beside me where he'd been. As I glanced around the empty clearing, a sliver of anxiety ran through me. Clay didn't take off on me like that. Getting rid of him was the problem. As I was looking, a sprinkle of cold water hit my head. I jumped to see Clay standing over me, grinning. Water dripped from his hands and glistened from his forearms. He was still naked; we hadn't bothered going back for our clothes the night before, not quite sure where we'd left them and even less certain they'd be in any condition to be worn again.

"Looking for me?" he asked, dropping down beside me.

"I thought that pack of wild dogs might have got you."

"You looked worried."

"I was. God knows what kind of indigestion you'd give the poor things."

He laughed and knelt on all fours, pushing me back down to the ground and kissing me. I kissed him back, entwining my legs around his, then jerking back as my feet touched his, ice-cold and wet.

"I was checking the pond," Clay said before I could ask. "I thought we might go for a swim. First of the season. It would definitely wake us up."

"Any food there?"

He chuckled. "That rabbit last night didn't quite do it?"

"Not by half."

"Okay then. Here's the deal. If you can't wait, we'll eat breakfast, then swim. Otherwise, come swimming with me now and I'll make you breakfast afterward, anything and everything you want."

I didn't hesitate long before agreeing to option two. Not because I wanted someone to prepare my breakfast, but because I knew if we went to the house first, we'd never come back out to go swimming. Something would happen. We'd remember that Logan was dead and there were three mutts in Bear Valley. Real life would destroy the fantasy world we'd built so carefully over the past night. I didn't want it to end. Just a few more hours, a little more time to pretend that it could really be like this, with no past or future to intrude on our utopia.

When I said yes to the swim first, Clay grinned and kissed me, then jumped to his feet.

"Race?" he asked. "Last one there gets thrown in?"

I pretended to think it over, then jumped to my feet and took off. Five seconds too late, I realized I'd picked the wrong route. As I raced into the clearing beside the pond, Clay stood on the north bank, grinning.

"Lose your way, darling?" he called.

I limped over to him, dragging my right foot.

"Damned vines," I muttered. "I think I twisted my ankle."

After all these years, you'd think he'd know better. You really would. But no, as I hopped onto the bank, he came forward to meet me, blue eyes clouding with concern. I waited until he bent down to check my ankle, then knocked him flying into the pond.

We stumbled back to the house later, still naked and not noticing or caring. After our swim, we'd made love on the edge of the pond, leaving us looking like we'd been mud wrestling, which wasn't entirely inaccurate. We'd done a quick washup in the pond, but Clay still had a smear of dirt across one cheek. He looked about twelve years old, eyes glowing with mischief, lips settled in a lingering grin that turned to a laugh every time we tripped over something in our path.

"Pancakes, right?" he said as he helped me up from a tumble over a hidden root.

"From scratch. No shortcuts."

"And ham, I assume. What else?"

"Steak."

He laughed and put his arm around my waist as the path widened enough for two. "For breakfast?"

"You said I could have whatever I wanted."

"Can I get you some fruit to balance that meal?"

"No, but you can dig up some bacon. Bacon and eggs."

"Dare I ask for a little help?"

"I'll make coffee."

He laughed again. "Thanks a hell of a—"

He stopped. We'd come to the forest's edge and stepped through to the backyard. There, on the back patio, less than fifty feet away, stood Jeremy . . . surrounded by five or six unfamiliar human faces, all of which turned the second we walked from the woods. Clay growled an oath and stepped in front of me, covering my nakedness. Jeremy wheeled around and ushered the group off to the side. It took a few seconds for them to move, and a few more for them to stop staring.

When the visitors had vanished around the side of the garage, I grabbed Clay's arm and made a run for the back door, not stopping until we were upstairs. Before he could say anything, I shoved him into his room and went to my own. I'd only put on panties and a bra before I heard Clay's door open. Expecting him to head downstairs to confront the trespassers, I hurried to my door and yanked it open, only to find him holding the handle.

"Hey," he said, grinning as he recovered his balance. "If you're that eager to let me into your bedroom, I should offer to make breakfast more often."

"I was— You're not— You're okay?"

"I'm fine, darling. Just coming to round you up for breakfast while Jeremy gets rid of our uninvited guests." He leaned forward, put a hand against my back, and kissed me. "And no, I'm not going out to help him. I'm in too good a mood to let a bunch of humans spoil it. Jeremy can handle them."

"Good," I said, putting my arms around his neck.

"Glad you approve. So let's get breakfast going, then we can dream up a few ways to distract ourselves until Jeremy's ready to tell us how he plans to deal with Marsten and Cain."

As he leaned forward to kiss me again, someone cleared his throat in the doorway. I peeked over Clay's shoulder to see Jeremy there, arms crossed, a slight smile on his lips.

"Sorry to interrupt," he said. "But I need Elena downstairs. Fully dressed if we ever intend to get rid of these men."

"Yes, sir," I said, disentangling myself from Clay. "I'll be right there."

"Hold up," Clay said as Jeremy turned to leave the room. "I need to talk to you."

They left. I could hear Clay apologizing for his behavior the night before, but quickly tuned them out, not wanting to intrude. I finished dressing, ran a brush through my hair, checked in the mirror, then went into the hall. Jeremy and Clay were still there.

"I'll start breakfast," Clay said, heading off down the stairs. "Have fun, darling."

"I'm sure I will," I said. As we went down the steps, I glanced over my shoulder at Jeremy. "Sorry about that. The walking naked from the woods thing. We didn't expect visitors."

"Nor should you," he said, steering me toward the back door. "There's no need to apologize. You should be able to come and go as you like here. It's these damned intrusions that . . ." He shook his head and didn't finish.

"What is it this time?"

"Another missing person."

"The boy from the other day?"

Jeremy shook his head as he held open the back door for me. "This time they're looking for one of the men who came on the property Friday. The middle-aged one. The leader."

"He's missing?"

"Not just missing, but missing after having left a message for a friend saying he was coming here last night to check things again. Something about this place was bothering him. He wanted another look around."

"Oh, shit."

"In a nutshell—exactly."

Mistrust

THERE WERE SIX PEOPLE IN THE SEARCH PARTY, THREE LOCAL COPS and three civilians. Jeremy, Peter, Nick, and I went out to help them look while Antonio returned to the house to keep an eye on Clay, in case his commitment to noninterference didn't last. The four of us played the role of good and concerned citizens, scouring the bushes while keeping our noses on alert for anything we didn't want the searchers to find. One thing I would have rather they hadn't found turned up early in the quest.

"Got something!" one of the men yelled.

"Is it Mike?" another called, rushing from our sides.

As everyone converged on the scene, Nick's voice rang out, choked with barely contained laughter. "Forget it. It's—uh—nothing important."

"What the hell do you mean?" the first man said. "Maybe this is all a joke to you, son, but . . ."

The rest of the sentence trailed off as we burst into the clearing to find one of the searchers bending over a ripped shirt. Torn clothing littered the ground, more hung from bushes. Nick held up half a pair of white panties and grinned at me.

"Wild dogs? Or just Clayton?"

"Oh God," I muttered under my breath.

I walked over to snatch the underwear from him, but he held it over his head, grinning like a schoolboy.

"I see Paris, I see France, I see Elena's underpants," he chanted.

"Everyone's already seen much more than that," Jeremy said. "I think we can safely resume the search."

Peter plucked Clay's shirt from a low-hanging branch and held it up, peering through a hole in the middle. "You guys can really do some damage. Where's the hidden video when you need it?"

"So this—uh—wasn't done by wild dogs?" one of the searchers said.

Peter grinned and tossed the shirt to the ground. "Nope. Just wild hormones."

The other men, who'd finally stopped casting sidelong glances at me after the "naked in the yard" incident, now looked me over with renewed interest. I smiled, trying hard not to bare my teeth, then hurried back into the woods.

Jeremy, two of the searchers, and I were beating the bushes in the northeast quadrant of the woods when we heard another shout, this time infused with enough urgency to make us run. When we got there, Nick and two searchers were standing over a body. Nick looked up, caught my eye and gave me a look that said he'd tried unsuccessfully to distract the men's attention. Jeremy and I walked to the body and looked down. It was the missing man. His shirt collar was torn and drenched with blood. Above the collar his throat was shredded, flaps of flesh hanging from the wound. Empty eye sockets stared up at us. Crows or turkey vultures had found him first, lying exposed in the clearing. Besides taking his eyes, they'd pecked at his face, leaving bloody holes where white bone peeked through. Bits of scattered flesh covered his shirtfront and surrounded his head, as if the searchers had scared the scavengers mid-meal.

"Like the others," one man said, then turned away from the sight.

"One difference," another said. "He wasn't eaten. Not by the dogs at least. Birds got to him though. Buggers don't waste any time."

A younger man bolted for the woods. Seconds later, the sound of retching filled the air. Two of the men shook their heads in sympathy, both looking a little green themselves. My stomach wasn't feeling so great either, though it had nothing to do with seeing a dead body.

When the younger man stopped throwing up, he was quiet a moment, then ran from the thicket.

"Come here! You guys have to see this!"

I knew what he'd found. I knew it and I dreaded stepping into that thicket to confirm my suspicions, but Jeremy prodded me on. When I stepped into the woods, the sickly sweet smell of vomit made my gorge rise. Then I looked down at the ground, following the path of the young man's finger. There, in the damp earth, were paw prints.

"Can you believe the size of those things?" the young man said. "Christ, they're as big as saucers. Just like those kids said. These dogs are huge!"

As I surveyed the thicket, my eyes caught sight of something snagged on a thornbush. A tuft of fur, shining golden even in the shadows. While everyone stared at the paw prints, I slipped over to the bush, stood in front of it, reached behind my back, and slid the fur into my pocket. Then I looked around for more. When I didn't see any, I glanced back at the paw prints, as recognizable as footprints from a familiar pair of shoes. As I stared at them, I felt sick. Then the disappointment turned to something else. Anger.

"I have to go," I muttered, turning from the thicket.

No one tried to stop me, the humans assuming it was a delayed reaction to the sight of the dead man, and the Pack not wanting to make a scene.

"Clayton!" I shouted as the back door slammed behind me.

Clay appeared in the kitchen doorway, wooden spoon in hand. "That didn't take long. Come in and get the coffee going."

I didn't move. "Aren't you going to ask if they found the missing man?"

"That would imply I give a damn."

"They found him."

"Good, so I presume they're leaving. All the better. Now come in and—"

"I found this by the body," I said, pulling the tuft of fur from my pocket.

"Huh. Looks like mine."

"It is yours. Your prints were there, too."

Clay leaned against the doorpost. "My fur and my prints in my forest? Fancy that. I hope you're not implying what I think you're implying, darling, 'cause if you recall, I was with you all last night, which is when Tonio says this guy went missing."

"You weren't with me this morning when I woke up."

Clay sputtered, nearly dropping the spoon. "I was gone five minutes! Five minutes to track and kill a guy? I'm good, but I'm not that good."

"I have no idea how long you were gone."

"Yes, you do, because I'm telling you. Come on, you know I didn't do it. Use your head, Elena. If I lost control and killed this guy, I'd have told you about it. I'd have asked for your help getting rid of the body and deciding what to tell Jeremy. I wouldn't have been frolicking in the pond while some dead human is lying in our forest waiting for another group of hunters to trip over him."

"You didn't expect an immediate search party, so you thought you had more time. You planned to hide the body later, after you got me out of the way."

"That's bullshit and you know it. I don't hide things from you. I don't lie to you. I don't deceive you. Not ever."

I stepped forward, lifting my face to his. "Oh, really? Somehow, I forget the discussion we had before you bit me, when you told me what you were planning to do. Convenient amnesia, I guess."

"I did not plan that," Clay said, looming over me. The wooden spoon snapped in two as he clenched his fist. "We've been through this before. I panicked and—"

"I don't want to hear your excuses."

"You never do, do you? You'd rather talk about things I *didn't* do, then toss that in for good measure when the opportunity arises. Why do I bother defending myself? You've made up your mind about everything I do and don't do, and the reasons I do them. Nothing I can ever say will change that."

He spun on his heel and stalked back to the kitchen. I turned the opposite way, strode into the study, and slammed the door.

As I sat in the study, I realized with some surprise that I had no urge to bolt. My fight with Clay hadn't left me with the usual overwhelming impulse to get free of Stonehaven. Yes, last night had been a mistake, but an instructive one. I'd let down my guard, given in to my most subconscious desire to be with Clay again, and what had happened? Within hours he was lying to me. Even while we'd been together in the woods, while I'd been sleeping, he was off indulging the darkest side of his nature. He wouldn't change. I couldn't change him. He was violent, selfish, and completely untrustworthy. If it took one regrettable night to remind me of that, it'd been worth it.

About twenty minutes later, the study door opened and Nick peeked around. I'd been curled up in Jeremy's armchair. When Nick opened the door, I unfolded myself and straightened up.

"Can I come in?" he asked.

"I smell food. If you can share, you're more than welcome."

He slipped into the room and put a plate of pancakes and ham on the footstool. The pancakes were plain, finger food without butter and syrup. I picked up one and gulped it too fast to taste it, not wanting to remember who'd made them and why.

"All done outside?" I asked.

Nick lowered himself onto the sofa and stretched out. "Pretty much. A couple more cops showed up. Jeremy sent Peter and me in."

Antonio walked through the door. "Are they investigating the scene?" he asked, pushing his son's legs off the sofa and sitting down.

Nick shrugged. "I guess so. They brought cameras and a bag of stuff. Someone from the morgue is on the way to pick up the body."

"Do you think they'll find anything?" Antonio asked me.

"Hopefully nothing that doesn't link this killing to a wild dog," I said. "If it seems clear-cut, they should wrap up the investigation pretty fast and devote their efforts to finding the dogs. No sense wasting time gathering evidence when the presumed killers will never see a courtroom."

"Just the business end of a shotgun," Antonio said. "If they see so much as a flash of fur in the woods, they'll shoot. When we need to run, we're going to have to find someplace far from here and Bear Valley."

"Damn," Nick said, shaking his head. "When we find out who's responsible, they're going to pay for this."

"Oh, I have a good idea who's responsible," I said.

I took the tuft of fur from my pocket and tossed it on the footrest. Nick stared at it a moment, confused. Then his eyes widened and he looked at me. I avoided his gaze, not wanting to see the disbelief I knew would be there. Antonio took one look at the fur, then sat back in his seat, and said nothing.

An hour or so later, I was alone again in the study, the others having drifted off to find less sedentary pursuits or more amiable companionship. As I sat there, my gaze wandered to the desk across the room. The top was still scattered with the piles of papers and anthropology journals Clay hadn't got around to reading yet. They reminded me of how I'd met Clay, how I'd come to be in this mess in the first place. While I was a student at the University of Toronto, I'd had a peripheral interest in anthropology. In my sophomore year I'd done a term paper on anthropomorphic religions, which was Clay's specialty, and I'd referenced enough of his work to recognize his name when I saw a notice on his lecture series in the student paper. His public appearances were so rare that the lecture series had been full and I'd needed to sneak in. Biggest mistake of my life.

I don't know what Clay saw in me to make him overlook his contempt for humans. He says it was a mirroring of something he recognized in himself. That's bullshit, of course. I was nothing like him or, if I was, I became that way after he bit me. Left on my own, I would have grown up, assimilated into the human world, and been a perfectly happy, well-adjusted person, leaving all my childhood baggage and anger behind. I'm sure of it.

"Blood," Clay said, swinging open the study door so hard it smacked against the wall and added to a decade's accumulation of dents. "Where was the blood?"

"What blood?"

"If I killed that guy, I would have had blood on me."

"You washed it off in the pond. That's why you made up the story about checking the water temperature, to explain why you were wet."

"Made up? Why the—" He stopped, inhaled, and started again. "Okay, assuming I cleaned up in the pond and decided it would be easier to invent some excuse for being wet instead of just drying off, you still would have smelled blood on me. The scent wouldn't wash off that easily."

"The smell would be weak. I'd have to be sniffing for it."

"Well, then sniff for it now. Come on." He locked my gaze and held it. "I dare you."

"You've had plenty of time to wash it off."

"Then check my shower. See if it's wet. Check my towels. See if they're damp."

"You'd have covered your tracks by now. You're not stupid."

"No, just stupid enough to leave a body in the woods with my prints and fur scattered all around. Why do I bother? Nothing I can say will change your mind. Do you know why? Because you want to believe I did it. That way, you can hole up in here and dwell on how wrong you were to come to me last night, curse yourself for having given in to me again, for forgetting what a monster I am."

"That's not what I'm—"

"It's not?" He stepped forward. "Look me in the eye and tell me that's not what you've been doing for the last hour."

I glared at him and said nothing. Clay stood there for at least a full minute, then threw up his hands and stormed out.

A while later, Jeremy came in. Without saying anything, he walked to the footrest, picked up the tuft of Clay's hair and looked at it, then put it down and sat in his chair.

"You don't think he did it, do you?" I said.

"If I say no, you'll try to convince me otherwise. If I say yes, you'll use that as ammunition against him. It's not important what I think. What's important is what you think."

"I once went to a therapist who talked like that. I canned him after two sessions."

"I'm sure you did."

I didn't know how to answer that, so I didn't. Instead, I feigned great interest in the patterns of the Turkish floor rug. Jeremy leaned back in his chair and watched me for a while before continuing.

"Have you called him?"

"Who?" I said, though I had a good idea who he meant.

"The man in Toronto."

"He has a name, though I'm sure you already know it."

"Have you called him?"

"I called the day before last. Yesterday was a bit hellish, if you recall, and I've been understandably preoccupied this morning."

"You have to call him every day, Elena. Make sure he knows you're okay. Don't give him any excuse for calling here or showing up."

"He only has my cell phone number."

"I don't care. You can't take any chances. Clay knows he exists, though he's trying to forget. Don't give him any reason to be reminded of it. And don't start accusing me of protecting Clay's feelings. I'm protecting the Pack. We can't afford to have Clay distracted now. And we certainly can't afford to have this man show up on our doorstep. We've had quite enough visitors as it is."

"I'll go call."

"Not yet. I've sent Nick to round up the others for a meeting."

"You can fill me in later."

"A meeting implies a group meeting," Jeremy said. "A group meeting implies that all the members of the group are expected to be there."

"What if I'm not a member of the group?"

"You are as long as you're here."

"I could remedy that."

Jeremy lifted his feet onto the footstool and leaned his head back against the headrest. "Beautiful weather we're having, isn't it?"

"Do you ever discuss anything you don't want to discuss?"

"It's the privilege of age."

I snorted. "It's the privilege of position."

"That, too."

Jeremy's lips curved in the barest of smiles and his black eyes flashed. I recognized the look, but it took me a few minutes to place it. Challenge. He was waiting for me to reengage in a debate we'd been grappling with since I first came to the Pack. As someone who'd once been a human in a democratic society, the idea of an all-powerful, unquestionable leader rankled. How many nights had Jeremy and I spent debating it, here in this room, drinking brandy until I was too tired and drunk to walk up to my room and fell asleep here, only to awaken later in my bed?

I'd missed him. Even now, living in the same house with him for almost five days, I missed him. Everyone else in the Pack had welcomed me back, no questions asked, no grudges held. Not Jeremy. He hadn't been unfriendly or even distant, but he hadn't been himself. He was keeping me at a distance, as if unwilling to recommit himself until he was certain I wasn't going to bolt again. The problem was that I wasn't all that certain of it myself.

I tried to think of a comeback, my brain rusty to the old argument, struggling to remember how it went. As I thought, Jeremy's eyes shuttered and his smile faded. I saw my opportunity skittering past and dove to catch it. As I opened my mouth, ready to say the next thing that came to mind, the door opened. The others came in and my moment alone with Jeremy evaporated.

The first issue of business at the meeting was that Jeremy forbade us to run on the property until this mess with the police had been settled. When the time came for a run we'd all go on a field trip to the northern forests. Now, I have nothing against group runs and, under normal circumstances, I love running as a Pack, but there's something about turning a Pack run into an organized and scheduled event that sucked the pleasure out of it. Next thing you know, we'd be renting a bus, taking bagged lunches, and singing "On Top of Old Smokey" on the way.

Issue two involved Jeremy's next plan of action. Once again, it didn't go over well with Clay. It didn't sit too nicely with me either, but I wasn't the one jumping to my feet and flipping out before Jeremy even finished.

"You can't leave me here," Clay shouted.

Jeremy's eyebrows went up the barest fraction. "I can't?"

"You shouldn't. It's stup— It doesn't make sense."

"It makes perfect sense. And you're not the only one being left behind."

I grumbled, but calmly and quietly and to myself, although Jeremy's eyes did flicker my way as I did it.

Jeremy continued, "I won't have you and Elena coming along when you're at each other like this."

"But I didn't do anything!" Clay said. "You haven't even accused me of killing that guy. You know I didn't do it. So why should I be punished—"

"It's not a punishment. Whether you did it or not doesn't matter. So long as you two are fighting, I want you here, where the only damage you can cause is to each other . . . and assorted pieces of furniture."

"Why leave us both?" I asked.

"Because I don't *need* either of you. I'm not intending to track or fight anyone. It's simple information gathering. Even if you two weren't arguing, I wouldn't take you. It's an unnecessary risk. I want to learn more about these mutts. I don't want to rely on secondhand information, so I'm going myself and I'm taking Tonio and Peter as backup. Nick isn't coming either and I don't hear him complaining."

"It doesn't sound like much fun," Nick said.

Jeremy smiled. "Exactly."

"But—" I said.

"It's past lunchtime," Jeremy said, getting to his feet. "We should eat before we leave."

He left before we could argue, which was probably the point. When he was gone, I got to my feet.

"I guess I'll make myself useful and fix something for lunch."

Nick offered to help. For once, Clay didn't. He didn't even follow us into the kitchen to supervise.

After lunch Jeremy, Antonio, and Peter left for reconnaissance duty. This was Jeremy's way of handling the curveball the mutts had thrown. The Pack was accustomed to dealing with only one mutt at a time. As I've said, mutts didn't team up. Not ever. This meant the Pack was ill-equipped to deal with the threat. Since Jeremy didn't have any experience handling a multiple-mutt onslaught, he was taking his time, gathering information before plotting a course of action. Logically, this made sense. Emotionally, it was infuriating. If I were in charge, I'd have been planning direct and immediate action against the mutts, risks be damned. That was why Jeremy was the Alpha and I was the lowly foot soldier.

Once they were gone, I retreated again, this time to my room, where I called Philip. I told him that I'd be a few days longer.

He inhaled. "Okay." A moment of silence. "I miss you."

"I—"

"I don't mean it as a guilt trip, hon. It's just— I miss you. I know you're doing the right thing and I wouldn't ask you to abandon your cousins. I just—didn't expect it to be this long." He paused, then clicked his tongue. "Got it. Brainstorm. I'll pop out there. How about tomorrow?"

My hands tightened around the receiver, brain shouting, *Oh shit!* I clamped my mouth shut until I'd forced the panic down. "And lose a vacation day?" I said as lightly as I could. "You promised me a week in the Caribbean. All-inclusive resort. Remember? As much as I'd love to see you, if it means giving up a week of all-you-can-drink booze and sun . . ."

He chuckled. "A day helping you baby-sit three kids is a poor substitute, eh? I can see that. Maybe I can swing something with James, work next Saturday instead . . . though it already looked like I'd be working Saturday, and probably Sunday."

"Uh-uh. Don't go making any deals or I may not see you for weeks even after I get home."

"Point taken. I'll survive a few more lonely days. But if it gets longer than that . . ."

"It won't."

We talked for a few more minutes, then signed off. A few more days. No longer. This time, I didn't have a choice. If I didn't get my butt back to Toronto in a few days, Philip might find a way to get that day off and show up in New York. That would be . . . well, it was more than I cared to contemplate.

After talking to Philip, I stretched back in bed and rested, dozing to catch up on two nights of minimal sleep. It didn't work. I worried about the possibility of Philip showing up at Stonehaven and my stress level jumped a half-dozen notches. Then I remembered why I was still at Stonehaven and thought about Logan, feeling the grief ooze back, filling my brain until I could think of nothing else, especially sleep. Finally, Nick came to my rescue, walking into my room unannounced.

"Do you ever knock?" I said, sitting up in bed.

"Never. I'd miss everything if I did that." Pulling back the canopy, he grinned wickedly. "Did I miss anything?"

"Everything."

"Guess I'll have to start something myself then," he said, thumping down beside me on the bed and letting the canopy swing shut. "It's nice in here. Nice and quiet and very private."

"Perfect for sleeping."

"It's too early to sleep. I have something better in mind."

"I'm sure you do."

He grinned and leaned over to kiss me, then ducked out of swatting range. "Actually, I was thinking of something else for a change. Since we're not allowed to run on the property, I thought maybe the three of us could drive somewhere for a run tonight."

"I ran last night."

"But I didn't and I'm going to need to Change soon."

"Then go with Clay. There's no reason all three of us have to go."

"I've already talked to him. He'll only go if you will. He doesn't want anyone staying here alone, in case the mutts make a surprise visit."

"I'm sure they wouldn't—" I stopped myself, realizing I wasn't so sure. The thought sent a chill through me. "Do you have to go tonight? It's been a long day and—"

"I was thinking of a hunt."

"I'm not sure I—"

"A deer hunt."

"Deer?"

He laughed. "Now her ears perk up. How long has it been since you hunted anything bigger than a rabbit? Not on your own, I'll bet."

"He's right." Clay's voice came from the other side of the curtains, startling us both. When I turned, I could see his silhouette, but he didn't pull the canopy back.

"A hunt would be a good idea," Clay continued. "Keep us busy while we're waiting for Jeremy. Nick needs to Change and he can't do that here. I'm not leaving you behind by yourself, Elena. I'm sure you can stomach my company for an hour or two."

I opened my mouth to reply, but he'd already left. I hesitated for a moment, then turned to Nick and nodded. He grinned and bounced from the room, leaving me to follow.

Stalking

WE TOOK MY CAR. NICK DROVE, AND CLAY SAT UP FRONT WITH him. I took the backseat and dozed so I wouldn't be expected to join in the conversation. I needn't have worried; Clay wasn't about to engage me in idle discussion, and Nick filled the void by chattering to anyone who would listen.

Nick was talking about his latest business venture, something to do with e-commerce and a new company he was backing. The question wasn't whether Nick's new venture would succeed, but how much it would lose. Exact dollar figures weren't important, since the Sorrentinos were wealthy enough to make Jeremy look middle-class. Antonio ran three multinational businesses. Nick had inherited none of his father's Midas touch. In fact, he'd been banned from all Antonio's business ventures. Nick was a playboy, plain and simple. He dabbled in an unending series of attempts at starting his own company, all of which succeeded in winning him nothing but friends and lovers, which was all he really wanted from life. How did Antonio react to this, watching his son squander his fortune? He encouraged it. Antonio recognized this lifestyle was the only thing Nick was truly qualified for, and if it made him happy and they could afford it, why not? Having scrimped and saved pennies for most of my life, I couldn't understand that philosophy. I envied it; not the idea of having so much money that you could throw it away, but the thought of growing up in a world where someone cared so much about your happiness and so little about what you accomplished in life.

Nick drove to the outskirts of a forest we'd used before. He took my car past a barricade and down an abandoned logging road, grounding out the bottom more times than I cared to count. My car wasn't in the greatest of shape and I suspected the undercarriage was more rust than steel, though I'd never worked up the nerve to test my theory. Jeremy kept offering to restore it for me or, better yet, buy me something else. I put up enough of a fuss that he was never tempted to surprise me with a new or newly restored car. Not that I'd mind getting my Camaro fixed up, if only to prolong its usefulness, but I was terrified that if I let Jeremy near it, it would come back a lovely shade of Mary Kay pink.

Farther into the forest, Nick stopped the car and put it in park. The engine died with a very unhealthy thunk. I tried not to think about that, namely because it might imply that it wouldn't start up again and that would definitely be a bad thing, stuck in backwoods New York, out of cell phone range, with a dead car and two guys who didn't know motor oil from antifreeze.

As we walked into the woods, Nick continued to talk.

"After this mess is cleaned up, we should do something. Go somewhere. Like a vacation. Maybe Europe. Clayton was supposed to go skiing with me in Switzerland this winter, but he backed out."

"I didn't back out," Clay said. He was walking ahead of us, cutting a path through the overgrown brush, maybe being helpful, more likely so he wasn't walking with me. "I never said I'd go."

"Yes, you did. At Christmas. I had to hunt you down to ask you." Nick turned to me. "He barely showed his face the whole week the Pack was at Stonehaven. He was holed up with his books and papers. He kept expecting you to show up and when you didn't—" At a look from Clay, Nick stopped. "Anyway, you did say you'd come skiing. I asked you and you grunted something that sure sounded like a yes."

"Huh."

"Exactly. Just like that. Okay, it wasn't really a yes, but it wasn't a no either. So you owe me a trip. The three of us will go. Where do you want to go when this is all over, Elena?"

"Toronto" was on the tip of my tongue, but I didn't say it. Squashing Nick's plans when he was trying so hard to smooth things over was like telling your kid there was no Santa Claus just because you had a bad day at work. It wasn't fair and he didn't deserve it.

"We'll see," I said.

Clay looked sharply over his shoulder and met my eyes. He knew exactly what I meant. With a scowl, he shoved a branch out of the way, then stalked off to find a place for his Change.

"I'm not sure this is such a good idea," I said to Nick after Clay was gone. "Maybe I should wait in the car."

"Come on. Don't do that. You can blow off some steam. Just ignore him."

I agreed. Well, I didn't actually agree, but Nick took off before I could argue and he had my car keys.

Just ignore Clay. Good advice. Really, really good advice. For practicality, though, it ranked up there with telling an acrophobic "just don't look down."

When I stepped from the thicket after my Change, Clay was there. He stood back, nose twitching. Then his mouth fell open, tongue lolling out in a wolf-grin as if we'd never argued. I searched for my own anger, knowing it should be there, but unable to find it, as if I'd left it in the thicket beside my discarded clothes.

I eyed Clay for a moment, then cautiously started to skirt around him. I was almost past him when he twisted and lunged sideways, grabbing my hind leg and yanking it out from under me. As I tumbled down, he jumped on top of me. We rolled through the underbrush, knocking into a sapling and sending a squirrel scampering for a steadier perch, chattering its annoyance as it ran. When I finally got out from under him, I leapt to my feet and ran. Behind me, Clay crashed through the brush. After no more than ten yards, I heard a yelp, then felt the ground shudder as Clay fell. I glanced over my shoulder to see him snapping and tugging at a vine caught around his forepaw. I slowed to turn around and go back for him, then saw him break free and lunge into a run. Realizing I was losing my lead, I turned forward and plowed into something solid, somersaulting over it and into a patch of nettles.

I looked up from my crash landing to see Nick standing over me. With a growl and as much dignity as I could muster, I got to my feet. Nick stood back and watched, eyes laughing as I disentangled myself from the nettles. Out of the corner of my eye, I saw Clay sneak up behind Nick. He crouched, forequarters down, rear end in the air. Then he pounced, knocking Nick flying into the nettles. As Nick was struggling to stand, I walked by him with a "serves you right" snort. He grabbed my foreleg and yanked me down. We tussled for a minute before I managed to get free and dart behind Clay.

While Nick extricated himself from the nettles, Clay rubbed his muzzle against mine, hot breath ruffling the fur around my neck. Nick walked around us, rubbing and sniffing a greeting. When he lingered too long sniffing near my tail, Clay growled a warning and he backed off.

After a couple of minutes, we pulled apart and began to run, Clay and I jostling for the lead, Nick content to stay at our heels. The forest was rife with smells, including the musky scent of deer, but most of it was old trails and long-dried spoor. We'd gone about a half mile before I caught the scent we wanted. Fresh deer. With a spurt of energy, I raced forward. Behind me, Nick and Clay ran through the woods in near silence. Only the rustle of dead undergrowth beneath their feet betrayed them. Then the wind changed and drove the scent of deer full in our faces. Nick yelped and raced up beside me, trying to take the lead. I snapped at him, catching a chunk of dark fur as he scrambled out of my way.

As I dealt with Nick, I realized Clay wasn't right behind us. I slowed, then turned and went back. He was standing about twenty feet away, nose twitching as he sniffed the air. As I loped over, he caught my eye and I knew why he'd stopped. We were close enough. It was time to plan. It might seem silly to think of deer as dangerous, but we're not human hunters who never get within a hundred feet of their prey. A slash of antlers can lay a wolf open. A well-aimed hoof can split a skull. There was a twelve-inch scar on Clay's thigh where he'd had his flank sliced by a hoof. Even real wolves know that a deer hunt requires caution and planning.

Planning obviously didn't mean discussing the matter, since such high-level communication was impossible as wolves. Unlike humans, though, we had something better: instinct and a brain ingrained with patterns that had proven successful for thousands of generations. We could assess the situation, recall a plan, and communicate it with a look. Or, at least, Clay and I could. Like many werewolves, Nick either wasn't in tune with the messages his wolf brain sent or his human brain didn't trust them. It didn't matter. Clay and I were the Alpha pair there, so Nick would follow orders without needing an explanation.

I walked to the east, sniffed the air and caught the deer's scent again. A lone stag. That meant we didn't have to worry about cutting a deer from a herd. Still, a stag was more dangerous than a doe, especially one with a full set of antlers. Clay moved up beside me and sniffed for the deer, then caught my eye with a look that said "what the hell, you only live once." I snorted my agreement and walked back to Nick. Clay didn't follow. He slipped into the forest again and vanished. The plan was set.

Nick and I circled through the woods, getting downwind before following the scent again. We found the stag grazing in a thicket. As Nick waited for the signal, he nudged me and rubbed against me, whining too low for the buck to hear. I growled low in my throat and he stopped. The stag lifted its head and looked around. When it returned to its feeding, I crouched and sprang. The deer paused only a millisecond before leaping over the bushes and breaking into a gallop. Nick and I tore after it, but the gap between us and the deer grew. Wolves are distance runners, not sprinters, and our only chance to catch a running deer from behind is to wear it down.

As often happened, the deer made the fatal error of throwing his energy into the opening spurt. We hadn't gone far when he started to slow, wheezing and snorting for breath, too frightened to pace himself. I was getting winded, too, having already expended a fair amount of energy finding and chasing the stag. What kept me going was the smell of the buck, the musky, tantalizing odor that made my stomach rumble.

I found Clay's scent in the air, and ran the deer toward him by veering out one way with a short burst of speed that sent it flying in the opposite direction. As we ran, the stag's fear escalated into panic. It galloped full-out, vaulting fallen trees and careering through undergrowth. The trees and bushes tore at its hide and the scent of blood seeped into the air. As we rounded a corner, Clay lunged from the bushes and caught the deer by the nose.

The stag slid to a halt and shook its head wildly, trying to dislodge Clay. Meanwhile, we caught up. I darted under the deer and sank my teeth into its stomach. I tasted the hot blood under a layer of fat and my mouth began to water. Nick attacked the deer's side, lunging and biting and skittering out of the way before the deer could aim a hoof or antler in his direction. Clay was being tossed from side to side, but he hung on. This was a ploy dredged up from deepest memory: bite the face of your prey and it'll be too busy trying to free itself from the most obvious danger to bother with the other attackers.

As I clung to the stag's underbelly, I ripped and sliced, dancing on my hind legs to keep out of hoofs' reach. When I'd torn a gaping hole, I released my grip and clamped down farther up. Entrails began to slide from the first hole and the smell nearly drove me mad. Blood was also dripping from Nick's lightning attacks, making the stag's coat slick and difficult to grasp. I bit harder, feeling my teeth slide through the skin into vital organs. At last the deer's front legs slid forward. Clay released his grip on its nose and tore into its throat. The deer thudded to the ground.

Once the deer was down, Nick backed off and found a place nearby to lie down. Clay lowered his head and looked at me. His muzzle was stained with blood. I licked it and rubbed against him, feeling the shudders of spent adrenaline coursing through him. Below us, the stag's limbs were still quivering, but its eyes stared forward, all life gone. As we tore into its side, steam swirled into the cool evening air. We began to feast, tearing off chunks of meat and gulping them whole.

When we'd eaten our fill, Nick approached and began to feed. Clay walked to a clearing and looked over his shoulder at me. I followed and dropped down beside him. Clay shifted closer, put one paw around my neck and started to lick my muzzle. I closed my eyes as he worked. When he'd cleaned the blood from my neck and shoulders, I worked on him. Once Nick finished eating, he curled up with us and we drifted off to sleep in a huddle of intertwined limbs and varicolored fur.

We hadn't been napping long when Clay jumped up, spilling Nick and me to the ground. I snapped awake when my head struck a rock. I scrambled to my feet, tense and looking for danger. We were alone in the clearing. Night had fallen, bringing with it only nocturnal sounds of nature, the calls of the hunters and the shrieks of the hunted. I growled at Clay and started settling back down to my nap. He knocked me in the ribs with his muzzle and made a show of sniffing the air. I glared at him, but did as he asked. At first, I smelled nothing. Then the wind shifted and I knew what had made him jump up. Someone was here. Another werewolf. Zachary Cain.

Clay was gone as soon as he knew that I understood. Behind me, Nick was still shaking off the groggy haze of interrupted sleep. I glanced back at him, then started to run, knowing he'd follow even if he wasn't sure why. At the edge of the clearing, Cain's smell grew stronger. I followed my nose to a thicket nearby. The trampled and flattened grass reeked of Cain's scent. He'd been lying here, close enough to us that he could stick his muzzle through the brambles and watch us sleep. Something about that scenario jarred, but I wasn't sure why. The human part of me wanted to sit back and contemplate the problem, but the wolf instinct shut my brain down and propelled my feet to action. There was an intruder to be dealt with.

Even if I hesitated near the thicket, Nick didn't. He stuck his nose in, took a deep breath, backed out, and raced after Clay. For once, I was left bringing up the rear. The other two were so far gone, I couldn't see or hear them and had to follow Clay's trail. It wove deeper into the woods, through trees so dense that they snuffed out the moon and stars. As good as my night vision was, I needed some light, even reflected light, with which to work. Here there was nothing. I could make out only the looming shapes of tree trunks and bushes, dark shadows against a darker canvas. Slowing, I put my nose to the ground and relied on Clay's trail instead.

On the other side of the dense hollow, the trees opened up to let in some moonlight. As I picked up speed, bushes crackled to the north, something big breaking through the undergrowth. It wasn't Clay or Nick. Even Nick moved through the woods with more finesse than that. Leaving Clay's trail, I veered north. I'd run about a quarter mile when I felt the vibration of running paws hitting the ground somewhere behind me. That was Clay and Nick. I recognized them without looking, so I didn't slow down. Since I was cutting the trail, though, I wasn't running as fast as they were, and before long, I heard Clay's rhythmic breathing at my heels. We skirted a large outcropping of rock. Branches snapped somewhere behind us. Twisting around, I saw a huge reddish-brown shadow burst from behind the rock and run in the opposite direction.

I dug my claws into the soft ground to stop, then pivoted and raced after Cain. Only one pair of footfalls followed: Nick. Clay was gone, taking another route in hopes of cutting Cain off like he had the stag. Cain followed the trail I'd cut, looping back the way he'd come. After a quarter mile, he swerved to the east. He was heading for the road, hoping to escape. I shot forward and got close enough for his tail hairs to brush my muzzle. Then my paw caught on an indentation in the ground, not a hole or anything large enough to make me trip, just the barest change in elevation that slowed me down enough for Cain to get that extra foot ahead. Nick raced up from behind me. As he started to overtake me, I eased back to conserve my energy. Ahead, the forest opened up as we approached the road. I swung to the left, hoping to gain a few feet by anticipating Cain's route. He didn't turn, though. He kept running, back into the forest.

Seeing what Cain was doing, I looked ahead and saw a clearer patch of land to the northwest. When Cain didn't head that way, I did. Nick stayed on Cain's tail, not so much trying to catch him as hoping to run him into the ground. My path led to a rocky hill. As I climbed it, I picked up traces of Clay's scent. The terrain got rougher as I ran, slowing me and making me curse my choice of shortcuts. Halfway up the hill, my forepaw slipped on some stones, one of them sharp enough to slice through my foot pads. I grunted, but kept moving. Once I was at the top of the hill, my effort seemed worthwhile. From here I could look down and see the whole terrain. To the east, I caught a flash of gold as Clay weaved through the trees. As a nearly black wolf, Nick wasn't so easy to spot at night, but after a moment, I saw some trees shake below me. I followed the path of the rustling trees and bushes. They were coming this way. I traced the line of their route and moved to the spot where I guessed they'd come out. I was rewarded by the crashing of undergrowth directly in front of me. Seconds later, a massive shape shot through the brush.

Seeing me in his path, Cain stopped. He growled and dropped his head. His green eyes blazed and his dark blond fur stood on end, adding a couple inches to his size. The extra size was superfluous; Cain didn't need it to look imposing. As a human, he stood over six-five, with the shoulders and sheer bulk of an all-star quarterback. As a wolf, he was literally more than twice my size. I pulled back my lips and snarled, but felt about as threatening as a Pomeranian facing down a pit bull. One part of my brain, soaring on adrenaline, insisted I could take Cain, whatever the size difference. Another part wondered where the hell Nick and Clay were. The loudest part just shouted: Run, you idiot, run!

As I was thinking this, Cain suddenly turned and . . . ran. For a moment, I couldn't move, unable to believe my eyes. Cain was running? From me? No matter how much my ego liked to think he was afraid of me, common sense told me otherwise. So why did he bolt? Again, my wolf instincts wouldn't let my brain ponder the question. As Cain disappeared down the hill, my instincts kicked in and I started after him.

I'd gone maybe a dozen feet when something landed on my back, knocking my legs from under me. I twisted to see Clay standing over me. I tried scrambling to my feet, but he held me down. Was he crazy? Cain was getting away. I snapped at him, catching his foreleg in my jaws and clamping down, growling. He grabbed me under the throat and pinned me. With each second, I pictured Cain getting farther away. I struggled, but Clay fought back and kept me down. Finally, I knew it was too late. Cain was gone. For a second, Clay hesitated. Then he bounded off, not after Cain, but in the opposite direction. When I was back on my feet, I raced after him. I followed his scent fifty feet to a clearing where I could smell his clothing. This was where we'd first Changed. I poked my muzzle through the undergrowth to see Clay in the midst of his Change, his back arched, his skin throbbing and pulsing, too immersed in the transformation to notice me. I paused, uncertain. Then I found my own clothes and Changed back.

When I stormed from the clearing, Clay was already there.

"Where's Nick?" Clay said before I could say anything. "Goddamn it! He's got the keys. Wasn't he right behind you?"

"What are you talking about?"

Clay strode into the bushes, looking around. "Don't you get it? He was distracting us, keeping us busy."

"Nick?"

"Cain." Clay was out of sight now, only his voice echoing from the forest. "We were asleep and he didn't attack us. We chased him and he didn't fight or try to escape. He just kept us going in circles. Nicholas!"

"But why—"

"Jeremy. They've gone after Jeremy. Goddamn it! They've probably been watching the house and we didn't even— There you are!"

"Hold on," Nick's voice emerged from the darkness. "Can I have a second to do up my pants?"

Clay crashed from the bush, dragging Nick by one arm. "To the car. Both of you. Move!"

We moved.

Ambush

ON THE WAY TO BEAR VALLEY, CLAY DROVE, NICK TOOK THE BACK-seat, and I sat up front where the safety restraints were better. As I'd feared, the Camaro wasn't eager to restart. When it hesitated, Clay rammed the gas pedal to the floor, revved the engine into the red zone, then slammed the gearshift into reverse, ignoring the clanking sounds coming from under the hood. Forced into a battle of wills, the car surrendered and meekly let him drive the shit out of it all the way to Bear Valley.

"No, take the next exit," I said as Clay started turning off the first road to Bear Valley. "Head for the east end. To the hotel."

"Hotel?"

"There's no sense chasing our tails all over Bear Valley if the mutts haven't even left their hotel room. If they are gone, maybe I can track them from there."

Clay's hands tightened on the steering wheel. I knew he was certain the mutts had gone after Jeremy and checking the hotel only meant precious minutes lost. Still, it made sense. Instead of answering me, he veered back onto the highway, darting in front of a fully loaded logging truck. I closed my eyes for the rest of the ride.

When we got to the motor lodge, Clay whipped the car into the handicapped spot beside the lobby and was flying out of his seat before the engine died. I grabbed the car keys from the ignition and went after him. This time, he made no effort to fool the desk clerk. Luckily, there wasn't anyone behind the desk. Clay ran up the stairs two at a time. At LeBlanc's room, he snapped the freshly repaired lock and barreled through the door without waiting to see if anyone was on the other side. I was mounting the last steps when he came out.

"Gone," he said, pushing past me back down the stairs. About halfway down, he realized I was still going up and turned around. "I said, they're gone."

"This isn't the only room," I said. "Marsten wouldn't be caught dead camping out on anyone's floor."

Clay growled something, but I was already heading down the hall, pausing at each door and trying to pick up Cain's or Marsten's scent. Clay came back up the stairs and strode down the hall toward me.

"We don't have time—"

"Then go," I said. "Just go."

He didn't. Three rooms past LeBlanc's, I stopped.

"Cain," I said, reaching for the door handle.

"Got it. Keep moving and find Marsten's."

Marsten had the next room down. While Clay was still checking Cain's room, I broke open Marsten's door and walked inside. Except for the Italian leather suitcase in the corner, the room looked uninhabited. The bed was made, the tables were spotless, and the towels were all neatly hung on the rack. Definitely Karl Marsten's room. If he had to stoop to taking a room in the Big Bear Motor Lodge, he wouldn't spend any more time there than necessary. I was about to leave the room when I caught another familiar scent.

"Jeremy," Clay said from behind me as he stepped into the room.

"He's gone," I said. "He must have been here checking things out."

Clay nodded and brushed past me on his way out the door. We went back to the car. Next, Clay cruised the parking lots looking for the Mercedes or the Acura. Actually, "cruise" is misleading; I should say he ripped into the lots, circled around sharp enough to induce whiplash, and tore out again. In the parking lot behind Drake's Family Wear, we found Marsten's Acura.

I was only guessing that the Acura belonged to Marsten, but it was a pretty safe bet. LeBlanc may have had a steady income while he was living in Chicago, but by the looks of his hotel room, he wasn't shelling out the big bucks on luxury cars these days. Marsten, on the other hand, was very successful at his career . . . if you call thievery a career. Stealing was the number one occupation among mutts. Their lifestyle didn't encourage them to stay in one town long enough to settle into a job. Even if they were inclined to lay down roots, it wouldn't last. The Pack routinely rousted mutts who seemed to be settling into a non-nomadic lifestyle. Making a home for oneself meant claiming territory and only the Pack could claim territory. So most mutts wandered from city to city, stealing enough to stay alive. Some did better than that. Marsten specialized in jewels, namely jewels from the necks and bedrooms of lonely middle-aged dowagers. He had money and he considered himself a cut above other werewolves. It didn't matter to the Pack that he could speak five languages and didn't touch wine younger than he was. A mutt was a mutt.

Clay slowed down behind the Acura, then hit the gas, and swung from the parking lot.

"We aren't tracking them?" Nick asked, leaning over the seat.

"I don't care where *they* are. I care where Jeremy is."

We found Antonio's Mercedes a couple blocks away in the paper-mill parking lot. This trail was easy for me to follow, the scents being so familiar that I could let my brain process on autopilot while I concentrated on looking ahead for clues.

The trail looped past the local newspaper office, The Donut Hole, the warehouse where the rave had been held, and a country-and-western bar just off the main street. I could follow Jeremy's logic as we passed each point: the paper for late-breaking news, the coffee shop for gossip, and the warehouse for any overlooked clues. The tavern was a bit trickier, until I picked up the acrid scent of stale urine where Cain had pissed on the rear wall, presumably after a round of drinking the night before. From there, the trail headed back toward the paper mill where Antonio's car was parked.

"They're heading back," Nick said. "I bet we just missed them."

We went about five steps when a cat hissed at us from a pile of garbage. Nick hissed back. The cat's eyes narrowed, tail shooting up into an affronted exclamation mark.

"Leave the kitty alone," I said. "He's too skinny to be more than a mouthful and a stringy one at that."

As I turned, I saw something sticking out from under the bags of garbage. At first it looked like a row of four pale pebbles peeking out from between two bags. The sight was so out of place that I stepped toward it, ignoring the reek of garbage that overpowered everything else. As I drew closer, I realized what I was really seeing: fingertips.

"Shit," I muttered. "Look at this. Either those mutts are getting careless with their kills or they're leaving them lying around on purpose."

"Twenty bucks on the latter," Clay said.

He stepped forward and nudged the top bag back for a better view. The fingertips were attached to a hand, which was attached to an arm. As Clay heaved the bag up, the lower bag slid out and the body tumbled to the ground. It rolled onto its back. The man's head lolled to the side at an impossible angle, neck broken. Unruly red hair glittered even in the dark.

"Peter," I whispered.

"No," Clay said. "Jeremy. No!"

Clay shot off into the darkness, running footsteps echoing down the alley. Nick's eyes widened and met mine. Then something behind them clicked as he remembered that Jeremy hadn't been the only one with Peter. He raced after Clay. I paused to hide Peter's body, then ran after them, my heart pounding so hard I couldn't breathe, gasping and choking for air as I ran. Twenty feet away, I saw a pool of thick red glimmering under the sick light of a half-dead light. From it, trails of blood tentacled out, then converged in a single thread leading into the distance. I followed the trail. Ahead, Nick's white shirt bobbed against the blackness. I could hear Clay's footfalls, but couldn't see him. The blood trail wove around two corners. As I wheeled around the second, I saw Clay and Nick just ahead, both stopping and circling back. They'd run past the trail, which ended in a puddle of blood just past the corner.

I bent, put a finger to the blood, then lifted it to my nose.

"Is it?" Clay asked.

"Jeremy's," I whispered.

"And there's plenty more here if you'd like a closer look," a deep voice said.

Clay's head shot up. We looked around, then saw a loading dock to our right. Clay hopped onto the three-foot-high ledge and disappeared into the darkness of the opening. Nick and I followed. At the back of the loading dock, Jeremy sat in the corner, propping his right leg on a broken crate as Antonio tore strips from his shirt. As we approached, Jeremy lifted his left arm to push his bangs back from his face, then winced and used his right hand instead, letting the left fall awkwardly to his side.

"Are you okay?" I asked.

"Peter's dead," Jeremy said. "We were ambushed."

"We were heading back to the car," Antonio said as he added another layer of bindings to Jeremy's leg. "I took off to find a bathroom. Five minutes. I must have barely turned the corner and—" He kept his eyes on his task, but self-reproach leached from every word. "Less than five minutes. While I'm taking a damned piss-break—"

"They were waiting for an opportunity," Jeremy said. "Any of us could have turned our back for a moment and they would have attacked the other two."

Antonio glanced over his shoulder as he worked. "The new one, the mutt that killed Logan, attacked Jeremy with a knife."

"A knife?" Clay glanced at Jeremy for affirmation, as disbelieving as if Antonio had said Jeremy was attacked with an antique Howitzer. "A knife?"

Jeremy nodded.

Antonio continued, "They jumped Peter and Jeremy. No one had time to react. When I showed up they took off. I'd have gone after them, but Jeremy was bleeding pretty badly."

"Not that I would have let you go after them anyway," Jeremy said. "We don't have time to rehash events now. We need to get things cleaned up and go."

He started getting to his feet. Clay hopped over a crate and helped him up.

"We left Peter at the scene," Jeremy said.

"I know," I said. "We found him."

"In the garbage," Antonio said, wiping a hand over his face. "That wasn't right. I'm sorry, but Jeremy was bleeding and I—"

"You needed to find a quick hiding spot," Jeremy finished. "No one's blaming you for that. We'll get him now and take him home."

Clay helped Jeremy down from the dock. I moved up on his left side to take his other arm, then remembered it was injured and settled for walking beside him, ready to catch him if his leg gave out. I gave Nick my car keys and he ran ahead to back up the Camaro to the end of the alley. When we got to the garbage heap, Antonio uncovered Peter and cleaned him off.

"Marsten's going to pay for this," Clay said, looking at Peter's body, hands clenching and unclenching at his sides. "He's really going to pay."

"Marsten didn't kill Peter. Daniel did."

"Dan—" Clay choked on the rest of the name. "Ah, shit."

I rode back to Stonehaven in Antonio's Mercedes, sitting in the backseat with Jeremy, in case the bleeding worsened. Antonio drove in silence. Jeremy stared out the window while holding the bindings tight on his leg. I tried to concentrate on something other than watching my car through the windshield and thinking about Peter's body in my trunk. Instead, I thought about the mutts.

So it was Daniel after all. That meant trouble. Big trouble. More than Marsten or Cain, Daniel knew how the Pack operated, how everyone in it operated. He'd been Pack, having grown up with Nick and Clay . . . or, more accurately, he grew up around them, "with them" sounding as if the three had been buddies, a definite misconception. Now, before Clay's arrival, Nick and Daniel had been semi-playmates, thrown together by their closeness in age, like two cousins who play with each other at family reunions because there's no one else to hang around with. Then came Clay. I was a bit fuzzy on the details, but I'd been told that Clay and Daniel loathed each other from the beginning.

The precipitating event seemed to have occurred when Daniel eavesdropped on Nick and Clay's conversation and raced off to regale the Pack with the story of Clay's expulsion from kindergarten, which had something to do with dissecting the classroom guinea pig to see how it worked, but like I said, I was fuzzy on the details—when I asked Clay about it, all he'd say was "it was already dead," which was apparently supposed to explain everything. Whatever the story, it embarrassed Jeremy, who'd been fudging the details when explaining to the others why Clay's school career had lasted only a month. By upsetting Jeremy, Daniel had earned Clay's eternal rancor.

In the years to follow the relationship between the two only grew more acrimonious as Daniel and Clay fought for supreme position among the younger generation. Or, I should say, Daniel fought for it. Clay simply assumed it was his and squashed Daniel's aspirations with the lazy contempt of someone batting away a mosquito. When the three were in their early twenties, Jeremy became Alpha. I may have given the impression that this was a bloodless ascension. It wasn't. Seven members of the Pack backed Jeremy and four didn't, including Daniel and his brother Stephen. The dissension crescendoed when Stephen tried to assassinate Jeremy. Clay killed him. Daniel insisted his brother had been innocent and that Clay had murdered him to quell opposition to Jeremy's leadership. When Jeremy was confirmed Alpha, Daniel decided there wasn't a place for him in the new Pack.

Unfortunately for all, that wasn't the end of the story. Even if they were no longer Pack brothers, Daniel and Clay had had plenty of runins since that time. After I came along, things got even worse. Daniel decided he absolutely had to have me, if only because I "belonged" to his archrival. When Daniel first approached me, I even thought he was a decent guy. I believed his stories about being mistreated and maligned by Clay—at the time I was quite happy to believe anything bad about Clay. One day I was in San Diego with Antonio delivering a warning to another mutt and, knowing Daniel had been living there a few months, I slipped away from Antonio to say hello to Daniel. When I got to his apartment, I caught him trying to hide a woman in the closet. It wouldn't have been so bad if the woman was still alive. Apparently, she had been, right up until I rang the doorbell, upon which Daniel snapped her neck and tried to stuff her into a closet so I wouldn't find him with someone. After that, I'd put a lot more credence in Clay's warnings about Daniel.

The woman in the closet wasn't the first of Daniel's kills. When he'd left the Pack, he'd abandoned its teachings and become a man-killer. Like all successful—and long-lived—man-killing mutts, Daniel learned the trick to killing humans, the same trick a wolf uses when confronted with a large herd of prey: cull from the edges. If you stick with the marginalized—the drug users, the teenage runaways, the prostitutes, the homeless—you stand a good chance of getting away with it. Why? Because nobody gives a damn. Oh sure, they say they do, the police and the politicians and everyone who's supposed to uphold justice, but they really don't. People can vanish and, so long as they stay gone, nobody will care. I'm not talking about third-world dictatorships or even American metropolises infamous for their crime rates. Vancouver had over twenty prostitutes disappear from a single neighborhood before authorities began to suspect a problem. Trust me, if these women had been students at the University of British Columbia, people would have perked up a whole lot quicker. That's where Thomas LeBlanc went wrong, picking the daughters and wives of middle-class families as his prey. If he'd stuck to hookers and runaways, he'd still be doing a booming business in Chicago. In all my arguments with Jeremy over the unfairness of the Pack's hierarchical system, I'd upheld the human democratic model for comparison, where everyone was supposedly equally important. It was bullshit, of course. Even though the Pack had a strict hierarchy, it would never let even the death of its omega member go unavenged.

Back at the house, Jeremy asked me to help dress his wounds. Maybe he assumed I'd be a gentler, more tolerable nurse than the men. Right. Jeremy may not have known much about women, but he'd learned enough about this particular one never to mistake me for Betty Crocker, Martha Stewart, or Florence Nightingale. More likely he thought that, given the choice between nursing and gravedigging, I'd be much happier donning a cute little white hat and dress. My last graveside episode wasn't one I cared to repeat any sooner than necessary. At least if I was looking after Jeremy, I could block out what was going on in the back field.

Normally, Jeremy would be the one doing the nursing. He was the Pack doctor. No, that wasn't a time-honored role passed down through generations of werewolves. It was something Jeremy took on when, as a child, Clay jumped five stories down a department-store elevator shaft (don't ask) and fractured his arm in several places. Not wanting to risk Clay's future mobility on a makeshift splint, Jeremy took him to a doctor. Although he was careful, citing religious reasons for not wanting blood work and other routine lab tests done, the doctor did them anyway. The results might have gone ignored, having little to do with a broken arm, but a bored lab technician on the night shift spotted something peculiar in the workups and called Jeremy at two A.M. Werewolf blood is screwed up. Don't ask me for the exact details—I barely passed tenth-grade biology. All I know is that we aren't supposed to let anyone draw and analyze our blood. Whatever the technician saw in Clay's workup made him think Clay had some life-threatening condition and he ordered Jeremy to bring Clay to the hospital immediately. The upshot of the whole mess was that both the technician and Clay's file were missing when the day shift arrived. After that, Jeremy bought and studied a shelf full of medical books. A few years ago I made the mistake of giving him a copy of the *St. John Ambulance Official Wilderness First Aid Guide*. He'd liked it so much he had me buy copies for all of us so we could keep them in our glove boxes and fix our own emergency amputations. Call me a wimp, but if I ever lose a limb and there's no one around, I'm a goner, even if the guide does have wonderful instructions (complete with helpful illustrations) for tying off the injury with a stick and a plastic garbage bag.

"Leg first?" I asked Jeremy as he took his box of medical supplies from the bathroom closet.

"Arm. I'll get the bone in place. You splint it."

That didn't sound too bad. Jeremy sat on the toilet seat and I crouched beside him as we worked. It was a clean break, not an open fracture, so there wasn't any of that nasty pulling the bone back under the skin stuff required. The break was just below his elbow. After he got it realigned, I placed the padded splint under his arm. Then I got the bandage roll out. Following Jeremy's instructions, I bound it first below his elbow, then above his wrist. Then I fashioned a sling to keep his arm elevated. It took a while, but it was fairly easy . . . compared to what he wanted me to do next.

"You'll need to stitch up my leg," he said.

"Stitch . . . ?"

"I can't do it with one hand." He stood and leaned against the vanity, undoing his jeans with his good hand, then struggling to get them off. "I could use some help with this, too, if it's not too much to ask."

"Sure," I said. "Undressing men, I'm good at. Sewing people up, though, is questionable. Maybe the cut isn't that bad."

I unwound the blood-soaked strips of Antonio's shirt from Jeremy's thigh. The skin and muscle parted like the Red Sea, an even more apt analogy considering the gush of blood that streamed out. I had no problem seeing Jeremy with his pants off, but this internal view was more than I wanted to see of anyone.

"Grab the facecloth," he said, sitting quickly and shoving a towel against the gash.

I wet the cloth, cleaned the wound, then applied antiseptic. I didn't work as fast as I should have, and by the time I was finishing, blood was gushing over my fingers.

"Get the tape," Jeremy said. "No, not that tape. The other—right."

Using the tape and some fancy maneuvering, we got the blood flow stopped before Jeremy passed out. He took something that looked remarkably like a needle and thread from the kit and handed it to me.

"Stop backing away, Elena. It's not going to bite. Take the needle and start. Don't think about it. Just try to make a reasonably straight line."

"Sounds easy, but you never saw my home economics projects."

"No, but I've had the privilege of experiencing your haircuts. As I said, *try* to make a straight line."

"I always cut your hair straight."

"If I hold my head on a certain angle, it's perfectly straight."

"Watch it. I've got a needle."

"And maybe if I get you mad enough, you'll actually jab me with it and get to work before I bleed out."

I took the hint. Despite what Jeremy said, it was not like sewing fabric nor could I pretend that it was. Cloth doesn't bleed. I concentrated on doing a good job, knowing that if I didn't, I'd be razzed about Jeremy's crooked scar for the rest of my life. It was nearly done when I felt a rush of anger that some mutt had dared do this to Jeremy, which made me think about how it had happened, which made me remember that Peter was dead. First Logan. Now Peter. Of all the Pack, they deserved it least. Jeremy never sent them to roust or kill any mutts, not even to deliver warnings. Their deaths weren't about revenge. They weren't about taking out the Pack's strongest fighters. Logan and Peter had been killed to make us sit up and take notice. Nothing more. My hands started to clench. The old serpent of rage started moving through me. I stopped, inhaled, and started again, but couldn't steady my fingers.

"So we're up against three experienced mutts," Jeremy said, breaking into my thoughts.

I swallowed back the clot in my throat and played along with the distraction. "Plus at least one new one."

"I haven't forgotten, though I'm more concerned about the experienced ones. Yes, they're good—my arm and leg prove that—but they're not on the same playing field as Daniel."

I broke off the thread. "That's because you know Daniel. And even if you don't know Marsten and Cain equally well, you know what to expect from them because they're like you. They think like you, they react like you, they kill like you. These new ones don't. Werewolves don't strangle people. That's how LeBlanc killed Logan and he succeeded because it's the last thing Logan would have expected. Then he pulled a knife on you. You'd expect that as much as a samurai would expect a kick in the balls. That's why LeBlanc is still alive. He threw you off balance. If—"

"We've dug the grave," Antonio said, coming into the bathroom. "I'm sorry. Did I interrupt something?"

"Nothing that can't be finished later," Jeremy said, getting to his feet and testing the stitches. When they didn't burst apart or gush blood, he nodded. "Perfect. I'll get dressed and we'll go out."

Conviction

I WENT TO PETER'S BURIAL SITE WITH JEREMY. IT WASN'T SOMEthing I particularly wanted to do, with my last graveside breakdown less than thirty-six hours old. Nor did Jeremy need my help making sure the grave was well concealed. He did, however, need my help in another way, though he'd never have admitted it or asked for it. With his leg freshly stitched, he was in no shape for walking without a supporting arm. So I helped him out to the backyard, though to an onlooker it would have appeared that Jeremy was the one helping me. That wasn't unintentional. The Pack Alpha could not show weakness, even if he was fresh from a fight for his life. Not that any of us would ever seize an opportunity to challenge Jeremy for leadership. Yet because the Pack placed its Alpha in total control, the idea that he might not be up to the task, even temporarily, would throw the whole Pack off balance.

Although Jeremy had to be in tremendous pain, he never showed it. He accepted my arm going to and from the grave site, but never put more than the minimum amount of weight on it. Only when we were heading back to the house did he pause for a second, presumably to catch his breath, though he pretended to be checking a crumbling stone in the garden wall.

"I guess we should grab some sleep now," I said, feigning a yawn. "I know I could use it."

"Go on," Jeremy said. "You've had a rough couple of days. I want to discuss what we found in Bear Valley before we were ambushed, but I can fill you in tomorrow."

"Everyone's probably exhausted. We can meet in the morning, can't we? I wouldn't want to miss anything."

"I'd like to get through it tonight. If you want to be there, claim the couch and you can doze while we talk."

Okay, forget subtlety. Full-frontal-assault time. "*You* need to sleep. Your leg has to be killing you, not to mention your arm. No one's going to think anything's wrong if you delay the meeting until tomorrow."

"I can handle it. Don't grind your teeth like that, Elena; I'm not qualified to do dental work. If you want to help, you can round up the others and get them into the study, if they're not already there."

"If you'd like me to really help, I can knock you unconscious until morning."

He gave me a wry half smile that said my suggestion sounded more tempting than he cared to admit. "How about a compromise? You can help by rounding up the others and fixing me a drink, preferably a double."

Before the ambush, Jeremy's information gathering had confirmed what Clay and I knew, that we had three mutts in Bear Valley. He'd also learned a few additional bits of information. Marsten had actually been the first of the three to arrive, before Cain and LeBlanc. He'd checked into the Big Bear three days ago, meaning he'd been in town before Brandon's death. After a few twenties loosened the desk clerk's powers of recall, he'd remembered a young man matching Brandon's description visiting Marsten at the hotel several times. Any doubt that Brandon had been involved with the others was now gone. I wondered if Marsten had been at the rave that night, enjoying a whiskey and soda as he watched Brandon and me, his scent and form hidden away in a dark, smoky corner. Yes, I was sure he'd been there. He'd seen Brandon start his Change, realized what was about to happen and slipped out before the chaos erupted, abandoning his protégé to his fate. Mutts may have been able to form relationships with each other, but they lasted only so long as proved advantageous to both parties. Once Marsten saw Brandon was in trouble, his only thought would be to get the hell out of there before he got sucked into the mess.

Cain and LeBlanc had checked into the Big Bear the night Brandon died. Presumably they'd either followed Logan from Los Angeles or met him at the airport. Waylaying him in Bear Valley would have been next to impossible. While we'd been chasing Brandon, Logan had already been dead, probably in the back of some rented car on his way to Bear Valley. Somewhere along the way, they must have found out from Marsten that Clay and I were in town and the prank of staging Logan's body near our car was born. I guessed that was LeBlanc's idea. Cain didn't have the wits to think of it and Marsten would consider such crude humor beneath him.

It wasn't quite seven when the doorbell rang. We all looked up, startled by the sound. The doorbell at Stonehaven rarely rang, the house being too remote for salesmen and Jehovah's Witnesses. Deliveries went to a post office box in Bear Valley. Even the Pack didn't ring the bell—except for Peter. I think we all remembered this as it rang. No one moved until the second buzz, then Jeremy got to his feet and left the room. I followed. From the dining room window we could see a police cruiser parked in the driveway.

"We don't need this," I said. "We really don't need this."

Jeremy shrugged off his arm sling and tucked it into the hall stand, then grabbed Clay's sweatshirt from the hooks. I helped him into it. The bulky shirt hid his splint and his pants covered his leg bandages. His clothes were clean and unwrinkled, since he'd changed only a few hours ago. That was more than I could say for the rest of us. One glance in the hall mirror told me that I looked like hell, clothes covered in dirt and blood, face blotchy, hair knotted from lying on the sofa.

"Get the others upstairs to dress," Jeremy said. "Tell Clay, Antonio, and Nick to stay up there. You can join me on the back porch."

"It's going to look suspicious if you usher them around the house for a second time."

"I know."

"Invite them in and offer them coffee. There's nothing here for them to see."

"I know."

"I'll meet you in the study, then?"

Jeremy hesitated. Knowing he should invite the police into the house was one thing, doing it was another. The only humans who came into Stonehaven were repairmen, and even that was done only when necessary. There was nothing at Stonehaven that would make anyone suspicious, no body parts in the freezer or pentagrams etched into the hardwood. The scariest thing in Stonehaven was my bedroom and I had no intention of inviting any cop up there, no matter how cute he looked in uniform.

"The living room," he said as the doorbell rang a third time. "We'll be in the living room."

"I'll make coffee," I said, and left before he could change his mind.

When I got back to the living room, there were two police officers with Jeremy. The older one was the town police chief, a burly, balding man named Morgan. I'd seen him around town, though he hadn't been with the search party the day before. With Morgan's arrival, things were obviously heating up, though in a town as small as Bear Valley, having the police chief show up at your house was a cause for concern but not panic. The other officer was young and bland-faced, the kind of guy you could see twenty times before you remembered him. According to his badge, his name was O'Neil. Neither the face nor the name triggered any recollection from yesterday, but he'd likely been there. The look he gave me indicated he remembered me, though he seemed disappointed to find me fully dressed. At least I came bearing coffee.

Jeremy and Morgan were discussing some local native land claim. Jeremy leaned back in a chair, feet on the ottoman, broken arm resting so casually against his leg no one would guess it was splinted. His face was relaxed, eyes alert and interested, as if he had policemen in his home every day and not only knew about the land claim, but was deeply concerned over it, mirroring the police chief's opinions with the ease of a consummate con artist. The younger officer, O'Neil, was unabashedly gawking around the room, taking in all the details to relate later to curious friends.

Conversation stopped when I entered. I set up the tray on an end table and started pouring coffee like a perfect hostess.

"Oh, I don't drink tea," Morgan said, eyeing the silver coffeepot as if it might bite.

"It's coffee," Jeremy said with a self-effacing smile. "You'll have to excuse us. We don't have many guests, so Elena has to use the teapot."

O'Neil leaned forward to take his coffee from me. "Elena. That's a pretty name."

"It's Russian, isn't it?" Morgan said, eyes narrowing.

"Could be," I said, smiling brightly. "Cream and sugar?"

"Three sugars. I didn't see your husband around. Is he sleeping in?"

I spilled scalding coffee on my hand and bit back a yelp. So Clay's marital fabrication had worked its way up the rumor chain to the police chief. Wonderful. Just wonderful. Common sense told me I should play along. After all, Bear Valley wasn't the kind of place that tolerated a woman romping naked in the woods with a man other than her husband. Actually, they probably didn't tolerate naked-forest-romping much at all, but that wasn't the point. The point was that this "placating the locals" was going too far. It was one thing to let them into our house, to tolerate their gawking, and to let them think we couldn't tell a teapot from a coffeepot, but to officially confirm the rumor that I was married to Clay? Branding me forever in Bear Valley as Clay's wife? Uh-uh. A girl's got to have limits.

"Yes, he's sleeping in," Jeremy said before I could speak. "Elena's always up early to get his breakfast ready."

I shot him a glare to say he'd pay for that. He pretended not to notice, but I could see the glimmer of laughter in his eyes. I dumped five sugars in his coffee. He'd have to drink it. After all, it would be impolite not to partake of social beverages with his visitors.

"Like I said," Morgan began. "I apologize for coming to see you folks so early in the morning, but I thought you'd want to know. Mike Braxton wasn't killed on your property. Coroner's one hundred percent certain on that. Somebody killed him elsewhere and dumped him on your land."

"Somebody?" Jeremy said. "Do you mean a person, not an animal?"

"Well, I'd still say it was an animal, but one of the human variety. Doesn't make a hell of a lot of sense to us. The other two were definitely animal kills, but the coroner says Mike's throat was slashed with a knife, not teeth."

"What about the paw prints?" I hated to ask, but we had to know what the police were thinking.

"We figure they're fake. Whoever planted the body stamped them into the ground to make it look like another dog kill. Guy made a mistake, though. They were too big. That was the tip-off. Dogs don't get that big. Well, my son says there's some kind of dog, a mastiff or something, that might leave a print like that, but we don't have any of those around here. Our hounds and shepherds don't grow that big, no matter how much we feed them. You'll recall I said yesterday that Mike left a message with someone saying he was coming here. Turns out, he left it with the fellow's wife, who now says she thought Mike sounded 'funny,' not like himself, but she figured maybe it was a bad phone connection. Seems fair to assume Mike didn't leave the message at all. Whoever killed him must have left it to make sure we hightailed it out to your place and found the body. Put all that together and I'm damned—sorry, ma'am—darned sure we've got a human killer."

"So we don't have wild dogs in our forest," Jeremy said. "That's a relief, though I can't say I prefer the idea of a human killer on the loose. Do you have any leads?"

"We're working on it. Likely someone Mike knew. Mike was a great guy and all but—" Morgan paused, as if thinking twice before speaking ill of the dead. "We've all got our problems, don't we? Enemies and such." Another pause. A slow sip of coffee. "How about you folks? Any idea why someone would dump Mike's body on your property?"

"No," Jeremy said, his voice unruffled but firm. "I was wondering about that myself."

"You haven't made any enemies in town? Maybe had a falling out with someone?"

Jeremy gave a small smile. "As I'm sure you're aware, we aren't the most sociable bunch in Granton County. We don't have enough contact with any of our neighbors to have a falling out with them. Either the killer thought blaming it on the 'outsiders' would divert attention from himself or he had no intention of involving us at all and simply thought this was a good place to dump the body."

"You're sure there's no one you folks have pissed off?" Morgan said, leaning forward. "Maybe someone who thinks you owe him money? Maybe a jealous husband"—Morgan shot a look at me—"or wife?"

"No and no. We don't gamble or do any business in credit. As for the other, I'm certain no one has ever seen me prowling the local singles bars, and Elena and Clayton have neither the inclination nor the energy to seek extramarital excitement. Bear Valley is a small town. If there were any rumors about us, you'd be asking more pointed questions."

Morgan didn't answer. Instead, he stared at Jeremy for two full minutes. Maybe this tactic worked on sixteen-year-old vandalism suspects, but it wasn't about to break down a fifty-one-year-old Pack Alpha. Jeremy just stared back, his expression calm and open.

After a few minutes, Jeremy said, "I'm sorry you had to make the drive out here two days in a row, but I appreciate you coming this morning to tell us."

Jeremy laid aside his mug and shifted to the edge of his seat. When Morgan and O'Neil didn't take the hint, he stood and said, "If that's everything . . ."

"We'll want to search the property some more," Morgan said at last.

"By all means."

"We may want to question your guests."

Morgan conducted another minute-long stare down. When Jeremy didn't so much as blink, he heaved himself to his feet.

"A killer dumped that body on your property," he said. "If I were you, I'd be trying damned hard to think of who might have done it and I'd be calling us if you come up with any answers."

"I wouldn't hesitate," Jeremy said. "I hope whoever dumped Mr. Braxton's body here hadn't any grudge against us, but if he did, I wouldn't want to ignore it and wait for his next move. No one here has any desire to tangle with a killer. We're more than happy to let the police do that."

Morgan grunted and swigged the last of his coffee.

"Anything else?" Jeremy asked.

"I wouldn't be hiking in those woods for a while."

"We've already stopped," Jeremy said. "But thank you for the warning. Elena, would you see our guests to the door?"

I did. Neither cop said a word to me, beyond Morgan's gruff goodbye. Obviously, as a female, I wasn't worth questioning.

After the police left, we realized Clay, Nick, and Antonio were gone. Had it been just Clay or even Clay and Nick, we would have worried. Since Antonio had gone with them, though, we knew they weren't planning any impromptu revenge in Bear Valley.

The police had been gone barely ten minutes when the Mercedes turned into the drive. Nick hopped out from the passenger side. I didn't notice who was driving, my attention being consumed by the sight of the large paper bag in Nick's hand. Breakfast. Not exactly hot and steaming after the drive from the highway diner, but I was too hungry to care.

Fifteen minutes later, the bag was empty, its contents reduced to the ghosts of crumbs and grease marks on plates scattered across the sunroom table. After the meal, Jeremy explained what the police had said. I kept expecting Clay to say something, proclaim his proven innocence and wait for me to apologize. He didn't. He listened to Jeremy, then helped Antonio clear the kitchen table while I escaped to the study, ostensibly to read the newspaper they'd brought back from town.

It took exactly three minutes for Clay to hunt me down. He walked into the study and closed the door behind him, then stood there, watching me read, for two minutes more. When I couldn't stand it any longer, I folded the paper noisily and tossed it aside.

"Okay, you didn't kill the man," I said. "For once, you were innocent. But if you expect me to apologize for thinking you were capable of doing it—"

"I don't."

I shot him a look.

Clay continued, "I don't expect you to apologize for thinking I could do it. Of course I could do it. If the guy saw us running or Changing or threatened us, I would have killed him. But I would have told you. That's what I'm pissed off about. That you'd think I'd sneak behind your back, hide the evidence, and lie about it."

"No, I guess it wouldn't occur to you that I might not *want* to know you did it. The thought of sparing me wouldn't enter your head."

"Sparing you?" Clay gave a harsh laugh. "You know what I am, Elena. If I pretended otherwise, you'd accuse me of trying to deceive you. I don't want you to come back to me because you think I've changed. I want you to come back because you accept what I am. If I could change, don't you think I'd have done it for you by now? I want you back. Not for a night or a few weeks or even a couple of months. I want you back for good. I'm miserable when you're not here—"

"You're miserable because you don't have what you want. Not because you want *me*."

"Goddamn it!" Clay swung his fist out, knocking a brass penholder off the desk. "You won't listen! You won't listen and you won't see. You know I love you, that I want *you*. Damn it, Elena, if I just wanted a partner, any partner, do you think I'd have spent ten years trying to get you back? Why haven't I just given up and found someone else?"

"Because you're stubborn."

"Oh, no. I'm not the stubborn one. You're the one who can't get past what I did no matter how much—"

"I don't want to talk about it."

"Of course you don't. God forbid any truth should complicate your convictions."

Clay turned and strode from the room, slamming the door behind him.

After Clay left, I decided to stay in the study—or hide out there, depending on the interpretation. I perused the selection on the bookshelves. It hadn't changed in the past year. Actually, it hadn't changed in the past decade. A motley collection of literature and reference books filled the shelves. Only a few of the reference books belonged to Clay. He bought every book and magazine related to his career, then trashed them as soon as he finished the last word. He didn't have a photographic memory, just the uncanny ability to absorb everything he read, making it pointless to save any form of the written word. Almost all of the books belonged to Jeremy. Over half of them weren't even in English, a throwback to Jeremy's early career as a translator.

Jeremy hadn't always been able to lavish sports cars and antique beds on his adopted family. When Clay first came to Stonehaven, Jeremy had been struggling to pay the heating bills, a situation deriving entirely from his father's spending habits and refusal to dirty his hands with any work that might generate income. Throughout Jeremy's twenties, he'd worked as a translator, an ideal occupation for someone with a gift for languages and a tendency toward reclusion. Later, the financial situation at Stonehaven took a drastic upswing, owing to twin circumstances of fortune: Malcolm Danvers's death and the launch of Jeremy's painting career. These days Jeremy sold very few paintings, but when he did, they brought in enough cash to keep Stonehaven running for several years.

While I was looking for something to read, Jeremy popped in to remind me to call Philip. I hadn't forgotten. I'd intended to do it before dinner and didn't appreciate the reminder, as if Jeremy thought I needed one. I didn't know how much Jeremy knew about Philip and I didn't want to know. I preferred the idea that when I left Stonehaven, I escaped to a foreign place the Pack knew nothing about. Okay, I was delusional, but it was a nice fantasy. I suspected Jeremy had investigated Philip, but I didn't bother to call him on it. If I did, he'd only claim he was protecting me from getting involved with some guy who had three wives or a history of battering his girlfriends. Of course Jeremy would never do anything simply to interfere with my life. Perish the thought.

No matter how much Jeremy knew about Philip, he didn't know how I felt about him. Again, I had no plans to enlighten him. I knew what he'd say. He'd sit back, watch me for a minute, then start talking about how difficult my circumstances were, with Clay and being the only female werewolf and all, and how he didn't blame me for being confused and wanting to explore my choices in life. Though he'd never say it outright, he'd imply that he was certain if he gave me enough latitude to make my own mistakes, I'd eventually see that I belonged with the Pack. Through the whole conversation, he'd be completely calm and understanding, never raising his voice or taking offense at anything I said. Sometimes I think I preferred Clay's rages.

The truth was that I cared about Philip more than Jeremy could imagine. I wanted to go back to him. I hadn't forgotten about him. I'd been planning to call him . . . later.

Now seemed like the perfect time for Jeremy to update us on his plans. When he didn't, no one else appeared to notice. More likely, they didn't care. Werewolves raised in the Pack are brought up with a certain set of expectations. One of those expectations was that their Alpha would look after them. Asking Jeremy what his plans were would imply that they didn't think he had any. Even Clay, as anxious as he was to take action, would give Jeremy plenty of plotting time before hinting about his plans. Such a trusting attitude drove me crazy. Not that I didn't think Jeremy was making plans. I knew he was. But I wanted in on them. I wanted to help. When I finally dreamed up a subtle way to ask, I found him outside with a pair of revolvers. No, he wasn't going after the mutts armed like Billy the Kid. Nor was he contemplating a quick end to his pain. He was target shooting, something he often did while he was deep in thought—not exactly the safest method of achieving mental focus, but who am I to judge? The revolvers were a gorgeous antique pair given to him by Antonio many years ago. Along with the guns, Antonio had given Jeremy a silver bullet inscribed with Malcolm Danvers's initials, a half-joking suggestion, which, of course, Jeremy never took. More seriously, Antonio intended the guns for their current purpose—marksmanship. By that time Jeremy had already mastered the longbow and crossbow and was looking for a new challenge. Don't ask me why he chose marksmanship for a hobby. He certainly never used the bows or guns off the target range. You might as well ask me why he painted. Neither was what you'd call a typical werewolf hobby. Then again, no one had ever accused Jeremy of being a typical werewolf. Anyway, when I went outside and saw him shooting, I decided it was an inopportune time to bug him about his plans. Urban survival rule twenty-two: never annoy an armed man.

Leaving Jeremy, I'd gone upstairs for a nap. A couple of hours later, I awoke and headed downstairs for lunch. The house was silent, all the upstairs doors closed as if everyone else was catching up on sleep, too. As I headed for the kitchen, Clay walked out from the study. His eyes were bloodshot and dark. Though he was exhausted, he wouldn't sleep. Not now, with two Pack brothers dead, his Alpha wounded, and none avenged. Once Jeremy gave us his plans, Clay would rest, if only to prepare.

He stepped in front of me. When I tried to squeeze past him, he braced his hands on either side of the corridor.

"Truce?" he said.

"Whatever."

"Love those definitive answers. I'll take that as a yes. Not that we're done with our little discussion, but I'll let it ride for now. Tell me when you want to pick it up again."

"Tell me when Satan starts a snowball fight."

"I'll do that. Lunch?"

When I finally nodded, he stepped back and motioned for me to go into the kitchen. I could feel him simmering, but he'd plastered on a happy face, so I decided to ignore it. In a crisis, we were both capable of summoning enough maturity to know that we couldn't afford to threaten the stability of the Pack with our fighting. Or, at least, we could fake it temporarily.

We gathered a cold meal from the kitchen, filling platters with meats and breads and fruits, knowing the others would wake up hungry. Then I sat down in the sunroom and loaded a plate. Clay did the same. Neither of us spoke as we ate. Although this wasn't unusual, the silence had a dead quality that made me eat a little faster, anxious to be done and out of the room. When I glanced over at Clay, he was dispatching his food just as quickly and with as little enjoyment. We were halfway through our meal when Jeremy and Antonio walked in.

"We need groceries," I said. "I'm sure that's the last thing on everyone's mind, but it won't be when we run out. I'll run into town and grab some."

"I'll call in an order," Jeremy said. "Assuming this mess with the police hasn't changed that arrangement. You'd best pick up cash, in case my checks aren't as welcome these days. Someone will have to go with you, of course. No one's leaving the house alone or staying here alone anymore."

"I'll go," Clay said around a mouthful of cantaloupe. "I've got a package waiting at the post office."

"I'm sure you do," I said.

"He does," Jeremy said. "The postman left a card the other day."

"Books I ordered from the U.K.," Clay said.

"Which you need right now," I said. "For a little light reading between maiming and killing."

"They shouldn't sit at the post office," Clay said. "Someone might get suspicious."

"Of anthropology texts?"

Antonio leaned over the table and grabbed a handful of grapes. "I've got a couple things to fax. I'll go with the two of you and run interference."

I pushed back my chair. "Well, then there's no need for me to go, is there? I'm sure you guys can handle the groceries."

"But you're the one who wanted to go," Clay said.

"I changed my mind."

"You're going," Jeremy said. "All three of you. You could use the diversion."

Antonio grinned. "And Jeremy could use a couple hours of peace and quiet."

When I glanced up, I swore Jeremy rolled his eyes, but the movement was so fast, I couldn't be sure. Antonio laughed and sat down to lunch. Just as I was about to start arguing again, Antonio launched into an anecdote about meeting a mutt in San Francisco last time he was there on business. By the time he finished, I'd forgotten what I'd meant to say, which was probably the point of the story.

An hour later, when Antonio and Clay were calling me to the car, I remembered that I didn't want to go and had been trying to find a way out of it when Antonio had interrupted. By then, it was too late. Jeremy was nowhere to be found, Antonio was waiting in the Mercedes, and Nick was ransacking the kitchen for his lunch, cleaning out what little food remained. Someone had to get the groceries, and if I didn't do it, I'd be cursing my stubbornness by dinnertime. So I went.

The bank was right across from the post office. Since Antonio was able to get a parking spot right in front of the bank, I convinced them that it was safe for me to go to the bank alone while Clay went to the post office alone. From his spot out front, Antonio would be able to see both Clay and me at all times. And it shaved a few minutes from the total amount of time I had to spend running errands with Clay.

Jeremy's bank account was also in my name and Clay's, allowing any of us to withdraw money for household needs. I used to have an ATM card for the account, but I'd trashed it last year when I left Stonehaven. Now I wished I hadn't. Bear Valley was the kind of town where people still used the tellers. As I stood in line for fifteen minutes, listening to an elderly man talking to the teller about his grandchildren, I gazed longingly at the shiny, unused ATM. When he started pulling out photographs, I began to wonder how long it would take to get a new bank machine card. With a sigh, I abandoned the idea. It would probably require filling out two forms in triplicate and waiting until the bank manager returned from his hour-long coffee break. Anyway, since I would be leaving Stonehaven in a couple of days, I wouldn't need it again.

Finally, I got up to the teller and had to produce three pieces of signed photo ID before she'd let me withdraw a couple hundred dollars from the account. I shoved the money into my pocket, headed for the door, and saw a brown pickup in the front parking spot. Thinking I must have been mistaken about where Antonio parked, I walked outside and looked around. The spot behind the pickup was empty. In front of it was a Buick. I searched up and down the road. There was no sign of the Mercedes.

Prisoner

THERE WERE AS MANY MERCEDESES IN BEAR VALLEY AS THERE were Porsches, so I didn't need to spend much time surveying the street to know Antonio's car wasn't there. I could imagine only two reasons for them abandoning me. One, the meter maid had been making her rounds and neither had a nickel for the meter. Two, they hadn't been able to see me in the bank, and when I'd been gone so long, they thought I bolted. There was a third possibility: Clay was *really* pissed off at me, knocked Antonio unconscious, and drove off, abandoning me to my fate. A nice dramatic twist, but not terribly likely.

There was a tiny dirt parking lot behind the bank for the employees and any customers unwilling to spend the dime-per-hour at the meters out front. I checked the lot and saw only a minivan and another pickup. I cocked my head to listen. Even these few feet from the road, quiet had fallen, as if the buildings lining Main Street were constructed to block all sound and limit it to the shopping district. In the distance, I heard the soft chugging of a well-tuned diesel engine. Definitely not a pickup. I closed my eyes and tuned out everything else. The Mercedes was less than a few blocks away, the sound of its engine fading, then growing, then fading as it seemed to be moving in slow circles. Where? Logically, another parking lot, where Antonio was circling, waiting for me. Had I missed some instruction? Was I supposed to meet them someplace else? That didn't make sense, since Clay hadn't even wanted to let me go into the bank alone. Well, whatever the reason, there wasn't any sense standing here thinking about it.

Narrow car tracks traced a path down an alley heading in the direction of the circling car. The passage was muddy and barely wide enough for the compact Mercedes to traverse without scraping the side mirrors, yet I knew Antonio wouldn't be worried about dirt or scratches. Clay and Antonio liked their expensive cars, but they were purely utility pieces, designed to get them from point A to point B with speed and comfort. Looking good wasn't a concern.

I started down the alley, sidestepping the puddles and deep muddy ruts. At one point, the alley branched right. I didn't need to follow the car's tracks to know that it kept going straight. Navigating a turn in these tight quarters would have taken off more than a few layers of paint. As I got farther and farther from the main road, the alley widened and rose up on a slight incline, turning from mud to gravel. Garbage Dumpsters lined the right side of the passage, but still left enough room for the Mercedes to pass. The drier ground only served to emphasize the amount of muddy water that had seeped into my shoes. With each step, my sneakers squelched and my mood sank. I was getting ready to storm back to the bank and call Jeremy for Antonio's cell number when I saw a glimmer of silver ahead. I stopped. Over a hundred feet away, the alley ended in a weedy vacant lot. As I watched, the Mercedes drifted past the alley opening. I waved my arms, but the car vanished behind the brick walls.

"Come on, guys," I muttered. "What's with the hide-and-seek?"

I tromped along in my soaked shoes, waving each time the Mercedes passed the alley and muttering increasingly nasty epithets each time it didn't stop. As I went by another branching alleyway, I heard a soft noise, but ignored it, being in no mood for idle curiosity. About ten feet later, gravel crunched behind me and the edge of a large shadow encroached on the left of my vision field. Clay. He was downwind, but I didn't need to smell him to recognize his flavor of practical joke.

As I whirled around, a hand grabbed the back of my shirt and sent me sailing face first to the ground. Okay. Not Clay.

"Get up," a voice said as a huge shape passed over me.

I lifted my head, spitting gravel and blood. "What? No witty riposte? No clever throwaway line?"

"Get up."

Cain grabbed my collar again and heaved me to my feet, setting me down so hard my ankle twisted beneath me. I made a show of wiping the dirt from my face and running my fingers through my hair.

"That's no way to greet a girl, Zack," I said. "No wonder you have to pay for it."

Cain stood there with his arms crossed, saying nothing. His shoulders spanned half the passage between buildings. Dark blond hair topped a face with bulldog features.

"Waiting for me to run?" I asked. "Or still trying to think up a comeback?"

He started forward. I wheeled and sprinted for the end of the alley. A mutt always stands his ground and fights. A Pack werewolf knows when to run like hell. I wasn't a match for Zachary Cain on my best days and today certainly wasn't one of those. I was half Cain's size, but twice his speed. If I could get to the end of the alley, I was safe. The Pack's two best fighters were there, and I wasn't stubborn or stupid enough to refuse help. Halfway there, the Mercedes passed the alley opening again. I lifted both arms to wave and my left foot hit the gravel wrong. As I fell, the silver car slowly vanished from sight.

I scrambled to my feet, but it was too late. Again, Cain reached out and caught me by the back of the shirt. This time, he swung me off the ground. My left foot smacked into a metal Dumpster and I swallowed a yelp. With his free hand, Cain grabbed me beneath the chin and smashed me backward into the wall. My head hit the brick, sending lightning bolts through my skull. He held me there, feet suspended off the ground. Then he reached up and tore my shirtfront open.

"Not much to see, is there?" I said, struggling to talk with a crushed windpipe. "I know, I know, they can fix things like that these days. Call me a feminist, but I think a woman's worth should be defined not by the size of her bust, but—"

I rammed my fist up into his Adam's apple. He grunted and stumbled back.

"—by the strength of her right hook," I said, throwing myself against his chest before he regained his balance.

Cain toppled to the ground. As he fell, I stayed on him, slamming my open hand against his neck and pinning him by the throat.

"Yes, I can talk and think at the same time," I said. "Most people can, though I suppose you wouldn't know that from personal experience."

With a roar, Cain swung one arm up toward me. In midair, a shoe shot down and stomped his hand to the ground.

"Uh-uh," Clay drawled above me. "Elena's played with you long enough. It's my turn."

I waited until Clay moved his foot to Cain's throat, then backed off. Antonio was standing to the side.

"Trap?" I asked.

Antonio nodded. "Clay saw him lurking in the alley. We figured you'd come looking for us."

"So you left a trail and circled that vacant lot waiting for me to take the bait, and Cain to take me as bait."

"Something like that."

Clay hauled Cain to his feet. The redness and dark circles had vanished from Clay's eyes. He was fully awake now. This was what he'd been waiting for.

Cain towered a good six inches over Clay and outweighed him by at least seventy pounds. It was a fair fight.

The two stepped back and looked at each other. Then Cain took a step left toward Clay. Clay mirrored the maneuver, but moving forward to the right. They repeated the dance steps, gazes locked, each watching the other for the lunge. The pattern for the ritual was ingrained in our brains. Step, circle, watch. To win, you either had to lunge without warning or catch the other about to lunge and sidestep. It went on for several minutes. Then Cain lost patience and dove. Clay dodged out of the way, grabbed him by the waistband, and flung him into the wall.

Cain recovered in a heartbeat and slammed into Clay's chest, knocking him to the ground.

I won't detail the fight, partly because it would be a boring recitation of hit, jab, grunt, stumble, recover, and partly because I wasn't watching it that closely. I wasn't *not* watching because I wasn't interested, but because I was too interested. Standing back and seeing Clay get pummeled and kicked and slammed into walls was a bit more than I could bear. Not that I didn't occasionally want to do the same to him myself, but this was different. I would have felt the same about watching any of my Pack brothers fight. It wasn't just Clay. Really.

Although I wasn't watching the fight, that didn't keep me from smelling it. I smelled Cain's blood first, but Clay's followed shortly. When I looked up, blood was streaming from Clay's nose and mouth, making him cough and sputter.

Antonio and I had to stand back and watch. This was how we fought. One-on-one, no weapons, no tricks. It was the wolf in us that dictated the rules of battle; the human side would goad us into winning at all costs. That wasn't to say we'd stand back and watch Clay get killed. If that seemed possible, loyalty to one's Pack brother overrode all codes of conduct. Still, there was a lot of blood and broken bones between life and death, and until that line was crossed, we couldn't interfere.

It finally ended with Cain sprawled facedown in the gravel. When he didn't get up, I thought he was dead. Than I saw his back rising and falling as he breathed.

"Unconscious," Clay wheezed, wiping his shirt over his bloody nose. "You can look now."

"I was watching," I said. "I turned away because I thought I heard something down the alley."

Clay grinned and blood gushed from his split upper lip.

"Don't start," Antonio said. "We need to get this mutt back to Stonehaven so Jeremy can question him. Elena, could you go down the alley to the car? Make sure no one's around? Clay, take the keys and open the trunk. I'll get this one."

As I'd thought, the alley ended in a vacant lot. Once there'd been road access to the north, but now it was barricaded with Dumpsters, leaving the long trip down the south alley as the only way in or out. The blocking Dumpsters left enough room for someone to walk through, so I went and stood by them to watch for passersby. Behind me, Antonio and Clay loaded Cain into the trunk. Then Clay walked over to where I was standing watch.

"You okay?" he asked.

"Other than a scraped cheek, a twisted ankle, a possible concussion, soaked sneakers, and a ruined shirt? I'm peachy. Feel free to use me for bait anytime."

"Glad you feel that way."

"Watch it or you'll have more than a bloody nose and split lip." I gave him a quick once-over. "Is that it?"

"Maybe a few bruised ribs. Nothing permanent."

He coughed and fresh blood spurted from his nose. He ripped off his shirt and wadded it up against the flow.

When we got back to the car, Antonio was closing the trunk. Cain's unconscious body took up every square inch of space.

"No groceries on this run, I assume," I said.

"Doesn't look like it," Antonio said. "I'll have to come back for them. We'll grab a snack on the way to tide us over."

I thought he was kidding. I should have known better. Before we left town, Antonio pulled into a strip mall and went in to get submarines and salads, leaving Clay and me half naked and bleeding in the car and Cain unconscious in the trunk. No wonder I was anxious to get back to Toronto. Spend too much time around these guys and you become a little too nonchalant about blood-soaked clothes and bodies in the trunk.

At Stonehaven, Antonio and Nick loaded the still-unconscious Cain into the basement cage while Jeremy inspected Clay's and my injuries. I got two aspirins for my head and iodine and sympathy for my scrapes and bruises. Clay got a plaster for his lip, binding for his ribs, and a few stiff words on the dangers of using me as bait. In spite of what I'd said to Clay, I wasn't upset about the bait thing. Getting Cain was worth a ripped shirt and a sore head. Clay knew I could handle it, and in a way,

I was glad of that. I'd be more pissed off if he thought I was too fragile to play with the big boys. Of course, I didn't forgive or defend him. Not out loud at least. If I had, Jeremy would have started worrying a lot more about that bump to my head.

After Cain was secured and Jeremy finished nursing, we had our snack. Then Nick and Antonio went back to town for the groceries while Jeremy, Clay, and I talked about what information we wanted from Cain. Around six o'clock, shouts and clangs from the basement told us that our prisoner was awake. Jeremy and Clay went down to the cage.

I stayed upstairs. I was welcome to go down and help, but I knew what was coming, so I stayed in the study, where I could hear what Cain said without seeing what made him say it. I'm squeamish about torture. Maybe that seems silly, considering how much violence I'd witnessed and participated in during my life. But there was something about being brutalized and unable to defend yourself that sent chills down my spine and nightmares to my sleep. Maybe it was vestiges of long-buried victim pathology from my childhood. Years ago, I went to see *Reservoir Dogs* with Clay. When it came to the infamous "Stuck in the Middle with You" scene, I covered my eyes and Clay picked up pointers. While I didn't think he'd tied anyone up and doused them with gasoline yet, he'd done things just as bad. I knew because I'd been there. I'd seen him do it, and what frightened me the most was the look in his eyes. They didn't burn with excitement or anticipation, like when he chased his prey. Instead, they were blue ice, frozen and impenetrable. When he tortured a mutt, he was completely methodical, showing no emotion at all. Of course, I'd be a whole lot more worried if he approached his work with glee, but there was something equally chilling about someone who could do things like that with such single-minded detachment. Most people torture for information. Clay did it for instruction. For every mutt he'd maimed and let live, five more would see and take a lesson from it. For every one he'd killed, a score heard the story. Those who thought of attacking a Pack member only had to recall these stories to change their minds. Most werewolves weren't afraid of dying, but there were worse fates than death and Clay made sure they knew it.

As I sat in the study and listened to the scene taking place below, I had to admit that there was another advantage to Clay's methods. The more his reputation spread, the less he had to do to uphold it. No bloodcurdling shrieks rent the air as Jeremy interrogated Cain. In the four long hours of questioning that followed, I heard exactly three pained grunts as Clay presumably hit Cain when he wasn't forthcoming with an answer. Just having Clay standing there and knowing what he *could* do was enough to make Cain talk.

Of the three experienced mutts in Bear Valley, Zachary Cain was the worst choice for an informant. Any plans Daniel and Marsten had deigned to share with him had since become lost in the empty wasteland of his brain. According to Cain, Jimmy Koenig was also part of the "revolution," but he hadn't shown up yet.

Cain had joined them because he was seeking "release from tyranny," a phrase doubtless assimilated through one too many viewings of *Braveheart.* As Cain so eloquently put it, he was "sick of having to watch my fucking back every time I piss the wrong way." Since the Pack has never taken any interest in the urinary habits of mutts, I assumed he meant that he was fighting for his right to kill humans without fear of reprisal, something I was sure was covered under the werewolf subclauses of the American constitution. According to Cain, Koenig wanted the same thing—the extermination of the Pack, much the way criminals dream of eliminating the police. Somehow the two of them were convinced that if the Pack was gone they'd be free to indulge their worst natures without fear of reprisal. Daniel had more grandiose plans, as always. He wanted to wipe out the Pack and start his own, probably envisioning some kind of werewolf Mafia. Cain wasn't clear on the details and wasn't interested in them. As for Marsten, Cain had no idea why he'd joined the fight. Again, he didn't really care.

Daniel had masterminded the new-recruit plan. He'd done the research, found the subjects, and played the psychopath's version of the Godfather—approaching them with an offer they couldn't refuse. If they helped him eliminate a few old enemies, he'd grant them the ultimate killer's body. None had refused. From there, Daniel had assigned a recruit to each of his comrades. Daniel had bitten and trained

Thomas LeBlanc. Marsten had taken Scott Brandon. We hadn't met Cain's protégé yet. Apparently, he was a man named Victor Olson who'd been waiting in the car the day Cain led us on a chase through the forest. Jeremy asked Cain what Olson had done in his human life. That was my question and I think Jeremy only asked it to humor me . . . and because he knew I was listening. Cain wasn't clear on the details, being as uninterested in Olson's past as he was in anything that didn't directly concern him. All he knew was that Olson had been in jail for "screwing around with a couple girls" and killing one of them. That sounded like a rapist moving up the ladder to a Thomas LeBlanc–type killer. Not exactly an experienced murderer, but Daniel must have seen some potential in him, since he'd sent Cain all the way to Arizona to break Olson out of jail.

So with Cain out of the way, we were down to two experienced and two new mutts. Right? I wish. As I said, Koenig hadn't arrived yet. His recruit was still recovering from being turned, but they'd be in Bear Valley soon. Fighting these guys was like battling a Hydra. Each time we lopped off a head, a few more appeared in its place. Clay tried to get more out of Cain, but didn't push it. So far, Cain hadn't tried to hold anything back, so it was unlikely he was starting now. His neck was on the line. He'd say anything to save himself from torture, even if it meant condemning his coconspirators to death. The loyalty of a mutt was an inspiring thing to behold.

It was past ten when Jeremy came upstairs. He stepped into the study where I was curled up in his chair.

"Anything else?" he asked.

I shook my head and he went back downstairs. There was a shout, a muffled sound, half anger, half pleading. Then silence. Seconds later, the basement door opened and I heard Jeremy's footsteps headed to the back patio. I knew to leave him alone for a while. When the door opened a second time, I peeked out from the study. Clay was rubbing a hand over his face. Specks of blood dotted his shirt. He looked exhausted, as if he'd been beating on Cain for the past four hours instead of playing silent enforcer. When he saw me, he managed a wan smile.

"Hey."

"Done?" I asked.

"Yeah. He's dead. We'll take him out tomorrow. He's in the cubbyhole for now." He rubbed the back of his neck. "Have you eaten?"

I shook my head. "Tonio made stew earlier. Do you want a bowl?"

"Right now, I want a shower, but if you'll heat up some, I'll be down before it's ready. Jeremy won't be hungry, so you'll be stuck with me. Okay?"

I nodded and he headed upstairs.

An hour later, Clay and I went into the study to find Jeremy already there, leaning back in his chair, eyes closed. He half opened one eye as we walked in.

"Sorry," I said. "Should we leave?"

He motioned us in with his good hand, then closed his eyes again. I sat on the couch while Clay fixed drinks. He laid one by Jeremy's elbow, but Jeremy made no move to take it.

"So we have four in town," I said to Clay as he sat beside me. "Plus two more on the way. The question is, what to do about it."

"Kill 'em all."

"Good plan," Jeremy murmured, not opening his eyes. "Very succinct."

"Hey, if you don't want to hear my ideas, don't be eavesdropping."

"I was here first."

"We thought you were sleeping," I said.

Jeremy raised one eyebrow, then fell silent, eyes still closed. Clay reached across me for his drink, took a sip, then left his arm behind my head, fingers dangling against my shoulder.

"We should take out Daniel first," he said. "He's the ringleader. No one else knows shit about organizing into a pack. Rip out the center and the whole thing falls apart."

"Right," I said. "That'll be easy. Daniel's such a pushover. The only reason you haven't killed him before now is that you still have a soft spot for your childhood playmate, right?"

Clay snorted.

"Exactly," I said. "He's still alive because he knows how you operate and he's not about to walk into a trap like Cain. I say we go after the two new ones first. They're the wild cards. Get rid of them and we know exactly what we're dealing with."

"I'm not wasting my time on a couple of brand-new mutts."

"Then I will. Without you."

"Ah, shit." He banged his head against the top of the sofa. "Jer, are you listening to this?"

"Now I'm asleep," Jeremy said.

He was silent for a moment. When we didn't resume our conversation, he sighed and opened his eyes.

"Clay is right to target Daniel," Jeremy said. "But killing him isn't that easy. I'll settle for talking to him."

"Talking to him?" Clay said. "Why?"

"Because I know what he's like and it might be easier to appease him than to risk more lives fighting him. With Daniel out of the picture, the others will break apart, as you said. Then we strike individually and destroy any future threat. I've put up with a lot from Daniel because he was Pack and his father was a good man. No more. We make him happy this once, then we keep our eyes on him. If he so much as kills a human in Australia, he dies."

"What makes you think Daniel will bargain?" I said. "Cain seemed to think he wants the Pack eliminated."

"Maybe so, but more than that, he wants revenge," Jeremy said. "He wants us on our knees. By offering to bargain with him, he'll see that he's succeeded. When he realizes Zachary Cain is dead, he'll start to worry. Jimmy Koenig hasn't shown up yet. All he has is Karl Marsten."

"And the two new mutts."

"They have no stake in this battle," Jeremy said, "They've been recruited for a war that doesn't concern them. They're only fighting because they made a deal with Daniel. They've got what they want from him. Once they see things falling apart, they'll leave. What motivation do they have to stay? They haven't had enough dealings with the Pack to want revenge. They haven't been werewolves long enough to develop a need for territory. Why would they fight?"

"For fun." I turned to Clay. "You saw Brandon in that bar. You saw how he killed that man, how much pleasure he took in it. Have you ever seen a werewolf act like that?"

"I'm not dismissing them, darling," Clay said. "LeBlanc dies for what he did to Logan and Jeremy. I won't forget that."

Clay's hand fell from the back of the sofa onto my shoulder and toyed with my hair. I leaned against him, feeling the effects of a stiff drink and sleepless nights. When Jeremy closed his eyes again, I did the same, letting my head fall on Clay's shoulder. He twisted toward me and reached his other hand over to rest on my leg. I could feel the warmth of it through my jeans. The smell of scotch wafted from his breath. I was drifting off to sleep when the door slammed open.

"What's this?" Nick said. "Bedtime?"

No one answered him. I kept my eyes closed.

"You look positively content, Clayton," Nick continued, thumping down on the floor. "That wouldn't have anything to do with the fact that Elena is cuddled up with you, would it?"

"It's cold in here," I murmured.

"Doesn't feel cold."

"It's cold," Clay growled.

"I could start a fire."

"I could start one, too," Clay said. "With your clothes. Before you get them off."

"That's a hint, Nicky," Antonio said from the doorway. "Take it. I have no desire to spend my waning years a childless old man."

I heard Antonio move across the room. Glasses clinked as he fixed two drinks. Then he settled into the other chair. Nick stayed on the floor, stretching out and leaning back against our legs. After a few minutes, quiet fell again, punctuated only by occasional murmurs of conversation. Soon the drowsiness that affected me spread its soft tentacles across the others. Voices turned to murmurs, conversation became sparse, then evaporated into silence. I spread my fingers across Clay's chest, feeling his heartbeat, and fell asleep.

Detour

WHEN I AWOKE, I DIMLY REMEMBERED HAVING FALLEN ASLEEP ON the sofa and began to adjust myself accordingly, putting my arms out and legs down to avoid sliding to the floor as I got up. Then I realized none of my limbs were where I expected them. My arms were folded under a pillow and my legs were entwined in sheets. The powdery scent of fabric softener filled my nostrils. I opened one eye to see the silhouette of dancing tree branches against my bed canopy. Surprise and surprise again. Not only was I in bed, but I was in my own. Usually if I fell asleep downstairs with Clay, he carted me off to his room like a caveman dragging his mate to his lair. Waking in my own room was a surprise close to a shock . . . until I roused enough to feel an arm over my waist and hear soft snoring against my back. As I moved, the snoring stopped and Clay shifted closer.

"Nice to see you remember how to make yourself at home in my bed," I said.

"I was with you when you fell asleep," he murmured drowsily. "Didn't see that it made much difference to stay with you."

I glanced down at my naked body. "As I recall, I was still dressed when I fell asleep."

"Just making sure you were comfortable."

"And making yourself equally comfortable, I see," I said, moving my legs and feeling his bare skin against mine.

"If you want to *see,* you need to turn over."

I snorted. "Not likely."

He snuggled against my back. His hand slid from my hip to my stomach. I closed my eyes again, my brain still adrift in the fog of near-sleep. Clay was warm against me, his body heat fighting off the chill of early morning. The canopy kept the bed dark and invited lingering. Outside the room, the house was silent. There wasn't any reason to get up yet and no need to invent a reason. It was comfortable here. We needed the rest. The thought and feel of Clay's naked body against mine sparked a few unbidden images and ideas, but he wasn't doing anything to provoke the need to fight them. His breathing was slow and deep, as if he was drifting back to sleep. His legs were entangled with mine, but they were staying still, as were his hands. After a couple minutes, he started to kiss the back of my neck. Still no cause for alarm. The back of my neck was hardly an erogenous zone, although it did feel good. Really good, actually. Especially when he moved his hand up to brush the hair from my shoulder and ran his fingertips across my jaw-line to my lips.

I parted my lips, flicking my tongue out to taste his finger, then ran my tongue across the roughness of his fingernail. As my lips parted, he moved his fingertip between my teeth. I nibbled at it, teeth grazing over the ridges of skin. He moved his lips down the back of my neck. His breath tickled the tiny hairs there and sent a shiver through me. As I nibbled on his finger, his lips and other hand moved over my back, raising goosebumps in their path. His hand slipped to the dip between my rib cage and hipbone and stroked the curve there. When his fingers slid down to my stomach, I turned toward him. He pulled me onto my side, facing him, then started to kiss me. The kisses were gentle and slow, their pace matching his hands as they explored my body, gliding across my sides, my back, my arms, my shoulders, along the back of my thighs and over my hips. I kept my eyes closed, floating between sleep and waking. Moving against him, I luxuriated in the heat of his skin and the smooth planes and sinews of his body. When I felt the hardness of him against my stomach, there was no question of what to do next. My body responded without instructions, shifting my torso up, easing my legs apart and . . .

"Did you call him yesterday?" Jeremy asked.

"Huh?" I was emptying the dishwasher. My mind was still in bed with Clay.

"Your . . . friend called before you woke up. You left your cell phone in the front hall."

My brain snapped out of the bedroom. "You answered it?"

"Would you have rather I waited until Clay answered it? You didn't call, did you?" He didn't wait for an answer. "Don't worry, I didn't say anything, so whatever story you're telling him is safe. It seems he was expecting you back today."

"I'll handle it."

"Elena . . ."

"I said I'd handle it."

I put away the last plate and headed for the door.

I hadn't called Philip because I forgot him. It sounded awful, but it was the plain truth. I loved this man, I knew I did, and that only made it worse. At least if I could say I wasn't in love with . . . In love? Was I in love with Philip? Damn it, that was such a trite, overworked cop-out. I loved him. There was no "in love." There was "in lust," "infatuated," and "in heat," three ultimately destructive emotions that had nothing to do with real, lasting love. I forgot Philip because that was how I was coping with this mess, splitting my life into two compartments, human and Pack. Philip belonged in the human world and to even think about him while I was in the Pack world somehow tainted what we had. Or at least, that was how I explained the oversight to myself.

As I was about to get my cell phone from the front hall, Clay showed up. Naturally, I couldn't excuse myself and run upstairs with my phone. So I left the phone where it was and went for a walk with Clay. I meant to call Philip when I got back. He'd left a message on my cell phone, but as we got in the door, Jeremy reminded us that we needed to dispose of Cain's body. From there, things got complicated, and in light of what happened that day, I think I could be forgiven if I forgot to call Philip . . . again.

Back in the good ol' days of lawlessness and circuit judges, the Pack could dump bodies wherever it pleased. As humans became more concerned with dead and missing people, the Pack had to start burying the mutts it killed. Today, with postmortems and computer-linked detective units, and DNA testing, disposing of a body was a full-blown event requiring a good half day of preparation and work. Every member of the Pack had been drilled in the procedures until we could dispose of a body better than the most forensics-savvy human killer.

We drove the Explorer an hour north, avoiding any dumping grounds used in the previous few decades. Another hour was spent navigating down a logging road and 4 × 4'ing deeper into the forest, then removing and dragging Cain's body to a suitable site where we stripped, washed, and examined it for injuries. The only marks on the body were two splotches under Cain's throat, bruises from Clay's thumbs when he'd snapped Cain's neck. To be safe, Clay excised the bruises with a penknife. Finally, we buried Cain. Then I replaced the sod while Clay rounded up two rocks too heavy to be lifted by a human, and placed them over the grave. We backtracked to the Explorer, covering our trail, then drove to site number two.

Site two was chosen with as much caution as site one, but it was over an hour away. Here we dug a pit, threw in Cain's clothing, ID, and the bags and cloths we'd used for transporting and cleaning his body. These were doused with kerosene and burned, keeping the smoke to a minimum. Once everything was reduced to ashes, Clay buried the remains and we declared the job complete. It wasn't foolproof, but no one would ever look for Zachary Cain. Mutts didn't leave mourners.

We were less than twenty minutes from Stonehaven when blue lights flashed in the rearview mirror. I looked up and down the road, certain the lights were meant for someone else. I knew I wasn't breaking any laws. The dumbest thing you could do after dumping a body is to break a few highway traffic laws making your escape, which is why I was driving instead of Clay. The cruise control was set to two miles over the speed limit—driving exactly on the speed limit always struck me as just as suspicious as speeding. I'd been traveling down a straight highway road for the past thirty miles, with no chance of making an illegal turn or missing a stop sign. I checked for other cars ahead and behind, but we were alone on the road. Clay glanced over his shoulder at the police car.

"Did the speed limit change here?" I asked.

"Speed limit?"

"Never mind. I'm pulling over."

"No big deal. Everything's clean."

I pulled onto the shoulder and hoped the cops would zoom past in pursuit of some emergency ahead. As the police car eased onto the gravel behind me, I swore under my breath.

"Everything's clean," Clay said. "Stop worrying."

One of the officers walked over to the passenger side and tapped on the window. Clay waited long enough to express annoyance, but not so long as to be disrespectful, then hit the button to roll down the window.

"Clayton Danvers?" the officer said.

Clay looked at the man, but said nothing.

The young officer continued, "My partner recognized the vehicle. We were hoping you were in it. Saves us a trip up to your place."

Clay continued to stare at the man.

"Could you step out of the car please, Mr. Danvers?"

Again, Clay hesitated the longest acceptable length of time before opening the door. I took off my seat belt and got out too, staying on my side. Panic nudged my memory for answers. The rear compartment was clean, right? We'd scrubbed our hands and inspected our clothes, right? We'd disposed of all the supplies, right? Check, check, and check. At least, as far as I knew. What if we'd missed something? Was there an overlooked scrap of fabric snagged in the back of the Explorer? Did our clothes smell as strongly of smoke to human noses as they did to mine?

The other officer, a solidly built man in his late thirties, wandered around the Explorer, looking in the back window, then putting his face close to the tinted glass and shielding his eyes so he could see inside.

"Lots of storage space," he said. "How much stuff can you fit in these things?"

"Stuff?" I blinked. "Oh, like baggage? Enough luggage for a week's vacation, I'd guess."

He laughed. "If you pack like my wife, that's saying a lot." He squinted inside. "Sure is nice and clean. You folks don't have kids, do you?" He laughed again and dropped to his knees, checking the tires and the undercarriage. "This is one of those new suburban assault vehicles, isn't it? A four-by-four that's not meant for four-by-four-ing."

"It'll go off-road," I said, struggling to stay calm as he continued to check under the Explorer. "But it's too bulky for serious 4 × 4'ing. Comes in handy in the middle of a New York winter, though."

"I bet it does." He looked over at Clay. "What's the towing capacity on one of these?"

"No idea," Clay said. He'd been standing to the side, letting me handle the niceties. One of his tricks for keeping his temper under control. Avoid confrontation.

"We've never towed with it," I said.

The older cop kept looking under the Explorer, maybe checking the suspension, maybe looking for something else. I waited as long as I could, then asked, "Was I speeding?"

"We had a tip," the younger officer said. He turned to Clay. "An anonymous tip telling us you know something about Mike Braxton's murder. We need you to come to the station to answer some questions."

Clay's jaw tensed. "You expect me to drop whatever I'm doing—"

He stopped. I didn't say anything, but he knew what I was thinking. Antagonizing the cops wasn't going to help. Taking the defensive might make them back off if they didn't have any reason to arrest him, but it was too risky. Piss them off and they might decide to search the Explorer and Clay himself. Small-town cops have a reputation for not always following proper procedure. Legally, they couldn't force Clay to talk to them, but at least they weren't likely to uncover any evidence of our morning's activities through simple conversation.

Clay allowed that he'd spare them an hour. He went to the station in the back of the police car. I followed in the Explorer. The anonymous caller had to be one of the mutts, making this a good bet for a trap. With me following in a separate car, the mutts wouldn't dare try an ambush. Once we were at the station, we'd be safe. They wouldn't attack in a building full of armed humans.

The police station waiting room was smaller than my bedroom at Stonehaven and had probably cost less than my silver vanity set to furnish. It was roughly ten feet square with one door and two windows. Actually, the south window was one-way glass looking into an even smaller room. The one-way glass didn't make much sense until you considered that the entire police station was originally a Depression-era home. Most rooms had to serve double duty. In the unlikely event that the police needed to watch a suspect or an important interview, they probably used the waiting area as an observation room. Clay didn't warrant that treatment; he'd been ushered off to a private interview room as soon as we'd arrived.

The second window was a barred opening into a cage where a twenty-something receptionist covered the phone, the front desk, and the waiting room, while fielding nonstop requests from the officers for typing, filing, and fresh coffee. Don't ask me why the window was barred. Maybe they were afraid she'd escape. The three chairs in the waiting room were upholstered with moth-eaten harvest gold velour and peeling duct tape. I picked the best one and sat down carefully, not letting any exposed skin touch the fabric and reminding myself to wash my clothes as soon as I got home. I sifted though the pile of magazines on a pressed-wood table. The word "Canada" on a copy of *Time* caught my eye. I picked it up, realized the article was about the Quebec referendum and put the magazine back. Not only was it a subject guaranteed to cure insomnia in ninety percent of Canadians but, unless something drastic had happened at home in the past week, it made the magazine over five years old. Very timely indeed.

I glanced up to see the receptionist watching me with the wary look people normally reserve for beggars and rabid dogs. Through the window, I could see the young officer who'd come out to Stonehaven leaning over the counter, talking to the receptionist. Since they were both staring at me, I assumed I was the topic of the conversation. Something told me they weren't discussing the disgraceful condition of my scuffed and graying Reeboks. Doubtless, he was retelling the story of my escapade in the forest. Just what I needed. Ten years of building a decent reputation in Bear Valley and I'd blown it all in a day, running around naked in the woods on a cold spring morning and having my clothing found shredded from some bizarre S/M ritual. Towns like Bear Valley had a special spot for women like me—as guest of honor at the annual summer picnic and bonfire.

As I was leafing through the magazines, the door to the waiting room opened. I looked up to see Karl Marsten walk through, followed by Thomas LeBlanc. Marsten was wearing chinos, thousand-dollar leather shoes, and a designer golf shirt. I didn't notice what LeBlanc was wearing. Beside Marsten, no one would notice. Marsten sauntered in with the casual, unstudied air of a man who'd spent years studying how to look that way. His hands were in his pockets, just enough to look relaxed, not enough to make his pants pull or sag unbecomingly. The half smile on his lips was the perfect mixture of interest, boredom, and amusement. When he turned that smile on the receptionist, she sat up straighter, hands straightening her blouse. He murmured a few words to her. She blushed and squirmed in her seat. Marsten leaned into the bars and said something more. Then he turned to me and rolled his eyes. I shook my head. Karl Marsten's sole redeeming feature was that he knew exactly how much of a fake he was.

"Elena," he said, taking the seat beside me. He kept his voice low, not whispering, but quiet enough that the receptionist couldn't eavesdrop from her cage across the room. "You're looking good."

"Don't practice on me, Karl."

He laughed. "I meant that you look surprisingly good for someone who had a run-in with Zachary Cain. I'm assuming that's where you got the scrape on your cheek. I'm also assuming he's no longer in the game."

"Something like that."

Marsten leaned back and crossed his ankles, obviously very concerned about his partner's passing. "I haven't seen you in a while.

What's it been, two years? Too long. Don't give me that look. I'm not practicing on you and I'm not hitting on you. God gave me a few ounces of brain. I simply meant that I've missed talking to you. If nothing else, you're always intriguing company."

LeBlanc had taken a seat on my other side. I was ignoring him. Given the choice, I'd much rather speak to Marsten than the man who had killed Logan.

"I read a couple magazine articles you wrote," Marsten continued. "Very well done. You've got quite a successful career, it would seem."

"Not as successful as some," I said, eyeing his Rolex. "Bought or stolen?"

His eyes glittered. "Guess."

I thought about it. "Bought. It would be easier—and cheaper—to steal it but you wouldn't wear someone else's jewelry. Though you wouldn't object to buying it with the money you made stealing someone else's jewelry."

"Dead on, as always."

"Business must be good."

Marsten laughed again. "I do well enough, thank you, considering I'm damned useless at everything else. And on that topic, I picked up something a few months ago that made me think of you. A platinum necklace with a wolf's head pendant. Gorgeous craftsmanship. The head is actually woven platinum filigree with emerald chips for eyes. Very elegant. I thought of sending it to you, but I figured it would end up in the nearest trash can."

"Excellent foresight."

"I haven't given it up, though. If you want it, it's yours. No strings attached. It would suit you, a nice twist of irony I'm sure you'd appreciate."

"You know, I'm surprised you're involved in this," I said. "I thought you didn't like Daniel."

Marsten sighed theatrically. "Must we talk shop?"

"I just never pictured you as the anarchist type."

"Anarchist?" He laughed. "Hardly. The others have their reasons for wanting the Pack dead, most of which have to do with allowing them to indulge some rather nasty, antisocial habits. The Pack has never given me any trouble. Of course, they've never done anything for me either. So, in a gesture of reciprocity, I don't care what happens to the Pack one way or the other. I only want my territory."

"If you had that, you'd back out of the fight?"

"And abandon my fellow anarchists? That would be the act of a despicable, unconscionable rogue, someone completely absorbed in furthering his own fortunes at the expense of others. Does that sound like me?"

LeBlanc made a noise of impatience beside me. Before I could resume the conversation with Marsten, he waved his hand at the other man.

"This one wanted to meet you," Marsten said. "When we saw you following the police into town, he decided he wanted to speak to you. I came along to provide the introduction. If he starts to bore you, scream. I'll be reading a magazine." Marsten pulled one from the pile. "*Hunter's Digest.* Hmmm. Maybe I can pick up a few tips."

Marsten settled into his chair and opened the magazine. LeBlanc shot him a look of pure contempt. He'd obviously decided before now that Marsten was a third-rate werewolf, barely deserving of the name. He was wrong. If I had to pick the most dangerous mutt in the country, it would be a toss-up between Marsten and Daniel. How did Marsten gain that reputation? By killing more humans than anyone else? By tormenting the Pack or causing trouble for us? No and no. Marsten was one of the few mutts who didn't kill humans. Like so many things, that was beneath him. As for the Pack, when he met us, he was as civil and personable as he'd been to me right now. Yet we kept a closer eye on him than on any mutt besides Daniel. Why? Because he possessed a single-minded strength of purpose that rivaled Clay's. When Marsten moved into a new town, he met with any werewolves in the area, took them out to an expensive dinner, chatted them up, gave them one warning to clear out of town, then killed them if they weren't gone by midnight. What Marsten wanted, Marsten took . . . with no compunction and no rancor. What he wanted now was territory. For several years, he'd been making noises about settling in one place, joking that he was hitting retirement age. The Pack had ignored him. Now Marsten was tired of waiting. Today he'd sit beside me, compliment me on my writing, and offer me jewelry. Tomorrow, if I got in his way, he'd take me out of the game. Nothing personal, that was just the way it worked.

Impressions

FOR AT LEAST TEN MINUTES LE BLANC STUDIED ME LIKE AN ENTOmologist examining some new kind of insect. I wanted to leave. Maybe that was the plan. Let this scumbag gawk at me long enough and I'd bolt to the bathroom to scrub my hands, where he and Marsten could corner me. I tried only to remember that LeBlanc had killed Logan and attacked Jeremy, but I couldn't. I kept thinking of the women he'd killed, the details I'd read in his scrapbook. For Logan, I wanted to kill him. For the others, I wanted him dead, but didn't want to do it myself, since that would require physical contact.

I forced myself to forget these things and concentrate on sizing him up. Life hadn't been good to Thomas LeBlanc in the past few years. He'd fallen a long way from the well-groomed man in his arrest photo. That wasn't to say he was greasy or unshaven, any of the things the average person expects of a serial killer psychopath. He looked like a thirty-something laborer wearing no-name jeans, a faded T-shirt, and sneakers from Wal-Mart. He'd put on weight since his photo. Unfortunately, it was muscle, not fat.

"You wanted to talk to me?" I said finally.

"I was wondering what all the fuss was about," he said, giving me a look that said he was still wondering.

He fell into silent bug-gazing mode again. It took all my strength to stay beside him. I fought to keep things in perspective: he was a new werewolf; I was an experienced werewolf. No sweat. But my frame of reference kept shifting. He preyed on women; I was a woman. No matter how much I rationalized, no matter how tough I tried to be, this man scared me. Scared me deep in my gut, where logic and reason couldn't intrude.

After a few minutes, a shadow of movement passed the one-way glass. Anxious for the distraction, I got up and walked over. Clay was in the other room. Alone. He sat at the table and leaned back in his chair, tipping the front legs off the ground. He wasn't cuffed or guarded or bruised and battered. Good. So far.

"That's him?" LeBlanc said from behind me. "The infamous Clayton Danvers? Say it isn't so."

I kept watching Clay.

"Jesus fucking Christ," LeBlanc muttered. "Where the hell did the Pack find you two? At a beach volleyball tournament? Great tan. Love those curls." LeBlanc shook his head. "He's not even as big as I am. He's what, six foot nothing? Two hundred pounds in steel-toed boots? Christ. I'm expecting some ugly bruiser bigger than Cain and what do I find? The next *Baywatch* star. Looks like his IQ would be low enough. Can he chew gum and tie his shoes at the same time?"

Clay stopped playing with his chair and turned to face the mirror. He got up, crossed the room, and stood in front of me. I was leaning forward, one hand pressed against the glass. Clay touched his fingertips to mine and smiled. LeBlanc jumped back.

"Fuck," he said. "I thought that was one-way glass."

"It is."

Clay turned his head toward LeBlanc and mouthed three words. Then the door to his room opened and one of the officers called him out. Clay grinned at me, then sauntered out with the officer. As he left, a surge of renewed confidence ran through me.

"What did he say?" LeBlanc asked.

" 'Wait for me.' "

"What?"

"It's a challenge," Marsten murmured from across the room. He didn't look up from his magazine. "He's inviting you to stick around and get to know him better."

"Are *you* going to?" LeBlanc said.

Marsten's lips curved in a smile. "He didn't invite me."

LeBlanc snorted. "For a bunch of killer monsters, the whole lot of you are nothing but hot air. All your rules and challenges and false bravado." He waved a hand at me. "Like you. Standing there so nonchalantly, pretending you aren't the least bit concerned about having the two of us in the room."

"I'm not."

"You should be. Do you know how fast I could kill you? You're standing two feet away from me. If I had a gun or knife in my pocket, you'd be dead before you had time to scream."

"Really? Huh."

LeBlanc's cheek twitched. "You don't believe me, do you? How do you know I'm not packing a gun? There's no metal detector at the door. I could pull one out now, kill you, and escape in thirty seconds."

"Then do it. I know, you don't like our little games, but humor me. If you have a gun or a knife, pull it out. If not, pretend to. Prove you could do it."

"I don't need to prove anything. Certainly not to a smart-mouthed—"

He whipped his hand up in mid-sentence. I grabbed it and snapped his wrist. The sound cracked through the room. The receptionist glanced over, but LeBlanc had his back to her. I smiled at her and she turned away.

"You—fucking—bitch," LeBlanc gasped, cradling his arm. "You broke my wrist."

"So I win."

His face purpled. "You smug—"

"Nobody likes a sore loser," I said. "Grit your teeth and bear it. There's no crying in werewolf games. Didn't Daniel teach you that?"

"I think you've outworn your welcome," Marsten said, getting to his feet and tossing the magazine back on the stack.

When LeBlanc didn't move, Marsten stepped toward him and reached for his arm. LeBlanc sidestepped before Marsten could touch him, glared once at me, then strode from the room.

"The joys of baby-sitting," Marsten said. "I'll be off then. Say hello to Clayton for me." Marsten left.

I stood there, heart pounding. I'd pulled it off, hidden my fear with false bravado and LeBlanc hadn't noticed the difference. Piece of cake. I could beat this mutt no problem. So why was my heart still jumping around like a rabbit in a trap?

Twenty minutes later, I was still in the waiting room, trying very hard to find something to read. A survey in *Cosmo* caught my eye. It was entitled: "Constructive Arguing: Are You Strengthening Your Relationship with Your Lover or Driving Him Away." Intriguing, especially the part about driving him away, but I forced myself to put the magazine down. *Cosmo* never speaks to my life. Its surveys always ask questions like How would you react if your lover announced he was taking a job in Alaska? and jumping for joy is never one of the options. Move to Alaska? Hell, my lover was thirty-seven and hadn't moved away from home yet. Where were the questions relevant to my life? What about How would you react if your lover's hair and footprints were found beside a dead man? Show me that in *Cosmo* and you have a subscriber.

I was searching for something else to read when Clay walked into the room. Again the receptionist perked up. She smiled and murmured something I couldn't catch. All she got in return was a level stare and a dismissive twist of the lip. As she deflated back into her typing, I almost felt sorry for her. Clay could be such a charmer.

"Death penalty?" I asked as he walked over to me.

"In your dreams. It was bullshit, darling. Pure bullshit and I missed lunch because of it."

"You should sue."

"I might do that." He walked back to the door and held it open for me. "So you had visitors?"

"Marsten and LeBlanc."

"What did Marsten want?"

"He offered me a necklace."

"In return for?"

"Nothing. Just Karl being Karl. As personable as ever, totally disregarding the small matter of being on opposite sides of a bloody battle to the death. Speaking of death, LeBlanc boasted he could kill me in the waiting room. I broke his wrist. He wasn't impressed."

"Good. What did he tag along for?"

"To stare at me, I think. Didn't seem too impressed with what he saw, either."

Clay snorted and we headed into the parking lot.

We parked in the drive at Stonehaven. Jeremy met us at the front door.

"You missed lunch," he said. "Did something go wrong?"

"Nah," Clay said. "I got hauled down to the police station for questioning."

"*After* we took care of Cain," I said, before Jeremy experienced any major chest pains. "I'd have called from the station, but the phone was too public. The police pulled us over on the way back from dumping the body. Looks like Daniel tipped them off that Clay might know something about Mike Braxton's death. Seems he hoped they'd catch us before we disposed of Cain's body. No such luck, though."

"How much did the police seem to know?"

"Not much," Clay said. "The questions were pretty general. A fishing expedition."

"Did they search the car?"

"Hard to say," I said. "One of them took a really good look through the windows and checked out the undercarriage. He acted like he was only interested in the Explorer in general, how much can it store, how does it do off-road, stuff like that. On the other hand, it may have been his way of doing a subtle plain-view search."

"Wonderful," Jeremy said, shaking his head. "Come inside and eat quickly. We need to leave."

"Have you figured out how to get a message to Daniel?" I asked.

Jeremy waved his hand. "That wasn't a problem. I've already conveyed my message."

"Did he reply?"

"Yes, but it doesn't concern what we're doing right now. Hurry up. We haven't much time."

"Where're we going?" Clay asked, but Jeremy was already in the house.

Less than an hour later, the five of us were in the Explorer. It was the first time the Pack didn't need to take multiple vehicles to travel together. There were only five of us left. Of course, I'd noticed that before, but I hadn't actually *realized* it until we were driving down the highway in one car. Five left. Four men and one woman who wasn't sure she even counted herself as part of the group. If I left, would there be a Pack? Could two fathers and two sons be considered a Pack? I shook off the thought. With or without me, the Pack would survive. It always had. Besides, there was no urgent need for me to declare my independence now or even in the near future. I planned to return to Toronto when this was over, but as Jeremy had said, there was no need to make a hasty decision on my Pack status.

We were going to the airport to meet Jimmy Koenig. Call it a surprise welcoming committee. Jeremy had found out that Koenig was arriving in New York City today on the 7:10 P.M. flight from Seattle. Don't ask me how he knew. I guessed the information came as the result of several phone calls, a few lies, and a heap of good manners. That was Jeremy's usual method. It was amazing what you could learn from airline clerks, motel reservation staff, credit card phone reps, and other customer service employees simply by telling a good story and being exceedingly polite doing it. Like I said, I assumed this was what Jeremy did. He didn't mention the how when parlaying the information. He never did. If it was anyone else, I'd suspect him of showing off, like a magician pulling the rabbit from the hat without revealing the trick. With Jeremy, I knew he had no such motive. He'd consider it showing off to give an explanation, as if expecting us to be wowed by his cleverness.

The plan was to meet Koenig at the gate, help him with his luggage, and escort him back to Bear Valley in high style after getting reacquainted over a few drinks at 21. Really.

Okay. That wasn't the plan.

The plan was to terminate the sorry mutt before he got his first look at the Empire State Building. The time for carefully exploring the problem was over. At last, we were taking action.

Vengeance

THE FLIGHT FROM SEATTLE WAS FORTY MINUTES LATE, WHICH WAS a good thing, considering that we didn't get there until twenty minutes after the plane was due to arrive. A jackknifed tractor trailer on the highway put us nearly an hour behind schedule. Antonio squealed into the airport at seven-thirty, weaved through traffic like a New York cabbie, and dropped us off at the front doors a couple minutes later. By the time he found a parking spot and joined us in the terminal, Koenig's flight was touching down. We'd made it, but barely. I wasn't sure whether to interpret that as a good omen or bad.

We stood well back from the crowd of welcoming friends and relatives, and watched the passengers disembark. Jimmy Koenig was easy to spot. He was tall and scrawny with a face that could be mistaken for Keith Richards on a bad day. He looked every day of his sixty-two years, his body's revenge for fifty years of being subjected to every stress test known to man. Too much booze, too many drugs, and way too many mornings waking up in strange hotel rooms beside even stranger women. The people who script Just Say No campaign ads should hire guys like Jimmy Koenig. Flash his face on television and any kid with an ounce of vanity would swear off booze and dope for life. Trust me.

Koenig wasn't traveling alone. He got off the plane with a guy who looked like his FBI escort—thirty-something, clean-shaven, and well-groomed, wearing a dark suit and dark sunglasses. Though his eyes were hidden behind the shades, his head turned from side to side as if constantly scanning his surroundings. I almost expected to see handcuffs linking him to Koenig. When they got to the bottom of the Jetway, they stopped. The two exchanged a brief flurry of words. FBI guy looked pissed, but Koenig wasn't backing down. After a few minutes, FBI guy stalked off toward the baggage claim area. Koenig headed for the waiting room and plopped into the nearest chair.

"Clay, Elena, take Koenig," Jeremy said. "Tonio and I'll go after his friend. Nick?"

"I'll stick with Clay," Nick said.

Jeremy nodded and he and Antonio started for the baggage area. After Clay and I discussed tactics, Clay and Nick headed off into the crowd. I waited until they were out of sight, then looped around a loud family reunion and walked behind Koenig. When I got to his seat, I stood in back of his chair and waited. It took a couple of minutes before his head jerked up. He sniffed the air, then slowly turned.

"Boo," I said.

He reacted as all mutts react when I confront them. He leapt from his chair and dove for the nearest exit, shaking in terror. In my dreams. He glanced at me and started looking for Clay. It never failed. Mutts only quaked when I appeared because it usually meant Clayton wasn't far behind. I was nothing but a harbinger of doom.

"Where is he?" Koenig asked, narrowing his eyes and surveying the crowds.

"It's only me," I said.

"Yeah, right."

I circled around the row of chairs and sat down beside Koenig. There was only the barest whiff of scotch on his breath, meaning he'd only imbibed a single drink on the plane. Again, I wasn't sure if this was a good sign or not. When sober, he was like a toothless lion, nasty but with little bite. It also meant, though, that his brain and reflexes were in perfect working order.

"Clay's gone to take care of your buddy with the shades," I said.

"Budd—" Koenig stopped and grunted.

"He figured I could handle you on my own."

Koenig's dark eyes snapped, obviously insulted. He muttered something. I was about to ask him to repeat himself when I saw Nick approaching from the other side. I watched him and swore under my breath. Koenig jerked his head around to look. When he saw Nick, his first reaction was relief. He started to relax, then tensed again. Nick might not be as bad as Clay but, as far as Koenig was concerned, he was definitely more cause for concern than me.

"Son-of-a-bitch," I muttered. "He wasn't supposed to interfere."

Nick grinned, not a friendly smile, but the predatory grin of a hunter scenting prey. His strides lengthened as he walked toward us. His gaze was fixed on Koenig.

"Nicholas . . ." I warned beneath my breath as I got to my feet.

Koenig fell for it. Thinking I was preoccupied getting ready to confront Nick, he bolted. Nick flashed a victory grin at me and we took off in pursuit. Although Koenig was running, he wasn't getting very far. It was like racing through a dense forest. He kept weaving to circumvent people and chairs and only succeeded in avoiding one to crash into the next. Nick and I pursued at a quick walk. Not only was it easier to dodge obstacles, but it wouldn't look as if we were chasing Koenig. Considering Koenig's appearance, no one seemed to think it was odd that he was tearing through the airport running from invisible pursuers. People probably figured he was drunk, stoned, or having one hell of a sixties flashback. They cursed when he mowed them down, but no one got involved.

Nick and I kept on opposite sides of Koenig. It was the same technique we'd used with the deer. Keep him running and steer him toward the finish line. And guess who was waiting at the finish line? I was almost surprised that Koenig fell for it. I say "almost," because I knew better than to be completely shocked that he'd fall for such an old ruse. Mutts didn't hunt deer. The pattern for the trick may have been in Koenig's brain, but he'd never bothered to use it so he didn't recognize it when it was being played on him.

I followed Clay's scent and we herded Koenig out of the crowded lobby, down a deserted hall, and behind a narrow stairwell. Clay jumped out from the stairwell, grabbed Koenig by the throat, and broke his neck. Anticlimactic, really, but we couldn't afford the risk of questioning him in a busy airport. Jeremy said to kill him, so that was what Clay did, with absolute efficiency. Before Koenig's body even went limp, Clay was stuffing him into the shadows under the stairwell.

"Are we leaving him here?" I asked.

"Nah. There's an exit door over there. I saw Dumpsters outside. If you guys stand guard, I'll move him."

"Do you need both of us?" I asked. "Tonio and Jeremy might need help."

"Good idea. Go on then. Nick can handle guard duty."

I took off.

By the time I got to the baggage claim area, most of the people from Koenig's flight had come and gone. All that was left were the inevitable stragglers standing by the conveyer belt, staring at it, transfixed. With each pile of luggage that passed, they perked up and checked it over, hoping against hope that their baggage was somehow there, hidden from sight, refusing to believe it had been devoured by the demon god of lost luggage. FBI guy was not amongst the believers. Nor were Jeremy and Antonio. I took one last look around, then headed back the way I'd come.

By the washrooms, I caught sight of FBI guy. I tried to pick up the werewolf scent, but it was lost amidst the stink of strangers. I also didn't smell Jeremy or Antonio, but that wasn't surprising. First, with all the human traffic that went up and down that hall every hour, I was lucky I could pick out any scent at all. Second, Jeremy was probably approaching from another angle, being far less inclined to childish stunts like walking up to his target and saying boo.

I followed the new werewolf's trail, staying well enough back that I wouldn't bump into him and screw up Jeremy's plan—whatever that was. I expected the mutt to walk back into the terminal where Koenig had been waiting. He didn't. Instead, he went out a side exit. I followed him onto some kind of laneway that looked like a loading zone. From there, he headed toward the parking lot.

Again his route didn't meet my expectations. Instead of going into the parking lot, he turned down another lane. As I started down it, a high-pitched bleating shattered the silence and I jerked around to see a forklift motoring up behind me. I jumped out of the way. As the machine scooted past, the driver stabbed a finger toward the parking lot, but didn't slow down, obviously too busy to worry about tourists wandering into what was probably a restricted area. After that, I kept close to the wall, ready to hightail it to a hiding spot if someone else appeared.

I raced to the end of the alley, but the mutt had vanished. I searched for his scent. It was still lost, now hidden by the smells of machinery and exhaust. I began to suspect that Jeremy and Antonio were nowhere nearby. The air was dense with oil and diesel fumes. They'd probably given up long ago. I was about to turn back when I rounded a corner and saw the mutt less than twenty feet away. I quickly stepped back out of sight, stopped, listened, and considered my options. If I was so certain Jeremy and Antonio weren't around, I should back off. Jeremy would tear a strip out of my hide if I went after the mutt alone, even if I succeeded in bringing him down. I knew this, but the temptation was too great. Telling myself I only wanted a better look, I crept forward.

When I got around the corner again, the mutt was gone. Keeping close to the building on my left, I slipped along the roadway and found him. We walked another fifteen or twenty feet. Then he stopped and looked around, as if getting his bearings. I flattened myself against the wall and waited. When he resumed walking, I stayed in my hiding place, letting him get farther ahead. I was so busy concentrating on my prey that I didn't hear footsteps behind me. Too late, I turned. An arm grabbed me by the throat and shoved me against the wall.

"Elena," LeBlanc said. "Fancy meeting you here."

I jerked my head to look down the alley, expecting FBI guy to be circling back. He was gone.

"Friend of yours?" LeBlanc asked.

"Yours, not mine."

LeBlanc's eyebrows went up, then he laughed. "Ah, I see. You were tracking him because you saw him talking to Koenig, so you figured he was one of us. Faulty deduction, girlie. Very faulty. Koenig's protégé didn't make it. Couldn't handle the Change. Died yesterday. Too bad, so sad. Daniel sent me to pick the old coot up. I saw your bunch lurking around, so I stood back and took in the show. Then I saw you take off and thought, huh, maybe this errand could be fun after all."

As he spoke, I tensed for attack, but before I could strike, he pulled something from his pocket. A gun. LeBlanc lifted the pistol and rested it against the middle of my forehead. The ground swayed beneath me, my knees threatening to give way. Stop it, I told myself. He's playing a game. Not the sort of game you're used to, but a game nonetheless. Sure, there was a gun at my forehead, but I'd find a way out of this. Mutts were predictable beasts. LeBlanc wouldn't kill me because I was a prize too valuable to waste on a few seconds of murderous pleasure. I was the only female werewolf. He might try to rape me or kidnap me or rough me up a bit, but he wouldn't kill me.

I swallowed my fear. False bravado had worked last time. Stick with the tried-and-true.

"Werewolves don't use guns," I said. "Weapons are for wimps. You guys realize that, right?"

"Shut up," LeBlanc said, tilting his gun up.

"Guess you were right about us not being too bright," I said. "If I was smart, I'd have broken your right wrist. How is it anyway? Giving you any trouble?"

"Shut up."

"Just making small talk."

"If you want to talk," LeBlanc said, "I'd suggest you start with an apology."

"For what?"

His face went deep red, eyes suffusing with an emotion it took me a moment to recognize. Hate. Pure hate, ten times stronger than what I'd seen at the police station that morning. Was he that angry with me for breaking his wrist? The thought came as something of a shock. Of course, most people would get a bit pissed about stuff like that, but mutts didn't normally make a big deal of it, especially if I was the one doing the damage. In fact, they usually laughed it off, as if in some perverse way they were pleased with me for having the guts to do it. Years ago, I'd bit off one of Daniel's ears. He didn't hold a grudge. If anything, he was proud of that missing ear, and would tell any mutt who asked exactly how he'd come to lose it, as if it proved we had some kind of close, personal relationship. Nothing says lovin' like permanent mutilation.

"Is it the wrist?" I asked. "You're the one who wanted to prove you could knife me. I was only proving I could defend myself."

"Bullshit. You thought it was funny. Humiliate the new guy. We got back to the house, what do you think Marsten does? Tells Daniel and Olson. Gave them a good laugh." He cocked the gun. "I want an apology."

I thought about this. Apologizing wasn't a big deal. Of course, I wasn't sorry I'd done it, but he didn't need to know that. The words stuck in my craw, though. Why should I apologize? Well, stupid, because the guy has a gun to your head. But if I was sure he wasn't going to use it. . . . It didn't matter. There was no sense escalating the matter.

"I'm sorry," I said. "I didn't mean to embarrass you."

"On your knees."

"What?"

"Apologize on your knees."

"The hell I—"

LeBlanc rammed the gun into my mouth. I clamped down involuntarily. Needles of pain ran though my jaw as my teeth hit metal. I tried to jerk away, but he had me backed against the wall. LeBlanc shoved the gun in until I gagged.

The taste of metal was sharp and foul. I tried to pull my tongue back, but the barrel was in too far. My heart was tripping, but I wasn't panicking. Whatever LeBlanc said, I knew he wouldn't kill me. He expected that the threat of death would be enough to make me do whatever he wanted. He'd realize his mistake soon enough. As soon as I figured out how to get his gun out of my mouth. Even as I thought this, I realized the answer was simple. I hated to do it, but it was the easiest way.

I lifted one leg, making a motion to show that I was ready to kneel. LeBlanc's lips twisted in an ugly smile and he pulled the gun from my mouth.

"Good girl," LeBlanc said. "Werewolf or not, I see you're still a woman. When push comes to shove, you know your place."

I gritted my teeth and kept my eyes down, which he seemed to take as proof that I'd been properly cowed.

"Well?" he said.

I tilted my head forward, letting my hair fall in a curtain around my face. Then I started to sniffle.

LeBlanc laughed. "Not nearly so cocky now, are you?"

Triumph rang from his voice. I sniffled some more and lifted a hand to wipe at my eyes. Through the blindfold of my hair, I could only see LeBlanc's lower half. It was enough. After a couple seconds of my crying, his arm dropped, letting the gun fall to his side. I lifted both hands to my face, covering it. Then, I pulled my hands down again, wrapped my left hand over my right fist and brought both hands slamming upward into LeBlanc's crotch. As he stumbled back, I lunged. I knocked him down and started running. Halfway down the alley, I heard the first shot. Instinctively, I flung myself forward to the ground. Something stung my left shoulder. I hit the pavement in an awkward half flip, managed to get back to my feet, and kept going. Two shots rang out in quick succession, but I was already rounding the corner.

As I ran, blood trickled down my shoulder, but the pain was minimal, no more than a nasty scrape. Left shoulder, I thought. And six inches or so below the left shoulder, my heart. He'd been aiming for my heart. I shook the thought and impending panic from my head. Behind me, I could hear his running footfalls. I took the first corner, then the next and the next, keeping my straight-out runs short so he wouldn't have a chance at another shot. It worked for about five minutes, then I ended up in a long alley with no exit except at the end. I leaned forward and sprinted like hell. It wasn't fast enough. LeBlanc rounded the corner before I got to the end of the alley. Another shot. Another dive. This time either the shot wasn't accurate or I'd moved faster. The bullet whammed into the side of a Dumpster. I veered left and made a headlong dash forward. A car was directly in front of me, and another one beside it, and another and another. Parking lot. A spark of joy zinged through me. A public place. Safety.

I raced around the corner, getting out of shooting range. As I ran, I tried to find the largest concentration of human activity. That was the key. Get near enough people that LeBlanc would be forced to hide his gun. If he didn't, I'd attract attention by screaming—a feminine ploy almost as universally effective as crying. In my first glimpse around, I didn't see anyone, but it was hard to take a good look while running full out. I swerved down a line of cars and slowed behind the shield of a minivan. I looked around. There was no one on the east side of the parking lot. I peeked over the passenger door and squinted through the window to check the west side. There was no one around. Absolutely no one. I was either in an employee parking lot or in long-term parking.

LeBlanc's scent floated over on the breeze.

I dropped to my hands and knees. Taking a deep breath, I controlled the returning panic and lowered my head to survey the lot from ground level. About fifty feet to my right were a pair of sneakers. LeBlanc. I rolled under the minivan and craned my neck to get a better look around. The rows of tires seemed to stretch to infinity in every direction. After a moment, I decided that the line of tires to my right seemed the shortest. Creeping on my stomach, I moved to the front of the minivan, stuck my head out and looked left. Beyond the parking lot, I couldn't see anything. As I watched, a car went by the end of the row. Then another. Some kind of road. Maybe only a service route, but where there were moving cars there had to be people. I eased out from under the minivan and started forward, staying doubled over behind the cars.

"Come out, come out, wherever you are," LeBlanc chanted.

A brief pause, then: "I don't like games, Elena. You make me look for you and you'll regret it. I can make you regret it. You took my scrapbook. You know what I can do."

I moved along the rear of a sedan and peered around the other side, checking before I dashed across an empty parking spot. A flash of motion caught my eye and I yanked my head back. Looking under the car, I saw LeBlanc's shoes. I froze and checked the wind direction. Southeast. I was upwind. I stopped breathing, but knew it wouldn't matter if

I didn't make any noise. He'd smell me. He had to. The sneakers passed the other end of the sedan and kept moving. LeBlanc didn't even pause. I closed my eyes and exhaled slowly. He wasn't using his nose. One less concern. I waited until his shoes vanished, then kept moving down the narrow passage between the two rows of parked cars. Each time I came to an empty space, I checked before crossing it. More than once there wasn't room to pass between the cars, the driver having pulled up within inches of the car in the opposite row. This was trickier than dashing across the empty spaces. I could go over or under. The first time, I tried to go over and set the car rocking. I spent a few breathless minutes standing there before I was sure LeBlanc hadn't noticed. After that, when cars abutted each other, I went under. Slower but safer.

I'd gone past fifteen cars and estimated another ten to go when I heard footsteps to my left. I dropped down, stopped moving, and listened. I knew LeBlanc was to my left, but at last check, he was left and rear. These footsteps came from left and front. They didn't sound like sneakers either. Hard-soled footsteps clacked across the pavement moving fast and coming almost straight for me. I fell to my stomach and looked out under the row of cars. Brown pumps were moving fast down the row immediately to my left. A woman hurrying to her car. I thought about standing up, waving my arms, calling attention to myself. Would one witness be enough to keep LeBlanc from firing?

"Aha," LeBlanc sang out.

My head jolted up and hit the undercarriage of the car with a thunderous bang. LeBlanc cursed and started running. I looked about wildly, trying to see his feet to figure out which way to escape. The woman. I had to take the chance and bolt toward her. But I couldn't hear her footsteps anymore. Was she already in her car?

"Fuck!" LeBlanc shouted. "I don't fucking believe it. Elena!"

I stopped moving. Why was he calling me? He knew where I was, didn't he? Even if he hadn't been calling out to me, he must have heard my head strike the car's underside. The sound had been so loud it had reverberated through the parking lot. LeBlanc was still cursing. I followed the sound and saw LeBlanc's sneakers about twenty feet away. And beside his shoes, the body of a woman, lying on the pavement, open eyes staring at me beneath a bloody crater in the middle of her forehead. When LeBlanc had shouted, it wasn't because he'd seen me. The bang I'd heard hadn't been my head hitting the car. He'd seen a motion, a woman moving fast, caught a glimpse of light-colored hair and fired. As I stared at the dead woman I started to shake. I told myself that my horror was for her, an innocent, gunned down in a parking lot. It wasn't true. The tightness in my throat and the pounding in my chest wasn't for her. It was for me. I looked at her body, staring sightless into eternity, and I saw myself lying there. It was supposed to be me. Killed in a second. One brief second. Alive and running. Then dead. Over. Everything. Would I have heard the shot? Would I have felt it? I could have died here, today, in this parking lot. I could still die. This morning could have been my last time waking up. Lunch my last meal. Thirty minutes ago in the airport, the last time I saw Antonio, Nick, Jeremy . . . Clay. The shaking got worse. I could die. Really die. Despite all my battles, I'd never thought of that before. Never really contemplated what it meant. The end could come in one impossibly short second. Now, thinking of it, I was afraid. More afraid than I'd ever been.

I felt stabs of pain in my clenched fists. I unclenched them and the pain lessened into a stretching, a pulsating as if something was moving under the skin. I ignored it. I had more important things to think about. Yet the sensation didn't go away. It got worse. I glanced down and saw my fingers retracting into my hands, hair sprouting from the backs. I hadn't done anything to precipitate a Change, hadn't even thought about it. I shook my hands sharply and flexed them, willing the transformation to stop. As I moved my fingers, fresh pain shot down my arms. Then my feet started to tingle. I closed my eyes and ordered my body to stop. My back arched. My shirt started to rip. No! my brain shouted. Not now! Stop! It didn't stop. My legs jerked and spasmed, wanting to pull under my body, but there wasn't room. I was jammed under a new VW Beetle with barely inches to spare. I couldn't get up on all fours. I couldn't move my legs and arms into position. I clenched my eyes shut and concentrated. Nothing happened. The first licks of alarm darted through me. As they came, the Change sped up, my clothing tearing and my body intent on moving itself into impossible contortions. The fear was doing it. Fear of being trapped in this parking lot with a killer had started the Change and now the fear of being trapped under the car was making it worse. I knew what I had to do. I had to get out. A fresh spark of fear made my torso jerk up, crashing my back into the underside of the car. This time I knew the resulting bang was real. Dimly I heard LeBlanc's shoes squeak against the pavement. Heard him say something. Heard him laugh . . .

I vaulted from under the Beetle. My nails scraped against the pavement. Halfway out my legs seized up and I fell face first to the ground. Every muscle in my arms and legs seemed to spasm at once. A howl of agony broke from my throat. I clamped my jaw shut. My eyes bugged out with the pain. It was too late to reverse the Change. I'd passed the midway mark; going back would take longer than going forward. I focused my energy on finishing, feeding it with fear. At last, the final phase hit with a shuddering wave of agony so blinding that I passed out. I came to as soon as my muzzle hit the pavement, then lay on my stomach, panting and gulping air. I didn't want to move. I could hear footsteps getting closer. He'd heard me. He knew approximately where I was and was narrowing his search, closing in. For a moment, I was too exhausted to care. Then I turned my head and saw the dead woman. Heaving myself to my feet, I started to run.

Any thoughts of a cautious, stealthy escape had fled from my brain, overpowered by the need to get away as quickly as possible. I tore out from between the cars, got onto the laneway and ran full-out. I didn't listen for sounds of pursuit. I couldn't waste the energy. I poured everything I had into running. A shout rang out behind me. Then a shot. It whizzed over my head. I didn't slow or veer from my course. I blocked out everything and kept going. Finally the row of cars came to an end. I was on a through road. A horn blared. A gust of air from a passing truck sliced through my fur. Still, I didn't slow down. On the other side of the road were two buildings. I ran toward them, no longer knowing where I was going, just that I had to get away.

As I was emerging from between the buildings, I heard a shout. Someone calling my name. The sound came from beside me. I hunkered down and ran faster. A brick wall suddenly popped up in my path. I tried to stop, but it was too late. My legs slid out from under me and I skidded into the wall with a bone-jarring thud. Behind me, LeBlanc was still running, shouting my name. I got to my feet and twisted around to see the shape of my pursuer at my back. There wasn't time to escape. Even as I was still turning, I launched myself at him. As I flew through the air, his arm went up, blocking his throat. I hit him full in the chest and we toppled over backward. I curled my lips. As I slashed down, the red fog of panic that blinded me cleared and I saw who lay beneath me. Not LeBlanc. Clay.

I yanked my head back just in time. The momentum of the sudden change in direction sent me tumbling sideways. When I tried scrambling up, Clay grabbed me and held me still. He whispered something, but I couldn't make it out. Not seeing any comprehension in my eyes, he waited a second, then spoke again, enunciating slowly.

"He's gone," he said. "Don't worry. He's gone."

I hesitated and looked back between the two buildings, certain LeBlanc would appear at any moment, gun in hand. Clay shook his head.

"He's gone, darling. When you crossed the road, he backed off. Too public."

I still waited, shaking. Clay buried his hands in my fur and tried to pull me against him, but I resisted. We had to be ready to run. He started saying something when footsteps echoed from somewhere nearby. I leapt to my feet, but Clay restrained me. Jeremy, Antonio, and Nick emerged from around the building. I stood there a moment, legs trembling, sniffing the air to make sure my eyes weren't betraying me. Yes, they were here. They were all here. I was safe. I paused for a second, then sank to the ground.

Promise

CLAY SAT BESIDE ME ON THE WAY BACK TO STONEHAVEN. I WAS still shaky, maybe even in shock, but he didn't try to pull me against him or comfort me. He knew better. Instead, he held my hand and glanced over from time to time, checking whether I wanted to talk about it. I didn't.

We were almost home when Clay broke the silence, leaning forward to catch Jeremy's attention in the front passenger seat. "You didn't tell us what Daniel demanded," he said. "It was Elena, wasn't it?"

"Yes," Jeremy said softly, not turning.

Antonio turned off the highway. "It's like an airplane hijacker asking for ten billion dollars. He knows we wouldn't consider it, so it's another way of saying he's not dealing."

"It's not just that," Clay said. "He's giving us a warning. He knows we would never give Elena up. He's telling us his next move. He's going to take her."

Jeremy nodded. "I should have realized that. We could have saved ourselves a very close call. I thought as Tonio did—that by asking for Elena, Daniel was saying he wouldn't bargain."

Nick asked, "So that mutt at the airport was trying to kidnap Elena?"

"No," I said. "He was trying to kill me."

"A mutt wouldn't do that, Elena," Jeremy began. "You're too valuable to them alive. It may have seemed—"

"You weren't there. A woman was hurrying through the parking lot. LeBlanc mistook her for me and blew a hole through her head. That's not an incapacitating shot. That's an execution."

Clay's hand tightened around mine. Jeremy pulled back into his seat. No one spoke for at least five minutes.

"Why would he do that?" Nick asked. "If Daniel wants you, he'd want you alive."

"LeBlanc doesn't give a damn what Daniel wants," I said. "Maybe it's because he's new or because he's been killing on his own for so long, but he doesn't seem to have the instinct to obey a stronger werewolf."

"But why kill you at all?" Nick said. "Like Jeremy says, these new mutts have no stake in this fight, other than some promise to Daniel. If Daniel doesn't want you dead, why go through all that trouble trying to kill you?"

"Thomas LeBlanc preys on women. He tortures them and rapes them and kills them. Men like that hate women and they're easily threatened by them. I forgot that. After all my talk about not treating these men like other mutts, I did exactly that. I humiliated him at the police station, taunted him, insulted him, and broke his wrist in front of Marsten. Now he wants to overpower me. He needs to."

Clay's thumb rubbed against my wrist, but he said nothing. Neither did anyone else.

When we got to Stonehaven, I went up to my room. As I climbed the stairs, I could hear Clay behind me, but I didn't say anything. I walked into my room, leaving the door open. He closed it behind him. I got partway to my bed and stopped. I stood there, Clay still silent behind me. A cold worm of fear wound up through my body and I started to shake. I gulped air and closed my eyes. I was okay. I was home and I was safe. And I'd almost been killed. The fear shot through me, mingling with anger and outrage, melding into something white-hot. I wanted to dive into my bed and hide under the covers. I wanted to throw something against the wall and watch it shatter. I wanted to storm back to those mutts and scream "How dare you!"

When I looked at Clay, I saw my emotions mirrored in his face, the anger and the outrage and something so rare I barely recognized it, a haunted look half hidden behind his eyes. Fear. He reached out and pulled me to him. I turned my face to his, found his lips and kissed him. His lips parted against mine. I kissed him harder, closing my eyes and pressing myself into him. Some spark of life penetrated the dead shock in my brain. I chased it, kissing him harder still, deeper, moving my body against his. The spark fanned into a flame, and all my senses jumped to life again. The world shrank and all I could experience, all I wanted to experience was him. I tasted him, smelled him, saw him, heard him, felt him, and reveled in the sensations like someone rising from a coma.

Moving backward toward the bed, our feet tangled and we tumbled onto the carpet. Once on the floor, I grabbed Clay's shirt and yanked it up, but his arms were still around me and I couldn't bear to make him pull back, as if that one second of broken contact would send me sliding back into fear and shock. I wrapped my fists in the back of his shirt and tore. As the material ripped, I stopped pulling. It was too much bother, too much wasted time. I moved my hands to his jeans, tore open the fly, and shoved them down over his hips. Still kissing me, he kicked them off, then fumbled with mine. I pushed his hands away and took off my pants myself. As I was pushing them down, Clay ripped my underwear and threw it aside. His hand moved from my rear to my inner thigh. He slid his fingers inside me.

"No," I said, twisting away from his hand.

I reached down and pulled him inside me. His eyes widened. I moved against him. When he drew back and thrust, I grabbed his hips and held him still.

"Don't," I panted. "Let me."

He shifted up and held himself motionless over me. I arched my hips to his and rubbed against him. Above me, Clay gasped. A shudder ran through him and I pushed his shoulders up off me so I could watch him. As I moved, he kept his eyes on mine, the tip of his tongue showing between his teeth as he fought to keep still. I thrust up against him and held myself there, relishing the control, the feeling of taking control after I'd lost it so completely a few hours ago. I moved one hand to his chest and held it against his heart. I could feel life there, tripping under my fingers.

"Okay," I whispered.

Clay buried himself in me and moaned. I arched up to meet him. We moved together. When climax threatened, I pulled back, not willing to give him up yet.

"Wait," I gasped. "Just wait."

I closed my eyes and inhaled. The smell of him was overwhelming, almost enough in itself to make me peak. I pressed my face against the hollow of his collarbone and inhaled greedily. As I breathed him in, the world seemed to stop and the jumble of sensations came apart, letting me experience each one untainted by the others. I could feel it all: the twitching of Clay's biceps under my hands as he held himself over me, the sweat trickling from his chest to mine, the scratchy pressure of his sock resting against my calf, the throbbing of him inside me. I wanted to hold everything right there until I'd committed it to memory. This was what it felt like to be alive.

I tightened myself around him, heard his answering groan, and felt my own response shudder through me. The perfection of the moment faded in a sudden need to attain another kind of perfection, another perfect image of life.

"Now," I said. "Please."

Clay bent his face to mine and kissed me hard as he moved inside me. I felt the waves of climax building, tasted it in his kiss. I wrapped myself around him, legs twisting with his, arms pulling him against me. Just as I was about to lose myself in him, he broke the kiss and reached up, entwining his hands in my hair. He didn't pull his head back, but kept his face above mine, eyes so close I could see nothing but blue.

"Don't ever scare me like that again," he rasped. "If I lost you . . . I can't lose you."

I moved my hands to his hair and kissed him. Again he stopped in mid-kiss.

"Promise," he said. "Promise me you'll never take a risk like that again."

I promised and he bent his face to mine as we let all remaining vestiges of control slide away.

Jeremy rapped on the door before dawn penetrated the trees outside my window. Clay opened his eyes, but made no move to get up or even respond.

"I need you two downstairs," Jeremy said through the closed door.

I glanced over at Clay and waited for him to answer. He didn't.

"Now," Jeremy said.

Clay was quiet for another thirty seconds, then grunted "Why?" in a tone I'd never heard him use with Jeremy. It threw Jeremy off balance too, and for a few long seconds, he didn't answer.

"Downstairs," he said finally. "Now."

Jeremy's footsteps receded down the hall.

"I'm sick of it," Clay said, throwing the covers off and shoving them aside. "We're not getting anywhere. All we've done so far is chase our tails. Chase, run away, chase, run away. And where has it gotten us? It's killed Logan, killed Peter, it almost killed Jeremy, and almost killed you. Now you're in danger and he'd better be planning to do something about it."

"I am," Jeremy's voice floated up from the stairway. "That's why I'm asking you to come downstairs."

Spots of red flared in Clay's cheeks. He'd forgotten Jeremy could hear him as well from the bottom of the stairs as from the bedroom door. He mumbled something that sounded apologetic and got out of bed.

Antonio and Nick were already in the study, grazing from a plate of cold meats and cheeses. As we walked in the door, Jeremy was laying out coffees by the sofa for us.

"I know you're worried about Elena, Clayton," Jeremy said as we settled in. "We all are. That's why I'm sending her away. Today."

"What?" I sat up sharply. "Wait a minute. Just because last night gave me a bit of a scare, it doesn't mean—"

"You weren't the only one given a scare last night, Elena. Daniel has targeted you and now it seems this LeBlanc has done the same. One wants to capture you. The other wants to kill you. Do you honestly think I'm going to sit back and wait to see which one succeeds? I've lost Logan and I've lost Peter. I won't take the remotest chance of losing anyone else. I made a mistake yesterday in letting you go with us after I knew Daniel wanted you. I'm not making another mistake by letting you stay one day longer."

I glanced at Clay, expecting him to protest as well, but he was holding his mug of coffee halfway to his lips, staring into its dark depths like a fortune-teller searching for answers in the bottom of a teacup. After a moment, he put the mug down, untasted. Even Jeremy looked over at him and paused, waiting for an argument that didn't come.

"Great," I said. "One panic attack and I'm a liability to be stashed away for safekeeping. Do I get to know where you're going to hide me? Or can't I be trusted with the information?"

Jeremy continued in the same even tone. "You're going to the last place the mutts would expect to find you. Back to Toronto."

"And what the hell am I supposed to do there? Hole up someplace by myself while the men fight the battle?"

"You won't be by yourself. Clay's going with you."

"Whoa!" I leapt to my feet. "You're kidding, right?" I turned to Clay. He hadn't moved. "Didn't you hear that? Say something, damn it."

Clay said nothing.

"What are we supposed to do in Toronto?" I asked. "Hide in a hotel room?"

"No, you'll do exactly what you normally do. You'll go back to your apartment, resume your job if you like, pick up the old routines. That's what will keep you safe. Familiarity. You know your apartment building, the routes you walk, the restaurants and stores you frequent. You'll be better able to spot potential danger than you would in an unfamiliar setting. And you'll be comfortable."

"Comfortable?" I sputtered. "I can't take Clay back to my apartment. You damn well know I can't."

Clay's head jerked up, as if snapped out of a deep sleep. "Why can't you?"

As I met his eyes, I realized he didn't know I was living with Philip. I opened my mouth to say something, but the look on his face froze the words in my throat.

"You'll have to get rid of him," Jeremy said. "Call him and tell him to leave."

"Get rid of who? Call—" Clay stopped. A sick look passed over his face. He stared at me for one long moment. Then he got to his feet and walked from the room.

Now, Jeremy had more talents than any person I knew and he was better at each of them than any person I knew. He could speak and translate in over a dozen languages, he could splint a broken bone so it healed as good as new, he could paint scenes I couldn't even imagine, and he could stop a two-hundred-pound charging wolf with a look. But he didn't know shit about romantic relationships.

"Thank you," I said after Nicholas and Antonio slipped out. "Thank you very much."

"He knows about this man," Jeremy said. "I assumed he knew about your living arrangement."

"And in case he didn't? You decided to humiliate him in front of Nick and Tonio?"

"I said, I thought he knew."

"Well, he does now, and you'll have to deal with it. He's not coming to Toronto with me, if I go at all."

"You are and he is. As for this man, he moved in with you, didn't he? It was your apartment first."

I didn't ask how Jeremy knew this. Nor did I answer.

"Then you can ask him to leave," Jeremy said.

"Just pick up the phone, call him and tell him I'll be home later today and I want him gone by then?"

"I don't see why not."

I gave a harsh laugh. "You don't dump someone you've been living with by phone. You don't sever all ties at a moment's notice. You don't give him a few hours to clear out of the apartment, not without damn good reason."

"You have a good reason."

"That's not—" I stopped and shook my head. "Let me put this in a way you'll understand. If I call him and tell him it's over, he won't leave. He'll want an explanation, and he'll stay until he's satisfied with it. In other words, he'll cause trouble. Is that a good enough reason?"

"Then don't break up with him. Move back in."

"With Clay?! Not in this lifetime. If you have to send a baby-sitter, send Nick. He'll behave himself."

"Clay knows Toronto. And nothing will distract him from protecting you." Jeremy walked toward the door. "I have you booked on an early afternoon flight."

"I'm not—"

Jeremy was already gone.

Clay was next in line to argue with Jeremy. I didn't eavesdrop, but I would have had to leave the house not to hear them. And since the conversation concerned my future, I didn't see any point in trying *not* to listen. Clay didn't like this arrangement any more than I did. His strongest instinct was to protect his Alpha and he couldn't do that from hundreds of miles away. Unfortunately, the instinct to obey Jeremy was almost equally strong. As I listened to them battle it out—Clay protesting loudly enough to drown out Jeremy's quiet insistence—I prayed Clay would win and we'd be allowed to stay. Jeremy stood firm. I was going and, since Clay had been responsible for bringing me into this life, he was responsible for ensuring I survived it.

I stood in the study and fumed. Then I made up my mind. I wasn't going back to Toronto and I wasn't taking Clay anywhere with me. No one could make me do it.

I walked into the empty hall, grabbed my keys and wallet from the hall table, and headed out the garage door. I started walking to my car, then stopped. Where was I going? Where could I go? If I left, I couldn't go back to Toronto and I couldn't come back to Stonehaven. Instead of choosing between two lives, I'd be abandoning both. My fingers clenched around my keys, digging the metal into my palm hard enough to draw blood. I inhaled and closed my eyes. I couldn't leave, but if I stayed, I'd have to obey Jeremy. No one could have that kind of power over me. I wouldn't let them.

As I walked around the car, I heard the squeak of shoe rubber on concrete and looked up to see Jeremy standing at the passenger door, holding the handle.

"Where are we going?" he asked calmly.

"I'm leaving."

"So I see. As I asked, where are we going?"

"We're not—" I stopped and glanced around the garage.

"Clay's car is right there," Jeremy said, his voice still even and unruffled. "You have the keys, but not the alarm remote. The Explorer's outside. No alarm, but it's about fifty feet away. The Mercedes is closer, but you don't have the keys. Shall we race to the Explorer? Or would you rather bolt down the drive and see if you can outrun me?"

"You can't—"

"Yes, I can. You're not leaving. The cage is downstairs. I won't hesitate to use it."

"This isn't—"

"Yes, it's terribly unfair. I know. No one would do this to you in the human world, would they? They'd understand that you have a right to kill yourself."

"I'm not—"

"If you leave here alone, you're committing suicide. I won't let you do that. Either you go to Toronto with Clay or I'll lock you up here until you agree."

I whipped the keys to the cement floor and turned my back on Jeremy. After a minute of silence, I said, "Don't make me take him. You know how hard I've worked to create a life there. You've always said you'd support that, even if you don't agree with it. Send me someplace else or send someone else with me. Don't make me take Clay. He'll destroy everything."

"No, I won't."

Clay's voice was as soft as Jeremy's, so much so that I hesitated, thinking I'd mistaken Jeremy for Clay. The door to the house clicked shut as Jeremy went inside. I didn't turn to look at Clay.

"Protecting you is the most important thing to me right now," Clay said. "No matter how angry I am, that doesn't change. I am capable of fitting in out there, Elena. Just because I don't do it, doesn't mean I can't. I've studied and practiced fitting in since I was eight years old. For fifteen years, I did nothing but study human behavior. Once I figured it out and knew I could fit in, I stopped trying. Why? Because it's not necessary. So long as I can modify my behavior in public enough that I don't have to worry about being attacked by mobs with silver bullets, that's good enough for Jeremy and the rest of the Pack. If I did more, I'd be betraying myself. I won't do that without reason. But protecting you is reason enough. This man may not think I'm the most pleasant person in the world, but he'll have no reason to think anything worse of me. I won't destroy anything."

"I don't want you there."

"And I don't want to be there. But neither of us has much say in the matter, do we?"

Again, the door clicked. When I turned, Clay was gone. Jeremy was back, holding the door open for me. I glared at him, then averted my gaze and walked into the house without another word.

That afternoon, Clay and I were on a plane to Toronto.

Descent

THIS WAS GOING TO BE A CATASTROPHE.

As the plane gained altitude, my mood plummeted. Why had I let Jeremy do this to me? Did he know he was about to ruin my life? Did he care? How could I bring Clay to the apartment I shared with Philip? I was about to bring the man I'd been sleeping with into the home of the man I'd made a commitment to. I could never believe stories I heard about people sneaking their lover into their homes as a housekeeper, a nanny, a gardener. Anyone who did something like that was morally bankrupt bottom-feeding trash . . . which was a pretty good description of what I thought about myself right then.

I'd called Philip that morning and told him I was bringing a guest home. I'd explained that Clay was my cousin, Jeremy's brother, and he was interested in moving to Toronto, so I'd agreed to put him up for a week or so while he looked for work. Philip was perfectly gracious about the whole thing, though when he'd said he'd like to meet my cousins, I suspected he meant inviting them to dinner, not sharing our tiny apartment.

And what about Clay? Jeremy had to know how much this would hurt him. Again, didn't he care? How were Clay and I supposed to get along under these circumstances? We had to live together in a one-bedroom apartment with none of the Pack to act as a buffer. So far, we hadn't spoken a word to each other since Clay came out to the garage that morning. Thirty minutes from Toronto and we were sitting side by side like strangers.

"Where do you live?" Clay said.

I jumped at the sound of his voice. I glanced over, but he was looking straight ahead, as if talking to the headrest in front of him.

"Where do you live?" he repeated.

"Uh—near the lake," I said. "South of Front Street."

"And work?"

"Bay-Bloor district."

It sounded like idle conversation, but I knew it wasn't. Behind Clay's eyes, his brain ticked, working out the geography and distances.

"Security?" he asked.

"Pretty good. The apartment building has a secured entrance. Nothing fancy. Just keys and a buzz-in system. Dead bolt and chain on my door."

Clay snorted. If a mutt could get past the front door, all the locks in the world wouldn't keep him out of my apartment. I'd once mentioned a security system to Philip, but he thought the only reliable home protection was a good insurance policy. I couldn't tell him I was worried about being attacked. That hardly fit the persona of a woman who took solitary walks at 2 A.M.

"At work there's a first-floor security guard," I said. "You need an ID card to get into my office. Plus it's a busy place. If I stick to regular working hours, no one's going to target me there. I don't even have to go back to work, really . . ."

"Stick to regular routines, like Jeremy said." Clay looked out the window. "So who am I supposed to be?"

"My second cousin. In town looking for work."

"Is that necessary?"

"It sounded good. If you're my cousin, then I'd be obligated to put you up—"

"I meant the looking for work part. I'm not going to be looking for work, Elena, and I don't want some elaborate script to follow. Say I'm in town doing work at the university—my normal work. I'll contact a few people there, stop by the department, maybe do a bit of research. Keep it real."

"Sure, but it would seem easier just to say—"

"I'm not playing a role, Elena. Not any more than I have to."

He faced the window and didn't say anything else for the rest of the flight.

No matter how much I'd brooded during the flight, the full impact of what we were doing didn't hit me until we were in the airport. We'd picked up our luggage and were heading to the taxi stand when I realized I was about to take Clay to the apartment I shared with Philip. My chest constricted, my heart pounded, and by the time we were at the entrance, I was in the middle of a full-blown panic attack.

Clay was a full pace ahead of me. I reached forward and grabbed his arm.

"You don't have to do this," I said.

He didn't look at me. "It's what Jeremy wants."

"But that doesn't mean you *have* to do it. He wants me safe, right? There's got to be another way."

Clay kept his back to me. "I said I'd stay with you. That's what I'm going to do."

"You can do that without going to my apartment."

He stopped and turned just enough so I could see his quarter profile. "How am I supposed to do that? Sleep in the alley outside your building?"

"No, I mean *we* don't have to go to my apartment. We'll go someplace else. A hotel room or something."

"And you'll go with me?"

"Sure. Of course."

"And you'll stay with me?"

"Exactly. Whatever you want."

I could hear the desperation in my voice and despised it, but I couldn't stop myself. My hands were shaking so badly that people around us were starting to stare.

"Whatever you want," I repeated. "Jeremy won't know. He said he won't contact us by phone, so he won't know whether we're staying at the apartment. I'll be safe and you'll be with me. That's what's important, right?"

For nearly a minute, Clay didn't move. Then he slowly turned toward me. As he did, I caught a glint of something like hope in his eyes, but it vanished as soon as he saw my expression. His jaw tightened and he locked my gaze.

"Fine," he said. "Anything I want?" He wheeled toward a bank of pay phones and grabbed the nearest receiver. "Call him."

"He said we can't call him. No phone contact."

"Not Jeremy. This man. Call him and tell him it's over. The apartment's his. You'll pick up your stuff later."

"That's not—"

"Not what you meant, right? I didn't think so. What's the plan then? You run back and forth between us until you've made up your mind?"

"I've made up my mind. Anything that happened at Stonehaven was a mistake, like it's always been a mistake. I never misled you. You knew there was someone else. It was the same damned thing that happens every time I go back to that place. I get caught up in it. I lose myself."

"In what? The house? A pile of bricks and mortar?"

"In that place," I said, gritting my teeth. "That world and everything about it, including you. I don't want it, but when I'm there, I can't resist. It takes over."

He gave a harsh laugh. "Bullshit. There is nothing in this world or that world or any world that you couldn't fight, Elena. Do you know what magical spell 'that place' has you under? It makes you happy. But you won't admit that because, to you, the only acceptable happiness comes in the 'normal' world, with 'normal' friends and a 'normal' man. You're bound and determined to make yourself happy with that kind of life, even if it kills you."

People were openly staring now. Alarm bells should have been going off in my head, telling me I was acting improperly for the human world. But they weren't. I didn't give a damn. I turned on my heel and glared at two elderly women tut-tutting behind me. They fell back, eyes widening. I strode toward the exit.

"When's the last time you called him?" Clay called after me.

I stopped.

Clay walked up behind me and lowered his voice so no one else could hear. "Not counting this morning when you called to tell him we were coming. When did you last call?"

I said nothing.

"Sunday," he said. "Three days ago."

"I've been busy," I said.

"Bullshit. You forgot him. You think he makes you happy? You think this life makes you happy? Well, then here's your chance. Take me there. Show me how happy it makes you. Prove it."

"Screw you," I snarled and strode to the door.

Clay came after me, but he was too late. I was out of the airport and in a cab before he caught up. I slammed the cab door, narrowly missing Clay's fingers, then gave the driver my address. As we pulled away, I allowed myself the small satisfaction of looking in the side mirror and seeing Clay standing on the sidewalk.

Too bad I hadn't been more specific when I told him where I lived. "Near" the lake covered a lot of real estate . . . with a lot of apartment buildings.

When I got to my building, I buzzed up to my apartment. Philip answered, sounding surprised when I announced myself. I hadn't lost my key. Don't ask why I buzzed to be let in. I only hoped Philip wouldn't ask either.

When I got upstairs, Philip was in the hall outside the elevator. He reached out and embraced me. I instinctively stiffened, then hugged him back.

"You should have called from the airport," he said. "I was waiting to pick you up." He looked over my shoulder. "Where's our guest?"

"Delayed. Maybe indefinitely."

"He's not coming."

I shrugged and feigned a yawn. "Rough flight. Lots of turbulence. You have no idea how glad I am to be home."

"Not as glad as I am to have you home, hon." Philip escorted me into the apartment. "Go sit down. I picked up roast chicken at the deli for dinner. I'll reheat it."

"Thanks."

I didn't even have my shoes off when someone pounded at the door. I thought of ignoring it, but it wouldn't do any good. Philip may not have had my sense of hearing, but he wasn't deaf.

I yanked open the door. Clay stood there holding our luggage.

"How did you—" I started.

He held up my overnight bag. Dangling from the handle was the tag with my name and address neatly printed on it.

"Pizza delivery kid held open the front door for me," he said. "Great security."

He walked in and threw our luggage by the coat rack. Behind me, the kitchen door opened. I tensed and listened to Philip's footsteps as he approached. The introduction jammed in my throat. What if Clay didn't go along with it? Was it too late to change my story? Was it too late to shove him out the door?

"You must be Elena's cousin," Philip said, walking up and extending a hand.

"Clay," I managed to get out. "Clayton."

Philip smiled. "Nice to meet you. Which do you prefer? Clayton or Clay?"

Clay said nothing. He didn't even glance at Philip, hadn't looked at him since he'd entered the room. Instead, he kept his eyes on mine. I could see the anger simmering there with the outrage and the humiliation. I braced for the outburst. It didn't come. Instead, he settled for unconscionable rudeness, ignoring Philip, his greeting, his question, and his outstretched hand, and striding into the living room.

Philip's smile faltered only a second, then he turned to Clay, who stood at the window with his back to us. "The sofa bed's right there," he said, waving at the couch, where he'd left a pile of bedding. "I hope it's not too uncomfortable. It's never been used, has it, hon?"

Clay's jaw tightened, but he kept looking out the window.

"No," I said. I struggled to think of something to add, some elaboration or change of subject, but nothing came.

"We're *supposed* to have a lake view," Philip said with a forced chuckle. "I think if you stand three paces to the left of the window between one and two in the afternoon, turn right, and squint a certain way, you can see a sliver of Lake Ontario. At least, that's the theory."

Still Clay said nothing. Neither did I. Silence deadened the room, as if Philip were talking into a vacuum, his words leaving no echo or impression.

Philip continued, "The other side of the building has a better view of Toronto. It's a great city, really. World-class amenities with a decent cost of living, low crime rate, clean streets. Maybe I can get off work a few hours early tomorrow and take you for a driving tour before Elena gets home."

"Not necessary," Clay said. The words came out so tightly clipped that his accent was lost, making him sound like a stranger.

"Clay used to live in Toronto," I said. "For a while. A—uh—few years ago."

"How'd you like it?" Philip asked. When Clay didn't answer, he forced another chuckle. "You came back, so I guess it wasn't a totally bad experience."

Clay turned and looked at me. "It has good memories."

He held my gaze for a moment, then broke eye contact and stalked into the bathroom. Within seconds, I heard the shower running.

"Just help yourself to the shower," I muttered, rolling my eyes. "Mr. Congeniality, eh?"

Philip smiled. "So it's not jet lag?"

"I wish. I should have warned you. Undiagnosed antisocial personality disorder. Don't take that crap from him while he's here. Either ignore him or tell him where to shove it."

Philip's eyebrows went up. At first I thought it was because of my description of Clay, but as Philip stared at me, I replayed what I'd said and heard the sarcasm and bite. Not the Elena Philip was used to. Damn Clay.

"Just kidding," I said. "It was a long flight with him. By the time we got to the airport, I lost my temper and we had a bit of a falling out."

"Lost your temper?" Philip said, walking over to kiss my forehead. "I didn't think you had one."

"Clayton brings out the worst in me. With any luck, he won't be here long. He's family, though, so I have to put up with it until then." I turned toward the kitchen and made a show of sniffing the air. "Smells like that chicken's done."

"Should we wait for your cousin?"

"He wouldn't wait for us," I said and headed to the kitchen.

The only good thing I can say about that evening was that it was short. Clay came out of the shower (dressed, thankfully), walked into the living room, and pulled one of my books from the shelf. We were still eating. I went into the living room and told him so. He grunted that he'd eat later and I left it at that. By the time we'd eaten and cleaned up, it was late enough for me to claim exhaustion and head off to bed. Philip followed and I quickly realized I'd forgotten one small thing about the living arrangement. Sex.

I was putting on my nightgown when Philip walked in. Now, I wasn't big on nighttime fashion, having slept in my underwear since I left my last foster family, but when Philip moved in and I noticed he wore pajama bottoms to bed, I figured maybe I was expected to wear something, too. I tried lingerie, all those sexy, skimpy things the women's magazines rave over. But the damned lace itched in places I'd never itched before and the elastic pinched and the shoulder straps twisted, and I decided maybe such nightwear was only meant to be worn before sex and discarded for something more comfortable afterward. Since Philip didn't get excited by black lace and red satin, anyway, I'd pitched the stuff and settled for oversized T-shirts. Then, for Christmas, Philip had bought me a white knee-length nightgown. It was very feminine and old-fashioned and a tad too virginal for my taste, but Philip liked it, so I wore it.

Philip waited until I started brushing my hair, then walked up behind me, leaned over, and kissed the side of my neck.

"I missed you," he murmured against my skin. "I didn't want to complain, but it was a longer separation than I expected. A few days more and you'd have had a guest in New York."

I covered a choking fit with an awkward wheezing laugh. Philip in Bear Valley. That was a scenario even more hellish than the one I was enduring now.

Philip's lips moved to the back of my neck. He pressed against me. One hand slipped under my nightgown and pushed it up to my hip. I stiffened. Without thinking I glanced at the bedroom door. Philip's gaze followed mine through the mirror.

"Ah," he said with a chuckle. "I forgot about our guest. We could keep it quiet, but if you'd rather wait for a more private moment . . ."

I nodded. Philip kissed my neck again, gave a mock sigh, and headed for the bed. I knew I should curl up in bed with him, cuddle, talk. But I couldn't.

I just couldn't.

This was going to be a catastrophe.

Settling

THE NEXT MORNING I AWOKE TO THE SMELL OF FRENCH TOAST AND bacon. I checked the clock. Nearly nine. Philip was normally gone by seven. He must have stayed late to make breakfast. A very pleasant surprise.

I padded out of the bedroom and into the kitchen. Clay stood at the stove, ramming a spatula under a mountain of bacon. He turned as I walked in. His eyes traveled over my nightgown.

"What the hell is that?" he asked.

"A nightgown."

"You sleep in it?"

"If I didn't, it would be a day-gown, wouldn't it?" I snapped.

Clay's lips quivered as if choking back a laugh. "It's very . . . sweet, darling. It looks like something Jeremy would buy you. Oh, by the way. He sent flowers."

"Jeremy?"

Clay shook his head. "They're by the front door."

I walked into the hall to find a dozen red roses in a silver-plated vase. The card read: "Thought I'd let you sleep in. Welcome home. Missed you. Philip."

See? Nothing had changed. Philip was as thoughtful as ever. Smiling, I picked up the vase and looked for a place to put it. The living room table? No, the flowers were too tall. Leave it on the hall table? Too crowded. The kitchen? I opened the door. No room.

"Bedroom," I murmured and backed out.

"Water," Clay called after me.

"What?"

"They need water."

"I knew that."

"And sunlight," he added.

I didn't answer. I'd have remembered water and sun . . . eventually. I must admit, I'd never quite understood the custom of sending flowers. Sure, they looked nice, but they didn't *do* anything. That's not to say I didn't appreciate them. I did. Jeremy always cut fresh flowers from the garden and put them in my room and I enjoyed them. Of course, if he didn't place them in the sunlight and keep them watered, I wouldn't have enjoyed them for long. I was far better at killing things than keeping them alive. Good thing I never planned to have children.

After watering and placing the roses, I went back into the kitchen. Clay put two pieces of French toast on my plate and lifted a third.

"That's good," I said, pulling my plate back.

He arched both eyebrows.

"I mean, that's good for now," I said. "Of course, I'll have more after I finish these."

"Is that all you eat when he's here? I'm surprised you make it to work without fainting. You can't eat like that, Elena. Your metabolism needs—"

I pushed my chair back. Clay stopped talking and dished out my bacon, then fixed his own plate and sat down.

"What time do you start work?" he asked.

"I called last night and said I'd be there by ten-thirty."

"We'd better move then. How long a walk is it? Thirty minutes?"

"I take the subway."

"Subway? You hate the subway. All those people stuffed in that tiny car, getting jostled around by strangers, and the smell—"

"I've gotten used to it."

"Why bother? It's an easy walk, over to Bloor and straight up."

"People don't walk to work," I said. "They bicycle, they Rollerblade, they jog. I don't own a bike or blades and I can't jog in a skirt."

"You wear skirts to work? You hate skirts."

I shoved my plate aside and left the table.

I tried to convince Clay that he could walk to my office and let me take the subway alone. He wouldn't have it. For the sake of my safety and in accordance with the express will of his leader, he would suffer through the torture of the underground train. I must admit I took a bit too much pleasure in watching him squirm throughout the excruciating seven-minute ride. Not that he literally squirmed. Anyone watching him would have seen a man standing in the crowded car, impatiently tracking our progress on the overhead map. But deep in his gaze, I could see the look of a caged animal, claustrophobia tinged with equal parts revulsion and impending panic. Every time someone brushed against him, he clenched the pole a bit tighter. He breathed through his mouth and kept his eyes on the map, looking away only to check the name of each station as the train slowed to a stop. Once he glanced at me. I smiled and made a show of relaxing in my seat. With a glare, he turned away and ignored me for the rest of the trip.

I had lunch with coworkers. As we were returning, I saw a familiar figure sitting on a bench outside my office building. I made some excuse for not going inside and circled back to Clay.

"What's wrong?" I asked as I came up behind him.

He turned and smiled. "Hey, darling. Good lunch?"

"What are you doing here?"

"Guarding you, remember?"

I paused. "Please don't tell me you've been sitting here all morning."

"'Course. I didn't figure I'd be welcome in your office."

"You can't just sit here."

"Why not? Oh, let me guess. Normal people don't sit on street benches. Don't worry, darling. If I see any cops, I'll switch to the bench across the road."

I glanced toward the building, making sure no one I knew was coming out. "I don't work in my office all day, you know. I'm covering a rally at Queen's Park this afternoon."

"So I'll come along. At a safe distance, making sure you don't have to endure the horror of publicly associating with me."

"You mean you'll stalk me."

Clay grinned. "A skill that can always use improvement."

"You can't just sit here."

"Back around we go . . ."

"At least *do* something. Read a book, a newspaper, a magazine."

"Sure, and let some mutt sneak past while I'm doing the daily crossword."

I threw up my hands and stalked into the building. Five minutes later, I returned to his bench.

"Miss me already?" he asked.

I dropped a magazine over his shoulder and onto his lap. He picked it up, glanced at the cover, and frowned.

"Rod World?"

"It's about cars. A good guy kinda magazine. At least pretend to read it."

He flipped through the pages, stopping on a photo of a bikini-clad redhead sprawled over the hood of a Corvette Stingray. He scanned the text, then examined the picture.

"What's the woman doing there?" he asked.

"Covering a scratch on the hood. She was cheaper than a new paint job."

He flipped through a few more pages of barely dressed women and classic cars. "Nick used to have magazines like this when we were kids. But without the cars." He rotated a photo sideways. "Or the bathing suits."

"Just pretend you're reading it, okay?" I said, turning back toward the doors. "You never know. Maybe I'll get lucky and you'll find something you like."

"I thought you liked my car."

I started walking away. "I wasn't talking about the cars."

After dinner, Clay and I hung out at the apartment and played cards. By the time Philip got home, I was ahead thirty dollars and fifty cents. I'd just won my fourth game in a row and was most immaturely crowing over it when Philip walked in. As soon as Philip asked to join us, Clay decided it was shower time again. At this rate, he was going to be the cleanest guy in Toronto. Philip and I played a few rounds together, but it wasn't the same. Philip didn't play for money. Worse yet, he expected me to abide by the rules.

That night, Jeremy contacted me to see if we were okay. Although he'd forbidden phone calls, that didn't mean we were out of touch. As I've said before, Jeremy had his own way of contacting us through a sort of nighttime psychic connection. All werewolves have some degree of psychic power. Most of them ignore it, finding it far too mystical for creatures accustomed to communicating with fists and fangs.

Clay and I shared a type of mental bond, maybe because he bit me. Not that we could read each other's minds or anything so earth-shattering. It was more like the heightened awareness of each other that twins often claim to experience, little things like feeling a twinge when he was injured or knowing when he was nearby even if I couldn't see, hear, or smell him. The whole thing made me uncomfortable, though, so it wasn't a skill I cultivated or even admitted to.

Jeremy's ability was different. He could communicate with us while we were sleeping. It wasn't like hearing voices in my head or anything so dramatic. I'd be sleeping and I'd have a dream about talking to him, but I'd subconsciously sense it was more than a dream, and I could listen and respond rationally. Quite cool, actually, though I'd never say so to Jeremy.

I awoke to the smell of pancakes. This time, I knew exactly who was making breakfast and I didn't mind. Food was food. For me, nothing beat a ready-made breakfast. I couldn't cook in the morning. By the time I got up, I was too hungry to mess with stoves and frying pans—sometimes even the toaster took too long. Even better than having someone cook breakfast for me was being able to crawl out of bed and go straight to the table, skipping shower, clothes, hair and teeth brushing, all those things necessary to make me a suitable eating companion.

With Clay, it didn't matter. He'd seen worse. I buried myself under the covers. When breakfast was ready, Clay would bring me a coffee. All I had to do was wait.

"This is really great. We don't get pancakes very often. Elena's not much of a breakfast person. Cold cereal and toast usually. I'm not sure she'll eat this, but I know I will."

I bolted upright. That was not Clay's voice.

"What do they call these in the South?" Philip continued. "Flapjacks? Johnnycakes? I can never keep it straight. That is where you're from, right? Originally, I mean. With that accent, I'm guessing Georgia, maybe Tennessee."

Clay grunted. I leapt out of bed and ran for the door. Then I caught a glimpse of my nightgown in the mirror. A housecoat. I needed a housecoat.

"Your brother Jeremy doesn't have an accent," Philip said. "At least, I didn't notice it when I spoke to him on the phone."

Shit! I rummaged through the closet. Where was that housecoat? Did I own a housecoat?

"My stepbrother," Clay said.

"Oh? Oh, I see. That makes sense."

I grabbed clothing and yanked it on, wheeling out of the bedroom and through the kitchen door. I skidded to a halt between Clay and Philip.

"Hungry?" Clay asked, still facing the stove.

Philip leaned over, kissed my cheek, and tried to smooth my tangled hair. "Make sure you call Mom this morning, hon. She didn't want to go ahead with Betsy's shower plans without you." He looked over at Clay. "My family is crazy about Elena. If I don't marry her soon, they're liable to adopt her."

His gaze lingered on Clay. Clay flipped three pancakes onto a growing stack, turned, and carried them to the table, face expressionless. A frown flickered across Philip's lips. Probably tired of making small talk and not getting any response.

"The butter's in the—" Philip started, but Clay already had the fridge open. "Oh, and the syrup is over the stove in the cup—"

Clay pulled from the refrigerator a fancy glass bottle of maple syrup, the kind sold in tourist shops for the price of liquid gold.

"That's new," I said, smiling over at Philip. "When did you pick it up?"

"I—uh—didn't."

I glanced at Clay.

"Grabbed it yesterday," he said.

"Oh, I'm not sure Elena likes—" Philip stopped, eyes going from me to Clay and back again. "Yes, well, that was very nice."

The phone rang, rescuing me from a fruitless struggle for something to say.

"I'll get it," Philip said, and vanished into the living room.

"Thank you," I hissed at Clay, keeping my voice low. "You just had to do that, didn't you? First breakfast, then the syrup. Make a big deal out of knowing what I like and embarrass him."

"Make a big deal? I didn't say a word. You brought up the syrup."

"You wouldn't have?"

"'Course not. Why would I? I'm not competing here, Elena. I noticed when I made French toast yesterday that you didn't have real syrup. I know how you complain about the fake stuff, so I figured you were out and bought you some."

"And breakfast? Tell me you weren't saying something by making me breakfast."

"Sure, I was saying something. I was saying that I'm concerned you're not eating right and wanted to make sure you got at least one decent meal. As your guest, I'm sure he only thinks I was trying to be helpful. I made enough for him."

"You made enough for the whole build—" I stopped, looking around and realizing there was only enough food out to feed three normal people.

"The rest is in the oven," Clay said. "I hid it when I heard him wake up. I'll pack it for you to take to work. If anyone comments, you can say you missed breakfast."

I struggled for something to say and, again, was saved by an interruption, this time by Philip coming back into the kitchen.

"Work," he said, pulling a face. "What else? Plan to come in late one morning and they call looking for me. Don't worry, hon. I said I'm having breakfast with you and I'll be in afterward." He pulled out a chair, sat down, and turned to Clay. "So, how's that job search going?"

I'd agreed to meet Clay for lunch. He bought a picnic box from a nearby deli and we went to the university grounds to eat. Going to the university wasn't my choice. I didn't even realize that was where we were headed until we got there. Although I worked only a few blocks away from the U of T, I hadn't visited the campus in all the months I'd been at the magazine. Nor had I gone there in all the times I'd visited Toronto in the past ten years. The university was where I'd met Clay, where I'd fallen in love. It was also the place where I'd been deceived, lied to, and ultimately betrayed. When I realized where Clay was headed for lunch that day, I balked. I thought up a dozen excuses and a dozen alternate places to eat. But none of them reached my mouth. Remembering what he'd said about Stonehaven, I was too embarrassed to admit I didn't want to go to the university. It was only a place, a "pile of bricks and mortar." Maybe there was more to it than embarrassment, though. Maybe I didn't want to admit how much emotional resonance that particular brick and mortar pile held for me. Maybe I didn't want him to know how much I remembered and how much I cared. So I said nothing.

We sat on benches beside University College. Exams were finishing up and only a handful of students sauntered around King's College Circle, the rush of classes a fading memory. A group of young men played touch football inside the circle, spring jackets and knapsacks abandoned in a heap near the goalpost. As we ate, Clay talked about his paper on jaguar cults in South America and my mind floated backward, remembering past conversations under these trees, between these buildings. I could picture Clay all those years before, sitting at a picnic table across the road in Queen's Park, eating lunch and talking, his focus so completely on the two of us that Frisbees could whiz over his head and he'd never notice. He always sat in the same pose, legs stretched out until his feet hooked behind mine beneath the table, hands moving constantly, flexing and emphasizing, as if some part of him always had to be moving. His voice sounded the same, now so familiar that I could follow the beat in my head, predicting each change of tone, each note of accentuation.

Even back then, he'd wanted to know my thoughts and opinions on everything. No flitting of my young mind was too trivial or boring for him. In time, I'd told him about my past, my aspirations, my fears, my hopes, and my insecurities, all the things I'd never imagined sharing with anyone. I'd always been afraid of opening up to anyone. I'd wanted to be a strong, independent woman, not some damaged waif with a background straight out of the worst Dickensian melodrama. I hid my background or, if someone found out, pretended it hadn't made a difference, hadn't affected me. With Clay, all that had changed. I'd wanted him to know everything about me, so I could be sure he knew what I was and that he loved me anyway. He'd listened and he'd stayed. More than that, he'd reciprocated. He'd told me about his childhood, losing his parents in some trauma he couldn't remember, being adopted, not fitting in at school, being ridiculed and shunned, getting into trouble and being expelled so often he seemed to go through schools the way I'd gone through foster parents. He'd told me so much that I'd been sure I knew him completely. Then I'd found out how wrong I'd been. Sometimes that deception hurt worse than being bitten.

Turbulence

WHEN PHILIP RETURNED FROM WORK IT WAS PAST MIDNIGHT. CLAY and I were watching a late movie. I was stretched out on the couch. Clay was on the recliner, hogging the popcorn. Philip walked in, stood behind the sofa, and watched the screen for a few minutes.

"Horror?" he said. "You know, I haven't seen a horror flick since I was in university." He walked around the couch and sat beside me. "What's this one?"

"Evil Dead II," I said, reaching for the remote. "I'm sure there's something else on."

"No, no. Leave it." He looked at Clay. "You like horror films?"

Clay was silent a moment, then grunted something noncommittal.

"Clay's not keen on horror," I said. "Too much violence. He's very squeamish. I have to switch channels if things get gory."

Clay snorted.

"This one's pure camp," I said to Philip. "It's a sequel. Horror sequels suck."

"Scream 2," Clay said.

"That's an exception only because the writers knew that sequels suck and played it up."

"Uh-uh," Clay said. "The idea—" He stopped, glanced at Philip who was following our conversation like a Ping-Pong tournament, and stuffed a handful of popcorn into his mouth.

"Pass it over," I said.

"I bought it."

"And cooked it in my microwave. Pass it."

"There's two more bags in the kitchen."

"I want that one. Pass it over."

He tossed the bowl onto the table and booted it toward me with his foot.

"It's empty!" I said.

Philip laughed. "I can tell you two knew each other as kids."

Silence ticked by. Then Clay heaved himself to his feet.

"I'll be in the shower," he said.

The next day was Saturday. Philip went golfing, leaving before I woke up. Golf was one sport I avoided. It demanded too little of me physically and too much behaviorally. Last fall, I'd agreed to try it, so Philip gave me two lists of course rules. One was on how to play the sport. The other was on how to dress and behave while playing the sport. Now, I was well aware that certain sports required certain modes of dress for protection, but I failed to see how wearing a sleeveless blouse on the course qualified as a safety hazard. God forbid the sight of my bare shoulders should send male golfers into a tizzy, knocking balls everywhere. I had enough to worry about in life without measuring the length of my shorts to see if they complied to course standards. Besides, after a couple rounds with Philip, I discovered golf really wasn't my thing. Whacking the hell out of a ball was great for working off aggression, but apparently it wasn't the point of the game. So Philip golfed. I didn't.

After golf, the three of us went out for lunch, undoubtedly marking the first time in ten years that I haven't enjoyed a meal. For twenty excruciating minutes, Philip tried to engage Clay in conversation. He'd have had better luck addressing his salad. To save him, I started a running monologue, which I then had to sustain until the bill arrived, thirty-eight minutes and twenty seconds later. At that point, Clay miraculously regained his voice, suggesting that we walk back to the apartment, knowing full well that we'd brought Philip's car, which meant Philip would have to drive back alone. Before I could argue, Philip suddenly remembered he had some work to do at the office, so if we didn't mind walking back, he'd drive straight there. This agreed, both men bolted for the exit like escaping convicts, leaving me to scrounge up the tip.

Sunday morning, while Philip golfed, Clay and I did the boring weekly chores like cleaning, laundry, and grocery shopping. When we returned from getting groceries, there was a message from Philip on the machine. I called him back.

"How was your game?" I asked when he answered.

"Not good. I was calling about dinner."

"You're not going to make it?"

"Actually, I wanted to ask you out for dinner. Something nice." He paused. "Just the two of us."

"Great."

"That's not a problem?"

"Not at all. Clay can fend for himself. He hates fancy meals. Besides, he didn't bring any dress-up clothes."

"What does he wear for interviews?"

Whoops. "It's academic," I said. "Very laid-back."

"Good." Another pause. "After dinner I thought we could take in a show. Maybe find half-price same-day tickets to something."

"Might not be easy on a holiday weekend, but we can manage something."

"I thought we'd"—throat clear—"go alone. The two of us."

"That's what I figured. Do you want me to make reservations? Get the tickets?"

"No, I'll handle it. I should be there by six. You might want to tell Clayton we'll be late getting in tonight. Dinner, a show, drinks or coffee afterward."

"Sounds great."

Philip was silent a moment, as if expecting me to say more. When I didn't he said good-bye and we signed off.

Dinner was another nightmare meal. Not that anything went wrong. I almost wished it had. If our reservations had been given away or if our food had arrived cold, at least we'd have had something to talk about. Instead, we sat for over an hour acting like two people on a first date after it became clear there wouldn't be a second. We didn't seem to know what to say to each other. Oh, we talked. Philip told me about the lakeside condo campaign he was working on. I told an amusing little story about a gaffe the premier had made at the latest scrum. We discussed Toronto's ideas for rejuvenating the harbor front. We complained about the latest talk of TTC fare increases. We discussed the Jays' early chances for the pennant race. In short, we talked about everything two near-strangers would discuss over dinner. Worse yet, we discussed these topics with the desperation of near-strangers terrified of dead silence. By dessert, we'd run out of subjects. Behind us, three men barely past acne were trumpeting their success with dot-com stocks loud enough that people on the street would know about their good fortune. I was about to make some eye-rolling comment to Philip, then stopped myself. I wasn't sure how he'd react. Would my remark sound overly negative? Snide? It was the sort of observation Clay would appreciate. But Philip? I wasn't sure, so I kept quiet.

As the server refilled our coffees, Philip cleared his throat.

"So," he said. "How much longer do you expect your cousin will be with us?"

"A few days probably. Is that a problem? I know he can be a jerk—"

"No, no. That's not it." He managed a wan smile. "I must say, he's not the most pleasant company, but I'll survive. It's just been . . . strange."

"Strange?"

Philip shrugged. "I guess it's because you two have known each other so long. There's a real . . . I don't know. I sense . . ." He shook his head. "It's just me, hon. I'm feeling a bit left out. Not the most mature response in the world. I don't know . . . " He tapped his fingers against his coffee cup, then met my eyes. "Was there something . . . ?" He trailed off.

"What?"

"Never mind." A sip of coffee. "Is he having any luck finding work?"

"He's setting some things in motion at U of T. Once that's a go, he'll move out."

"So he's staying in Toronto?"

"For a while."

Philip opened his mouth, hesitated, then took another swig of coffee.

"So," he said. "Did you hear Mayor Mel's latest pronouncement?"

We hadn't been able to get last-minute tickets for any decent shows, so we ended up seeing a movie instead, then going to a jazz bar for drinks. By the time we returned to the apartment, it was almost two. Clay wasn't there. While Philip went into the bedroom to get his cell phone and retrieve messages, Clay wheeled in the door, cheeks flushed.

"Hey," he said, gaze darting past me to look for Philip.

"He's in the bedroom," I said. "Did you go for a run?"

"Without you?"

Clay walked into the kitchen. Seconds later he returned with a bottle of water, uncapped it, gulped half, and held the rest out to me. I shook my head.

"Please tell me you were exercising downstairs in the gym," I said.

Clay took another drink of water.

"Damn you," I muttered, dropping onto the sofa. "You promised you wouldn't follow me tonight."

"No, you told me not to follow you. I didn't answer. My job here is to protect you. That's what I'm gonna do, darling."

"I don't need—"

Philip reappeared from the bedroom. "Bad news." He looked from Clay to me. "Oh, am I interrupting something?"

Clay guzzled his water and headed for the kitchen.

"What's the bad news?" I asked.

"Emergency meeting tomorrow." He sighed. "Yes, it's Victoria Day. I know. I'm really sorry, hon. But I called Blake and bumped our golf game up to eight o'clock, so I'll have time to play and take you out to lunch before the meeting. I'd really hoped to spend more time with you this weekend."

I shrugged. "No big deal. Clay and I can keep ourselves amused."

Philip hesitated, seemed ready to say something, then glanced toward the kitchen and shut his mouth.

At noon Monday, as I waited for Philip to pick me up, he called to say there'd been a mix-up at the golf course and his party had been over an hour late teeing off. They'd just finished their game. So, no lunch date.

After Philip called, Clay and I decided to hike to Chinatown for lunch. We spent the rest of the day slacking off, discovering unexplored neighborhoods, looping down residential streets, then jogging along the beach before returning to the apartment with supplies for a steak dinner. Around seven someone buzzed the apartment. I was in the washroom, so I yelled for Clay to get it. When I came out, he was holding another vase of flowers, this time a mix of irises in an earthenware jar.

"He's sorry for missing lunch," Clay said. "You want them in the bedroom with the others?"

I stopped, watching him hold the flowers and waiting.

"Say it," I said.

"Say what?"

I snatched the flowers from his hand. "I know what you're thinking. If he really regretted it, he'd have cut his golf game short."

"I wasn't going to say that."

"You were thinking it."

"No, you were. You said it."

I marched toward the bedroom.

"Water," he called after me.

With a growl, I veered into the bathroom. I sloshed water into the pot, dislodging a bunch of green marbles. Three plinked into the sink, more onto the floor. I scooped the ones from the sink, gave a cursory look for the others and decided to leave them for cleaning day.

"Unlike some people," I said as I strode back into the hall, "Philip doesn't feel the necessity for a couple to lead their lives joined at the hip. That's fine with me. At least he sends flowers."

Silence returned from the living room. I plunked the vase on my nightstand, beside the roses, and stalked back to Clay. He was perched on the sofa back, reading the rough notes I'd brought home from work Friday.

"Say it," I said.

He glanced up from the notes. "Say what?"

"You've been waiting all week to tell me what you think of Philip. Go ahead. Get it out."

"My honest opinion?"

I gritted my teeth. "Yes."

"You sure?"

I ground my teeth. "Yes."

"I think he's a decent guy."

My teeth were starting to hurt. "What's that supposed to mean?"

"Exactly what I said, darling. I think he's a decent guy. Not perfect, but who is? He obviously cares for you. He tries to be considerate. He's very patient. If I were him, I'd have kicked my ass out of here days ago. He's been nothing but polite. A nice guy."

"But what?"

"But it's not going to work." He held up a hand against my protest. "Come on, Elena. You do know why you've picked this guy, right? I don't mean because you're looking for a home and a family and all that. You think I don't know that's what you want? I do. And I'd tell you it's right under your nose, but you wouldn't listen. The question is: why have you picked this particular guy to fulfill those fantasies? You do know, don't you, darling?"

"Because he's a good man. He's—"

"Good and patient and caring. Doesn't that remind you of someone?"

"Not you."

Clay slid off the couch back, laughing. "Definitely not me." He laid my portfolio on the table and studied my face. "You really don't get it, do you, darling? Well, when you do, you'll know why it can't work. You can care for this guy, but it'll never be what we have. It can't be. As decent as he is, you've picked him for all the wrong reasons."

"You're wrong."

He shrugged. "Always a first time. How about those steaks? The barbeque should be ready. Pass them to me and you can get the veggies cooking."

We went for a long walk after dinner. When we got back to the apartment, Philip had stopped by and left a note on the table saying the partners had invited him to a meeting in Montreal the next morning. He'd stopped by to pack an overnight bag and was already on a train to Quebec.

"So he'll be gone all night?" Clay asked, leaning over my shoulder to read the note.

"Looks that way."

"Damn shame. Guess we'll have to find something else to do." He walked over to the calendar. "Let's see. Six days since you Changed. Eight for me. You know what that means."

Time for a run.

Fireworks

WE DEBATED WHETHER TO DRIVE OR WALK TO THE RAVINE. ALthough it was a long hike, neither of us minded walking there—it was walking back after an exhausting run that wasn't nearly so appealing. We'd almost agreed to drive when I made the mistake of mentioning that the car belonged to Philip, and Clay decided it was such a beautiful night it would be a crime not to walk. I didn't argue. Taking Philip's car was often more bother than it was worth. Finding an overnight parking spot near the ravine was tough and I was always worried I'd get ticketed or towed and would have to explain to Philip what I was doing in that part of town in the middle of the night.

It was midnight when we got to the ravine. We split up. I found a thicket and undressed. As I crouched to start my Change, I was struck by something I'd never felt before, at least not in Toronto. I was getting ready for my Change with all the mental preparation that I'd use brushing my teeth. While my brain was occupied with other thoughts, my body was moving into position as if what I was doing was the most natural thing in the world. Now after ten years the routine should've become pretty automatic and it did . . . when I was with the Pack or at Stonehaven. Not that it hurt any less, but mentally, the transition was smooth. One minute I was human, the next I was a wolf. No big deal—I'm a werewolf, right? Yet Changing here in Toronto was another matter. Ninety-five percent of the time I lived like any normal human. I got up, went to work, took the subway home, ate dinner, spent the evening with my boyfriend, and went to bed. A perfectly normal routine interrupted by the occasional need to change into a wolf, run through the woods, hunt down a rabbit, and bay at the moon. The juxtaposition was so jarring that I often got to the ravine, took off my clothes, and stood naked thinking I'm supposed to be doing *what?* I half expected to get down on my knees, concentrate on Changing, and have nothing happen . . . except maybe to wake up wearing a straitjacket with a nice doctor telling me for the millionth time that people cannot change into wolves.

When I started getting into position that night, it felt perfectly natural. That probably had a lot to do with Clay being there. He was like a bridge between the worlds. If he was there, I couldn't forget what I was. Not that this was a big surprise. The shock was that I didn't mind, even that I felt good about it. For so long, I'd been trying to suppress that side of my nature, certain that I had to become someone else to fit into the human world. Now I was seeing the possibility of another option. Maybe Clay was right. Maybe I was trying too hard, making things more difficult for myself than necessary. With Clay around, it was nearly impossible to maintain the "human" Elena persona for long. I'd been my usual self—snappish, willful, argumentative. And the earth hadn't crashed and burned around me. Maybe I didn't have to be the "good" Elena, nice and demure and quiet. Not that I should start flying into a rage when Philip left the toilet seat up or sucker punching strangers who stepped on my feet in the subway, but maybe I didn't have to back down every time a confrontation threatened. If I let some aspects of my normal personality slip into my "human" persona, living in the human world might be easier, might even come to feel natural. Perhaps that was the key.

The bushes rustled, snapping me back to reality. I caught a glimpse of Clay's fur passing by the thicket. He gave a low growl of impatience. I laughed and dropped back into position to start my Change, thinking how odd it was that the person who most loathed the human world might be the one who most helped me live in it. Clay growled again and poked his muzzle into the clearing.

"Hold on," I said.

I shook my head, clearing it, then prepared for the Change.

After our run, we Changed back and lay in a grassy clearing, resting and talking. It was the darkest and quietest part of the night, long after evening had passed and still long before dawn arrived. Despite the chill in the air, neither of us had dressed. The run had pumped our blood so hot we could probably lie in a snowdrift until sunrise and not notice. I lay on my back, luxuriating in the sensation of the cool wind against my skin. Overhead, the trees blocked out the stars and moon. Only enough light filtered in to keep total darkness at bay.

"Got something for you," Clay said after we'd rested awhile. He reached behind him into the darkness, pulled two long wire rods from his discarded jacket and flourished them over his head.

I sat up. "You brought sparklers?"

"This is a fireworks weekend up here, isn't it? Did you think I'd forget your sparklers?"

I loved sparklers. Okay, I was probably the only thirty-year-old in the world who got giddy over sulphur-coated sticks, but I didn't care. At least, I didn't care when Clay was around. He didn't know that grown people didn't normally play with sparklers and I didn't care to enlighten him. One of my few memories of my parents was of a Canada Day party. I only knew that it was Canada Day because, in my memory, I could see a cake in the shape of the flag. I also saw fireworks, lots of fireworks. I heard music and laughter. I smelled sulfur and old camp blankets. I remembered my father handing me a sparkler, my first. I remembered my mother and me dancing barefoot on wet grass, waving the sparklers like magic wands, giggling and spinning around, watching the trail of fairy light we left behind.

Clay pulled a book of matches from his jacket and lit the first sparkler. I scrambled to my feet and took it. Sparks of orange shot out in a star, sizzling and sputtering. Lifting it, I drew an experimental line through the air. Too slow. I did it quicker and the image stayed for a few seconds, a line of fire in the darkness. I spun it in a circle, watching the sparks flash and spin. I wrote my name in the sky, the first *E* vanishing before I finished the *A*. I tried it again, faster. This time my name hung there for an eye-blink.

"Almost done," Clay called after me. "Throw it and make a wish."

"That's birthday candles," I said. "Only you blow them out, you don't throw them."

"You threw them once. Cake and all."

"I threw them *at* you. And the only wish I made can't be repeated."

Clay laughed. "Well, you always throw the sparklers, so you might as well make a wish. A new werewolf superstition."

As I drew my arm back, the sparkler winked out. Clay lit the other one and handed it to me. I lifted it over my head and spun a figure eight, then brought my arm down and twirled around so fast I nearly tripped over Clay. He laughed and put a hand on the back of my calf to steady me. When I recovered, he didn't take his hand away. I looked down at him, lying on his back beneath me.

"I love you," he said.

I blinked and froze.

"Bad timing?" he said with a small smile. He took his hand off my leg. "Better?"

"I—" I started, then stopped. I didn't know what I'd been going to say, didn't know what I wanted to say.

"I'm not trying to seduce you, Elena. The run, the sparklers, they're not leading up to anything. The last few days, I've been trying to keep things easy for you. No tricks. No pressure. I want you to see things clearly. When you do, you'll be able to make your choice. The right choice."

"Which would be you."

He waved a hand at my sparkler. "Better hurry up. It's almost gone. That's the last one until next fireworks day."

I looked down to see that the glow had almost reached the end of the sparkler. I looked up into the trees above, then pulled back my arm, and threw it high. The glowing ember shot into the sky, arced, then came tumbling down, end over end like a falling star. I glanced down at Clay. He was watching the sparkler and grinning with as much childlike joy as I'd felt, dancing around the grove with my fairy wand. I looked back up at the light, closed my eyes, and made my wish.

I wished I knew what I wanted.

Possibilities

WE SLEPT IN THE FOREST UNTIL DAWN, THEN DRESSED AND headed out before morning hikers and joggers intruded on our domain. We found a tiny bistro near Yonge and had breakfast on the front patio. Business was brisk, but it was all takeout, commuters stopping to grab a double espresso and biscotti on the way to the office. No one had time to stop and sit. We had the patio to ourselves and the staff left us alone even when we'd been there more than an hour. I was leaning back in my chair, eyes closed, fingers against my warm coffee cup, listening to Clay's running commentary on the morning traffic of cars and people rushing by.

"You look happy," he said suddenly.

"I am," I said, not opening my eyes. I tilted my head back and felt the heat of the sun on my face. "You know, I couldn't imagine living somewhere without seasons."

"Yeah?"

"Real seasons, I mean. I'd miss the changes, the variety. Especially spring. I couldn't live without spring. Days like today are worth every snowstorm and slush puddle. By March, it seems like winter will never end. All that snow and ice that seemed so wonderful in December is driving you crazy. But you know spring's coming. Every year, you wait for that first warm day, then the next and the next, each better than the last. You can't help but be happy. You forget winter and get the chance to start over. Fresh possibilities."

"A fresh start."

"Exactly."

Clay hesitated, then leaned forward as if to say something, but then stopped, pulled back, and said nothing.

We got back to the apartment after nine. I was late for work, but I was in too good a mood to care. I could always work through lunch or stay late. No big deal.

As we headed up the elevator, Clay told me how some street punks had tried to steal his car on a trip to New York City last winter. By the time I got to the apartment, I was laughing so hard I nearly fell inside as we walked into the apartment.

"Seriously?" I said as I closed the door.

Clay didn't answer. When I glanced at him, he wasn't laughing. He wasn't even looking at me. His gaze was trained somewhere over my shoulder. I turned to see Philip sitting on the recliner, arms crossed, looking like a parent who'd been waiting up all night for an errant child. I opened my mouth, but nothing came out. My brain raced, wondering how long he'd been home, what excuse would be appropriate. Had he come back that morning? If so, I could say we'd gone out for breakfast. As we stepped farther inside, Philip stood.

"I'd like to talk to Elena," he said.

Clay headed for the bathroom. Philip stepped in his path. Clay halted, shoulders tightening. He started turning his gaze toward Philip, then stopped, looking somewhere past him. He tried stepping around, as if he didn't see anyone there.

"I said, I want to talk to Elena," Philip said. "I'd like you to leave."

Clay turned and headed for the sofa. Again, Philip stepped in front of him and again Clay tensed. His hands clenched once at his sides, then relaxed. Philip was challenging him and it cost every ounce of self-control to ignore it. I was about to step in when Clay turned and looked at me.

"Please," I said.

He nodded and headed for the door, murmuring, "I'll be downstairs," as he passed me. When the door closed, I turned to Philip.

"When did you get back?" I asked.

"I didn't go."

"So you—"

"I was here all night."

I stalled as I struggled to think up an excuse. "The meeting was canceled?"

"There was no meeting."

I looked up sharply.

"Yes, I lied, Elena," he said. "I had to prove to myself that my suspicions were wrong."

"You think Clay and I are—"

"No. I wondered, but you wouldn't have needed to leave the apartment for that. Something's going on, it's just not the obvious." Philip paused. "You know he's in love with you, don't you?"

As I opened my mouth, he held up his hand.

"Don't," he continued. "It doesn't matter whether you know or not, or agree or not. He is. It's there for anyone to see, every time he looks at you, the way he talks to you. I don't know how you feel about him. I can't tell. Whenever I walk into the room, you two are arguing or laughing or doing both at the same time. I don't understand it. I don't understand a lot of things since you got back."

"He'll be leaving soon."

"Not soon. Now. Today."

He turned and walked into the bedroom. As I debated going after him, he returned with a handful of papers. He handed them to me. I looked at the top one. It was a real estate listing sheet for a house in Mississauga. I leafed through the papers and found three more listings for houses in the suburbs.

"I didn't go golfing Sunday," he said. "I was looking at houses. For us."

"You want to move into a house?"

"No, I— Yes, I do want to move into a house but—" He paused, crossed, then uncrossed his arms. "I mean that I want to get married. That's what a house means to me. Commitment, marriage, children someday. The whole nine yards. That's what I want."

I stared at him. Philip stepped toward me, then stopped, crossing and uncrossing his arms again, as if he couldn't figure out what to do with them.

"Is it such a surprise?" he asked softly.

I shook my head. "It's just . . . sudden. Clay and I were drinking last night and I'm still a bit . . . I'm not sure I can . . ."

"Don't answer, then. Give me time to buy a ring and do things right."

He shoved his hands in his pockets and stood there looking, despite his words, as if he still expected a reply. I said nothing.

"Go to work," he said. "Think about it."

We stood there for another awkward moment, then I broke away. I headed for the door, then hesitated, went back and embraced Philip. He hugged me back, holding on for a second or two after I let go. I kissed him, mumbled something about being home by seven, and made my getaway.

I went to work in a such a daze I was amazed I got off the subway at the right stop. I was sitting at my desk when I remembered Clay. He hadn't been outside the apartment when I'd left and I hadn't looked for him. It wouldn't take long before he figured out I'd gone to work and followed. What would I do when he showed up? What would I say? I shook the questions from my head. I didn't want to think about Clay now.

Philip had proposed.

Marriage.

The thought resuscitated hopes and dreams I thought had died ten years ago. I knew I couldn't get married, but the point had been moot for so long that I'd forgotten how much I'd wanted it. Did I still want it? The ache in my chest answered my question. I told myself I was being silly, old-fashioned. Marriage was for women who wanted someone to take care of them. I didn't need that. I didn't want it. But there were things I did want. Stability. Normalcy. Family. A permanent place in the human world. Marriage could give me that. Philip could give me that. But I couldn't get married. Or could I? I'd lived this long with Philip. Was it possible to sustain it forever? A small voice in my head asked if I wanted to be with Philip forever, but I stifled it. I loved

Philip. Right now, the question wasn't whether I wanted to marry him, but whether it was a possibility.

Was it possible?

Perhaps.

I could adapt better if we had a house. I could make sure we bought one near a forest or maybe a place in the country with some acreage. I could work from home and Change during the day so I'd never need to disappear from our bed in the middle of the night. The voice surfaced again, this time asking if I could imagine a life Changing by daylight, sneaking out and hurrying through it, not daring to run or hunt or anything else that would be too dangerous in the day. Again, I silenced the voice. I was considering my options, not making decisions.

Maybe I could continue hiding my secret from Philip, but would I want to? While I'd never felt the urge to tell him the truth before, maybe someday the deception would weigh so heavily on me that I couldn't bear it any longer. I remembered Clay when we were dating, painstakingly revising his history, in hindsight so obviously uncomfortable with it. How would I have reacted if Clay had told me the truth? I would have accepted it. I'd loved him enough that I wouldn't have cared. Philip said he loved me, but did he love me that much? Even if he accepted what I was, would he resent all the lies between us? I jumped to my own defense, insisting that there had been no other way. As much as I cared for Philip, it would have been impossible to tell him the truth. Then why did I still blame Clay for his lies? I pushed past that question. This was about Philip, not Clay. It wasn't the same. I'd never bite Phillip. The thought was unfathomable. But what if he wanted that, wanted to join me? A cold shiver went through me. No. Never. Not even if he wanted it. That was a part of my life I'd never bring Philip into.

My desk phone rang. As I lifted the receiver, I knew who was on the other end. I knew and I answered it anyway.

"Where are you?" Clay said in greeting.

"At work."

Pause. "Dumb question, right? If I call you at work and you answer, it should be pretty apparent where you are. I'm surprised you didn't pick up on that one."

I said nothing.

"What's wrong?" he asked.

"Nothing."

"Darling, anytime you miss a chance to slam me, there's something wrong."

"It's nothing."

Another pause. "It's those papers. For the houses. I saw them on the table when I went up looking for you. I'd hoped . . . That's it, isn't it?"

I didn't answer. Clay pulled the phone away from his mouth and swore. The line hissed and twittered as if the receiver was being jerked. I heard a thump and crackle. Then silence. I started to hang up when Clay's voice came back, muffled, then clear.

"Okay," he said. "Okay." He inhaled, the sound echoing down the line. "We need to talk. I'll be right there and we'll talk."

Again, I didn't answer.

"We need to talk," he repeated. "No tricks. I promised and I'm sticking to it, Elena. No tricks. I don't want to win that way anymore. We'll go someplace public, wherever you're comfortable, and we'll talk. Hear me out, then you can leave whenever you want."

"Okay."

"I mean it. I know—" He stopped. "Okay?"

"That's what I said."

He hesitated, then hurried on. "Give me ten minutes, fifteen tops. I'll take the subway and meet you in front of your office."

He hung up without waiting for a reply.

As soon as I got off the phone, I went downstairs. I wondered what I was doing. Why had I agreed to meet Clay? What did I expect him to say: "Philip asked you to marry him? —that's great, darling, I'm so happy for you"? Still, I didn't turn around and go back inside. It wouldn't do any good. I couldn't hide. I didn't want to hide. I shouldn't need to hide.

My stomach began to churn. Anxiety. I closed my eyes and tried to relax, but the nausea got worse. The ground beneath me grew rubbery, unstable. I stumbled to one side, then righted myself, glancing around to make sure no one had noticed. My body jerked up, suddenly tense, alarmed. I looked around, but saw nothing out of the ordinary. As I turned to look behind me, I felt a brief moment of light-headedness. Everything went black.

A middle-aged man grabbed me as I fell. At least, that's what I assume. One second I was standing on the sidewalk feeling light-headed, the next I was reclining backward looking up into the worried face of a stranger. My rescuer and his wife led me to a bench and sat me down. I mumbled something about skipping breakfast. They made sure I was okay, secured my promise to eat something and get out of the sun, then reluctantly moved on.

I went into the building, stood inside the doors, and checked my watch. Fifteen minutes had passed since Clay had called. He should be here any moment. My stomach was still churning. It was definitely anxiety, but I couldn't pin it down to a cause. Sure, my mind was spinning after Philip's proposal and I didn't really want to talk to Clay, yet for some reason the anxiety didn't seem linked to either of these stressors. It floated there, oddly disconnected and distant.

I focused back on Clay. He'd promised not to trick me. That vow would last only as long as he got his way. If I decided to marry Philip or even to stay with him, Clay would go ballistic, all bets off, all promises forgotten. I knew that but, to my surprise, I wasn't afraid of what he'd do. After all these years, I knew his tricks so well that they were no longer tricks. Whatever he tried, I could anticipate it. I would be ready for it. He'd said last night that I needed to make a choice. He was right. *I* needed to make that choice. I wasn't going to let him do it for me.

A clock somewhere sounded eleven chimes. I double-checked my watch. Yes, it was eleven. Clay had called at ten thirty-five. The anxiety pushed to the surface. Don't be silly, I told myself. Twenty-five minutes wasn't unreasonable. Maybe he couldn't face the subway after all and had decided to walk. Something's wrong, the voice from earlier whispered inside me. No, I told it. Nothing's wrong.

I waited ten minutes longer. The anxiety was worse, my stomach roiling now. I had to go. Back to the apartment.

Discovery

AS I SWUNG OPEN THE APARTMENT DOOR, IT STRUCK SOMETHING and bounced back toward me. I pushed it again. It opened a few inches, then stopped. I pushed harder. Whatever was in the way was heavy, but it moved, making a swishing sound against the carpet. Looking down, I saw a leg stretched across the floor. I squeezed through the narrow opening, nearly tripping over the leg in my haste to get inside.

It was Philip. He was sprawled behind the door. As I looked at him, my brain refused to register what I was seeing. I stood there, staring down, perversely thinking not, Oh, my God but, How did he get there. Even as I saw the blood pooled at his side, dripping from his mouth, smeared in a bloody trail across the carpet, my brain would only accept simple and ridiculous explanations. Had he passed out? Fainted? Heart attack? Stroke? Seizure? Still numb, I dropped to his side and started going through the motions for basic first aid. Conscious? No. Breathing? Yes. Pulse? Neither strong nor weak. I lifted his eyelids, but didn't know what I was checking for. As I pulled back his shirt, my fingers grazed across his side and slipped into a gaping wound. I pulled my hand back and stared at my bloodied fingers.

Clay.

I gagged, yanking back from Philip as if afraid of soiling him, and vomited a thin string of bile onto the carpet. The shock passed in a second and I started to shake, alternating between fear and rage. Clay did this. No, he couldn't have. Yes, he *could* have, but he wouldn't. Wouldn't he? Why wouldn't he? What would stop him? I hadn't been here to stop him. But no, he wouldn't do something like this. Why not? Because he'd been sweet and even-tempered for a few days? Had I forgotten what he was capable of? Not this. Never this. Clay didn't attack humans. Unless they were a threat. But Philip didn't know what we were, so he wasn't dangerous, wasn't a threat to the Pack, to our way of life. Maybe not to the Pack's way of life, but to Clay's . . . ?

Philip stirred. I jumped to my feet, suddenly remembering the most basic first aid response. I ran to the phone, lifted it, and dialed 911. It took a few seconds to realize I wasn't hearing anything on the other end. I jammed the plunger up and down and dialed again. Still nothing. I looked down. The phone cord snaked around the table leg. The end lay a foot away, colored wires sticking out. Cut. Someone had deliberately cut the phone cord. I knew then that Clay hadn't done this to Philip. He wouldn't leave him alive, bleeding to death, then cut off the phone. Whatever else Clay was, he wasn't a sadist.

I raced to the hall closet and flung it open. Philip's briefcase was on its usual hook and his cell phone was inside its usual spot. I punched in 911, then told the operator that my boyfriend was wounded and unconscious, that I'd come home to find him like that and had no idea how badly he was hurt or how it had happened. I didn't know if she believed me and I didn't care. She took the address and promised an ambulance. That was good enough.

After turning off the phone, I ran to the closet, grabbed a sheet, and ripped it into strips. As I bound Philip's side, I bent close enough to smell who had touched him, who'd done this to him. The scent that wafted up from his clothes wasn't Clay's, but it was someone I knew, someone whose smell registered without a moment of surprise. Thomas LeBlanc. In the back of my brain, I wondered how he'd found me, where he was now, whether he'd return, but I didn't waste time pondering the questions. First priority was Philip. Second priority was finding Clay and warning him.

I checked Philip's breathing and pulse again. Still the same. I leaned over him, braced his neck with one hand, and lifted him to check for any hidden wounds. As I shifted myself upward to kneel, I caught a glimpse of something under the hall table. A hypodermic needle. Fresh alarm surged through me. Had LeBlanc injected Philip with something? Poisoned him? Easing Philip down, I scrambled to the table. I was about to bend over to pick up the needle when I saw the ring on the tabletop. A gold band so familiar that I knew what it was without a closer look. Clay's wedding band. Beneath it was a sheet of torn paper with a scribbled note. For a brief second, I thought Clay had taken off his ring, that he'd come up here before LeBlanc had arrived, removed the ring, written the note, then left—left me. Some emotion surged through me, but before I could analyze it, I realized the writing wasn't Clay's. My hands started to shake. I lifted the note. The ring slipped off and fell, tumbling toward the carpet. I lunged to grab it, my hand closing around the cool metal before it struck the floor. I turned back to the note.

Elena,
Big Bear Motor Lodge. Rm. 211. Tomorrow. 10 A.M.
—D.

A sick feeling settled in my gut. Even as I bent to pick up the syringe, I knew what I'd smell on it. Daniel's scent on the plunger. Clay's on the needle.

"No," I whispered.

I yanked out the plunger and sniffed inside. A strong medicinal smell clung to the empty casing, but I couldn't place it. Not poison, I told myself. Daniel wouldn't use poison. LeBlanc might, but not Daniel. If it was poison, they would have left Clay, not just his ring. The ring and note were a sign. Clay was still alive. Still alive? The thought went through me like an icy knife, not that he was alive but that I would even need to consider the alternative.

"Oh, God," I whispered and swayed, grabbing the table to steady myself.

Get a grip, I told myself. Clay was okay. Daniel gave him something to knock him out. That's why I'd fainted earlier, a manifestation of the sympathetic bond between us. Daniel drugged Clay and took him away but he was okay. I'd know if he wasn't. Oh, God, I hoped I'd know. I looked at the note again. A meeting. Daniel had Clay and he wanted me to meet him tomorrow at ten in Bear Valley. And if I didn't show up . . .

I dropped the paper and turned to run out the door. Philip's body was still blocking the way.

"I'm sorry," I whispered. "Very, very sorry."

I bent to move him out of the way. As I touched him, his eyes flew open and his hand clasped around my wrist.

"Elena?" he said, looking around in confusion, eyes not focusing.

"You're okay," I said. "I've called an ambulance."

"There was a man . . . Two men . . ."

"I know. You're hurt but you'll be okay. An ambulance is coming."

"Asking where you were . . . Didn't tell them . . . Then Clayton . . . Fighting . . ."

"I know." Panic was edging into my voice. I had to go. Now. "Wait here. I'm going down to wait for the ambulance."

"No . . . Could still be there . . . Looking for you . . ."

"I'll be careful."

I tried to pry Philip's fingers from my wrist but he tightened his grip. As gently as possible, I wriggled free, then got to my feet. He lifted himself a couple inches and fell back again, blocking the door. He put a hand on my leg.

"No," he said again. "You can't go."

"I have to."

"No!"

His eyes blazed with fever and pain. A pang of anguish went through me. I'd done this. I'd brought this to him. I had to stay and help. If he got upset, he might make himself worse. A few more minutes wouldn't make any difference. My hands clenched at my sides. Clay's ring jabbed into my palm and I jerked upright.

Ten o'clock. I had to be there by ten o'clock.

Philip said something, but I didn't hear it. Panic flooded through me.

I had to leave. I had to leave now.

I tried to reason with myself, calm myself down, but it was too late.

My body was already responding to the fear. A sudden jolt of agony doubled me in half. I was dimly aware of Clay's ring falling to the floor, of Philip saying something. My head shot down, pulling back into my chest. A wail split the air, leaving my throat raw. I gasped, choking, sputtering for air. As I toppled forward, my arms went out to break my fall. I tried to pull into myself, keeping my head down, but my legs spasmed and my head jerked back. Through the fog of pain I saw Philip's face in front of mine, saw his eyes, saw the revulsion and horror there. I fell to all fours, hunching into myself. My back went up. My shirt split. I wailed again, this time an unearthly howl. The Change was coming so fast and so strong I couldn't even think of stopping it. My brain went blank, filled with nothing but fear and agony. My body convulsed once, then again, seizures so powerful that I felt I'd be ripped in half and I didn't care, aware only that it would stop the pain. Then it ended.

I lifted my head and knew that I was a wolf. There was one moment of total exhaustion that vanished as quickly as it came. Panic and terror instantly took its place. I looked up. Philip lay on the floor a few feet away. All I could see were his eyes, staring at me in helpless horror.

I turned, ran across the room, closed my eyes, and plunged through the balcony doors. The glass exploded. Shards of glass sliced through my fur and skin, but I barely felt them. Without pausing or even thinking, I vaulted up and over the railing. For a moment, I was airborne. Then I hit the grass four stories below. My left front paw twisted. Pain shot through my leg. Someone shouted. I ran.

I tore around the building and into the underground parking garage. Ducking behind the first car, I listened for following footsteps. When none came, I shook myself and tried to relax and concentrate. Even if no one came after me, I was stuck. So long as I was anxious and panicked, I couldn't Change back. Even if I did, I'd be naked in a parking garage. I might be able to find clothes, but then what? My wallet, with money, credit cards, and ID, was in the apartment. Without them, I couldn't get out of Toronto. Not only would I need to find clothing, but I'd need to go back up to the apartment. I couldn't do that. Philip has seen me and the ambulance would be here any minute. Maybe if I waited . . . For how long? When, if ever, would it be safe to go back? Daniel's note flashed in my brain. Ten A.M. tomorrow. The deadline. Anxiety surged again, shoving all rational thought from my brain.

Go.

Go now.

I hesitated only a moment, then obeyed.

I took the back alleys where I could and side roads where I couldn't. People saw me. I didn't care. I kept running. When I got out of Toronto, I raced across fields and forests and open pastures. Logically, my flight made no sense. I would have been better off waiting in the parking garage, sneaking back up to the apartment after an hour or so, and catching a plane. Yet this never occurred to me. Every fiber in me rebelled at the thought of waiting. My gut told me to act and I did.

My brain shut off as I ran, letting instinct control my muscles. Hours later I arrived at an obstacle that my instincts alone couldn't handle: the Niagara Falls border crossing. I spent nearly an hour pacing behind a warehouse, my thoughts slipping and sliding like a car on ice, whirring uselessly. Finally, I regained enough control to contemplate the problem and come up with a solution. There was a huge line of trucks backed up across the bridge, slowed down in customs by some new U.S. entry regulation. Thanks to bureaucratic red tape, I had time to pick out a truck with a canvas-covered trailer and sneak on board. Thankfully the cargo wasn't checked at the border and the truck continued unhindered from Niagara Falls, Ontario, to Niagara Falls, New York. The truck left the city and headed south toward Buffalo. My gut screamed, Wrong Way! and I found myself flying off the back of the truck before my brain had time to protest. I hit the curb hard and rolled into a ditch. As I got to my feet, the paw that I'd hurt leaping from the balcony buckled under me. My stomach growled, reminding me I'd missed lunch and dinner. I thought of slowing down, finding a patch of woods and hunting for dinner, but the panic switch in my head went on, shutting down all higher reasoning. Run, it said. So I did.

By nightfall I was moving on pure fear and momentum. No matter how hungry I was, I was certain that if I stopped, I'd never get started again. Ten o'clock, my gut screamed each time I thought of pausing to rest or eat. Ten o'clock. Stop even for a second and you'll never make it. And if you don't make it . . . I refused to think of that. It was easier to keep running.

It must have been nearly midnight when a thunderous roar in my head sent me pitching forward into the grass. As I got back up, the boom came again. I whined, lowered my head and shook it, scratching at my right ear with my forepaw. Got to run. Can't stop. I lurched forward.

"Elena!" The boom in my head took on a voice and words. Jeremy. His voice roared again, splitting my skull with its intensity. "Elena! Where are you?!"

I lowered my head again and whimpered. Go away, Jeremy. Go away. You're making me stop. I can't stop.

"Where are you, Elena? I can't contact Clay! Where the hell are you?"

I tried to answer, if only to shut him up, but my brain wouldn't form words, only images. Jeremy went silent and I stood there, dazed and wondering if I'd heard him at all. Was I hallucinating? I was awake, wasn't I? Jeremy couldn't contact us when we were awake. Was I sleeping or losing my mind? It didn't matter. Ten o'clock, ten o'clock, ten o'clock. You'll never make it. Run.

I stumbled forward and ran. Soon I started blacking out. I was still moving, but everything kept fading in and out. My legs were numb. I could smell the blood trailing from my torn pads. One minute the ground was like a bed of nails beneath my paws, the next it was like cotton and I was floating above it, racing faster than the wind. It was suddenly day, then night again. I was running through a town. No, I was running through Toronto, the CN Tower beckoning in the distance. I heard voices. A shout. A laugh. Clay's laugh. I strained to see through the night. Fog had rolled in from Lake Ontario, but I could hear him laughing. The concrete turned to grass. The fog wasn't from the lake, but from a pond. Our pond. I was at Stonehaven, bounding through the back acres. Clay was running ahead of me. I could see snatches of gold fur bobbing through the trees. I dug my claws in and ran faster. Suddenly, the ground ended. I was running through the air. Then I was falling. I scrambled for a foothold, but there was nothing around me but inky blackness. Then there was nothing at all.

Caged

I AWOKE TO THE SENSATION OF COLD. AS I SHIVERED, I FELT WET grass beneath my bare skin. I opened one eye. Trees. Long grass. A meadow. I tried lifting my head but couldn't. Clay. That was my first thought, but I didn't know why. Had I been running with him? I couldn't smell him. Why couldn't I raise my head? There was nothing holding me down. My muscles just refused to respond. Was I dead? Dead. Clay. I remembered and my head shot up. Blinding pain pierced my skull.

Something warm and soft fell around my shoulders. I jerked up, crying out in pain as I moved. A jacket lay over my bare torso, the smell of it so familiar, yet so impossible. Was I dreaming? Hallucinating? I felt hands slipping under me to lift me up, the touch as familiar as the scent on the coat.

"Elena?"

A face bent over mine. Jeremy, dark hair falling over his forehead, shoved back with an impatient hand. Not possible. Not here. I closed my eyes.

"Elena?" Sharper now, worried.

I tried to move, but it hurt too much. Deciding to abandon myself to the hallucination, I lifted one eyelid.

"H—" I croaked, wanting to ask how he'd got there. "H—" Nothing more would come.

"Don't try to talk," he said. "And don't try to move. I'm going to carry you to the truck. It's right over there."

"C—Cl—"

"They have him, don't they?" His arms tightened around me.

"T—ten—o'clock," I managed to get out, then everything went dark again.

This time I woke to warmth, artificial heat blowing across my face. I heard the humming of a motor, felt the vibration and small bumps of a car moving over a smooth road. I smelled old leather and shifted beneath the jacket slung around me. I stretched my legs, but the pain made me whimper and pull back.

"Is that too hot?" Nick's voice. I felt his arm move over me and reach for the vent. He tilted it away from my face.

"Is she awake?" Jeremy somewhere nearby. In front of me. The front seat.

"I'm not sure," Nick said. "Her eyes are closed. You can probably turn down the heat. She's got her color back."

The click of a dial. The harsh blowing fell to a quiet drone. I opened one eye, then the other. I was propped half-reclining in the back seat of the Explorer, my head resting near the side window, legs curled beside me on the seat. Scenery and cars sped past. Antonio was in front of me, in the driver's seat. His eyes flickered toward me through the rearview mirror.

"She's awake," he said.

A seat belt clicked open. Then the whir of denim on the cloth seats. Nick bent over me.

"Is it warm enough?" he asked. "Can I get you anything?"

"T—ti—"

"Don't talk, Elena," Jeremy said. "Grab the water bottle from the cooler, Nick. She's dehydrated. Let her sip it, but not too much."

Nick rummaged around in the cooler. Then a cold plastic straw touched my lips. I pulled back and gave a small shake of my head that sent lightning bolts through my skull.

"Ti—" I croaked. "Ti—me. Wha—ti—me."

"What time?" Nick lowered his face to mine. "What time is it?"

I nodded, sending a shower of burning sparks through my head this time. Nick still looked confused, but he checked his watch.

"Eleven-twenty . . . almost eleven-thirty."

"No!" I shot upright. "No!"

Nick jerked back. The Explorer swerved and Antonio swore, then yanked the steering wheel back on track. I fought to get out from under Jeremy's jacket.

"Elena." Jeremy's voice came from the front seat, calm and firm. "It's okay, Elena. Calm her down, Nick, before she gives your father a heart attack."

"She just surprised me," Antonio said. "Nicky, make sure—"

I didn't hear the rest. I struggled free of the jacket and flung it aside, then fumbled to undo the seat belt. Every movement ripped through me. My hands were bruised and torn. I didn't care. I was late. I had to go. I had to get there. Now.

Nick grabbed the seat belt fastener away from me, but I already had it open and was squirming out of the restraining strap. Nick grabbed my shoulders.

"No!" I shouted and flung his hands off.

He grabbed me again, harder this time. I fought, baring my teeth and scratching any part of him I could reach.

"Stop the car," I shouted.

The Explorer slowed to half speed, but no more, as if Antonio was deciding what to do.

"Keep going," Jeremy said. "She's delirious. *Keep going.*"

Nick struggled to keep me in my seat, his face hardening with resolve. I heard a sound in the front. Over Nick's shoulder, I saw Jeremy getting up from his seat, reaching back to restrain me. I gathered all my strength and control, drew back my fist, and punched Jeremy in the stomach. His eyes went wide and he doubled over. Some deep part of me was horrified, but I didn't care. The fever in my brain incinerated any pangs of conscience. I had to get out. I was late. Nothing else mattered.

I shoved Nick away and flung myself past him toward the opposite door. Grabbing the handle, I thrust it open and looked down. Gravel flew by in a gray blur. Nick shouted. The brakes squealed. The Explorer veered right. I tensed to jump. Two sets of hands grabbed me, one by the back, the other by the shoulders, and yanked me inside. I felt Jeremy's hands go around my neck, then pressure on the side of my throat, then blackness again.

I awoke in a memory. Every part of my body ached. I'd Changed last night. The recollection was dim, a montage of images—pain, fear, rage, disbelief. Yet I hadn't been running through New York State. I'd Changed in a 8′× 6′ cell, manacled hand and foot. My seventh Change. Seven weeks since I'd come to this place. I had no idea what day it was, but I knew how many times I'd gone through hell and marked the time by that. When I awoke, I was still in the cage. I'd been in it for five weeks now, five Changes since the man gave up trying to keep me in a bedroom upstairs. I knew his name: Jeremy, but I never used it, not to his face, not even when I thought of him. To his face, I called him nothing. I refused to speak to him. In my mind, he was simply "he" or "the man," a designation devoid of thought and emotion.

I awoke feeling the scratchy fabric of a mattress beneath me. There had been sheets once, soft flannel sheets and a comforter. Then he caught me tearing them into strips and thought I was planning to hang myself. I wasn't. I wouldn't give him the satisfaction of seeing me dead. I'd torn up the sheets for the same reason I'd destroyed the magazines and clothing he'd brought for me, and the pretty pictures he'd affixed to the stone cage walls. I wanted nothing from him. I would accept nothing meant to make this cage seem like anything other than the hellhole it was. The only offering I accepted was food and I ate that only because I had to keep my strength up for when I escaped. That was what kept me going, the thought of escape. Soon I would get away, back to the city, to people who could help me, heal me.

I opened my eyes to see a figure on the chair outside the cage. At first I thought it was him. He sat there most of the day, watching me and talking to me, trying to brainwash me with the insanity that spilled from his lips. When my eyes focused, the figure became clearer, bent over, elbows on knees, gold curls shining in the artificial light. The one person I hated more than the man. Quickly, I closed my eyes and feigned sleep, but it was too late. He'd seen me. He got to his feet and started to talk. I wanted to stop up my ears, but it would do no good. I could hear too well now. Even if I could block his words, I knew what he'd be saying. He said the same things every time he came, sneaking in when the man was out. He tried to explain what he'd done, why he'd done it. He apologized. He pleaded with me to obey the man so that I could get out of the cage. He wanted me to talk to the man, to ask that his banishment be revoked so he could come back and help me. But there was only one way he could help me. Each time he came, each time he swore he'd do anything to make it up to me, I told him the same thing. The only words I'd speak to him. Fix me. Undo what you did.

"Clay."

The sound of my voice woke me from my memories. I was on my back, staring up at a naked lightbulb on a whitewashed cement ceiling. I turned my head and saw solid stone walls. No windows. No ornaments. Beneath me, I felt the scratchy twin-size mattress. The cage.

"No," I whispered. "No."

I turned my head and saw the bars. Beyond them, someone was sitting on the chair. My heart leapt. Then the figure stood, black eyes meeting mine.

"No," I whispered again, sitting up. "Damn you, no."

"I had to, Elena," Jeremy said. "I was afraid you'd hurt yourself. Now, if you're feeling better—"

I threw myself at the bars. Jeremy stepped out of arm's reach, cautious but not surprised.

"Let me out of here!" I shouted.

"Elena, if you'd—"

"You don't understand!"

"Yes, I do. Daniel has Clay. He took him in Toronto. He wanted you to show up at the hotel at ten today. You were talking in your sleep on the way back."

"You—" I stopped and swallowed. "You know?"

"Yes, I—"

"You know and you're keeping me in here? How could you?!" I grabbed the bars and strained against them. "You knew Clay's life was in danger and you put me in here?"

"What do you think Daniel planned to do, Elena? Take you and let Clay go? Of course not. If you went there, we'd lose you both."

"I don't care!"

Jeremy rubbed a hand over his face. "You do care, Elena. You're just too upset to think about this logically—"

"Logically? Logically? Are you really that cold? You raised him. You mean the world to him. He's spent his life protecting you. He's risked his life protecting you, risks it constantly for you. You'd sit back, logically assess the situation and decide it's not worth the gamble to save him?"

"Elena—"

"If he's dead, it's your fault."

"Elena!"

"It's my fault. If he's dead because I didn't get there on time—"

Jeremy grabbed my arm through the bars, fingers cutting to the bone. "Stop it, Elena! He's not dead. I know you're upset, but if you'd calm down—"

"Calm down? Are you saying I'm hysterical?"

"—calm down and think about it, you'll know Clay isn't dead. Think about it. Daniel knows how important Clayton is to the Pack. To you. To me. He's too valuable as a hostage."

"But Daniel doesn't know why I didn't show up. Maybe he thinks we don't care, that we've abandoned Clay, given him up for dead."

"Daniel would know better. To be sure, I've sent him a note. Last week he gave me a post office box to contact him through. Antonio and Nick dropped off a letter saying that we weren't letting you make that appointment, but that I'm willing to negotiate so long as Clay's not harmed. I'm sure Daniel already knows that, but I wanted to make it clear. I'm not taking any chances with Clay's life, Elena."

On some level I knew Jeremy was right. It didn't help. I kept thinking, What if he's wrong? What if Clay had never even made it back to

New York? What if he'd woken up and they'd fought and he was lying in a Dumpster in Toronto? What if Daniel couldn't resist the opportunity to destroy his lifelong enemy while he was drugged and powerless? Even if Daniel managed to keep it together, what about LeBlanc? He'd already proven he didn't give a damn what Daniel wanted. If Clay angered LeBlanc, he'd kill him. Even if Clay didn't do anything to LeBlanc, he might kill him just because he could. As all the possibilities ran through my mind, my aching legs surrendered and I slumped to the floor, still clutching the bars.

"You didn't warn me," I said.

Jeremy crouched down, putting one hand over mine. "I didn't warn you about what, sweetheart?" he asked softly.

"I didn't think. I should have known."

"Known what?"

"That he was in danger, too. He was looking after me. But I wasn't looking after him."

I dropped my head to my knees and felt the first prick of tears behind my eyes.

Jeremy left me in the cage overnight. As much as I wanted to believe otherwise, I knew he wasn't being heartless or unfeeling. After my crying jag, one might have expected me to give up the fight and meekly accept Jeremy's will. At least, anyone who didn't know me very well might expect that. Jeremy knew me better. When I was sobbing on the floor, he'd reached through the bars to comfort me, but didn't unlock the door. After I'd had a good cry and wiped away the tears, I flew into a rage. I broke the bed, it being the only breakable thing in the cell. I kicked the toilet, but that didn't break anything except maybe a couple of my toes. I flung my dinner on the floor. I cursed Jeremy at the top of my lungs. And once it was all over, I should have felt better, right? I didn't. I felt stupid. I felt like I'd had a fit of hysterics and made a fool of myself. I needed to get a grip and take control. Throwing tantrums wouldn't help Clay.

Of course, just because I was ready to leave the cage didn't mean Jeremy was prepared to let me out. He left me in there all morning, stopping by periodically to make sure I hadn't resumed my *Exorcist* imitation. When he came down with my lunch, he brought a letter-size manila envelope. Before giving me the food tray, he wordlessly passed me the envelope.

Inside was a Polaroid shot of Clay. He was sitting on the floor, knees pulled up, feet bound together, and arms behind him. His hands were out of sight, but judging by his position they must have been tied or manacled. His eyes were half closed and so clouded by drugs they looked gray instead of blue. Though I couldn't see any sign of bars, I knew he was in a cage. No werewolf would capture Clay without making damn sure he couldn't Change and break out. Keeping him secure would mean drugs, bindings, and/or a cage. Daniel would use all three. He'd fought Clay before and he wouldn't take any chance on an accidental rematch.

I looked at the picture again. Bruises covered Clay's arms and bare torso, an ugly slice bisected his left cheek, his lips were swollen and split, and he had one blackened eye. Despite his condition, he stared into the camera with a look of bored annoyance, like a supermodel who's had one too many photographers in her face that day. Showing defiance would have only set Daniel off. Clay knew better.

I reached inside the envelope again and found it empty. I looked up at Jeremy. For the first time since he'd brought me back, I really looked at him. His eyes were underscored with purple and his bangs fell lankly against his forehead, as if he hadn't slept or showered in days. Tiny lines had appeared around his eyes and mouth. He almost looked his age.

"Where's the letter?" I asked, more gently than I'd intended. "I know Daniel must have sent a letter. Can I see it?"

"It says they have Clay, which is obvious, and that he's not in great shape, but he's alive, both equally obvious. If you check the background of the photo, you'll see a newspaper hanging on the wall. It's today's *New York Times,* presumably to prove the picture was taken today."

"What does Daniel want?"

"Clay's in no immediate danger."

"Are you going to give me a direct answer to any of my questions?"

"I've sent a note back. I'm demanding daily pictures while we negotiate."

I scowled and stomped to the other side of the cell, reminding myself that I had to play nice. Another tantrum wouldn't get me out of the cage anytime soon.

"I know I lost it yesterday," I said. "But I'm fine now. I want to help. Can I come out?"

"Eat your lunch. I'll be back in a while to see if you're still hungry."

Jeremy slipped the tray through the slot near the floor and went upstairs. I bit my tongue to keep from calling him anything I might regret . . . at least until he was out of earshot.

Plans

JEREMY LET ME OUT LATER THAT AFTERNOON. BEFORE WE WERE even up the stairs, I asked about his plans. He made me wait until after dinner, probably testing how far he could stretch my patience before I snapped. I'll admit, by mealtime I was getting close, but I managed to hold it together. While Antonio and Nick cleaned up the dinner mess, Jeremy took me into the study for our talk. The *Reader's Digest* condensed version of our hour-long talk was this: Jeremy had a plan for getting Clay back and I wasn't allowed to know anything about it or allowed to help him carry it out. As one might expect, I accepted this news with grace and understanding.

"That is the stupidest idea I've ever heard!" I snarled for the dozenth time that hour. "I won't just sit here and do nothing."

"Would you prefer to sit in the cage and do nothing?"

"Don't threaten me."

"Then don't threaten me."

Something in Jeremy's voice made me clamp my mouth shut and settle for pacing.

"I can help," I said, keeping my voice low and, I hoped, calm. "Please, Jer, don't shut me out. Maybe you blame me for what happened in Toronto, but don't punish me like this."

"You didn't do anything wrong in Toronto. If it's anyone's fault, it's mine. I thought Toronto was safe. I didn't realize Daniel was gone until Tuesday morning, when he was already there. I'm not going to tell you how I plan to get Clay back because then you'll want to help and if I don't let you, you'll go ahead and try anyway."

"But—"

He leaned forward. "I'm being honest with you, Elena. More honest than I'd dare be with anyone else. Everything is falling apart. I wasn't prepared to handle this. If I've been a good Alpha all these years it's because I've never been tested. Not like this. I started slow, feeling things out, gathering information. Peter and Logan got killed. I changed course and took off again, going after Jimmy Koenig. You almost got killed. I sent you two away where I thought you'd be safe. Less than a week later, Daniel found you. Now he has Clay."

"But—"

Jeremy stood and smiled down at me, a crooked half smile, and brushed a lock of hair off my shoulder. "I'm sorry, sweetheart. I really am. But this is how it has to be."

Before I could respond, he was gone.

Despite Jeremy's orders, I had no intention of sitting on my hands and doing nothing. After all, he hadn't specifically forbidden me to do anything. So I started to plan.

Step one: find an ally. This was easy. Well, there wasn't a lot of selection, but even if there had been, Nick would be the obvious choice. Not only was he Clay's best friend, but he'd been shut out of the rescue plan as well, and was as unhappy about it as I. Jeremy claimed he needed Nick to guard me, but even Nick was smart enough to know that Jeremy wasn't telling him anything for fear he'd take it back to me. I persuaded Nick by saying I only wanted to gather information, so we could prove our value to Jeremy. Not that this was a lie. I had every intention of sharing any information I uncovered with Jeremy. And if he still refused to let me help? I didn't worry about that. I could always renegotiate my arrangement with Nick later.

Step two: plot a course of action. Jeremy would be trying to find where the mutts were keeping Clay. It didn't take a genius to figure this out. Bargaining with Daniel would only be a cover to keep him busy while Jeremy figured out where they were staying. Nick confirmed this.

Yesterday, before he was cut out of the plan, Jeremy had sent him and Antonio to the Big Bear Motor Lodge. Everyone except Daniel had checked out of the motel on Monday. Daniel had checked out Wednesday. So the conclusion I'd drawn, and likely the same one Jeremy had drawn, was that the mutts had found another hiding place and had taken Clay there upon his return from Toronto. Since I didn't want to interfere with Jeremy's plans—or, more realistically, I didn't want to get caught interfering—I'd have to leave the mutt tracking to him and find another way to discover where they were hiding Clay.

Step three: divert attention from my activities. Had it been anyone but Jeremy, I'd have played the role of the cowed subordinate. To Jeremy, though, that would be a sure sign that I was up to something. So, I bitched and complained and made his life hell. He expected nothing less. Every chance I got, I demanded, begged, or wheedled to be let in on his plans. Finally, after an evening and morning of being in his face at every possible opportunity, I gave him an ultimatum. If he didn't find Clay in three days, I was going after him with or without Jeremy's permission. He therefore assumed that he had three days before I started raising hell again, so he relaxed. An ingenious ruse if I do say so myself.

Although Nick had agreed to help me, he refused to disobey Jeremy's order of house arrest, so I couldn't actually go anywhere. Well, I could knock Nick over the head and make a run for it, but I wouldn't do that to him. Besides, Jeremy would only find me and bring me back and Nick wouldn't be too enthusiastic about helping me again if he was suffering from a concussion.

The first thing I did was call the hospital. No, I didn't call the local hospital on some premonition that they might have Clay or know where he was. I called St. Michael's Hospital in Toronto. I hadn't forgotten that I'd left Philip bleeding on the floor of our apartment. I'll admit I might not have spent as much time dwelling on it as I should have, but I knew his injuries weren't life threatening, at least not after I'd stopped the bleeding and called for help, and Clay's situation was far more dire, so I think I can be excused if my attentions weren't evenly divided between the two. Philip wasn't at St. Mike's. The emergency room had been closed to new arrivals last Tuesday afternoon, not an uncommon occurrence after years of health care budget cuts. Philip had been taken to Toronto East General and was still there. I spoke to the nurse on his floor, introducing myself as his sister, and learned that he'd suffered some internal injuries and had required surgery, but he was recovering and was expected to leave on Monday, which meant he'd actually be feeling better by next Wednesday or Thursday—budget cuts again. She offered to put me through to his room to speak to him, but I declined, claiming I didn't want to disturb his rest. The truth was I was too much of a coward to speak to him. Even if he forgave me for abandoning him, there was the small matter of having watched me Change into a wolf. I settled for sending him flowers with a note saying I'd see him soon, and hoped that didn't scare him back into intensive care.

The next thing I did was call the local real estate office. No, not because I was planning to move out and needed a place to stay. Tempting idea, but I knew I wouldn't get far. If Jeremy had tracked me to a field in upstate New York—and he still wouldn't tell me how he'd accomplished that—then he could certainly find me living in Bear Valley, either before or after the mutts found me. Either way, I wasn't suicidal. I called the real estate office to check for homes rented or purchased in the past couple of weeks, particularly houses in the rural area. Only three homes had been sold in the Bear Valley district recently. Two were bought by young families and the third by a retirement-age couple. There were more rentals, but all to longtime Bear Valley residents.

When the house idea didn't pan out, I looked for a possible cottage rental. The bad news was that we lived in cottage country. The good news was that it was still early in the season and the Bear Valley area itself wasn't prime cottage land, having too many trees and too few lakes and waterways. I called the Bear Valley Cottage Association. With a little ingenuity, a lot of lying, and even more politeness—Jeremy had taught me well—I discovered that only four local cottages were being rented, three to honeymooning couples and the fourth to a bunch of middle-aged men from New York who came up every May for some kind of male-bonding-in-the-wilderness therapeutic retreat. Another dead end. I'd have to try another tack. I just wasn't sure yet what that might be.

Purposeful action made the hours fly past, leaving little time to brood over Clay's situation. By evening though, I was left alone with my thoughts. I was tending the fire in the study. It didn't need tending. It didn't even need to be lit, the temperature outside still hovering in the mid-seventies. But there was comfort sitting on the hearth, poking at the logs and watching the fire dance and spark. Unnecessary action was better than no action. Besides, staring at the flames had a mesmerizing effect, giving me something to concentrate on other than the thoughts and fears that kept slipping past the mental barriers I'd carefully erected in the past twenty-four hours.

I wasn't alone in the study. Nick was there, half dozing on the couch. Every so often he'd open his eyes and say something. We'd talk for a few minutes, then the conversation would begin moving dangerously close to Clay and we'd both fall silent. As the clock on the mantel chimed midnight, Nick woke again. He tilted his head backward over the arm of the sofa and looked at the window.

"Full moon coming," he said. "Two, three days?"

"Two."

"I'll need to run. How about you?"

I managed a small smile. "You know perfectly well that I don't need to run, since I did more than enough of that three days ago. What you really want to know is: will I run with you and save you from the horrifying prospect of having to run alone."

"I don't know how you did it in Toronto all those months," he said with a shudder. "I had to do it a couple times last winter. Tonio took off on business and Logan was wrapped up in some court case and Clay— Anyway, I had to Change by myself."

"Poor baby."

"It was awful. It was, like, walk out to the woods, Change, stand there until enough time passed, Change back. It was about as much fun as taking a shit."

"Nice analogy."

"I'm serious. Come on, Elena. Admit it. That's what it's like if you're by yourself. I remember when I was a kid, before my first Change, and Clay used to—"

He stopped. This time, he didn't pick up again. Silence fell and I turned back toward the fire, poking it and watching the sparks cascade from the logs. The door opened. I heard Jeremy come in, but didn't turn around. A moment later, the sofa springs groaned as Nick got up. He walked across the room and the door closed again. Jeremy sat beside me on the hearth. His hand touched the back of my head, hesitated, then stroked my hair.

"I know how difficult this is for you, Elena. I know how scared you are, how afraid you are of losing him."

"It's not that. I mean, of course I'm afraid of losing him. But if you think it's because I've suddenly realized how much I love him and that if—when we get him back, I'll come home and everything will be fine, then you're wrong. I'm sorry. I know you want that, that it would be easier for you and everyone else, but it's not going to happen. Yes, I care about him. Very much. And yes, I want him back. I want him back for you and for Nick and for the Pack. I'm upset because I hold myself responsible."

Jeremy said nothing.

I looked over my shoulder at him. "So you hold me responsible, too?"

"No, not at all. I didn't answer because I thought it best to hold my tongue about the rest. If you think that's why you're upset—"

"It is."

He was quiet for a moment, then reached over to rub my back, fingers moving to the tight ball between my shoulders. "Whatever the reason for your worry, I don't hold you responsible for what happened. We've been through this before. I should have sent you two someplace else. I thought I was being clever, but I didn't even realize something happened until I tried contacting Clay that night—"

"Have you done it since?" I asked, straightening up and turning to face him. "Have you contacted Clay since he's been captured? You've tried, haven't you? What did he say? Is he—"

Jeremy put his fingers to my lips. "Yes, I've tried. Tried and tried again. But I can't get through to him. It's the drugs."

There was another possible reason why Jeremy couldn't get in touch with Clay, but I didn't dare speak it. Jeremy seemed to read it in my face, though, and shook his head.

"Don't think that. You saw today's picture. He doesn't look good, but he's alive."

He sounded so tired. The Pack was under siege, and the mutts were ripping down the defenses as fast as Jeremy could erect them. It was wearing him out. I wished I didn't see that. I wished I could believe, as Antonio and Nick did, that the Pack Alpha was indestructible. That's the way Pack werewolves were raised, secure in the knowledge that no matter what happens, their Alpha will protect them. That was wrong. Plain wrong. It worked great under normal circumstances, when the Pack was never troubled by more than one mutt at a time and the Alpha's job was more focused on settling internal dissent and presenting a united front against the mutts. Faced with a problem of this size, though, the Alpha needed help, not just in fighting the threat, but in deciding how to fight it. Such collaboration was unthinkable. Jeremy might bounce his ideas off Antonio, but he'd never think of asking for advice, nor would any Pack member dream of offering it. I did. I wanted to tell Jeremy what I thought and try to help him, but I knew I couldn't. If he felt overwhelmed now, having me second-guess his plans would only make things worse. Like Antonio and Nick, Jeremy was bound by the same misconception of leadership. The responsibility of saving the Pack fell squarely on his shoulders. The only way I could help was to plot strategies on my own.

Awakening

THE NEXT MORNING, JEREMY AND ANTONIO TOOK OFF AGAIN. I went to work. Or, at least, I prepared to go back to work. I called the hospital to check on Philip, then sat at the desk in the study, fired up Clay's laptop and sat there, looking from the phone to the laptop and back again. These were my only tools for finding Clay and I had no idea what to do now with either one. I pulled out a pad of paper and reviewed what I knew, hoping some new avenue of exploration would leap out at me.

We had two experienced mutts left, half of the original number. This was reassuring, until I reminded myself that we'd eliminated the lesser mutts, leaving the more dangerous ones alive. Not so good. We also had two new mutts. LeBlanc, I knew, and understood how he worked. Again, I felt a momentary burst of complacency before remembering that I hadn't even met Cain's protégé, Victor Olson. So there it was, the next step: find out more about Olson. Of course, deciding *what* I was going to do wasn't the same as determining *how* I was going to do it. Of the two tools I had available, the Internet seemed the best bet, namely because I wasn't sure where to even begin with the telephone.

Cain had said that his protégé's name was Victor Olson and that he'd broken him out of jail in Arizona where he'd been imprisoned for sex crimes. Since Daniel had found Olson, his crimes must have been big enough to warrant media attention. A simple search on the name and city brought up seven complete matches. The first one was for some long-dead city father named Victor Olson. The next four matches were for Vic "Mad Dog" Olson, which sounded promising, until I clicked on one site and found an advertisement for a personal injury lawyer. On the last two I hit pay dirt. Victor Olson had escaped from jail four months ago, cutting short a life sentence for raping and killing a ten-year-old-girl. I reread his victim's age several times. Cain said Olson had been in jail for "screwing around with a couple girls." I'd assumed by "girls" he really meant women. Obviously not. Suppressing my revulsion, I read the article. Olson was a lifetime pedophile who'd been charged several times with acts of indecency, but the charges had always been dismissed when the judge ruled his victims' testimony "unreliable." With the last victim, the judge had to admit the testimony provided by her dead body was reasonably reliable. I skipped to the news article on the other site and discovered why Daniel had chosen Olson. He was a stalker. He chose his victims with care and trailed them for weeks before making his move. One detective said he'd never seen someone so skilled at "the hunt" —his choice of words, not mine.

I spent another hour going over what I knew. When that led nowhere, I tracked down Nick in the exercise room and repeated everything to him, hoping either he'd think of something or the very act of verbalizing it would help me think of something. Nick listened, but didn't have any ideas. Nick wasn't used to having ideas. That sounded worse than I intended. What I meant was that he was accustomed to following the plans of others. He was an enthusiastic lieutenant and a loyal friend, but he wasn't exactly—how do I put this nicely—not exactly a deep thinker. Talking to him didn't help me think of anything either. So I put aside my papers, turned off the laptop, and did the most mind-numbing, menial chore I could imagine. I did the laundry.

No one had done laundry since we'd gone to Toronto, probably because it was the last thing on anyone's mind. I didn't realize the full implications of that until I was folding the first load and came across one of Clay's shirts. I stood there in the laundry room holding the shirt. Clay had worn it the day before we left. I don't know why I remembered that.

It was a dark green golf shirt, one of the few departures from Clay's plethora of plain white and black cotton T-shirts. It must have been a gift from Logan, who'd considered it his thankless job to add some fashion to Clay's wardrobe. I stared at the shirt, thinking about Logan and the grief surged fresh. Then I thought about Peter, remembered him ribbing Clay about his monochromatic wardrobe, threatening to give him a stack of the most garish concert T-shirts he could find. Blinking hard, I tucked the shirt under a stack of Nick's pants and kept going.

After I'd folded the first load, I took it upstairs to put the clothes away. I left Clay's pile for last. For several minutes, I stood outside his closed bedroom door and screwed up the courage to go inside. I rushed through the job, stuffing shirts, underwear, and socks into his drawers. His jeans went in the closet. Yes, he hung up his jeans, probably because if he didn't, there wouldn't be anything in there. I was putting the jeans on hangers when I saw the pile of wrapped presents on the closet floor. Without even checking the tags, I knew what they were. Part of me wanted to slam the door shut and run. I didn't want to see them. Yet I couldn't resist. I reached down and picked up the top gift. It was wrapped in Christmas paper, bright candy canes and bows. On the tag, one name scrawled across, obliterating the TO: and FROM: label. Elena.

Nick had said Clay expected me back. I'd half expected to come back last Christmas myself, not through my own volition, but magically, as if I could fall asleep in Toronto on Christmas Eve and wake up in Stonehaven the next morning. Easter, Thanksgiving, birthdays, they'd all passed unnoticed, untainted by the urge of return. Christmas was different.

Growing up, I'd hated Christmas. Of all the holidays, it was the one that most glorified the family, all those movies and TV specials and advertisements and magazine covers showing happy families going through the rites of the season. That's not to say I was deprived of the normal trappings of Christmas. My foster families weren't complete ogres. I got presents and turkey dinners. I went to parties and midnight mass. I sat on Santa's knee and learned to sing "Up on the Rooftop" for the school concert. But without real family bonds, all the rituals of the season were as phony as sprayed-on snow. So when I moved out on my own at eighteen, I stopped celebrating. Then I met Clay. That first year together, I finally felt that a true Christmas was possible. Sure, I wasn't surrounded by parents and grandparents and aunts and uncles, but I had someone. I had the first link to everything else I wanted so bad.

I should say that Clay had no idea how to celebrate Christmas. It wasn't an official werewolf holiday. Okay, there were no official werewolf holidays, but that wasn't the point. The Pack recognized Christmas only as a time to get together as they did umpteen other times a year. They exchanged presents, the same as they did on birthdays, but that was the extent of the celebration. So what did Clay do when I hinted that I wanted a full-blown Christmas? He gave me one.

Although I didn't know it at the time, Clay spent weeks researching the holiday. Then he gave me Christmas with all the trimmings. We went out and cut down a tree—then realized the impossibility of getting it back to his apartment on his motorcycle. We had the tree delivered and decorated it. We made shortbread, gingerbread, and sugar cookies, and discovered how hard it is to form gingerbread men without a cookie cutter. We made a fruitcake, which was probably still on the balcony of his old apartment, where we'd eventually used it to hold open the door. We bought lights for the balcony, then had to go back to the hardware store for an extension cord, then had to go back for wire cutters to snip a hole in the screen to slip the cord through. We listened to Christmas music, watched *How the Grinch Stole Christmas* and rented *It's a Wonderful Life,* though Clay fell asleep during the latter—okay, we both fell asleep during the latter. We drank eggnog by the fire, or by a magazine photo of a fire that Clay stuck on the wall. No tradition went unobserved. It was the perfect Christmas. We didn't make it to Easter.

There was no Christmas the next year. I assume Christmas still occurred in the outside world, but at Stonehaven, it passed unnoticed. I'd barely got out of the cage by winter. Clay was still banished. Logan came to see me, but I drove him away, as I'd driven him away the half-dozen other times he tried to visit. Nick sent a gift. I threw it out unopened. Before Clay bit me, I'd met both Logan and Nick, had even started considering them friends. Afterward, I blamed them for not warning me. So, Christmas came and went and I barely realized it.

The next year, Clay was still banished. I was well on the road to recovery by then. I'd forgiven Logan and Nick and even Jeremy. I'd started getting to know Antonio and Peter. I was coming to accept life as a werewolf. Then came Christmas. I expected it would pass again with little fanfare, like the year before. Instead, we had a full-blown Christmas, complete with presents under the tree, colored lights sparkling against the snow, and a turkey on the table. The whole Pack came to Stonehaven for a week, and for the first time, I knew how hectic, stressful, loud, and wonderful a family Christmas could be. I thought this was how the Pack normally celebrated Christmas, when they didn't have an angry new female werewolf to contend with. It wasn't until January that I learned the truth. Clay had contacted Jeremy and asked him to do this for me. That was his gift to me. My gift to him was to ask Jeremy to repeal his banishment.

For every year after that, we had a full Christmas at Stonehaven. The Pack indulged my fantasy completely, without ever making me feel that they were only doing it to humor me. I can't say that every Christmas was a good one. Sometimes Clay and I were getting along, more often we weren't, but we were always together. If this last Christmas away from Clay had been hard, one thing had made it bearable: knowing he was out there, somewhere. As I stared at the pile of presents in his closet, I realized this applied to my life every day of the year, not just at Christmas. Somehow, knowing Clay was there, waiting for me should I ever return, gave me a cushion of comfort in my life. In a perverse way, he was the most stable thing in my life. No matter what I did, he'd be there. What if he wasn't? The thought filled me with something so icy cold that my breath seemed to freeze in my lungs and I had to gasp for air. I hadn't lied to Jeremy the night before. This wasn't one of those fairy-tale romances where the heroine realizes her undying love for the hero after he's placed in mortal danger. There were no heroes or heroines in this story and there would be no happily ever after ending, even if we got Clay back. I still couldn't imagine living with him, nor could

I envision my world without him. I needed him. Maybe that was unspeakably selfish. It almost certainly was. But it was honest. I needed Clay and I had to get him back. I looked at the gifts again and I knew I wasn't doing enough.

"I'm going to Bear Valley," I said.

It was the next day. Nick and I were on the back patio, lying on lounge chairs, luncheon plates on our laps. Jeremy and Antonio had left an hour ago. Since then, I'd been trying to figure out how to tell Nick what I'd planned. After a half-dozen false starts, I went with the blurt-it-out approach.

"I told Daniel I wanted to see him," I said.

"Is that what was in the note?"

When Antonio and Nick had gone to deliver Jeremy's latest missive to Daniel's post office box, I'd slipped Nick a note to add to Jeremy's. Nick hadn't asked what the note said, probably because he didn't want to know.

"Yes," I said. "I'm meeting him at two o'clock."

"How'd he get back to you?"

"He didn't. I said I was meeting him at two. He'll be there."

"And Jeremy's okay with this?"

I could tell by Nick's tone that he knew perfectly well I hadn't mentioned it to Jeremy. The question was his way of prudently broaching the topic. Or maybe he was just hoping against hope that this was something I'd already planned with Jeremy and we'd both somehow forgotten to mention it to him.

"I'm not sitting around anymore," I said. "I can't do it. I tried, but I can't."

Nick swung his legs over and sat on the edge of his lounge chair. "I know how hard this is for you, Elena. I know how much you love him—"

"That's not it. Look, I've already been through this with Jeremy. We need Clay back. Whether or not you want to help is up to you."

"I want to help get him back, but I'm not going to help you get yourself killed doing it."

"What's that supposed to mean?"

"Just what it sounds like. I saw the way you were a few days ago—"

"Is that what this is about? Because I flipped out three days ago? Look at me now. Do I seem flipped out?"

"No, and that probably scares me more than if you were."

"I am going," I said.

"Not without me."

"Fine."

"But I'm not going. So neither are you."

I got up and started for the back door. Nick leapt to his feet and blocked my path.

"What are you going to do?" I asked. "Knock me out and lock me in the cage?"

He looked away, but he didn't move. I knew he wouldn't do anything. If it came down to it, Nick wouldn't use physical force to stop me. It wasn't in his nature.

"Where's this meeting?" he asked at last. "Is it in a public place? Because if it's not—"

"It's in The Donut Hole. As public as I can make it. No matter what you might think, I'm not doing anything that might endanger myself. I wouldn't do anything to endanger *you.* The only risk I'm taking is in breaking Jeremy's orders. And I'm only doing that because he's wrong to exclude me."

"So you'll meet Daniel in the coffee shop and I'll be there. We'll park right out front. We won't go anyplace with him, even for a walk down the street."

"Exactly."

Nick turned and walked to the house. He wasn't happy, but he'd do it. I'd make it up to him someday.

As I pulled into a parking spot in front of the coffee shop, I could see Daniel through the window. He was sitting in a booth. His shoulder-length auburn hair was pushed back behind his left ear—his only ear, actually, after that little biting mishap a few years ago. His profile was sharp, high cheekbones, pointed chin, and thin nose, not unhandsome in a feral way, but his looks were more fox than wolf, which better complemented his personality.

As I got out of the car, his green eyes followed me, but he didn't acknowledge me in any other way, having learned long ago that I didn't respond well to fawning. His body was lean and compact. Standing, we'd be on perfect eye level, making him no more than five feet ten. Once, when I'd needed to meet Daniel to deliver a warning from Jeremy, I'd worn two-inch heels and had quite enjoyed the sensation of talking down to Daniel, until he told me how sexy I looked. Since then he'd never seen me in anything but my oldest, grubbiest sneakers.

Today Daniel was wearing a plain black T-shirt and blue jeans, which was pretty much what he wore all the time. He copied Clay's monochromatic, construction-worker-casual wardrobe as if it would lend him a certain cachet. It didn't.

Marsten sat across from Daniel. As usual, he was groomed and dressed like he'd stepped from the pages of *GQ*, which only made Daniel look like a slob in comparison. Okay, Karl Marsten made everyone look like a slob.

As Nick and I walked in, Marsten stood and strolled to the door to meet us.

"You came," he said to me. "I'm surprised Jeremy let you. Or does he know?"

I mentally kicked myself. I hadn't thought how it would look if I showed up against Jeremy's wishes. Dissension in the Pack. Wonderful. Trust Marsten to pick up on it in five seconds flat.

"You look good, Elena," Marsten continued, not waiting for me to answer. "Tired, but that's to be expected. Hopefully all this will be over soon."

"That depends on you," I said.

"In part." He turned to the server behind the counter. "Two coffees. Black for the lady and—" He looked over at Nick. "One cream, two sugars, correct?"

Nick only glared at him.

"One black. The other with one cream, two sugars," Marsten repeated to the server. "Put it on my tab." He paused, then turned to me with a wry smile. "I can't believe I just said that in a doughnut shop. I have to get out of this town."

I looked away.

"It's been a long time, Nicholas," Marsten continued. "How's your father? I invested in one of his companies last year. Thirty percent return. He certainly hasn't lost his touch."

Ignoring him, Nick sat on a stool at the counter and studied the doughnut display. Marsten took the stool beside him and waved me toward Daniel.

"I'll keep Nicholas company," he said.

Daniel didn't look up as I walked over. He stirred his coffee and acknowledged me only with the barest nod. The server delivered my coffee. I pushed it aside and sat on the bench across the table from Daniel. He kept stirring. For a few seconds, I sat there. Under any other circumstances, I would have waited to see how long he could stretch this coffee-stirring feigned indifference before he cracked and looked at me. But the time for games was over.

"What do you want?" I asked.

Still stirring, eyes on the mug as if it might skitter away if he stopped watching it. "What do I usually want?"

"Revenge."

He glanced up and met my gaze, then broke eye contact to give me the usual slow once-over. I gritted my teeth and waited. After a few seconds I was tempted to snap my fingers in front of his face and tell him there wasn't *that* much of me to look at.

"You want revenge," I repeated to get his brain back on track.

Daniel leaned back in his seat, pulling one leg up to look oh-so-cool and relaxed. "No, I don't. I've never wanted that. Whatever the Pack did to me, I'm over it. They're not worth my time. But you are."

"Here we go," I muttered.

Daniel ignored me. "I know why you're with them, Elena. Because you're afraid to leave, afraid of what they'll do, and afraid of what will happen to you without their protection. I'm trying to show you that they can't hurt you and they can't protect you. If you want a partner, a true partner, you deserve better than some freak who has to turn around three times before he lies down. I can give you better."

"So this is all about winning me? Bullshit."

"You don't think you're worth it? I thought your self-esteem was higher than that."

"My IQ is higher than that. This isn't about me. It never has been. It's about you and Clay. You think he has me, so you want me. Your motivation is as complex as that of a two-year-old seeing another kid with a shiny toy. You want it."

"You underestimate yourself."

"No, I don't underestimate how much you hate him. What happened? Did he always get the bigger slice of birthday cake?"

"He made my life hell. Him and Tonto over there." Daniel glared toward Nick. "Poor little Clay. He has problems. He's had a tough life. You should be nice to him. You should make friends with him. That's all I ever heard. All they saw was a cute little runt of a wolf cub. He bared his teeth and they thought it was cute. He ordered us around like a miniature Napoleon and they thought it was cute. Well, it wasn't cute from where I was standing. It was—"

I held up my hand. "You're ranting."

"What?"

"Just wanted to let you know. You're ranting. It's kinda ugly. Next thing you know, you'll be laying out your plans for world domination. That's what all villains do after they rant about their motivation. I was hoping you'd be different."

Daniel took a swig of coffee, then shook his head and gave a small laugh. "Well, you've put me in my place. You've always been good at that. You say bark and I say how loud."

"I say let Clay go . . ."

Daniel made a face. "And I say why bother? Okay, there's a limit to my obedience training. I won't let him go just because you want it, Elena. You could pout and bat your eyes and plead and, while I'd find that damned arousing, it wouldn't make me release him. I'll make you the same exchange offer I made to Jeremy. You for Clay."

"Why?"

"I already told you."

"Because I'm so damned irresistible. Uh-huh. Give me a better explanation or I'm out of here."

Daniel was silent for a moment, then leaned forward. "Have you ever thought of starting your own Pack? Not recruiting a bunch of half-wit mutts, but creating a dynasty? We aren't immortal, Elena, but there is a way to ensure our immortality."

"I really hope you're not implying what I think you're implying."

"Children, Elena. A new breed of werewolves. Not half-werewolf, half-human, but complete werewolves, inheriting the genes from both parents. Perfect werewolves."

"Wow. You really do want to rule the world."

"I'm serious."

"Seriously crazy. Sorry, but this womb isn't for sale or rent."

"Not even for the price of a life? Clay's life?"

I pulled back and pretended to think about it. Time to call his bluff. "So I agree to go with you and you'll release him?"

"Right. Only, I'm not just going to trust you to come with me and stay with me, so let's get that straight right off. I've got a place I plan to take you, someplace suitably remote and secure. You'll be confined. Something like the cage at Stonehaven, but far more luxurious. You give me what I want, everything I want, and you won't be in there very long. Once I've convinced you that I'm the better choice, I'll let you out. If you try to run, I'll put you back in."

"Gee, doesn't that sound tempting."

"I'm being honest, Elena. It's an exchange. His captivity for yours."

I pretended to think about it, staring out the window. Then I turned back to Daniel. "Here's my condition. I want to see him released. You'll do it in broad daylight and in a public place. I'll be there with you to watch it happen. Once he's free, I'm yours."

"That's not how it works. Once you're mine, he's free."

"You have no intention of letting him go," I said. "That's what I thought."

I got to my feet, turned, and walked out of the coffee shop. Both

Nick and Daniel hurried after me. When I got to the car, Daniel's hand shot out and held the door shut.

"You've seen the photos, haven't you?" he asked.

I stopped, but didn't turn around.

"I know you've seen the photos," Daniel continued. "You've seen what kind of shape he's in. You've seen that it's getting worse. How much longer do you think he can hold out?"

I turned around slowly. I turned and I saw Daniel's face and I saw the satisfaction in his eyes and I lost it. For the past half hour, I'd been struggling not to think about Clay. As I'd talked to Daniel, I'd fought not to remember that he was the one holding Clay captive, that he'd drugged him and beaten him until there was scarcely an inch of skin left unmarked. I'd concentrated on talking to Daniel as I'd talked to him a hundred times before, as it if was just another message I was conveying from Jeremy telling him to shape up or face punishment. I'd really, really, really tried to forget what was actually happening. But when he stood there and threatened Clay, I couldn't pretend anymore. The rage inside me bubbled over before I could rein it back.

I grabbed him by the shirtfront and threw him against my car so hard the driver's window shattered into a million bits of safety glass.

"You sniveling hyena." I pressed myself against him until our faces were only inches apart. "You kidnap him with a hypodermic needle. You chain him up so you can beat him. But that's not good enough. You have to drug him first. You have to make absolutely certain he can't even summon the strength to spit in your face. Then you beat him. Did it feel good? Did it make you feel like a man, beating your enemy to a pulp when he can't lift a finger to fight back? You're not a man and you're not a wolf. You're a hyena, a bottom-feeding coward. If you lay another hand on him, I'll do something to you that will make that ear bite look like a paper cut. And if you kill him, I swear to God and the devil and anyone who will listen, if you kill him, I will hunt you down. I will find you and I will inflict on you every torture I can imagine. I'll blind you and I'll castrate you and I'll burn you. But I won't kill you. I won't let you die. I'll put you in hell and I'll make you live there for the rest of your life."

I threw Daniel aside. He stumbled, recovered, and turned to face me. His mouth opened, closed, opened again, but he couldn't seem to think of a suitable reply, so he settled for turning on his heel and stamping back into the coffee shop, where it looked as if every one of the dozen customers had suddenly taken a window seat. As I looked away I heard a low whistle and turned to see Marsten leaning against the back of the car.

"The bitch is back," Marsten said. "Well, well. This might get interesting."

"Go to hell," I snarled.

I threw open the car door, got in, and started it up as Nick jumped into the passenger side. The Camaro roared from the parking spot, tires squealing. I didn't look at the speedometer the whole way back to Stonehaven.

I'd been right about one thing. The time for games was over.

Regression

I LEFT STONEHAVEN AFTER EVERYONE HAD GONE TO BED. I dressed in the dark, jumped out my window, then rolled my car a half mile down the road before starting it. I hadn't told Nick my plans. He was better off not knowing.

I'd gone to my room early and spent the evening in bed, thinking. My meeting with Daniel had been a mistake. By refusing his offer, I'd only made things worse. Jeremy had been buying time for Clay. I'd stolen it away. To fix things, I had to act now.

For several hours that evening, I'd tried mentally contacting Clay. Of course it didn't work. I wasn't even sure how to do it, but I'd held out some small hope that our connection might be enough. Maybe it would have been, but it was like demanding special effort from a muscle I'd ignored for too long. Nothing happened. When I couldn't get into Clay's mind, I decided to work on getting into the minds of the mutts who held him captive. Get into their minds figuratively, I mean. If I put myself in their position and tried to imagine what they'd be feeling or thinking, maybe I could find a weakness. Daniel and Marsten were easy to understand. I knew what they wanted and I knew how they operated. Marsten wouldn't leave any openings for me to slip through. Daniel's weakness was his obsession with Clay and with me. I could work on that, contact him again and try reeling him in with lies and smiles, but it would take time and I didn't have time. That left the new mutts. Here I was on unfamiliar ground. They weren't werewolves, I reminded myself. Not real ones. So how could I get inside their heads?

For the longest time, I lay in bed, staring at the ceiling, overwhelmed by the impossibility of understanding these two. Then it came to me. They weren't werewolves, but they were human. I'd been human. I was still trying to be human. Why couldn't I get into their heads? All I had to do was strip away my wolf side, something I'd been trying to do for years already. Yet there was more to understanding these killers than that. I couldn't be the sort of human I'd been trying to be—even-tempered, passive, and caring. I had to be what I had been before.

Every defense mechanism in my brain threw up barriers at the thought. Be what I'd been before Clay bit me? But I'd been even-tempered, passive, caring. Clay had changed that. Before him, I was different. I wasn't like *this.* That's what I wanted to believe, but I knew it wasn't true. I'd always had the capacity for violence. Clay had seen that. The child-werewolf looked at the child victim and saw a soul mate, someone who understood what it was like to grow up alienated, our odd behavior scrutinized by adults and mocked by children. By the age of seven Clay was a full werewolf with an inherent capacity for violence and a temper to match. By the same age my foster families had taught me how to hate, developing my own capacity for violence, though I'd been better at hiding it, turning it inward and struggling to show the world the passive little girl it expected to see. It was time I confronted that. Clay didn't make me the way I was. He only gave me an outlet for the anger and the hate. I had to go back there, back to the mistrust and the hatred and the impotence and the rage, most of all the rage, against everyone who had wronged me. There I'd find the mind of a killer, a human killer.

LeBlanc hated women. Maybe he'd been mistreated by his mother or laughed at by girls in school or maybe he had such low self-esteem that he needed to feel superior to some group of people and chose women instead of blacks or Jews. If it was self-esteem, I could use that. But to find the truth, I'd need to research his life, looking for some road sign to his psychopathology. Again, I didn't have time.

What about Victor Olson? I started to dismiss the idea without a second thought. After all, I'd never even met the man. But did I need to? I pulled the two Internet article printouts from my dresser drawer and studied them. What did they tell me about Olson? He was a stalker. A compulsive stalker. In one article, he'd admitted to going out every night to watch his victims sleep, said that seeing their peaceful sleeping faces relaxed him and helped his insomnia. Would becoming a werewolf cure that compulsion or that insomnia? Of course not. Which meant there was a very good chance Olson hadn't abandoned his old patterns, that he was still watching young girls sleep, here in Bear Valley.

I'd left Stonehaven to find Olson. The articles said he targeted girls from middle-class homes. I assumed he'd be looking for single-story homes, so he could peek through a first-floor window. There were only two such subdivisions in Bear Valley. All I had to do was cruise the streets and sniff him out.

After driving around Bear Valley for over an hour, I began to realize how big a task this was. Sure, there were only two subdivisions, but each contained a dozen or more streets with at least a hundred homes. I only had several hours before dawn. To cover as much ground as possible, I drove slowly with all the windows down—except the smashed driver's window, which was now permanently down. Sometimes the wind favored me. Mostly it didn't and the only thing I smelled was the musty interior of my little-used car. Making matters worse, the police were out in full force, still looking for a killer. They were pulling over every car out that late that night, so I spent as much time avoiding them as looking for Olson. After two hours, I finished both subdivisions. No sign of Olson. For all I knew, he wasn't even out that night.

I was circling the second subdivision one last time when I saw a lone car in the parking lot of a convenience store, now conveniently closed for the night. As I passed, I noticed the rental sticker on the car's back bumper. Of course. If the mutts weren't hiding in town, Olson would need transportation to Bear Valley. I swung my car down a side road, parked and got out. I didn't even make it halfway to the convenience store when I caught the scent of an unfamiliar werewolf.

I jogged around the corner and stopped short. A heavyset, middle-aged man in a windbreaker walked along the sidewalk, less than twenty feet from the corner. Fortunately, Olson had his back to me. He was heading toward his car. I hurried back around the corner and ran for my car. He drove by as I was turning the car around in a driveway. Keeping my headlights out, I followed.

As we drove out of Bear Valley, my heart pounded. I was right. They were staying in the countryside. Olson would lead me right to them. We'd been heading northwest for almost twenty minutes when Olson turned into an overgrown drive carved into deep forest. He stopped the car past the edge of the woods. I was about to enact part two of my plan when I realized Olson wasn't getting out of his car. Staying well back, I killed the engine and waited. Ten minutes passed. I could see the outline of his head in the car. I leaned over, carefully opened my passenger door, and slipped into a ditch.

I crept to the end of the drive. The forest was black. Even when my eyes adjusted, I could see no sign of a house. As I turned back toward Olson's car, I saw that the driveway went nowhere. It was only a turnaround or a one-car parking spot for a nature trail beyond. I moved into the woods and snuck closer to the car. When I was parallel to the driver's side, I stopped and squinted through the darkness. Olson's head was resting against the headrest. His eyes were closed. Asleep. I briefly wondered why, but the question was irrelevant. Maybe he couldn't sleep near the others. Or maybe he liked to be alone after his spying trips. It didn't matter. Victor Olson wasn't leading me back to Clay. At least not tonight. But I couldn't wait until morning. Come morning, Jeremy would know I was gone. The Pack would be looking for me. Even if I managed to elude them for another day, that would be another twenty-four hours for Daniel to kill Clay. And what if Olson wasn't just taking a break from the mutts? What if he wasn't ever going back to them? He knew where Clay was. I had to know—tonight.

A plan formed in my head as I watched Olson sleep. Even as I contemplated it, I rebelled at the thought. I hesitated, then forced myself forward out of the trees before I could change my mind. I crept to the side of the car, then pulled my fist back and smashed the driver's side window. Even as Olson was bolting awake, I was reaching through the window. I jerked the seat belt. It slid through my fingers as it tightened around him. He snapped his head back, away from my hand, but I was already reaching past him. Leaning into the car, I grabbed the seat belt buckle, twisting the metal and breaking the plastic, jamming the buckle closed. Then I pulled my head out of the car.

Olson whipped his head around, following my hand as it moved past him. He looked up at me. For a moment, he just stared, fixing me with the wide eyes of a coward bracing for the first blow. Even as I stepped away, he flinched. When he realized I was backing off, his brow furrowed, then his eyes lit up with a flash of malevolent cunning and he started to smile. Keeping his eyes on me, he lowered his right hand to the seat belt lock. He pushed the release button, but nothing happened. Realizing what I'd done, he grabbed the seat belt strap and yanked, but it was locked tight against his chest.

I knew what I had to do, but again I hesitated. Could I do it? Thoughts of Jose Carter flashed in my brain. This was different, I told myself. This wasn't some human con man, but a killer. Still, what I was about to do was beyond what I'd done to Carter. Way beyond. This was Clay's territory. Could I do it? Detach myself from my feelings and do it? Olson's a killer, I told myself. More than a killer. A sick pervert who'd preyed on little girls, little girls like the one I'd been so many lifetimes ago. I closed my eyes and concentrated, feeling the serpent of anger whiplashing through my body.

Olson struggled against the seat belt, but it held, the fabric made to withstand more punishment than even a werewolf could deal out. I ignored him and focused all my energy into my left hand. It started to throb, then twist, the pain shooting up my arm. I opened my eyes and watched. When my hand was half changed, I stopped. With my right hand, I reached into the car and grabbed Olson's right wrist. I slashed it with the claws on my left. He screamed, a high-pitched rabbity squeal. A red line opened on the underside of his wrist. Blood gushed. I grabbed his left hand and did the same. He screamed again and squirmed wildly. Blood sprayed the steering wheel and dashboard.

"Moving will only make it worse," I said, keeping my voice calm and willing my hand back to normal. "If you want the bleeding to slow down, hold your hands up."

"Wh—wh—?"

"Why? Why am I doing this? Or why am I telling you how to slow it down? I shouldn't need to answer the first. Obviously you know who I am. That's answer enough. As for the second, I'm not trying to kill you. I just want information. If you give it to me, I'll undo the seat belt. You can bind your wrists and probably have time to get to the hospital. If you don't tell me what I want to know, you'll be killing yourself."

"Wh—" Olson gulped. "What do you wa—want to know?"

"Again, I shouldn't have to answer that. But since you might be going into shock and not thinking too clearly, I'll humor you. Where's Clayton?"

I won't report the rest of the conversation. Olson was in no shape to bargain or argue and he knew it. As I expected, he didn't give a damn about the others. Only his own life mattered. He told me everything I needed to know and more, babbling madly as if every word he spoke would improve his chance of survival.

When he was done, I left him sitting in his car. I thought about undoing the seat belt and giving him a fighting chance to escape. After all, I'd promised him that. I'd never reneged on a deal before. Then I thought of all the girls he'd victimized and imagined all the times he'd made promises to them, promising not to hurt them, promising never to do it again. He hadn't kept his promises. Why should I?

I walked away and left Victor Olson to bleed to death in the forest.

Confrontation

I STOPPED AT A GAS STATION AND CALLED STONEHAVEN. THE FIRST two times, the machine picked up. On the third round, Nick answered. He was half asleep and I had to repeat myself twice before he clued in that I wasn't somewhere in the house. No one had noticed my disappearing act yet. I gave him instructions and had him write them down then read them back to me. By then, he had finally realized what I was saying and what I planned to do. I hung up when he started yelling.

Ten minutes later, I was knocking on the front door of the mutts' hideaway. It was a rundown cottage set so far back in the woods that no light penetrated the canopy of trees. As I stood on the front step, I listened for the rustle of the wind or the chirping of crickets, but heard nothing. The silence and the dark were complete.

Several minutes passed without a response. I knocked again. More minutes ticked by, but I didn't doubt Olson's directions. This was the right place. I could feel Clay here.

I pounded on the door. Finally the barest shimmer of light shone from between heavy front drapes. Footsteps sounded on a wooden plank floor. I looked down at the door handle and saw it was broken. Above it was a hole and fresh splinters where a dead bolt had been. Did I really expect the mutts to buy or rent a cottage when they could break into one? How stupid I'd been. How much time I'd wasted.

The door opened. I glanced up. It took a second to recognize the man standing there was Karl Marsten, partly because of the dim lighting and partly because of his attire. He wore only pajama bottoms, his bare chest showing muscles and battle scars normally hidden by expensive shirts. He squinted and blinked at me, then swore under his breath and quickstepped out the door, closing it behind him.

"What the hell are you doing here?" he said in a whispery growl.

I looked around him at the closed door. "Afraid I'll wake up your wife?"

"My—?" He glanced over his shoulder at the door, then turned back to me, his scowl smoothed over, studied nonchalance firmly back in place. "I'm sure this is a wonderful plan, Elena, but I really must advise against it. If you go in there, you'll leave in chains or a body bag. Neither would suit you."

"So you came out here to warn me? Wow, chivalry isn't dead after all."

"You know me better than that. I see an opportunity, I take advantage of it."

"So you'll let me leave in return for . . . ?"

"What I came for." His eyes glittered, something hard piercing the sangfroid. "Territory. Promise me that and I'll let you go. I'll leave, too. One less 'mutt' for the Pack to worry about."

"To hell with the others?"

"Daniel would do the same to me. I didn't hear my name being bandied about in that deal he offered you at the coffee shop."

I shook my head. "It doesn't matter. I'm not leaving."

I reached around him for the door handle. Marsten grabbed my wrist, squeezing hard enough to bruise.

"Don't be stupid, Elena. You're not getting him out that way."

"What way?" Daniel's voice was smooth and cool as he swung open the door. He met Marsten's eyes. "What way, Karl?"

"Sleeping soundly enough, Danny-boy? Christ, the whole Pack could be howling on your doorstep before you woke up." Marsten threw Daniel a contemptuous look and pushed me into the cabin. "It's an ambush, you moron. Elena wouldn't show up alone. Get your flunky out there searching the woods. Make himself useful for once."

I don't know if Daniel argued. I was too busy picking myself up off the floor after a shove from Marsten that sent me flying across the room. Before I could recover, Marsten had a knee on my back and had pinned me to the floor. I expected to be tied up. I wasn't. Maybe Marsten didn't think I posed enough of a threat. Moments later, footsteps sounded behind me. I smelled LeBlanc join Daniel and Marsten.

"Olson's gone," Daniel said.

"Gone for good, I would assume," Marsten said. "How else did you think she found us? It's a great loss for the cause, though. One never knows when a kiddie raper would come in handy."

"He had other—" Daniel began, then snapped his mouth shut. "Thomas, outside. Look for the others."

The front door slammed behind LeBlanc.

"That's one loyal pup you've got there," I said, lifting my mouth from the floor. "You know he tried to kill me at the airport. Before I left for Toronto."

A moment of silence. Then Daniel laughed. "Nice try, Elle. Sowing dissension?"

"Doesn't seem like I need to."

"Now, now, Elena," Marsten said, knee pressing me further into the floor. "As much as we all admire that tongue of yours, this is not the time to use it."

"Don't forget who's downstairs," Daniel said. "You're in no position to defend him now."

I shut my mouth and calculated how long it would take Jeremy, Antonio, and Nick to arrive. At least fifteen minutes to wake up, dress, and get into the car, another thirty to drive here. When LeBlanc came in after ten minutes, I knew he hadn't found anyone. The others wouldn't have arrived yet.

"No one out there," he said, knocking dirt off his boots.

"Take the car," Daniel said. "Drive around and make sure. Look for a vehicle by the side of the road. They would have driven."

For a moment, LeBlanc didn't move. I thought he was going to tell Daniel where to stuff it. Instead, he grabbed a ring of keys and tramped out the door. This time he was gone at least twenty minutes, during which neither Daniel nor Marsten said a word. When LeBlanc finally returned, I managed to turn my head to the side and saw him grinning.

"What?" Daniel said.

"Oh, you're gonna love this. The cavalry has been detained." He turned his shark's grin on me. "They're on Pinecrest, just off the highway, enjoying the hospitality of the local P.D. Cops nailed them. Don't know what for, but they're taking the car apart bolt by bolt. What do you think of that?"

"I think it's bullshit," I said.

His grin broadened. "Green Ford Explorer? Three guys? All dark-haired. Two over six foot, thin? Oldest shorter than me, quarterback shoulders? When I drove by, the young guy was trying to slip into the woods. Cops grabbed him and had him spread-eagled when I circled back."

"Bullshit," I said.

LeBlanc laughed. "Not quite the same air of certainty that time."

"Enough," Marsten said, yanking me to my feet. "They won't be detained forever." He jerked my wrists behind my back and clamped one hand around them. "Tommy, bring our other guest upstairs. Time to move."

LeBlanc turned to stare at him. "Move? This is what you guys wanted, isn't it? To take down this 'pack'? We've got two here. The last three on the way. Three against three and we've already been forewarned. We have the upper hand."

"Bring Clayton upstairs," Daniel said.

"What the fuck?" LeBlanc looked from Marsten to Daniel. "This is it. Showdown at the OK Corral. Killing time. Don't tell me you guys don't have the balls—"

"We have more brains than balls," Marsten said. "That's why we're still alive. Now get Clayton. We have him and we have Elena. That guarantees you'll get your fight soon, with odds of our making, not theirs."

LeBlanc shot a glare of pure contempt at Marsten, marched into a side hall, and vanished.

I gritted my teeth and focused on my plan. Were the others really detained by the cops? I didn't believe it. I couldn't. But I'd seen the police presence out here. If they'd come roaring down the highway, driving the very vehicle that the police had expressed such interest in the other day . . . ? Why hadn't I warned Nick?

Okay. Relax. Time to switch to plan B. If only I had a plan B.

As I was frantically working on an alternate plot, Marsten swung me around. Daniel sat on the arm of an overstuffed recliner that stank of mildew. Two figures emerged from another room. One stumbled forward and tripped. A flash of gold curls glinted in the dim light.

"Clay!"

Without thinking, I dove toward him. Still holding my wrists, Marsten swung me backward, jolting my arms so hard I gasped. Clay was on his knees, hands bound behind him. He struggled to lift his head. He met my eyes. For a second, he stared, his eyes struggling to focus. Then recognition broke through the drugged haze.

"No," he whispered, his voice paper-thin. "No."

He made a move, so slight I barely saw it. Behind him, LeBlanc's foot came up and kicked him square in the back, sending him sprawling face first to the floor.

"No!" I shouted.

I lunged at LeBlanc. Again, Marsten yanked me back, nearly dislocating my shoulders. I didn't care. I kept pulling. LeBlanc grabbed Clay by the handcuffs and dragged him to his feet.

"Leave him there," Marsten said. As LeBlanc sauntered by, Marsten whipped out his free hand and snagged something from LeBlanc's waistband. His gun. "Aren't you ever going to outgrow your security blanket?"

LeBlanc grabbed for the pistol. Marsten held it out of reach.

"A werewolf with a handgun?" Marsten said. "This is a sorry day. Brilliant idea, Daniel. Turn a bunch of human killers into werewolves. Now why didn't I think of that? Maybe because . . . it's stupid. You're never going to wean him off his weapons, Danny-boy."

To my left, I could hear Clay breathing. I forced myself not to look at him. While Marsten and Daniel discussed their next move, I cast a surreptitious glance at my watch. Five-fifty. If the cops had stopped Jeremy, how long would they hold him? How much longer did I have to wait? Was that all I could come up with for a backup plan? Wait it out until help arrived? Not good enough. For all I knew, they could be taken to the precinct and kept there for hours. Jeremy would be frantic, but the only alternative would be to kill the police and he wouldn't do that unless absolutely necessary. He'd know Daniel would hold Clay and me as hostages, not kill us—at least not right away. Since the danger wasn't immediate, Jeremy would wait out the police procedures. Yet by the time he arrived, we might be gone. No, strike that. We would be gone. Daniel was already gathering his wallet and car keys.

I looked at Clay. He was still lying facedown on the floor. His back was a quilt-work of purple, yellow, and black bruises with red welts and cuts sewing the pieces together. His left leg buckled awkwardly to the side, as if it was broken and he'd been forced to walk on it. His back rose and fell with shallow breaths. I looked at him and I knew what I had to do.

"We had a deal," I said, turning to Daniel. "I'm here. Let him go."

No one answered. Marsten and Daniel stared at me as if I'd lost my mind. An hour ago, this was exactly the reaction I'd anticipated. I'd planned to show up at the front door and turn myself over to Daniel. They'd be shocked, of course. Somewhere between the surprise and the eventual self-congratulations, the Pack would arrive. My version of the old Trojan horse trick. Only the warriors weren't coming. The gift was in the enemy camp and there was no taking it back now.

"Don't. You. Dare." Clay's whisper floated up from the floor.

He raised his head enough to glare at me. I looked away. Everyone else ignored him. For the first time in Clay's life, he was with a group of mutts and no one was paying the least attention to him. They'd stolen not only his strength, but his dignity. It was my fault. I was supposed to stay with him in Toronto, but I hadn't. What had distracted me so much that I'd gone to work and left Clay behind? A marriage proposal from another man. My stomach clenched at the memory.

I turned back to Daniel. "You wanted me, you have me. You wanted

Clay on his knees. You have that. Now live up to your end of the bargain. Let him go and I'll go with you willingly. Right now." I twisted to look over my shoulder at Marsten. "Make sure he leaves Clay here and you'll get your territory. When Jeremy shows up, Clay will tell him that I made the deal. He'll honor it."

More silence. Marsten and Daniel were thinking. I was offering exactly what they wanted—territory for Marsten and my willing self for Daniel, sealing his revenge against Clay and the Pack. Was it enough? They didn't want a showdown. Time was already ticking past, each second increasing the likelihood that Jeremy, Antonio, and Nick would arrive. I'd fight before I let them take me out of here. They knew that. They'd have to subdue and restrain me, then haul both Clay and me into the car.

"No deal."

I jerked my head up. The answer had come from Daniel's direction, but it hadn't sounded like him. From behind Daniel, LeBlanc stepped forward, hands in his pockets.

"No deal," he repeated. His voice was soft, but it sliced through the silence.

Marsten gave a low chuckle. "Ah, the peasants revolt. I suppose—"

Before he could finish, LeBlanc's hand darted from his pocket. Silver winked in the lamplight. His hand shot in front of Daniel's throat and sliced sideways. For a millisecond, it appeared as if nothing had happened. Daniel stood there, looking slightly confused. Then his throat split open in a slash of crimson. Blood spurted. Daniel's hands flew to his neck. His eyes bugged disbelieving. The blood gushed over his fingers and streamed down his arms. His mouth opened. He blew a bubble of pink, like some macabre bubblegum, then slid to the floor.

I stared at Daniel, blinking, as unable to believe his death as he. Daniel was dying. The mutt who'd plagued the Pack for over a decade, who'd outwitted plots by both Clay and me to make him screw up enough to deserve execution. Dead. Not killed in some long, dangerous fight. Not killed by Clay. Not even killed by me. Killed by a new mutt with a knife. Killed in an instant. In a trick so cowardly and so completely human that all Marsten and I could do was gape.

As Daniel lay gasping and dying on the floor, LeBlanc stepped over him as if he were a fallen log. He held up the switchblade. It was almost clean, discolored only by specks of crimson.

"No deal," he said, advancing on Marsten.

Marsten snatched the gun from the table and pointed it at LeBlanc.

"Yes, I know. I said real werewolves don't use weapons. But you'll find I'm quite adaptable, particularly when it comes to saving my own hide." Marsten smiled, lips curving, eyes ice-cold. "Is this your 'showdown at the OK Corral'? Knife versus gun? Any bets on the outcome?"

LeBlanc jiggled the knife, as if contemplating throwing it. Then he stopped.

"Smart man," Marsten said. "What do you say we save ourselves some bloodshed and make a deal? An even split. I get Clayton. You get Elena. We go our separate ways from here."

When LeBlanc didn't respond, Marsten continued, "That's what you want, isn't it? That's why you killed Daniel, because Elena humiliated you and you want revenge."

From the look that flashed across LeBlanc's face, I knew he hadn't killed Daniel to get me. He hadn't killed him to get anything at all. LeBlanc had joined this battle because he liked to kill. Now as a cease-fire had been nearing, he'd turned on his comrades, not out of anger or greed, but simply because they were there, more lives to take before the fun came to an end. Now he was weighing his options. Should he take me and be satisfied? Or could he get Marsten and Clay in the bargain?

"You don't want her?" LeBlanc asked. "I thought all you guys wanted her."

"I've never been one for following the crowd," Marsten said. "While Elena certainly has her attractions, she wouldn't suit my lifestyle. I want territory. Clayton is the better bargaining chip. And I'm sure you'll have more fun with Elena."

"You son-of-a-bitch," I snarled.

I whipped around, yanking my arms free from Marsten's grasp. I aimed a fist at his stomach, but he twisted at the last moment and my knuckles only grazed his abs. His foot shot out and hooked mine, flipping me to the floor. My head struck the corner of an empty gun rack.

I blacked out for a moment. When I came to, Marsten's gray eyes were boring into mine. I blinked and tried to get up, but he held me down. He pushed my chin forward so I faced the wall.

"She's unconscious," he said, getting to his knees. "All the better. We're getting low on sedatives."

Unconscious? I blinked again, slowly, feeling my eyes close, then re-open. I was staring at a line of mouse turds along the bottom of the wall. I was definitely awake. Hadn't Marsten seen me open my eyes? I began to lift my head, then thought better of it and lay still. Let them think I was unconscious. I needed all the advantages I could get.

Marsten stood. I heard him move a few feet away.

"What are you doing?" LeBlanc asked sharply.

"Taking my booty and getting the hell out of here, which is what I suggest you do as well. If Elena isn't enough of a reward, you're more than welcome to take any money you can find in Daniel's and Vic's belongings."

"Stop untying him," LeBlanc said.

Marsten sighed. "Don't tell me Daniel made you paranoid, too. Clayton is barely breathing. He wouldn't be a threat to a Chihuahua. I'm in a hurry. If he can walk, I want him walking."

"I haven't agreed to the deal yet."

Eyes closed, I inched my chin down, then peeked. Marsten was bent over Clay. He'd pulled him onto his knees. Clay swayed. Only a hint of blue showed from narrowed eyes. The gun lay ten feet away, abandoned. I doubted Marsten would know how to use it anyway.

"I said, stop untying him," LeBlanc said.

"Oh, for Christ's sake," Marsten muttered. "Fine."

He straightened up. Then, before Marsten was even fully standing, he lunged at LeBlanc. Marsten and LeBlanc fell to the floor. While the two fought, I got to my hands and knees and crept toward Clay. As I took hold of his handcuffs, his head jolted up. He looked over his shoulder at me.

"Go," he rasped.

I grabbed the two cuffs and yanked hard on the chain. The links stretched, but didn't break.

"No time," he said, trying to twist toward me. "Go."

As I met his eyes, I knew how wrong I'd been. I didn't come here to get him back for Jeremy or the Pack. I came to get him back for me. Because I loved him, loved him so much I'd risk everything for the faintest hope of saving him. Even now, as I realized he was right, that there wasn't time to get him out, I knew I wouldn't leave him here. I'd rather die.

I looked around wildly for a weapon, then suddenly stopped. Weapon? I was looking for a weapon? Had I lost my mind? I already had the best possible weapon. If only I had time to get it ready.

I dropped to my hands and knees and concentrated. Dimly, I heard Clay growl my name. I moved away. The Change started at its normal pace. Not good enough. Not enough time! My thoughts flitted in panic for a moment. I started trying to rein them in, then realized my Change was gaining speed. Throwing control aside, I let my fears run wild. If I failed, I was dead. If I failed, Clay was dead. I'd screwed up so badly, so completely. Fear and pain twisted through me. I doubled over and surrendered to it. A blinding flash of agony. Then victory.

I stood. Ahead, I saw LeBlanc bent over Marsten's prone form. He lifted his hand. The switchblade flashed. I growled. LeBlanc stopped in mid-strike and looked back at me. I flew at him. He dropped the knife and rolled out of the way. I'd put too much into the leap and hit the floor crooked, somersaulting into the wall. By the time I recovered, LeBlanc was gone.

I heard a voice and jerked my head toward it. Marsten was sitting up, wheezing. He pointed to the open back door and coughed blood. More blood trickled from slashes on his arms and chest. I glanced at the rear door. I couldn't let LeBlanc escape. A woman had made him turn tail and run. He wouldn't rest until he'd had his revenge. Marsten said something, but I couldn't understand him. Blood pounded in my ears, urging me to go after LeBlanc. I started for the door. Behind me, Clay grunted and I heard scuffling as he tried to stand. Remembering him, I turned back to Marsten. I wasn't leaving him with Clay. Lowering my head between my shoulder blades, I snarled. Marsten froze. His lips moved. Only a jumble of meaningless sound reached my ears. I crouched.

"Elena!" Clay said.

I could understand him. I stopped. Clay was on his feet now.

"Don't. Waste. Time," he said.

I looked at Marsten. He said one word. I still couldn't understand him, but I could read his lips. Territory. It was all he wanted. All he cared about. He'd known perfectly well that I was conscious on that floor. I'd played right into his plans. He was a single-minded, treacherous bastard, but he wouldn't hurt Clay. Killing Clay wouldn't get Marsten his territory. Keeping him alive and safe would.

I growled once more at Marsten, then tore out the door after LeBlanc.

LeBlanc's trail was easy to find. I didn't even have to track his scent. I could hear him thundering through the thick brush. Fool. I dove into the forest and started to run. Branches snagged in my fur and whipped against my face. I closed my eyes to slits to protect them and kept running. LeBlanc had trampled a path through the undergrowth. I stuck to it. Minutes later, the woods turned silent. LeBlanc had stopped. He must have realized that his only hope was to Change. I lifted my nose and sampled the breezes. The east wind held traces of his scent, but when a draft from the southeast hit me, it was full of him. I lifted one forepaw and brought it down on a pile of dead undergrowth. It was damp with the morning dew and barely whispered under my weight. Good. I turned southeast and crept forward.

Night had passed. Dawn lightened the thick blanket of trees overhead, sending shards of sun through to the forest floor. As I stepped in one pool of light, I could feel it warm my back with the promise of a sultry late spring day. Mist rose from the long grass and shrubs, the cool night earth rising to meet the warm morning. I inhaled the fog, closing my eyes to enjoy the clean nothingness of the smell. An eastern bluebird started singing somewhere to my left. A beautiful morning. I inhaled again, drinking it in, feeling the fear of the night give way to the anticipation of the hunt. It would end here. It would all end here, on this most beautiful of mornings.

When I heard LeBlanc's breathing, I stopped. I tilted my head and listened. He was crouching behind a thicket, breathing hard as he worked at his Change. I inched forward until I was outside the edge of his thicket and peeked through a fringe of fern. As I'd guessed by the height of his breathing sounds, he was crouching. But I'd been wrong about one thing. He wasn't Changing. He hadn't even undressed. A tremor of excitement raced through me. He was afraid, but instead of giving into the fear, he was fighting the Change. I pushed my muzzle through the fern and drank in the mead of his fear. It warmed me, fanning the spark of excitement into near-lust. LeBlanc might have scared me in the airport parking lot, but this was my arena.

LeBlanc shifted his weight and leaned forward to peer from the thicket. Use your nose, I thought. One sniff and you'd know the truth. But he didn't. He eased one leg back. His knee cracked and he froze, breath coming in shallow spurts. His head moved from side to side, listening and looking. Lifting the switchblade, he snapped it open, then waited for the sound to bring me to him. Something padded through the undergrowth beyond, a cat or a fox or something equally small and silent. LeBlanc tensed, raising the knife. Fool, fool, fool. I was growing tired of this. I wanted to run. I wanted to chase. I crept backward a dozen feet. Then I lifted my muzzle to the trees and howled. LeBlanc broke from the thicket and ran. I pursued.

LeBlanc had a head start. I let him keep it. We wove through the bushes and trees, jumping logs, trampling wildflowers, and sending two pheasants into the sky. He kept going deeper and deeper into the forest. Finally, he stopped running. As I realized I couldn't hear him any longer, I was bursting through into a clearing. Something slashed across my hind leg. I tumbled forward into the long grass. As I fell, I twisted around to see LeBlanc standing behind me, legs apart, switchblade raised, poised like a fighter waiting for the next round. He sneered and said something. I didn't need to hear the words to know what he said. Come and get me. A shudder of pleasure ran through me. He really was a fool.

I crouched and leapt at him. I didn't bother trying to figure out how to avoid the switchblade. It didn't matter. I felt the blade nick the side of my neck and slide across my shoulder. Blood welled up, hot against my skin. But there was no gushing, no pain worse than an irritating tingle. My fur was too thick. The knife had only scratched me. LeBlanc's arm went back to stab again, but it was too late. I was already on him. He flew backward, the blade arcing from his hand and vanishing in the trees. As my face came down to his, his eyes widened. Shock. Disbelief. Fear. I allowed myself one long moment to drink in his defeat. Then I ripped out his throat.

Ready

JEREMY, ANTONIO, AND NICK DID EVENTUALLY SHOW UP AT THE cabin. They came through the door as I was using Clay's bindings to tie up Marsten. Naturally, Jeremy was incredibly impressed by how well I'd handled things on my own and vowed never to shut me out of anything ever again. Yeah, right. His first words were nonrepeatable. Then he said that if I ever, ever did anything so stupid again, he'd—well, that part was unrepeatable, too, though Clay, Antonio, and Nick were quick to repeat it, each adding their own threats. So, the brave soul who saved the day was forced to slink from her victory site and ride home in the backseat of her own car. It could have been worse. They could have put me in the trunk. Actually, Nick suggested that, but he was kidding . . . I think.

Jeremy gave Marsten his territory. Wyoming, to be exact. When Marsten complained, Jeremy offered to switch it to Utah. Marsten left muttering something about ten-gallon hats and rhinestone pants. Of course, he wouldn't settle for retiring on a dude ranch. He'd be back in search of territory more amenable to his lifestyle, but for now he knew when to shut his mouth and take what was offered.

Clay took a while to heal. A long while, actually. He had a broken leg, four broken ribs, and a dislocated shoulder. He was so bruised and battered that he was in pain lying down, sitting, standing—basically every moment he was awake. He was exhausted, starved, dehydrated, and pumped full of enough drugs to fell a rhino for days. I spent a week living in a chair by his bed before I was convinced he was going to make it. Even then, I only left his room to make meals and only because I decided Jeremy's cooking was doing Clay more harm than good.

I had to go back to Toronto. I'd known it since that day in the cabin, but I postponed it, telling myself Clay was too sick, Jeremy needed my help around the house, the Camaro was low on gas, pretty much any excuse I could come up with. But I had to go back. Philip was waiting. I had to confront him with what he'd seen, find out how he planned to handle it. Once that was done, I'd come back to Stonehaven. There was no longer any question of which home I'd choose. Maybe there never had been.

I belonged at Stonehaven. The idea still rankled. Maybe I'd never be entirely at peace with this life because I hadn't chosen it and I was too stubborn to ever completely accept something that had been forced on me. But Clay was right. I was happy here. There would always be a human part of me that would see fault with this way of living, a human morality appalled by the violence of it, vestiges of Puritanism that rebelled at such total immersion in satisfying primal needs. Yet even when Stonehaven didn't make me happy, when I was raging at Jeremy or at Clay or at myself, I was in a perverse way still happy, content at least, content and fulfilled.

Everything I'd chased in the human world was here. I wanted stability? I had it in a place and people who would always welcome me, no matter what I did. I wanted family? I had it in my Pack, loyalty and love beyond the simple labels of mother, father, sister, brother. So, realizing that everything I ever wanted was here, was I prepared to cast aside my human aspirations and bury myself in Stonehaven forever? Of course not. I'd always have the need to fit into the larger world. No amount of therapy or self-analysis would change that. I'd still hold down a job in the human world, maybe escape there for vacations when the insulated life of the Pack overwhelmed me. But Stonehaven was my home. I wouldn't run from it anymore.

Nor could I keep running from myself. I don't mean the werewolf part of me. I think I accepted that years ago, maybe even embraced it because it gave me an excuse for so many things in my life. If I was aggressive and snappish, it was the wolf blood. If I lashed out at others, wolf blood again. Ditto for any violent tendencies. Moody? Angry? Hot-tempered? Hell, I had a reason to be that way, didn't I? I was a monster. Not exactly a condition to invoke peace and inner harmony in the best of people. Yet I had to admit the truth. Being a werewolf didn't make me that way. Look at Jeremy, Antonio, Nick, Logan, Peter. Each one might have shared some of my less attractive characteristics, but so would almost any stranger pulled off the street. Being a werewolf made me more capable of acting on my anger, and living with the Pack made such behavior more acceptable, but everything that I was, I'd been before Clay bit me. Of course, knowing that and accepting it were two different things. I'd have to work on the accepting part.

It took almost a month from that day in Toronto for me to realize what Clay had meant when he'd said he knew why I picked Philip and why it couldn't work. The first two weeks after we recovered Clay were hell, some days not knowing if he'd make it to the next. At least, it seemed that way to me. I'd watch him lying unconscious in bed and be sure his chest had stopped rising. I'd call for Jeremy. No, strike that. I'd scream for Jeremy and he'd come running. Of course, Clay was breathing fine, but Jeremy never made me feel I'd overreacted. He'd murmur something about a temporary shortness of breath, maybe minor sleep apnea, and he'd examine Clay thoroughly before settling into the bedside chair to watch for a "relapse." By the third week, Clay was regaining consciousness for longer periods and even I had to admit the danger finally seemed past. That wasn't to say I stopped camping out at his bedside. I didn't. I couldn't. And as long as I insisted on being there, Jeremy insisted taking over bedside watch while I slept or went for a run, even though we both knew such constant vigilance was necessary only for my peace of mind.

Near the end of the third week, I came back from my shower to find Jeremy in my post by Clay's bed, in the exact same vigilant pose I'd left him in twenty minutes before. I stood in the door, watching him, taking in the circles under his eyes, the gaunt prominence of his cheekbones. I knew then that I had to stop, get a grip, and admit to myself that Clay was doing fine and would continue to do fine—if not better—without constant surveillance. If I didn't, I'd run myself into the ground and Jeremy would follow without a word of protest.

"Feeling better?" he asked without turning.

"Much."

He reached back as I approached, took my hand, and squeezed it. "He'll be awake soon. His stomach's growling."

"God forbid he should miss dinner."

"Speaking of which, we're going out tonight. You and I. Someplace requiring a suit and tie and a shave—at least for me. Antonio is driving in with Nick. They'll look after Clay."

"That's not nec—"

"It's very necessary. You need to get out, get your mind off this. Clay will be fine. We'll take your cell phone in case anything happens."

As I nodded and sat in the chair beside Jeremy, the answer to Clay's puzzle hit me with such force I had to gasp. Then I had to beat myself over the head for not having seen it earlier. Why had I chosen Philip? The answer had been staring me in the face since I'd returned to Stonehaven. Who did he remind me of? Jeremy, of course.

In my defense, Jeremy and Philip did not, outwardly at least, have much in common. They looked nothing alike. They didn't share the same gestures. They didn't even act the same way. Philip didn't have Jeremy's emotional control, his authoritarianism, his quiet reserve. But these weren't the qualities I most admired in Jeremy. What I saw in Philip was a shallower reflection of what I valued in Jeremy, his endless patience, his consideration, his innate goodness. Why did I subconsciously seek out someone who reminded me of Jeremy? Because in Jeremy I saw some girlish vision of Prince Charming, someone who would bring me flowers and care for me no matter how badly I screwed up. The problem with this fantasy was that I had absolutely no romantic feelings for Jeremy. I loved him as a friend, a leader, and a father figure. Nothing more. So in finding a human version of my ideal, I'd found a man I was certain to love, but never with the passion I'd feel for a lover.

Did that make me feel better? Of course not. In excusing my inability to fall in love with Philip, I wanted to be able to say that it was because of some problem in him, something he lacked. The truth was that the fault was entirely mine. I'd made a mistake and, as good and as decent as Philip was, he had to suffer for it.

After five weeks of postponing my return to Toronto, I decided to do it. Clay was taking an afternoon nap. I was lying beside him, half dozing, when I realized I had to leave right then, before I changed my mind. I got up and scribbled a note for Clay. Jeremy was out back fixing the stone wall. I didn't tell him where I was going. I was afraid he'd want me to eat dinner first or wait until he could drive me to the airport or some other delay that would give my resolve time to weaken.

I didn't call to tell Philip I was coming. Hearing his voice was one more thing that might make me change my mind. I went straight to the apartment and let myself in. He wasn't there. I settled onto the couch to wait. An hour later, he returned, panting from a run in the early July heat. He swung through the door, saw me, and stopped.

"Hi," I said, managing a weak smile.

I saw the fear in his eyes then and knew it never would have worked between us. No matter how close I got to any human, if they ever learned the truth about me, there would always be fear. You couldn't get past that.

"Hello," he said at last. He hesitated, then closed the apartment door, and mopped off his face. After giving himself time to recover, he laid his towel on the hall table and stepped into the room. "When did you get back?"

"Just now. How are you feeling?"

"Fine. I got your flowers. Thank you."

I inhaled. God, this was awkward. Had it always been this way? I couldn't even remember how we used to talk. Any sense of familiarity had flitted away.

"Your—uh—side must be better," I said. "If you're out jogging."

"Walking. Not jogging. Not yet."

He sat in the recliner opposite me. I inhaled again. This wasn't working. There was no easy way to do this.

"About what you saw that day . . ." I began.

He said nothing.

"About what you—uh—saw me do."

"I didn't see anything." His voice was soft, barely audible.

"I know you did and we need to talk about it."

He met my eyes. "I didn't see anything."

"Philip, I know—"

"No." He spat the word, then pulled back and shook his head. "I don't remember anything about that day, Elena. You went to work. Your cousin came up looking for you. Two other men came up looking for you. Someone stabbed me. Then it's all a blank."

I knew he was lying. For the safety of the Pack, I should pursue it, get him to admit what he'd seen, and find a way to explain it away. Yet something told me that this was better for Philip. Let him explain it his own way. I owed him that much.

"I should go now."

I got to my feet. He said nothing. I saw my bags stacked in the hall, next to a few boxes of his own stuff.

"I've subletted the apartment," he said. "I—" He rubbed the bridge of his nose. "I would have called you, your cell phone. I was . . . working my way up to it."

"I'm sorry."

"I know." He met my eyes for the first time since I'd arrived and managed the barest ghost of a smile. "It was good, still. A mistake, but a good one. If you come back to Toronto someday, maybe you can look me up. Have a drink together or something."

I nodded. As I lifted my bags, my gaze flitted to the hall table.

"It's in the drawer," Philip said softly.

I turned to say something, but he was heading into the bedroom, his back to me. He closed the door.

"I'm sorry," I whispered.

I pushed open the lobby doors and walked out carrying two small pieces of luggage. I'd left a note for Philip to give the rest to charity or throw it in the garbage. There was nothing there I needed. I only took the two bags so he wouldn't think I was abandoning my things in anger. There was only one item in that apartment I'd really wanted back, the item I'd retrieved from the hall table drawer. I still had it in my hand. As I stood in the building vestibule, I put down the luggage, and opened my fist. Clay's wedding band gleamed in the streetlights.

Clay.

What was I going to do about Clay?

Despite all we'd been through, I still couldn't give him what he wanted. I couldn't promise my life to him, swear I'd be by his side every waking and sleeping minute, 'til death do us part. But I loved him. Loved him completely. There would be no other men in my life, no other lovers. I could promise him that. As for the rest, well, I'd have to offer what I could and hope it would be enough.

"You're here."

I looked up sharply. Clay stood in the wavering yellow light of a streetlamp. For a moment, I thought I was imagining things. Then he stepped forward, his left leg dragging, not completely healed after his ordeal.

"Didn't you get my note?" I asked.

"Note?"

I shook my head. "You shouldn't be here. You're supposed to be in bed."

"I couldn't let you leave. Not until I talked to you."

I glanced at the luggage by my feet and realized he must have thought I was waiting to get inside the apartment building, instead of leaving it. Hmmm. Never let it be said I passed up the opportunity to milk something for all it's worth. Yes, I can be cruel, even sadistic on occasion.

"And what did you want to say to me?" I asked.

He stepped forward, putting one hand on my elbow and moving so close I could feel his heart beating through his shirt. It was pounding, but that might have just been from the exertion of the impromptu trip.

"I love you. Yes, you've heard that before, heard it a million times, but I don't know what else to say." He lifted a hand to my face and touched my cheek. "I need you. This last year, when you were gone, it was hell. I made up my mind that when you came back, I'd do whatever it took to get you back. No more tricks. No more tantrums. I know I didn't do a great job. Hell, you probably never even noticed the difference. But I was trying. I'll keep trying. Come back home with me. Please."

I looked up into his eyes. "Why did you go back up to the apartment?"

He blinked. "Huh?"

"The day you were attacked. You saw Daniel and LeBlanc go up to the apartment, didn't you?"

"Right . . ."

"You knew I wasn't up there. You'd just spoken to me on the phone."

"Right . . ."

"So you knew the only person in the apartment was Philip. Yet you went up there and tried to protect him. Why?"

Clay hesitated, then said, "Because I knew it was what you'd want me to do." He stroked his thumb across my cheek. "I know that's not the answer you want to hear. You want me to say I had a sudden flash of conscience and went up there to save Philip. But I can't lie. I can't feel the things you want me to feel. I didn't care whether Philip lived or died. I saved him because I knew you'd want me to, because I knew if anything happened to him, you'd be hurt."

"Thank you," I said, kissing him.

"That was a good answer?" A hint of his old grin slipped into his voice and his eyes.

"The best I can hope for. I know that now."

"So you'll stay?"

I smiled up at him. "I never planned to leave, which you'd know if you'd bothered to read my note before charging all the way here to stop me."

"You—" He stopped, threw back his head, and laughed, then caught me up in a bone-jarring kiss and hug. "I guess I deserved that."

"That and more." I grinned and kissed him, then pulled back and watched him.

"What is it?" he asked.

"When you were gone, I was thinking this story wouldn't have a happily ever after ending. Maybe I was wrong."

"Happily ever after?" He grinned. "As in 'forever after'?"

"Well, maybe not 'forever after.' Maybe 'happily ever after for a little while.' "

"I could live with that."

"Happily ever after for a day or two, at least."

"A day or two?" He made a face. "I was thinking of a bit longer. Not forever, of course. Just eight, maybe nine decades."

"Don't push your luck."

He laughed and lifted me up in another hug. "We'll work on it."

"Yes," I said, smiling down at him. "I'm ready to work on it."

Printed in the United States
by Baker & Taylor Publisher Services